DEFIANCE
A WORLD WAR II STORY

OTHER BOOKS AND AUDIO BOOKS
BY A. L. SOWARDS

The Rules in Rome

The Spider and the Sparrow

Espionage

Sworn Enemy

Deadly Alliance

The Perfect Gift

DEFIANCE

A WORLD WAR II STORY

a novel

A. L. SOWARDS

Covenant Communications, Inc.

Published by Covenant Communications, Inc.
American Fork, Utah

Printed in the United States of America
First Printing: April 2017

23 22 21 20 19 18 17   10 9 8 7 6 5 4 3 2 1

ISBN 978-1-52440-215-0

With love, for George and Paula,
who have taught me a great deal about love, family, and second chances

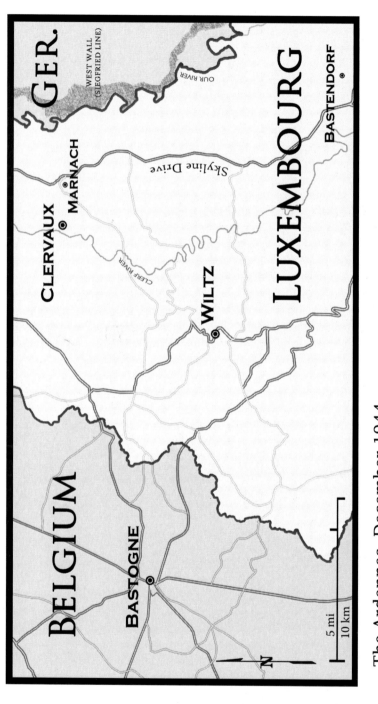

The Ardennes, December 1944

Central/Eastern Germany, 1945

PART ONE: CIVILIAN
SUMMER 1944
VIRGINIA, USA

CHAPTER 1

I wasn't supposed to be riding my brother's motorcycle the day I graduated from high school. If he found out I'd taken it, he'd give me a stern lecture about how it was wrong to borrow someone's prized possession without asking and how it was irresponsible to waste gasoline during a war. But since he'd gone off to Europe and disappeared, I didn't think there was much of a chance that he'd notice.

I pushed the 1937 BSA M20 to 65 miles per hour. The rushing air cooled my skin but still wasn't softening the trio of frustrations that had sent me outside with a yearning for speed and solitude. I was angry that Bastien had stopped writing, angry that I couldn't go to Belle's graduation party because her father had threatened to shoot me with a shotgun, and angry that President Roosevelt had ended voluntary recruitment and instituted a universal draft. For years, I'd planned to volunteer with the air corps the day after graduation; now I had to wait until the draft board called me up, and they'd probably send me to whichever branch of service was most in need of fresh bodies. I loved flying along the road on a motorcycle, but flying in the air sounded so much better. With my luck, I'd end up on a graves registration crew. Or maybe worse, get sent to the Pacific. I was plenty mad at the Japanese, but I'd been wanting to get back at the Nazis since I was nine and the Gestapo took my dad away.

Thick green trees lined the twisting Virginia road, creating the illusion that I was all alone, which suited my current mood. A few hours ago, I'd thought it lame to come home after commencement to a party of two: my mom and me. Next door, all of Belle's extended family and most of our friends gathered to celebrate. It was quite the contrast, but unlike Belle, I wasn't Fairfax High School's class of 1944 valedictorian, and most of my family was gone, one way or another.

I took a turn too sharply and felt the bike wobble, but I kept my balance. Even if I hadn't caught myself, I wore a helmet, thanks to Bastien. My brother was big on things like wearing helmets and not playing with matches. He was overprotective, but I listened to him most of the time. When he was around to talk.

He had shipped overseas a year and a half ago. He'd told my mom and sisters all sorts of kind things in parting. Then he'd looked at me and said, "Lukas, don't do anything stupid while I'm gone." He'd still had a German accent, so it had sounded more like *vile* than *while*, but it was his tone that still stuck in my head. It was as if he thought that since I procrastinated my homework and always lost my watch, I must be too immature to be the man of the house. I swear he still thought of me as the ten-year-old boy he'd brought to America eight years before. My sisters had started treating me like an equal when I'd surpassed them in height, and even Mom seemed to recognize that I'd grown more responsible. But with Bastien, it was like nothing ever changed.

I took the next turn slower than the last. Same with the one after as the road curved through the trees. As I came around the corner, I heard another engine. I moved to the right edge of the lane in case the other driver was sloppy during turns, but I didn't think much of it. Not until the truck came into view, driving straight at me on the wrong side of the road.

I jerked the handlebars, forcing the motorcycle to the road's shoulder and barely missing the big Deuce and a Half army truck barreling along in *my* lane. A second later, I was off the pavement, driving over weeds and loose gravel.

I pumped the brake with my right hand so I wouldn't skid and told myself not to panic despite the pack of trees looming ahead of me. I dodged a tree to the left, then two to the right as I fought to slow down. Then I hit a root. The motorcycle toppled to the side and slid out from under me. It bashed into one tree, and I banged into another. The air rushed out of my lungs in one big whoosh, and I had to gulp a few times before I had enough air to exhale again. My head hurt. My shoulder hurt. My right hip and leg hurt. But I didn't experience horror until I saw the Beeza broken into pieces and wrapped around a tree.

Footsteps sounded behind me, and I turned toward the noise. I instantly regretted it. Moving hurt.

"Are you all right, lad?"

I squinted to get a better look at the man leaning over me. A glance back at the truck proved he was the driver. His voice and uniform said he was

British. The three four-pointed stars on his shoulder straps told me he was a captain. Now, don't get me wrong. I was glad the British were fighting the Nazis, and I was sure the man had a very good reason for being in America, but what idiot handed him a set of car keys in Virginia? I managed a grunt and tried to sit. The captain helped me, which was painful since my back was bruised.

The hammering in my head grew worse. "You know, you're supposed to drive on the right side of the road around here."

He cleared his throat. "Yes, I suppose I forgot where I was. Sorry about that. Can I offer you a ride somewhere?"

"No offense, but I've seen how you drive, sir. Not sure I want to get in a truck with you." It was rude, and I shouldn't have said it because it would be a long walk home. Probably take me until dawn, and in the meantime, my mom would be all sorts of worried.

To my relief, he laughed. "I would offer you the keys, but seeing as how you knocked your head quite soundly, I think you best accept my offer." When I didn't answer right away, he continued. "Be a good chap and agree to a ride. I can't in good conscience leave you bleeding on the roadside with a ruined motorbike and no way to get home."

I tugged off my helmet and felt along my forehead. My hand came away sticky and red. I stared at the pieces of the motorcycle again. I'd ruined it. If Bastien was still alive, he was going to kill me.

I didn't have much of a choice, so I accepted the ride. The captain checked my injuries and asked if I wanted to go to the hospital. The cut in my head stopped bleeding after a few minutes, and I hadn't been knocked unconscious, so I told him no. I was already late with June's rent; the last thing I needed was a hospital bill.

The captain opened the tailgate and found a piece of wood to use as a ramp. Between the two of us, we pushed the remnants of the Beeza into the back of the truck beside some unmarked wooden crates. The rest of the pieces were small enough to lift individually. I wasn't sure why we bothered. The thing was destroyed. I slunk into the passenger seat as the captain started the engine.

"I'm Captain Cunningham, by the way." He kept his eyes on the road as he drove and kept the truck in the right lane.

"I'm Luke. Lukas Ley."

Other than telling him where to turn, we drove in silence for a while. Something inside my head thumped, and I was afraid I was going to lose the apple pie my mom had made to celebrate graduation. It was my favorite dessert, but I was pretty sure it wouldn't taste as good on the way up as it had on the way down.

"So, why are you in Virginia?" I asked.

"I am working in an advisory role."

"Advising on what, exactly?"

His lips tightened, then lifted into a smile. "There are a few things we have a bit more experience with. Driving in the right lane probably can't be counted among them."

"You got that right." I watched the trees go by for a while, then looked back at the road. I wanted to make sure he was on the correct half of it. "I'm sorry," I finally said. "I haven't been very polite. Thank you for stopping, and thank you for the ride. It would've taken me a long time to walk home."

"A ride is the least I could offer. I am rather embarrassed that I fouled up like that."

"I guess that's what you're used to in England." I could relate. When we'd first moved to the US, I'd taken all sorts of cultural missteps. It had taken me three years to get good at pronouncing a *W*.

"Yes. I spent time in Shanghai too. We drove on the left there as well."

"Did you like Shanghai?"

He nodded. "Most of the time."

"Do you like Virginia?"

"It has its pleasant moments. The traffic rules are a bit backward."

I laughed. The sun disappeared behind the trees, and I realized I'd been squinting. "Turn left at the next cross street." As he turned, I remembered he hadn't told me about his job. "So you don't by chance advise the army air force or anything, do you?"

"No. Why do you ask?"

"I want to be a fighter pilot."

"Ah." He glanced at me, then back at the road. "You and every other seventeen-year-old boy in America."

"I'm eighteen," I said. "And not everyone wants to be a pilot. Ray and Frank want to join the marine corps because they figure it's a sure ticket to combat. Bob and Wally want to join the navy. And Arthur wants to drive tanks." I realized he had no idea who I was talking about, so I shut my mouth. But then I opened it again because the motorcycle ride hadn't been long enough to banish my frustration, and the wreck had added to it. "Not that it matters. They'll put us where they need us."

"Maybe you'll be lucky enough to get what you want."

By then, we'd made it to my house, a three-bedroom brick rambler on the outskirts of Fairfax. It had a big porch out front and a blue-star banner hanging in one window. The house had been the perfect size when we'd moved in five years ago, but since then, both my sisters and Bastien had moved away, and I planned to follow them soon. It was bigger than what my mom and I needed, and so was the rent.

"I'll put the motorcycle parts in there, I guess." I pointed to the detached garage. "But if you have to be somewhere, we can put them on the grass for now."

"I can spare a few minutes."

We'd just set up the ramp again when my mom burst through the front door. Her mostly-gray hair was pulled back in a bun, and she wore a blue apron. She zeroed in on my cut forehead and gasped. Instantly I wished it were dark.

"Are you all right, Lukas?" she asked in German.

Cunningham's eyebrows lifted slightly. He probably thought we were Nazi spies.

I answered in English. "I'm fine, Mom."

"What happened?" By then, she was right beside me, trying to get a better look. She didn't seem to notice that I'd mangled Bastien's bike or that she was blocking the way to the garage.

"Um, had a little crash. So I'll just put this in the garage, and I can tell you all about it later."

She stepped out of the way, but I could tell she was eager to give me a thorough interrogation. She stood there watching, her hands on her hips and her mouth drawn tight as the captain and I unloaded the broken bits of the Beeza and stacked them in the garage.

"Your mother is German?" the captain asked.

I nodded.

"And you? Obviously you understand the language. Do you speak it?"

"Yeah, I lived there till I was ten." I picked up the last piece of the Beeza, part of the exhaust pipe, and carried it to the garage. When I turned around, he was still watching me. "I know what you're thinking, that we're a couple of German agents. But that's not how it is. My brother's in the army. One of my sisters is married to a marine, and the other just married a guy in the navy. We came to the US after the Nazis killed my dad. Trust me, no one hates Hitler more than we do."

Captain Cunningham tilted his head to the side. "What is your brother's name?"

"Bastien Ley. He's a captain now."

"I think I remember him. Talented chap. I daresay you look a great deal like him."

"You know Bastien?"

Cunningham nodded. "We did some training together. Back in '42, I believe it was. How is he?"

I swallowed before answering. "It's been awhile since we've heard from him."

A tightness crossed Cunningham's face, and he glanced at my mom, then back at me. "I'm sorry to hear that. I hope you have good news of him soon." He grabbed his wallet and removed a few crisp American bills. "Here, for the repairs."

I hesitated. I didn't have the funds to fix the motorcycle myself, but I didn't want to take advantage of Cunningham's good nature.

He stretched his arm out. "The wreck was my fault. And since I am transporting those crates for official purposes, I can claim it as a work expense."

I accepted the money. "Thanks."

He climbed into his truck.

"Thank you for bringing my son home," my mom said in English. She knew a lot of English, even if it didn't always sound English.

He nodded politely. "Yes, ma'am."

After the captain drove away, I stared at the motorcycle. It was my brother's favorite thing in the whole world, and I'd smashed it into twenty-seven pieces.

"Lukas, what happened?" My mom switched back to German.

I glanced from the BSA to my mom. She studied my forehead. I brushed my hand along my hairline. It was sore, but it wasn't bleeding anymore. "I told you, Mom. I had a little crash."

"Little?"

I sighed. "No, I guess not. Look at it. It's ruined." I turned and walked into the house.

Mom followed me. I sank into the second-hand sofa, leaned over, and rested my head in my hands. My headache was getting worse.

"You are more important than the motorcycle." She sat beside me and pushed my hair back so she could see my cut. "Where else are you hurt?"

"It's not bad. Just bruises and scratches. I think I've had worse beatings playing football."

"You were lucky, then. Or blessed."

I scoffed. "I just destroyed Bastien's motorcycle. You call that lucky? Or blessed?"

My mom rubbed my back. I bit my lip to keep from wincing as her hand went over a sore spot. "Motorcycles can be replaced or repaired."

"Not that one."

"Even that one. It was old when he bought it, remember?"

I remembered all right. And I remembered all the hours my brother had spent restoring it. That made it even worse. "I think he's going to kill me."

"Nonsense."

She had a point—he wasn't really going to kill me. He already had some weird guilt about when my other brother had accidentally started a fire and they'd both gotten caught in it when they were young. Bastien had lived. Hans hadn't.

"Right. He'll just hate me forever." He'd probably never speak to me again, but I was starting to get used to that. For the last eight months, his letters had been so rare that he might as well have been not talking to me.

"That's not true either. Has he ever lost his temper with you?"

"I haven't ever wrecked his motorcycle before." I rubbed my eyes like I usually did when I was tired, but then I stopped because it hurt. "I shouldn't have taken it out."

"No, you shouldn't have. But you can't change what happened." She patted my knee. "Why don't you have another piece of pie? Everything seems a little better after dessert, yes?"

I ate the pie with a tall glass of milk. But I didn't feel much better.

CHAPTER 2

THE RING OF MY ALARM clock startled me awake the next morning at five thirty. Three dozen bruises howled at me when I reached over to switch it off. I groaned and stayed in bed. It wasn't like I had to get up that early. I normally milked the Montgomery cow before breakfast, but it wasn't an official obligation, especially not the morning after a wreck. Annabelle Katherine Montgomery was perfectly capable of milking her own cow. Mr. Thompson expected me at 8:00 a.m. sharp to help on his farm, but it took only ten minutes to get there on my bicycle, and it was a Saturday, so I didn't have to deliver newspapers. I could sleep another two hours and still get to work on time.

I closed my eyes and told myself missing one day wasn't that big a deal. But ten minutes later, I decided missing one day maybe was kind of a big deal, so I threw the blankets back and stepped out of bed and almost tripped over a pile of dirty laundry. I brushed my teeth but not my hair before leaving through the kitchen door at the back of the house, shutting it softly so it wouldn't wake my mom. Most days she was up as early as I was, but not Saturdays.

I crossed the grass and hopped over the white picket fence from our yard into Belle's. A grove of trees lined the edge of the property, old and thick and great for concealment. I waited there for a few seconds.

I was late, but she was still singing. I could hear her voice, clear and low. "Behind the door, her daddy kept a shotgun. He kept it in the springtime and the merry month of May. And if you asked him why the heck he kept it, he kept it for that soldier who was far, far away. Far away, far away. He kept it for that soldier who was far, far away."

"You know, there's a version of that song without the shotgun verse," I said as I stepped into the barn.

"I'm quite aware of that. I already sang that version, but your tardiness forced me into singing this version too." She looked up from the cow she milked. Her eyes were the color of a spring sky, and her hair was the color of a late-summer wheat field. Her smile was all sunshine and freckles until she saw my face. "Luke! What happened to your head?"

I rubbed a hand over the scabs, accidentally aggravating the swelling under my eye. "Now that I'm done with school, I figured I didn't need it anymore."

She stepped in for a closer inspection. "What did you do? My daddy didn't find you, did he?"

Belle's dad hadn't always hated me. As recently as football season, Mr. Montgomery had been an ardent fan of my season-total ten touchdowns. But sometime during basketball season, I'd changed from his favorite wide receiver to a dirty kraut. It wasn't my basketball skills. I wasn't the star of the team, but I usually started. I think the change in attitude had more to do with Belle's brother getting killed by the Germans somewhere in Italy and Belle's dad catching me giving Belle her first kiss.

"I haven't seen your dad in weeks."

"Then what happened?"

"I wrecked the motorcycle."

She grimaced. "Your brother's motorcycle?"

"Yeah."

"Oh dear."

"Oh dear is right." The bruises on my legs ached in protest as I sat on the stool to milk the cow for her.

"How badly are you hurt?"

"Does it matter? Bastien's going to come home and kill me."

"Yes, it matters. And I'm pretty sure your brother isn't going to kill you. If I remember right, he's kind of fond of you.'"

"He might be fonder of that motorcycle."

Belle ran her fingers through my hair. "I doubt that."

I closed my eyes and let her massage my scalp. Her fingers were light enough that I barely even noticed when they went over a scrape. She smelled like a bouquet of flowers—I could pick it out even over the cow. "Did you get new perfume?"

"Yes. A graduation present from my aunt."

"It's nice."

"Nice, huh?"

"Yeah. But you always smell good, so it's not that different, I guess."

Her fingers moved to my neck. Normally I liked her neck rubs, but this morning I was sore, and I couldn't hold back a wince.

"Hmm. So you are hurt."

"I never said I wasn't."

"Then tell me where."

When I didn't answer right away, she slapped my shoulder.

"Ow!"

"Then start talking, mister."

I turned one of the cow's teats toward her and squirted milk in her direction, slow enough that she had time to duck away.

"That only distracted me for two seconds."

I didn't mind telling Belle what had happened. It was just fun teasing her for a while first. "I got run off the road by a British captain driving like he was still in London. Then I hit a root, and the motorcycle slid out from under me. I bruised my right side pretty bad. And I smacked into a tree and got a few cuts. Not any worse than what I got at our Homecoming game."

"You have a habit of looking a little beat up for important occasions. A black eye for our first date. An ugly scab for enlistment."

I finished with the cow and felt the scab on my forehead. "Ugly, huh?" I asked as I stood.

"Just the scab. The rest of your face is nice enough." She gave me that sunshine-and-freckles smile again, and I kissed her on the cheek. "Thanks for milking the cow for me."

"Sure," I said. I would milk the cow for her anytime, as long as her daddy wasn't around. Kisses and neck rubs were just an added bonus. "See you tomorrow, Belle."

* * *

I spent the day working on the Thompson farm. It was always hard work, and that day it was extra miserable because I was sore from the wreck. Add in the Virginia humidity and the bugs, and I could barely push the bicycle pedals when I finally got home.

I should have been grateful I had a job. The money Captain Cunningham gave us was exactly how much we were short for June's rent. But July would come soon enough, and Bastien's motorcycle probably needed all sorts of new parts. Or maybe it would have to be replaced entirely. I needed the work, but I was still in a bad mood.

Mom cleaned houses to bring in extra money. I worked for Mr. Thompson and had a paper route. We still ate a lot of cheap food, like grits, beans, and rice. Things had been worse before, like when we'd spent all our savings getting to the US and arrived in the middle of a depression. But they'd also been better before, like when Bastien had sent home most of his earnings, first as a lieutenant and then as a captain. Captains made decent money, but Bastien's allotments had stopped coming six months ago, which was about the time Mom had gotten sick and hadn't been able to work for a few weeks. We'd been living paycheck to paycheck ever since.

We could have moved somewhere cheaper, but neither of us really wanted to. First we put it off because all of Mom's work was nearby. Then we put it off until I finished school. It was time to find somewhere smaller and more affordable, but I was hesitant to move. Leaving would sever our last ties to the time when my sisters had still been around and my brother hadn't been missing.

I checked the mailbox as I rode past. It was empty. "Mom, did you get the mail?" I asked when I came inside.

"*Ja.*"

"Anything from the draft board?"

"*Nein.*"

I frowned.

She laughed. It was a sound I didn't hear too often. "Are you so eager to leave me?"

"No. I'll probably start missing you on the bus to the reception center. For sure by the time they give us our first chow." We ate cheap, but Mom somehow made it taste good. I looked through the window to the yard and thought of all the work she'd have to do when I left. "Are you going to be okay here all by yourself?" I didn't want to back out now that I was finally old enough to join the war effort, but Mom had never lived alone. She'd married young, and when my dad had gone away to war, she'd had Bastien and Hans to keep her busy. Now she was a widow, and her youngest child was about to leave, and I suddenly felt guilty.

Mom wrapped her arm around my waist. The top of her head came level with my shoulder. "I'm not so helpless. I'll manage. Especially if I don't have you dirtying the laundry and losing your homework."

I slung my arm across her shoulders and rolled my eyes. "I haven't lost any homework for at least two months."

"Well, when you get to be a pilot, we can hope you fly something too big to misplace."

I gave her my best *that's not funny* look and steered the conversation a new direction. "Maybe you should go live with Hannah or Stefanie."

She shrugged. "We'll see."

"You know you want to go meet your grandson." My sister Hannah had given birth to a baby in March.

"Yes, I would like to meet little Freddy. Maybe I'll visit after you're inducted." She turned and started for the kitchen. Right on time, my stomach started to rumble. "The postman brought something else today."

"What?"

"Come see. On the table."

"A picture of Freddy?"

She didn't answer. I guess she actually intended to make me walk over there to see for myself. When I stepped around the corner into the kitchen, I saw a telegram on the table and froze. Telegrams weren't common. Hannah's husband had sent one when the baby was born, but most telegrams began with the words *The Secretary of War desires me to inform you that . . .* and then went on to say that a son, husband, or brother was wounded, missing, or dead.

I'd been worried about Bastien for a long time. From November until February, his letters had been mailed with precision every two weeks. But the letters were odd. They never mentioned the news, and he'd stopped responding to our questions. No acknowledgment of my sister Stefanie's engagement. No congratulations when Freddy was born. And no reaction to the question I ended every letter with: *Can I have your motorcycle now?* It was like he wasn't getting our letters. Or like he had written a bunch all at once and someone else was mailing them. Then in March they'd stop coming altogether, and I'd concluded he was dead.

I picked up the telegram, expecting it to confirm my fears. Instead it read: *COMING HOME WITH A FEW SURPRISES STOP DATE OF ARRIVAL UNCERTAIN STOP LOVE BASTIEN.*

"Holy cow, he's alive!"

"Of course he's alive." Mom had never doubted, and I'd never pointed out all the evidence to the contrary.

I whooped in celebration. Then I remembered I'd crashed his Beeza and I wouldn't have money to replace it for at least six months. My brother was alive, and he was going to be livid when he got home and saw what I'd done to his motorcycle.

* * *

The next morning I waited in the trees, straining to hear Belle. She always sang "She Wore a Yellow Ribbon" to let me know it was safe to come milk the cow for her. Maybe her dad was around today. She didn't think he'd really shoot me. I wasn't so sure. I wanted to see her, but I didn't want my head blown off, so I waited.

I listened to the birds chirping for a few minutes before I finally heard it.

"Around her hair she wore a yellow ribbon. She wore it in the spring-time and the merry month of May. And if you asked her why the heck she wore it, she wore it for her soldier who was far, far away. Far away. Far away. She wore it for her soldier who was far, far away."

I met her in the barn as she finished the chorus. "And who's late this morning?"

"Maybe you were early." Belle blew me a kiss and handed me the milk pail. "Although I stayed up late finishing a book last night, so I'm a little sleepy still."

"Was it any good?"

She shrugged. "The bad knight died. The good knight lived and got to marry the lady he wanted to marry. But I think he might have been better off with the other girl."

"Hmm. Too bad school's over. If it wasn't, I bet you could write an award-winning essay on why he should have chosen the other girl instead."

Belle laughed. Then she held my chin and examined my face. "I think your bruises are worse today."

My legs ached as I sat on the stool, confirming her words. "Yeah. And I still haven't heard from the draft board. But something else came yesterday."

"What?"

"Bastien's alive, and he's coming home. He sent a telegram."

I glanced back and saw her grinning. She'd met Bastien only once, but she knew how much I worried about him. "When's he coming home?"

"He didn't say."

"Will it be before you leave for training?"

"I don't know. I still don't even have a date for the pre-induction exam. And then it's at least three weeks before I report." I let some of my frustra-tion seep into my milking, and the cow bellowed in protest.

"Well, you've only been graduated from high school two whole days."

"But they knew when I'd graduate. They could have set the date for next week and sent the notice during finals."

Belle's fingers found their way to my hair. "They'll get you soon enough. Unless you found a job vital to national defense yesterday and your skills there are irreplaceable."

I tried to relax. The scalp massage helped. "Yeah. I'm single, and just about anyone can take over my paper route. And it's not like Mr. Thompson's crops are being turned into K rations or anything. No chance of getting a deferral, thank goodness."

"I'm kind of hoping you won't report till after my birthday."

"Yeah, it might be rough having to actually do your chores yourself instead of shoving them off on me."

Belle kicked the stool just hard enough for me to feel the vibration. "It's the loss of company I'm lamenting, not the extra work. But if you're still here when I turn eighteen, you could baptize me." Belle had gone to church every Sunday for a year, but her dad wouldn't let her get baptized until she was eighteen. He didn't mind most religions, as long as he didn't have to attend services, but he found Mormonism distasteful, and the fact that I was part of the congregation made it even worse.

"Maybe I'll get leave and come back for it. Or you could hop on a bus and come visit me at whatever base I'm at."

"My aunt goes to Norfolk once a month. If you joined the navy instead of the army, maybe you'd get stationed there."

"Me, in the navy? Not a chance."

"Why not? The navy has pilots too." She bent forward to wink at me, and her braid brushed the top of my ear.

"I want to shoot Nazis, not Japs." I finished milking and turned around to face her.

"Yeah, I know." She held out her hands to help me up, but instead, I pulled her onto my lap.

"Don't look so sad about it," I said into her ear. "I'll write to you all the time."

"All the time, huh?"

"Yep. And find out who's trying to make a pass at you and write them letters ordering them to cease and desist."

"And how do you plan on figuring that out?"

"I'll think of something." I kissed her on the cheek and let her stand again.

She walked to the barn door and peeked around the corner, checking to see if her dad was around. "It's clear."

I gave her another kiss on my way out, enjoying the smoothness of her lips and the scent of her perfume for a few blissful seconds.

"Luke?"

"Yeah?"

"Don't be in such a hurry to get in on the fight. We barely landed in France, and it's a long way to Berlin."

"Yeah, but training to be a pilot takes a long time."

She shook her head. "Sometimes you're too determined for your own good."

"I thought that was one of the reasons you found me so irresistible. That and my willingness to crawl out of bed before the sun most mornings to do your chores for you."

She smiled but only halfway. "You better get out of here while it's still clear. See you at church, Luke."

CHAPTER 3

I GOT MY NOTICE THE next week and reported to the induction station a week after that. They weren't going to induct me yet—they just needed to do the physical exam and give me a list of things to complete before I reported for duty, most of which didn't apply to an eighteen-year-old with no debts, no assets, no wife, and no children.

Plenty of my friends had joined the service, and I'd been reading everything I could get my hands on about the war since it started, so I knew what to expect. First they talked a bunch about what would happen after I was inducted. Then they weighed me: 175 pounds. They measured my height: six feet two inches. They took a urine sample, X-rayed my chest, and examined my throat, ears, and nose. Everything went smoothly until I got to the eye exam.

"Do you wear glasses, son?" the man pointing to a chart with rows of gradually smaller letters asked. I assumed he was a doctor or an optician.

"No."

"Did you have problems seeing the chalkboard in school?"

"No." I always sat by Belle, and she always sat up front.

"Hmm. Let's check your right eye now."

I switched the blinder from my right eye to my left and tried to read the letters on the chart twenty feet away. When I finished, I waited while the doctor wrote something on my paperwork. "Well?"

"20/70 in both eyes."

"What does that mean?"

"It means that at twenty feet, you can see what most people see at seventy feet."

"You aren't going to reject me, are you?" The last thing I wanted was to be classified as 4F—unfit for service due to physical, mental, or moral deficiencies.

"Only if we can't get at least 20/40 with glasses."

I spent the next fifteen minutes repeating the exam with different lenses in front of my eyes. I didn't know enough about the chart to tell if I was doing better or not. Had I thought the eye exam was going to be a problem, I would have found a chart and memorized it.

The doctor grunted with satisfaction after the last pair of lenses. "20/30 in both eyes with that prescription. Good enough for general service. I'll write your prescription out in case you want to get glasses at once. If not, the army will provide a pair once you've been inducted."

I wondered if the hole in my left shoe or the patches on my collar had given away the fact that I didn't have extra money to spend on glasses. Either way, I was grateful I wouldn't have to buy them myself. I'd gone through school without glasses, so a few more weeks couldn't make much of a difference.

Later, I sat across from a pair of officers to talk about my background. Lieutenant Patterson represented the army and Ensign Edwards was from the navy, but he also answered questions about the marines and the Coast Guard.

"You were born in Germany?" Patterson asked.

"Yes, sir. Moved here when I was ten."

"Do you have any concerns about joining the service?"

"No, sir, not really." I sat up straight in my chair. "I was a little nervous about leaving my mom alone, but one of the Red Cross ladies gave me some paperwork to see that she gets a dependency allotment, so I'm set. I would have joined up earlier if my mom hadn't insisted I finish high school."

"Finishing school is fine. We have you now, and that's soon enough." The navy officer looked up from my paperwork. "You seem to have been a successful athlete."

"Good enough for the high school teams."

"Any mechanical experience?"

I thought of the bits of motorcycle still piled in the garage. I'd looked at them a few times but hadn't made any progress in putting them back into something that functioned. "A little. I keep my mom's car running. That thing's almost as old as I am. Something seems to break on it every other week."

"And what are you doing now that high school is finished?" the army man asked. "Other than waiting to be drafted?"

"I have a paper route, and I work on a farm. But it's a small farm, and Mr. Thompson has a couple of kids. They're younger, but now that school's out, they'll be able to help him more. He knows I'm trying to get into the service as soon as I can, and he won't request an agricultural deferment or anything."

Lieutenant Patterson rested his elbows on the desk and leaned forward. "Have you given any thought to which branch you'd like to join? We can't guarantee anything, but we'll take your preference into consideration."

"Yes, sir. I'd like to join the army and be a pilot in the air force."

He glanced at my paperwork and frowned. "Pilot cadets are required to have normal vision."

His words echoed through my brain. *Pilot cadets are required to have normal vision.* I sat there, stunned. With one sentence, he'd stolen my dream.

"What about becoming a navigator or a bombardier?" I couldn't be a pilot, but maybe I could still fly.

"Those positions usually require an advanced understanding of mathematics—beyond the normal high school level."

"What about aerial gunnery school?" I was starting to get desperate.

"I'm sorry, son, but that requires normal vision too." Patterson set the papers down. "Look, you're obviously motivated, and other than your eyesight, you're in good physical shape. Have you considered the infantry? Being able to speak German would be a huge asset to your unit. Give it some thought."

I thought about it for a few seconds, but infantry work meant being down on the ground instead of up in the air, so I turned to Ensign Edwards. "What are the requirements for navy pilots?"

He offered a half smile. "I'm afraid our pilots need good vision too. But if you want to be sure to see some action, the marine corps might be just the thing for you."

"I have the utmost respect for the marines, sir, but don't they usually end up in the Pacific?"

He nodded. "Is that a concern?"

Patterson cleared his throat. "Why waste a German speaker in the Pacific or at sea?"

"Because he's motivated and fit. Perfect match for the marine corps. And if he'd rather be a sailor, he's got some mechanical ability—we could put him in an engine room on a destroyer somewhere."

Patterson looked like he was going to make another argument, but I spoke first. "Sir, nine years ago, I was living in Germany. I woke up one morning and found out the Gestapo had arrested my father the night before. I never saw him again. He died of typhus in some camp called Sachsenhausen, and all he did was write a few things that weren't so flattering about the Nazis. Things haven't always been easy since we moved to the US, but we've done okay, you know? America gave us a chance. So if my country needs me to help invade Japan, I'll do it. But if there's any way I can serve in Europe and get back at the men who took my dad away, that's what I want to do, even more than I want to fly."

Edwards looked at me and then at the army rep. "Well, that being the case, I guess we better put you down for the army."

The army man stood and shook my hand. "Sometime in the next few weeks you can expect a notice in the mail telling you when to report. You'll go to a reception center, then basic training. Pick up a flier on your way out. It has a checklist of things to do. You'll have at least three weeks before you report."

I picked up all the paperwork and went to wait for the bus that would take me home. Once I was outside, it really hit me. I wasn't going to fly. Not as a pilot, not as a crew member. I'd always known the standards were high for pilots, but I'd assumed I'd at least have a chance to prove myself. I'd been waiting for years, and now, because of one measly eye exam, I was out.

I sulked while I waited. Recruiting posters covered a nearby wall. I could read them just fine. If my eyes were good enough to read posters, weren't they good enough to pick out an enemy plane?

One of the posters caught my attention. *Become a paratrooper,* it said. *Jump into the fight. Soldiers between the ages of 18 and 32, inclusive, who believe they have the qualifications for this thrilling service, may apply for parachutist training.* The poster said, *Jump into the fight.* But it might as well have said, *Fly into the fight.*

Joining the air corps wasn't the only way to get on a plane.

* * *

Five days later, I still hadn't received my induction date. As each day went by with no news, I got more and more antsy. Mom told me to be patient. Belle told me to relax. Mr. Thompson said he was glad to have me for a few more weeks and showed me how to clean his old Springfield rifle. He said I could shoot it too, if I could scrounge up some ammo. But I was worried about July's rent, so we never got around to testing my marksmanship.

I finished at the Thompson farm and rode home. When I arrived, Vivien Leigh was digging through my mom's mailbox. It wasn't really Vivien

Leigh—this lady wore normal clothes, not some big *Gone with the Wind* gown. Her skin was more olive than ivory, and she had a big birthmark on her cheek, but she still looked a lot like a movie star, from the victory rolls in her hair to the high heels on her feet.

"Can I help you?" I asked, propping my bicycle against the fence and eying the letters she held. I wasn't going to let anyone steal our mail, pretty face or not. That pile of letters might contain my summons to the army or something from one of my sisters. Maybe something from Bastien.

Vivien met my eyes and smiled. "You must be Lukas."

"Yeah," I said, assuming she'd gotten my name from the mail. I reached for the envelopes. "Why don't I take those?"

She ignored my hand and sorted through the mail. Eventually, she plucked a letter from the stack and handed the rest to me.

"I'd like that one too," I said.

"Actually, this one is for me."

"I don't think so."

"No, it is. See?" She flipped the envelope around so I could read it. It was addressed to *Mr. & Mrs. Ley*, which was a little odd. My dad had never lived in the US, let alone at our house in Virginia. But not everyone trying to sell insurance or war bonds knew that, so sometimes we got letters for him.

I snatched the envelope from her and headed for the house. *Crazy girl.*

"Will you at least tell me what it says?" she asked. "It's from a landlord in Alexandria, and if he has an apartment for us, I'll need to drive there now and put down a deposit."

I took another look at the mental case by the mailbox and kept walking to the house, wondering if I'd need to call the police. Or maybe the insane asylum.

"Lukas, is that how I taught you to treat a lady?" The male voice coming from the shadows on the porch sounded familiar.

I squinted as I ran up the steps to make sure I wasn't imagining it. Bastien was home, sitting on the porch bench. He grabbed a crutch and stood. I stopped, staring at his leg. Part of the left one was missing, and his pants were pinned up where I would have expected his knee to be. "Bastien?" I made it a question, even though I knew it was him.

His smile wavered as he followed my gaze down to his missing leg.

I closed the distance between us, feeling like a jerk for staring at his leg like that. I didn't care what was wrong with it. I didn't care that a loony girl was stealing our mail. I didn't even care that Bastien was probably going to strangle me when I told him about his Beeza. He was alive, and he was home. I gave him a hug, gripping him tightly to make sure he was really there. The telegram hadn't been enough, but with him solidly in my arms, a flood of relief washed over me.

He hugged me back and then released me, looking me over from head to foot. "When did you get so tall?" He was still taller than I was, but the difference in height had shrunk in the last eighteen months.

I shrugged and coughed back the tightness in my throat. "When did you get back?"

"Ship sailed in the day I sent the telegram. They let me out of the hospital this morning." Bastien held his hand out for the stack of letters, and I handed them over. He took the one Vivien Leigh had tried to swipe and opened it. He read it, then handed it to the woman as she joined us on the porch. "Lukas, I'd like you to meet my wife."

Bastien's wife smiled at me. *Mrs. Ley. Mrs. Bastien Ley.* She wasn't a movie star, and she wasn't a mail thief. She was my new sister-in-law.

"I'm sorry," I said.

She quirked one eyebrow. "Most people tell us congratulations."

"No, that's not what I meant. I'm sorry about the mail. And I'm glad you're married. At least, I think I am. The last girl Bastien brought home was a conniving idiot." The instant the words were out of my mouth, I realized my mistake. What if his wife didn't know he'd been engaged before, twice? My cheeks went hot. "But I'm sure his taste in women has improved since then." That didn't make it much better, but I was afraid if I said anything else it would be just as stupid.

My sister-in-law laughed.

Bastien grinned. "She knows more about my previous girlfriends than you do, so you haven't exposed any dark secrets. And we've yet to find an apartment, so it seems we'll be staying here awhile. Long enough for you to realize she's neither conniving nor an idiot."

Vivien Leigh held out a hand. "I'm Gracie," she said.

"I'm Lukas."

That smile came to her face again. "I know. Bastien talks about you a lot."

I hoped that wasn't a bad thing.

Bastien grabbed a second crutch from where it leaned against the house. I was about to ask what happened when Gracie caught my eye and shook her head slightly.

Bastien didn't seem to notice. "Mom said you had your induction exam last week. Do you still want to be a pilot?"

"Yeah, but I failed the eye test."

"I'm sorry to hear that." He glanced at his leg. I followed his gaze, wondering if there were things he wanted to do but couldn't because of whatever had happened. Maybe he understood how disappointing it was to be told you couldn't have your dream because some part of you wasn't perfect and there wasn't anything you could do to fix it.

Another thought crossed my mind, and I wondered what else Mom had told him. "Did Mom say anything about your motorcycle?"

"No. Why?"

I'd never been so desperate to take back something I'd said. *Welcome home, Bastien, I ruined your prized possession.* It was too late to go back now. Time to get the confession over with. Maybe Bastien wouldn't pound me too badly in front of his new wife—at least I assumed she was new. "How long have you been married?"

"Three weeks. And what were you going to say about my motorcycle?"

I swallowed and looked at my shoes. "I crashed it. Pretty bad. I don't think it's fixable."

I didn't really think Bastien would pummel me, even if Gracie weren't there, but I braced myself for a bawling out, for some type of lecture. It didn't come.

"Oh."

I risked looking at his face. He didn't seem mad. It was almost like he didn't care.

"Lukas, will you do me a favor?" Bastien asked.

"Sure." I hoped he wasn't about to tell me to go drown myself as punishment for the motorbike.

"Will you push Stefanie and Hannah's beds together? Gracie and I will be staying in their room."

I glanced at his leg one more time, then nodded and went inside.

In the corner of my sisters' old room was a small trunk, an army-issue duffel bag, and a prosthetic leg. My brother was crippled, and I wasn't sure what that meant for the future. I stared at the fake limb for a good minute before turning to the furniture.

Gracie followed me into the bedroom. "Let's put the beds in the middle, leaving an aisle on either side. More space by the door so Bastien has room to maneuver with the crutches. We can move the dresser under the window."

I nodded and pulled a drawer from the dresser so it would be easier to move. "Gracie, what happened to his leg?"

"The left one's been amputated just above the knee."

"Why?"

She set the prosthetic leg on one of the beds and moved the rest of the luggage to make a path for the dresser as I dragged it across the floor. "Because the doctors couldn't save it."

"Obviously not. But how did he injure it?"

"He got shot a few times."

A few times? "Will he always need crutches?"

"No, but he's only had his prosthesis about a week, and he's still getting used to it. Sometimes the crutches are easier, especially by the end of the day."

"And he doesn't like talking about it?"

Her lips pulled into a half smile. "Depends on the day, but I think telling your mother was enough for now."

"Does it hurt him?"

"He doesn't say. But the prosthesis gave him blisters, and they haven't healed yet. He had it on most of the day. Took it off a little before you got home. If it hadn't been bothering him, I suppose he would have left it on."

I lifted one side of Stefanie's bed and helped Gracie move it away from the wall, and then we did the same thing with Hannah's bed. "How did you two meet?" I asked.

"I was working for the War Department in Europe. So was he."

"Have you known each other long?"

She opened the window to let in the breeze. "Long enough."

That wasn't the answer I was looking for, but I let it go. "You from around here?"

"I was born in Italy. Came to America when I was eleven, went to Salt Lake City. I was in Virginia before I went overseas, and I'll be working here again." She pulled the blankets up to the top of the bed, but even when the bedding was smooth, her hands kept in constant motion.

"Salt Lake. Does that mean you're a Mormon?"

She nodded.

That was at least one thing she and my brother had in common. An important thing. "So what do you do for the War Department?"

She took her time answering. "Communications. Do you know where the pillows are?"

I grabbed them from the closet. I almost asked what type of communications, but she spoke first.

"I think your mother has supper about ready. Will you make sure there's a chair for Bastien with a few feet of space around it?"

I left Gracie to finish making the beds and went to shift the kitchen table out from the wall and set four places. My mom smiled as she ladled chicken dumpling soup into bowls. It was Bastien's favorite.

I filled the glasses with water. "Did you know he was coming today?"

"*Nein*. Not until he knocked on the door."

"Did you know he was married?"

"I didn't even know he met someone." She pursed her lips briefly. "But I like her. More importantly, he likes her. I haven't seen him this happy in a long time."

I watched my brother and his new wife when they came to eat. She seemed to know exactly what he'd need help with, offering him a hand as he sat. He'd put his fake leg back on. The knee didn't seem to bend very well, but the two of them made the movement smoothly, as if they'd practiced. It was odd to think of him as crippled and imperfect. But even more strange was seeing my brother, the man who never needed help with anything, accepting Gracie's assistance and even smiling about it.

Bastien's leg wasn't the only thing that had changed while he was away.

CHAPTER 4

"It's great having him back," I told Belle over the sound of milk squirting into the empty pail. "But it's strange too." Bastien had been home for two days, but Belle hadn't been singing the day before because her father was replacing the squeaky hinge on the barn door.

"Why's that?"

I stopped milking as I pinpointed my reply. "He got married without telling us. That's kind of a big deal. I would have expected him to write a letter or something."

"Do you like her?"

"Sure. But I barely know her. And to have them show up like that without any hint that he even had a girl . . . And it's weird to see him letting someone help him."

Belle ran her hands through my hair. "That's right; he's always been the one taking care of the rest of you."

"He still is. I said I was worried about Mom keeping up with the yardwork when I enlisted, so yesterday he found her a job at a bakery in town. The owner's son went into the service six months ago, and the daughter-in-law went to live with her parents, so there's an empty apartment on the second story. Mom can live there and won't have to mow a lawn, won't have to drive, won't have to clean houses anymore. It's perfect."

"If it's perfect, why do you sound so sad about it?"

The silence hung in the air, broken only by a bellow from the cow. "Why didn't I think of something like that ages ago?"

"It wouldn't have worked ages ago because you were still in school."

I grunted. "Maybe. I guess I'm just feeling a little redundant with Bastien back. Mom doesn't need me if Bastien's looking out for her."

Belle's hands moved to my shoulders. "You've been doing just fine taking care of your mother. Bastien's just had a little more practice at it."

"Yeah." He'd been twenty-three when our dad died. Mom had mostly deferred to him ever since. He'd been the breadwinner from the day our dad was arrested until the dependency payments had stopped coming six months ago.

"Have you decided what you want to do in the army yet?"

That brought a smile to my lips, which was probably the reason she'd asked. "Airborne sounds exciting. And if I'm going into battle, it would be nice to go with a bunch of people who volunteered to jump out of a plane instead of with a bunch of people who're only fighting because they were drafted. The extra pay doesn't sound too bad either."

"And you'd look right smart in a uniform and jump boots."

I huffed. "Yeah, and glasses." I'd never made fun of people who wore glasses, but that didn't mean I was eager to join their ranks.

The barn door slapped against the frame, and I jerked around.

Belle's dad stood in the doorway with his shotgun on his shoulder, and he didn't look happy to see me. "I thought I told you to stay away from my daughter."

I shot to my feet. Belle positioned herself between me and her dad, her back to me. I tried to move her out of the way, but she resisted.

"He won't shoot me," she whispered.

"Get out of the way, Annabelle. You know better than to associate with a kraut." Her dad still had the shotgun slung across his shoulder. Could I make it to the door before he aimed?

Belle grabbed my hands and inched toward the barn's only exit, keeping me behind her. "Daddy, you're overreacting. Luke's not a kraut. He's just about to join the army."

"Hmph. Which one? Ours or the Nazis'?"

"Ours, of course. He'll probably win a medal."

Her dad scowled. "Get out of the way, Annabelle."

"I'm not going to let you shoot him."

We were ten feet from the door. I squeezed Belle's hands before I let go and sprinted for the opening. I kept running despite the noise behind me. It felt wrong to leave her, but Belle was right; her dad wouldn't shoot her. But they were sure yelling at each other as I dashed around the barn and ran for the copse of trees.

I heard Mr. Montgomery behind me. I doubted he was as quick as I was, but he didn't have to be, not when he was armed. His footsteps tore through the overgrown grass. If they weren't gaining on me, they weren't falling farther behind either.

"Daddy, no!"

An instant after Belle's shout, the shotgun exploded. A second later, I tumbled to the earth as pricks of pain tore into my back and burned from my shoulders to my waist.

"Luke!" Belle sounded desperate. I turned my head to look back. Her dad was dragging her to the house. "Luke!" I could tell she wasn't crying out for rescue. She wanted to know if I was still alive.

For her sake, I forced myself to stand, even though moving made everything hurt more. When I twisted my neck around, splotches of blood were visible on my shoulders. I tumbled over the white picket fence and headed for the back door of my house, hunched over in biting pain. It would have been easier to collapse on the grass, but I didn't want Belle to worry. Nor did I want her dad coming around for a second shot. Besides, I'd read more than one story about soldiers carrying on despite serious injury. Only later did they keel over. I needed to go somewhere safe before my adrenaline wore out. Mom would have left already, but the newlyweds would be home still.

The kitchen door burst open before I reached it, and Bastien limped toward me. "I heard a gunshot."

"Yeah. Mr. Montgomery's shotgun."

His eyes widened. He grabbed my arm and pulled me inside. He stayed behind me, probably checking the damage. "Gracie, will you make sure my pistol is loaded?"

Gracie nodded. "Should I go for the police?"

"No," I said. "It's probably just bird shot, or I'd still be lying out there."

Bastien followed me to my room, navigating around the clutter on the floor. "Take your shirt off and lie on your stomach."

I had to bite my lips to keep from whimpering as I stripped off my shirt. My back burned. "How bad is it?"

"It can't be too serious if you're still standing."

Gracie peeked into the room as I crawled onto the bed.

Bastien turned to her. "I'll need tweezers, rags, water, and iodine."

"Where should I look?"

"In the bathroom under the sink," I told her.

As soon as she left, Bastien sat on the edge of the bed. "Drop your pants. I need to see how far down it goes."

I grimaced.

"Come on, I used to change your diapers. And you won't get any privacy in the army."

I thought about arguing, but Bastien usually got his way, and I didn't want to have my rear end exposed when Gracie got back, so I undid my belt and fly and pushed my pants down a little. My brother grabbed my waistband and jerked it down a bit more.

"Clear." He pulled my pants back up just before Gracie returned. "Thank you," he told her. He got to work. I squeezed my eyes shut as the wet rag cleaned the blood away. I couldn't quite hold back a groan when he started with the tweezers.

"What is it?" Gracie asked.

I glanced at my brother. He held a small, blood-covered something in the tweezers. He wiped at it with a rag, then held it to his tongue. "Rock salt."

I hadn't realized how scared I was until Bastien gave his diagnosis. Rock salt. It hurt, but it wasn't going to kill me. I sighed with relief.

"Why did Mr. Montgomery shoot you with rock salt?"

"Because I was in his barn milking the cow for Belle."

"His daughter?" Bastien dug another piece out of my back.

I had to let my breath out slowly as he worked with the tweezers. "Yeah, he told me to stay away from her."

"Then why didn't you?" Another piece came out.

"'Cause we like each other."

Bastien removed a few more pieces in silence. "Lukas, have you gotten Annabelle in some type of trouble? Is that why her father shot you?"

"Yeah, she'll probably be in plenty of trouble. Grounded for a few months, I imagine. Maybe all summer."

"That's not what I meant."

Gracie picked up some of the bloody rags. "I'll go rinse these out."

"Then what did you mean?" I asked.

He extracted a particularly painful bit of rock salt and then another. "Annabelle isn't expecting a baby, is she?"

"What? No!" I was hurt that he'd even consider something like that. "I go to church, you know. And I've read the scriptures a few times."

"Plenty of people go to church and read the scriptures. That doesn't mean they don't sometimes stray, either deliberately or in a moment of passion."

"I thought you knew me better than that. I've kissed her a few times. That's it."

He was quiet for a few more pieces of rock salt. "Sorry to doubt your integrity. But I haven't seen much of you the last few years."

"Yeah."

"If Mr. Montgomery didn't shoot you because you got his daughter in trouble, why did he shoot you?"

"'Cause I'm a dirty kraut. And a Mormon too, which might be even worse." My back still burned, and so did my temper. Most of the people I'd graduated with took America for granted. Not me. I might not have been born in the US, but that just meant I appreciated her more. And I didn't see anything wrong with the religion my parents joined in 1921. It wasn't like Belle's dad was a preacher somewhere else. He might have been baptized at some point into some church, probably as a baby, but I doubted he'd been back since.

"Do you often spend mornings in the barn with her?"

"Most days. Unless her dad's around."

"When did you get old enough to have a girlfriend?" Bastien wiped the tweezers and then started on my back with an iodine-soaked rag.

I didn't think my cuts could sting any worse than they already did, but I was wrong. I waited until he was done before I trusted myself to talk again. "It didn't start out like that. We both needed a friend at the same time, I guess. Her mom died a little over a year ago. A couple days after the funeral, I noticed her crying out by those trees, so I went and talked to her. Belle was the smartest kid in school, but she didn't know anything about heaven, so I invited her to church. It was Easter, so I thought it would give her hope about her mom, you know? I didn't mean to convert her. Or turn her into my sweetheart. It just kind of happened."

"Is she worth it?"

"Sure. It's not like milking a cow's all that hard. My arms were pretty sore for a few weeks, but they're used to it now."

Bastien chuckled softly. "Worth getting shot for?"

"Well, seeing as how it was just rock salt." I shrugged, which was a big mistake. The pain flared so intensely that I almost puked. "Man, my back feels like it's on fire."

Bastien glanced at his scarred hands, marred during the fire when he was a boy. I'd said the wrong thing, again, just when it seemed like he was going to accept that I was old enough to risk my neck for a girl. He gathered up the supplies and left me on my bed, staring at the ruined shirt I'd been wearing. I needed to start my paper route, and I needed to get to the Thompson farm. But I didn't feel like moving.

A few minutes later, I glanced at the clock. 7:15. I sat up and winced. As I hobbled into the hallway, I heard Gracie's voice.

"Are you sure this is a good idea?"

I came around the corner. Bastien was in full uniform with his pistol in its holster. "Where are you going?" I asked.

"I'm going to have a few words with Mr. Montgomery."

"Whoa—I don't think that's such a good idea," I said. We'd both been born in Germany, but Bastien still sounded German. All he had to do was mispronounce one *the* as *ze* and Belle's dad might give him the same treatment he'd given me. And if he didn't have any shells with rock salt, he might throw in a few with buckshot instead. "He hates Germans, even American ones, especially since his son got killed fighting them."

"I'm a uniformed American officer, and I was wounded while in the US Army. I think he'll respect that."

"Bastien, you still sound like a kraut. And Mr. Montgomery is as stubborn as they come."

"Which is why I'm bringing my pistol."

"Can you hold your pistol and your crutches at the same time?" I was thankful those words came from Gracie, not from me. I didn't want to remind him that he was crippled, but surely he'd listen to his wife.

He brought his hand up to caress her cheek. "It was rock salt, not lead. He may be pigheaded and prejudiced, but I don't think he wants a murder on his hands. And I'm not the one stealing kisses from his daughter."

"Then why don't you let me come along?" Gracie put one hand on her hip.

"Because if I'm wrong about our neighbor, I want you to be safe."

"I'm quite capable of helping."

Bastien grinned. "I know. Stay here anyway, please?" He kissed her on the forehead. "How do I look?"

"As intimidating as ever, *mein hauptmann*." *My captain.* I hadn't known Gracie could speak German.

If his wife couldn't keep him from walking over to the madman's house, I should have known I couldn't convince him. But I tried anyway. "Bastien, you shouldn't go. He's warned me a couple times. And it doesn't hurt that bad." The truth was, my back still stung in a dozen different spots, and I felt like I was going to fall over, but Bastien didn't need to know that.

"He shot my brother. I'm not going to pretend it didn't happen. What if you'd looked the wrong way when he fired? He could have blinded you.

And since I'm taking your word that you've been a perfect gentleman with Annabelle, he was in the wrong."

He shuffled out the front door on his crutches, and Gracie and I followed him onto the porch. We watched him limp across the grass and around the fence, moving slowly over the uneven ground. I hated that he was risking his life for me, and I hated that he wouldn't listen to me when I told him it was a bad idea.

When he disappeared behind the barn, I sneaked a glance at Gracie. Her lips were drawn into a thin, tense line, her eyes were focused on the side of the Montgomery house, and her hands were balled into fists.

"I'm sorry, Gracie." It came out as a whisper.

She glanced at me and folded her arms. "Bastien can take care of himself. I'm just worried about his new leg. If things go badly, he might try something on reflex before he realizes he can't do it anymore."

"I don't know why he's so insistent on walking into that hornet's nest. Mr. Montgomery might not shoot him, but he's not going to listen to him either."

"He doesn't want to see you get hurt, Lukas." Her face was serious, but her tone was kind.

"If he doesn't want to see me get hurt, he should have been easier with the iodine."

One side of her lips curled up. I had to hand it to Bastien. He knew how to pick a pretty wife. "How bad is it?"

"It feels like somebody poked a bunch of holes in my back and then poured salt in them. My paper route is gonna be hell today. Same with the farm work." There was still no movement from the Montgomery place. "Sorry. Bastien would tell me not to use language like that around a lady."

That brought a full smile to her lips. "You didn't use it as a curse, and even if you had, I spent a week on a ship full of soldiers not too long ago. I'd hardly call *hell* a swear word."

"He'd still tell me not to say it. I don't know if you've noticed, but he's a little bossy."

"He's the oldest, and he's an officer. What do you expect?" She shifted her hands and leaned against the porch railing. "Although I would take that same trait and call him confident and decisive."

I guess that meant my brother knew how to pick a loyal wife too.

He was probably gone only ten minutes, but it felt like a few hours. As soon as he came into sight, Gracie went to meet him at the property line. He even let her take one of his crutches, and he wrapped an arm around her shoulders for support.

I held the door open for them when they reached it. "Well?" I asked as they came inside.

"Mr. Montgomery and I have come to an understanding. He won't threaten you with a firearm again. But no more milking his cow."

I frowned. "And Belle? Is she all right?"

"You really like that girl, don't you?" he asked.

"Yeah." I left it at that. He'd already finagled more about my relationship with Belle than I would have told him under different circumstances.

"Well, she seems to like you too. Climbed out the window and ran after me when I was done talking to her father. Seemed quite concerned about your injury, even though her father already told her it was rock salt. She said she's not allowed to go anywhere without him until you're inducted. But they're going to see the new Ingrid Bergman movie tomorrow evening. She'll sneak out after the newsreel."

CHAPTER 5

THE NEXT NIGHT I SAT in the dark movie theater a few rows from the back entrance. I'd arrived early so I could watch everyone file in. *Gaslight* had been out awhile, so the theater wasn't crowded. I sat hunched over, both to hide my face and to keep my back from pressing into the seat. My rock-salt-torn flesh wasn't as bad as it had been the day before, but it still hurt. Mr. Thompson had given me two days off. Gracie had driven me around for my paper route, but even with a ride, delivering papers had been painful.

Belle and her dad came in right before the newsreel began. She'd said her dad didn't like people sitting in front of him. He walked right to the first row. I was more interested in the newsreel about Normandy than I was in the movie, and I almost missed Belle as she walked out to the lobby. I counted to twenty and then followed her.

Dozens of people milled about the lobby, but it didn't take long for me to spot Belle because she practically ran to me. "Luke, are you okay?" She didn't wrap her arms around me—thank goodness—but she curled up next to my chest, making it easy for me to hold her without aggravating my back.

"I'm great. I got to sleep in this morning instead of getting up early to milk someone else's cow." Her arms moved like she was trying to get one free so she could slug me, so I pulled her closer. "Naw, I actually missed you."

"How's your back?"

"It hurts. Your dad ruined one shirt with rock-salt holes, and I've got two others that I bled all over." I was going to run out of clothes if the stains didn't come out, but the army would give me stuff to wear, so I wasn't too worried. "Nothing's very deep. It just stings, but not as bad as it did yesterday."

"I was so worried about you."

"You grounded?"

"Mostly. No church. No going into town unless Aunt Edith's with me. No movies unless Dad's with me."

I wasn't surprised, but I was disappointed that church was off limits. I liked seeing her there and talking with her afterward. "I bet that birthday of yours can't come soon enough."

"Sixty-five days left."

"You counted?"

"Yeah. Yesterday." She rested her head on my chest and sighed. "I told Daddy I was going to the ladies' room. If I'm gone too long, he might come looking for me. I better go."

I didn't want to let her go, but I didn't want to face an angry Mr. Montgomery in the lobby either. Rumor was the 29th Division had gotten a little chewed up during the landings in Normandy. The 29th Division had originally been a National Guard unit from Virginia, so Mr. Montgomery wasn't the only local resident with a personal reason to loathe krauts and kraut immigrants. He might find a few buddies to join him if he wanted to teach me another lesson. But I wasn't sure when I'd see Belle again. "I'm going to miss you."

"I always get the mail, so you can write to me."

"Yeah, but I can't kiss a letter." I wasn't sure what else to say. She lived next door, but there was a possibility I'd never see her again. I didn't want to say anything mushier than I already had, so I just kissed her cheek and relaxed my arms. "Guess you better go before your dad comes looking for you."

"Be careful once you get in the army, okay?"

I nodded and watched her walk back into the theater. I pulled my ticket from my pocket and looked at it, but I wasn't really in the mood for noir. Saying good-bye to Belle was depressing enough.

I rode my bicycle home from the movie theater, grateful my rear end hadn't gotten the rock-salt treatment. I wondered how long the rest of me was going to hurt. I was hungry, so after I put my bike away, I went around back to the kitchen door.

The window was open, and Bastien's voice floated through the screen. "He said something about wanting to be a paratrooper."

"Jump school will keep him in training longer," Gracie said.

"Yes, but then he'll be dropped right in the middle of a battle. If not in Europe, then in Japan."

"Artillery?"

"Maybe. It would be safer than the infantry, but he'd be a target for enemy shells, not to mention the damage to his hearing. It would be nice to get him on someone's staff. Someone high up who keeps his distance from the front line. What were his grades like?"

"Better this last semester. I think he was trying to impress Belle. But overall, just average." I recognized my mom's voice, so it seemed all three of them were having a conversation about me.

"Unlikely he'll be picked up for officer's training, then, at least at first," Bastien said. "I could ask around when I go back to work. Someone might need a clerk who speaks German. But then he might get pulled into something else."

"What about a supply company?" Gracie asked.

"That would be ideal, but they don't exactly seek out volunteers. Maybe—"

I yanked the door open and cut my brother off. "And even if they asked for volunteers, I don't want a safe job in the rear with the gear." I glanced around at each of their faces. Bastien frowned, Gracie studied the tabletop, and Mom just looked sad. "I don't want to avoid combat."

I stomped through the house to my bedroom. I hadn't cracked the window earlier, and it was stifling. I kicked aside a pile of clothes and shoved the window open. But the room was still stuffy, and my temper matched the heat. I went out to the front porch instead, wondering why everyone felt the need to baby me. I might be the youngest in the family, but I was eighteen now, and there was a war on. A war my family understood better than most. I kicked a stray piece of gravel from the porch and leaned against the railing.

A minute or two later, Bastien opened the front door. He stood in the doorway for a while, then came out to stand next to me, leaning his crutches on the rail. "Did you ever think how hard it would be for Mom to send you off to war?"

His words cut deeper than I wanted to admit. Mom was the last person in the world I wanted to hurt. Dad had left. Bastien had left. Stefanie and Hannah had left. And Belle was grounded. But Mom had always been there, had always held the family together, even when the family was scattered, even when we were poor, even when it was just her and me. "Right. So you can go off to war and get shot a few times, but I'm supposed to try and weasel my way out of service?"

"I'm not suggesting you become a conscientious objector, but if the chance for a safe assignment comes along, would it be so awful to take it?"

"Is that what you did?"

"I made commitments to the army before the war started. I promised Dad I would take care of the family, and the army helped me do that." He kept his tone and volume calm and reasonable, but that only made me more frustrated.

"Sure, so you went off and almost got killed. 'Cause you'd be able to take real good care of Mom and the rest of us as a ghost."

"She was the beneficiary on my life insurance. And she was getting a dependency allotment in the meantime."

"Well, the dependency allotment stopped coming in November. Mom was sick most of the winter and couldn't work. I was paying rent with my paper route and farm work, and the only reason we had food money was because Belle talked her aunt into hiring me for a landscaping project."

Bastien swore.

"How come you can say that, but you always tell me not to?"

He ignored my question. "I made arrangements so you'd be taken care of."

"Well, someone fouled up."

"Yes, and I have a good idea who. If he wasn't safe in Europe, I'd kill him."

I opened my mouth to say something, but I wasn't sure if he was joking or not. "Well, now you're here, and you can take care of Mom while I take your place on the front lines."

"Lukas, war isn't some grand adventure."

"I never said it was. But just because it's hard doesn't mean I should sit it out."

"German bullets won't be packed with rock salt."

"Yeah, I know." I tried to keep my words as level as his, but I wasn't succeeding.

He looked at me, every muscle in his face tight and hard. "Fine. You don't like our ideas from the kitchen. What do *you* want to do in the army?"

I shrugged. "I hear they mostly need infantry. Airborne sounds good."

"You can't even keep track of your watch. How are you going to keep track of a rifle?"

"I'll figure it out."

"And what about your eyesight? You can't shoot the enemy if you can't see him."

"I'll get glasses. And if my marksmanship's still off, I can be part of a tank crew. A loader or something."

Bastien pushed off the railing. "Do you know the nickname for Sherman tanks? Ronsons. Because just like the cigarette lighter, they light every time."

"So they should put someone with a wife and a couple of kids in there instead? And let him get killed instead of me? Because that's what it's coming down to. They're inducting guys like me, fresh out of high school, and guys with kids. You're acting like I have a choice. But you know what, I'm going to be in the service whether I like it or not. I can step up and try to make a difference, or I can get dragged in kicking and screaming."

Bastien looked away as a breeze ruffled both our nearly identical hair. "You think you'll make a difference as cannon fodder?"

"Look, I know the risks. I may get on that bus to boot camp and never see Mom again. I said good-bye to Belle tonight. I might never see her again either. But I'm going to do my part because I remember how rotten it was to have Dad arrested for no good reason and then have him disappear. I'm not going to let the Nazis win."

Bastien opened his mouth and turned to face me. In the process, he knocked his crutches over. One fell on the porch, and the other tumbled onto the lawn.

I'd watched him accept help from Gracie, but I wasn't sure he'd accept help from me. "Want me to pick those up for you?"

"No." His answer was immediate. Then he sighed. "Yes."

I grabbed them both and leaned them against the rail within easy reach. I was tired of arguing, and I had a feeling his pride was battered enough that he was sick of it too.

"Lukas, you don't know how awful war can be."

"I'll find out soon."

His eyes focused on mine, stern and serious. "Lukas . . ."

I shook my head in frustration. "Bastien, you've been acting like my dad for years. But you know what? I'm not a kid anymore." I shoved my hands into my pockets and walked away. I needed space and time and more of that soft summer breeze blowing through my hair and cooling off my anger. Maybe Bastien felt the same way, because he didn't call me back.

I walked around for about an hour. I didn't know where my watch was, so I couldn't be sure. But the funny thing about bumming around alone with nothing but the chirp of crickets and the occasional shuffling of a raccoon was that I couldn't escape my thoughts.

Bastien had been gone for a lot of my life. He served a Church mission when I was seven and eight, then he was in the army when I was eleven, twelve, thirteen, and fourteen. He'd gone to college for a little bit, but he'd stayed in the National Guard and been called up before Pearl Harbor. Since then, he'd been training, first in the States, then in Europe. Then he'd disappeared for a while. I'd missed him every single time he'd gone away, so why was it so hard to talk to him now that he was here? He was the closest thing to a dad I had left, so why was I throwing his protective instincts back in his face like they were something bad?

By the time I meandered back to the house, I was ready to apologize. Not for my desire to join the army but for arguing. Mom didn't have to know I was so eager to fight the Nazis. Maybe I could stop talking about enlistment for a while. It would still happen, of course, but it might be easier on her. And easier on Bastien. And maybe if I could keep my temper in check, it would be easier for them both to see me as an adult.

When the porch came into view, Bastien was still there, with Gracie. I decided my apology could wait because I didn't want to interrupt the rather involved kiss they were sharing. I tiptoed along the side of the lawn, as far from the porch as I could get on our property. I wanted to give them privacy, but I couldn't help looking, and frankly, I could think of a few movie stars who could have taken lessons. The perfect mix of passion and tenderness left an impression on me. I'd never kissed Belle like that, but seeing how complete the two of them seemed together made me hope that someday I'd find the same thing. And in the meantime, I was happy for Bastien. More than anyone I knew, he deserved that type of joy.

I went inside through the back door. The kitchen was deserted. There were a few dishes in the sink, so to make up for the pain I was causing everyone, I filled the sink with soapy water and scrubbed them clean. I was drying the last one when I heard something and turned around.

Bastien stood in the doorway, watching me. "I worry about you because I love you. You know that, don't you?"

I smiled. He'd beaten me to the apology, and not for the first time. "Yeah, I guess I do know that."

* * *

Bastien was waiting outside with an envelope in his hand when I rode my bicycle back from the Thompson farm the next day. He gave it to me when I stepped onto the porch. He'd had the decency not to open it, but we both knew what it was.

It took effort to hold my hands steady as I broke the seal and took out the letter. *ORDER TO REPORT FOR INDUCTION* was printed across the top. I whispered the words as I read them. "*The President of the United States, to Lukas Jürgen Ley. Greeting: Having submitted yourself to a local board composed of your neighbors for the purpose of determining your availability for training and service in the land or naval forces of the United States, you are hereby notified that you have now been selected for training and service therein.*"

"When?" Bastien asked.

"July 10." It was earlier than Mom or Belle wanted, later than I'd planned.

He gazed past me in silence. "July 10," he finally said. "I suppose you ought to tell Mom."

"Yeah, I guess so." I went inside and found her in the kitchen setting the table. "Mom?"

"*Ja?*"

I held the letter out to her. "I report July 10."

She bit her lower lip as she read. Maybe it was just the lighting in the kitchen, but her skin seemed to turn paler. She put her hand on my arm. "Sometimes I wonder when I will stop losing things to that madman."

"I'm not lost, Mom."

"At the very least, I will lose time with you—weeks, months. Maybe years. And at the worst . . ." She swallowed and looked away.

"Mom, you understand better than most people. Hitler has to be stopped."

She patted my arm again. "Yes. It is right to fight him. But a mother worries. I am not sure how many prayers I can expect the Lord to answer. I may have worn Him out with all my pleas for Bastien."

"Mom . . ." I wanted to promise her I'd come back, but I couldn't guarantee that. I could only try. "I'll do my best to come home again."

She nodded. I guess she knew that was the most I could do. The truth was Hitler had already taken a lot from her. Her husband. Her house. Most of her possessions. Bastien's leg. And maybe my future.

"Mom?"

"*Ja?*"

"Do you remember what you told me when we found out what happened to Dad? You said Dad's body was gone, but his soul would never die. And you said if we were good, we would be a family forever. Do you still believe that?"

"*Ja.*"

"So do I. So if everything goes according to plan, I'll whip up on those Nazis and be back safe and sound before you know it. And if not, I'll just get to see Dad again before you do." The words tumbled off my tongue easily, and I meant them. But even though I missed my dad, I wanted to come back to my mom, and with my induction notice, the possibility that I might not return was suddenly real.

CHAPTER 6

AFTER SUPPER, BASTIEN PUSHED HIMSELF upright and put his hand on my shoulder. "Let's go outside for a bit."

I glanced at the tabletop. It had been my job to tidy up after meals for a couple of years. Some days I even did it without grousing.

Gracie piled up the plates and silverware. "I'll handle the cleanup."

"Thanks, Gracie," I said. Sharing the home's single bathroom with a sister-in-law was an adjustment, but I liked sharing a kitchen with her.

I followed Bastien out the back door, hoping he hadn't found something new to lecture me about.

"Since you're going to end up in this war regardless of my wishes, I want to help you be ready."

That sounded good to me, but as he walked onto the grass with only one of his crutches, he had a hard time balancing. If his leg was having a bad day, I didn't want to make it worse. And I was tired after working at the Thompson farm. "You know they still have basic training, right?"

"Yes. But none of your drill sergeants will care as much about your safety as I do. And, frankly, I probably have more experience than most of them."

I swatted away a mosquito. "So you want to go over what they'll teach me beforehand?"

"Not necessarily. Have you had any firearms training?"

"No. Mr. Thompson said I could practice with his rifle, but I have to get my own ammo."

"What type is it?"

"Springfield," I said.

"1903?"

I nodded.

Bastien considered it. "They'll probably issue you an M1, but any practice should help. Gracie's leave is over in a few days. I'll ask her to pick up some ammunition."

"Gracie can pick up ammunition at work?"

"Probably. We'll start with hand-to-hand combat. I don't suppose you've had much training in that?"

I shrugged. "Not unless you count football."

Bastien lifted his left hand and held it out to the side, bent at the elbow. "Give me your best jab."

"You want me to punch you?"

He wiggled his hand. "Right here. As hard as you can."

I glanced at his half leg and hesitated, but I figured he knew what he was doing. I balled my fist up and whacked his outstretched hand.

"Boys!"

Mom stood at the kitchen door, hands on her hips and eyes wide in shock. I guess she thought we were fighting, which was so ridiculous it was funny. I'd roughhoused with my sisters, but the age gap between Bastien and me meant we'd never gotten physical with our disagreements. When I was younger, I'd known I wouldn't stand a chance against him, and he wasn't the bully type as a brother or the corporal-punishment type as a stand-in father.

"Just a little practice, Mom," Bastien said. "I thought I'd give him a head start on his training."

Mom didn't look pleased, but she went back inside.

Gracie had stepped outside too. "Take it easy on him."

I gave my sister-in-law a big smile. "Don't worry, I will."

Gracie cleared her throat. "I was actually talking to Bastien."

I didn't know Gracie well enough to tell if she was joking or not, so I didn't laugh. I didn't want to insult my brother. He was taller and his muscles were bigger, but he had only one full leg. I wasn't all that worried.

I turned back to Bastien for a clue about whether she was teasing. I couldn't tell what he thought of her comments, but I could tell what he thought of her. "You're whooped."

He raised an eyebrow. "Is that a challenge? Because I've seen worse punches, but you're hardly a professional."

I laughed. "No, I'm not talking about me." I nodded to the back door. Gracie had gone inside. "She's got you wrapped around her finger."

"Said the boy getting up before the sun and risking a gunshot to milk Annabelle's cow."

I waved away another insect. "I'm not doing it anymore. And it's only before sunrise in the winter."

Bastien chuckled. "Right. Let's get going. First rule of hand-to-hand combat: if at all possible, get a weapon. A gun or knife is preferable, but if that's not feasible, a stick, a rock, a chair—just about anything is better than nothing."

I nodded.

"For now, we'll work on what to do if you find yourself unarmed. Your fists are useful, but it takes time and practice to develop a punch powerful enough to knock someone out. If you have a chance to do any boxing at boot camp, do it. In the meantime, I think we can get you ready with a few other strikes by the end of the week."

He held his crutch to his side with his elbow and pointed to a spot between the little finger and wrist of his other hand. "Keep your fingers straight and thumb extended. Use the edge of your hand to chop at your opponent." He demonstrated with smooth, slow motions. "Wrist, fore-arm, biceps, neck, right below the Adam's apple, kidneys, base of spine."

"Adam's apple?" I pressed against my throat. "That sounds like it could do permanent damage."

"Rule number two: Normal rules of decency don't apply when some-one is trying to kill you. You've got to kill or be killed. It's ugly, but you can't hesitate, or you'll lose your chance."

We practiced edge-of-the-hand blows, with Bastien critiquing my form, making sure I kept my palm down and swung out when I hit hori-zontally, reminding me to keep my elbow bent when I chopped toward his wrist.

"Now do it faster."

By the time the sun set, we'd moved on to chin jabs with an open fist.

"Once you've knocked his chin, don't hesitate to go for the eyes."

"Okay." It was brutal, but after my brother's previous tips, it didn't surprise me.

"Don't draw back first, or you'll lose the element of surprise. Speed is everything. And if your opponent isn't in a good position for this strike, aim for between his legs with your knee. Even if you miss, you'll draw his chin forward and down."

"Have you ever tried this in real life?"

Bastien smiled slightly. "Rule number three: Don't ask what I did in Europe. But everything I'm teaching you will work if done correctly."

I nodded, trying to hide my disappointment. He always changed the subject when I asked about his time overseas. It was like he thought I wasn't mature enough to hear about war.

He must have noticed my mood change. "We'll go over one more thing before we call it a night. How to sneak up on a sentry. Might prove useful if you end up as a rifleman and some fool officer sends you off to capture a prisoner."

"All right. What do I do?"

"First, prepare. No loose clothing, no unnecessary equipment. Darken your face with oil or dirt; cover your hair. Wear rubber shoes, or put a pair of socks on outside your boots. Then observe. Wait till your target is relaxed. Approach him from behind. Strike his neck with your forearm bone and at the same time punch him in the small of his back. If you hit his throat, he'll inhale and be unable to call for help. Then slap your hand over his mouth and nose." Bastien acted it out as he explained. "Turn around."

I obeyed, and he went through the motions on me without any force in his blows.

"Now you try."

I wiped my sweaty hands off on my pants as I approached him from behind. I didn't worry too much about stealth or speed; I just focused on going through the movements correctly. Sneak up behind my opponent, strike the throat and back at the same time, clap my hand over the mouth. Even though he was taller than I was, I seemed to manage okay. "So now I just cart you back to camp for interrogation, huh?" I moved my hand from Bastien's mouth so he could answer.

"Usually. If you've hit hard enough, your opponent will probably be half conscious. If you haven't hit hard enough, make sure he doesn't do this to you."

In less than a second, Bastien broke my hold and somehow ducked underneath me. He flipped me over his back and flung me to the ground, with one of my arms still in his grip and his false foot resting on my chest. The rock-salt wounds throbbed with the impact, and the grass tickled my neck as I looked up at him. "How did you do that?"

Bastien released me so I could get back to my feet. "We'll go over that tomorrow."

I rubbed my rear, sure I was going to have a bruise there. "Didn't Gracie tell you to go easy on me?"

Bastien chuckled and accepted his crutch when I handed it to him. "You aren't really whining about a little bruise, are you?"

"I'm not whining. I'm just asking a question."

"Mmm."

"Where did you learn all that? Do they go over that in basic?"

We'd reached the back porch. "No. I'd been in the army awhile when I got that training. From a couple men who helped run the Shanghai riot squad."

"Shanghai?"

"Yes. In China. Before the Japanese took over, there was a large international section with their own rules. I gather typical police procedures weren't quite enough to keep the peace."

"I know where Shanghai is," I said. "In fact, I think I met one of your instructors. He helped ruin your motorcycle because he was driving like he was still in the International Settlement."

"Oh? Who?"

"Captain Cunningham."

"And he didn't offer to fix it after he ran you off the road?"

"He gave us some money. But we were short for rent . . . I'm sorry."

Bastien smiled and put his hand on my shoulder. "I think you made the right choice. And I'd say that even if I thought I might someday ride a motorcycle again."

* * *

A high-pitched scream woke me in the middle of the night. The moon shone through my open window, illuminating the handle of my baseball bat half buried under a pile of dirty clothes. I grabbed it as I ran from my room and turned left toward Bastien and Gracie's room. I wasn't always clearheaded in the middle of the night, but I was certain the scream had come from a woman, someone younger than my mom.

I rammed through the doorway, baseball bat over my shoulder, where I could swing it at anyone threatening my brother and sister-in-law. But no one was inside except Bastien and Gracie, sitting up in bed with the blankets askew around them. Gracie gasped for air like she'd just completed an obstacle course, and her dark hair was wet with perspiration.

The lacy nightgown she wore to survive the sweltering summer night didn't cover her shoulders. Bastien pulled a blanket around her. "It was just a dream," he whispered. He glanced up at me. "Will you get her a glass of water?"

I nodded and lowered my baseball bat. I caught Mom on my way to the kitchen. She was still tying her robe. "Gracie had a nightmare or something," I explained.

My mom looked past me toward their room and hesitated. "I will go back to bed, then."

I took a few ice cubes from the freezer and added them to a glass of water. I was thirsty, and my heart was still marching double-time from being startled awake like that, so I drained the glass, then got a new one for Gracie.

I knocked on the wall next to the doorway to warn them I was back. Gracie thanked me for the water, and I turned to go, dragging my baseball bat with me.

"You found a weapon," Bastien said.

I looked at the baseball bat and shrugged.

"Either you have good instincts, or you remembered our lessons." Bastien turned back to Gracie, tucking her hair behind her ear and rubbing her back. They'd turned the lamp on while I was in the kitchen. Bastien wasn't wearing anything but a pair of shorts. For the first time, I got a good look at what was left of his leg. Just a smooth stump with a few lines, still red from the sutures. And I noticed scars on the back of both his shoulders. Before he left, we'd slept in the same room whenever he was home, and he usually slept without a shirt in the summer. As long as I could remember, Bastien'd had scars on his hands and his feet, but before the war, his back had been smooth.

Those scars were new.

* * *

Gracie went back to work a few days later. She left before I started my paper route and came back after I finished at the Thompson farm. Some days it was a lot later. She never said anything about her job, even when she made it home in time for supper, but it must have been important, or she wouldn't have had enough gas rations for the drive. I figured she couldn't be too high in the chain of command, though, or someone would have found her and Bastien a place closer to work, despite the housing shortage. I didn't mind having them around—I was glad for it. But she looked tired.

As soon as I finished work each afternoon, Bastien and I went to the backyard to practice hand-to-hand combat.

"You're getting better at that," he said about a week after Gracie's nightmare. I'd just finished practicing how to break someone's back. Gracie had sewn some sacks into a straw dummy, so it was the current victim.

"It's not very heavy." I plucked the dummy from the grass and held it upright.

"Leave it." Bastien nodded toward the dummy. "I think you've got that down. Let's try something new."

I let the stuffed bags fall to the ground and braced myself for a new set of rules. Bastien kept throwing them at me. *Don't let go of your weapon. Stay on your feet. Keep your knife sharp because a clean cut will bleed more. Keep your firearm spotless because dirt can slow reloading.*

They each sounded useful, but it was hard to remember all of them, and each time we learned something new, I ended up with a bunch of bruises. I'd landed flat on my back more times than I wanted to count over the past week. For a guy with only one working leg, my brother was pretty good—a lot better than I was. He said I was improving, but I wasn't sure I believed him.

"Say someone holds you up with a pistol. What do you do?" Bastien asked.

"Surrender, I guess. Try to escape later."

"If he hasn't already shot you, chances are he prefers you alive or doesn't want to shoot because it will make too much noise. He'll hesitate, so you have a fraction of a second to work with."

"That's not much time."

Bastien nodded. "That's why you have to practice."

"Okay, show me." I held my hand out like it was a pistol and pointed it at him.

"First, let him think you're really surrendering. Raise your hands and wait for him to get close."

I stepped in next to him.

"Swing your right arm down and across to grab his right wrist. At the same time, turn sideways. If you manage it correctly, the pistol will be pointed clear of you by the time he fires." Bastien demonstrated with rapid, precise motions as he spoke. "Grip the pistol with your other hand

and knee him between the legs. Now try it on me. Remember, it has to be quick."

"All right."

He pointed his finger at me, and I put my hands up. Then I took a deep breath and focused. I brought my hand down to grab his wrist and twisted my torso at the same time. I hadn't meant to do it hard, but I was trying to be fast, and I ended up with more force than I'd planned for.

Bastien tottered for an instant and then his good leg went out from under him, and he landed on the ground.

"Sorry!"

He looked up at me and laughed. "You managed good results for only half the move."

"I'm sorry," I said again.

"Bound to happen sometime. Help me up." He reached a hand out, and I grabbed it. But the second he put weight on his fake leg, his face twisted in pain. "On second thought, I think I'll rest a minute."

The hinge on the kitchen door squeaked, and Gracie came outside. "Are you two ready for supper?"

I didn't answer, but a knot of worry tightened in my stomach as she approached. I'd teased Bastien about how much his world revolved around Gracie, but the same seemed true in reverse. Gracie was crazy about my brother. Would she be mad that I'd hurt him?

Bastien waited until she was only a foot away before answering. "Let's have a picnic instead."

"A picnic?" Gracie raised an eyebrow for an instant. Then she glanced at his leg and folded her arms across her chest. "What happened?"

"I knocked him over," I confessed. "I'm sorry. Something hurt when he tried to put weight on it."

She gave me a glance, then focused on Bastien. "Well?"

"I think the prosthesis got whacked out of alignment is all. But I'll have to take my pants off to check."

"Then we better get you inside. Don't put any weight on it for now." Gracie waved her hand at me. "Take the left side."

When we opened the back door, Mom dried her hands and came over for a closer look. "What happened?"

"Nothing worth interrupting your cooking for," Bastien said.

I think Mom knew better, but she pursed her lips and didn't follow us to Bastien's room. As soon as I helped him to the bed, he asked me to get his crutches. I retrieved one from the grass outside and the other from the kitchen. When I came back, I propped them next to the bedroom door and waited. "Is he all right?" I asked when Gracie came into the hallway.

She lifted her hands and then dropped them. They rarely stayed still when she spoke. "I think it's just bruised. We'll have to keep an eye on it to make sure the swelling doesn't get any worse."

Bastien joined us, the left side of his pants pinned up the way it had been the first day he'd come back. He took the crutches when Gracie handed them to him. "It's just a convenient reason to avoid my prosthesis for a few days."

"And a convenient reason to end sparring lessons?" Gracie's tone made it clear she wanted them to stop.

Bastien shrugged as she cuddled in next to him. "Maybe so." He brushed his lips across her forehead and glanced at me. "Tell Mom we'll be there in a few minutes."

CHAPTER 7

OUR LESSONS DIDN'T END COMPLETELY, but I didn't learn anything new, and I had to practice by myself with the dummy. Bastien sat on the back porch and gave me pointers. As our second week of lessons passed, the movements felt natural. I was getting better with Mr. Thompson's rifle and Bastien's pistol too. As I sparred with the stuffed sacks, I thought of all the reasons I hated the Nazis. It was enough motivation to keep me pushing through scrapes, blisters, and sore muscles.

I finished a flying jump on the dummy and stood back, satisfied. Rule forty-something said flying jumps were better than using the toe of your boot to kick an opponent on the ground. The only way he could escape was by rolling, and he'd have to do it fast.

"How about a break?" Bastien asked.

I picked up the dummy and brought it to the porch.

"Are you nervous?" he asked.

I shrugged. Tomorrow was my induction date, and I was equal parts worried and excited.

"Are you packed?"

"They said not to bring much. Toothbrush, razor, change of clothes. I have my bag out."

Bastien grabbed his crutches and stood. "I can talk while you pack."

I didn't think it would take more than a minute or two to put my stuff in a bag, but tidying up so I didn't leave a mess for Mom would be a little more labor-intensive. I followed Bastien into the room we used to share and grabbed a shirt, a pair of pants, and two sets of underwear.

"Are you still shooting for airborne?" Bastien balanced by the closet, flipping all the hangers so they faced the same way.

"Yeah."

"I jumped from a plane a few times. Make sure you learn how to roll when you land. It's almost impossible to stay on your feet, but if you roll right, you won't end up tangled in your parachute harness."

"I didn't know you were a paratrooper."

"I wasn't. Part of me wishes I had been so I could give you better guidance. But I've never jumped into a firefight." He seemed sad as he fastened the top button on a shirt about to fall off its hanger.

"I thought only paratroopers jumped out of planes." It was easy to imagine Bastien as a paratrooper, but it was hard to come up with any other reason for him to bail out of an undamaged airplane. I almost brushed it off. Maybe everyone rotated through jump school and learned unorthodox hand-to-hand combat techniques if they stayed in as long as Bastien had. Except I'd never heard of anyone else doing either.

"The point is, I've never been in normal combat, so I can't give you firsthand advice on what to expect."

"What exactly did you do in Europe that involved all the tricks you taught me *and* jumping out of planes *and* getting shot a bunch of times but not fighting in battle?"

"If I remember correctly, one of the first rules I gave you was not to ask about my time in Europe." He shuffled away from the closet and sat on the edge of the bed. "I can't talk about it."

I almost asked if he was a pathfinder—one of the paratroopers who went in early to mark drop zones, but that didn't fit because pathfinders ended up in battle too, if they lived that long. Bastien was being evasive, and I wanted to know why. I tried a different tactic. "What did Gracie do?"

He seemed surprised by the change of subject, but he answered. "She was a secretary."

"Hmm." I sorted through the piles of paper on my desk and threw away a few sheets of old homework. "She told me she worked in communications."

"Secretaries are involved in communications."

"Yeah, I guess." It didn't sound like my brother was lying to me, not exactly, but it was a little weird that he and Gracie had given different answers. I thought of other possibilities for Bastien's work and came up with only one thing that made sense. I'd had my back to him while I'd cleaned the clutter off my desk, but I turned to face him, to watch his expression. "You weren't a spy or something, were you?"

He didn't answer immediately. "*If* I was involved in irregular warfare, I wouldn't be allowed to talk about it."

"Irregular warfare?"

"Sabotage. Intelligence work. That sort of thing."

"But you know all about it?"

Bastien chuckled. "Not even Roosevelt knows all about it."

"And Gracie? I don't suppose nightmares like the doozy she had a few weeks back come from sitting at a desk in some bureaucracy. And I don't suppose most secretaries, even ones working for the War Department, can bring home boxes of ammunition for their brother-in-law's target practice."

"Think what you like, Lukas. I'm not at liberty to confirm your guesses. But don't mention your theories to anyone else."

"Anyone else, like Mom?"

Bastien picked up a baseball from a pile on my bed and tossed it a few feet in the air before catching it again. "No one. Including Mom." He motioned toward me with the ball and tossed it when I held out my hands. "What I'm trying to say is I don't know everything you're going to face. But I can make a few guesses. So will you listen if I give you some advice?"

I sat beside him. "Yeah, I'll listen."

"Good. First thing, get used to being called a sissy."

"What? Why?"

"Unless boot camp has changed, people will make fun of you because you don't drink, you don't smoke, you don't chase women, and you rarely cuss. You won't be the only one, so I imagine you can put up with it. There will be other things to keep you busy—sports, movies, letters. But once you get overseas, it might be tougher."

"Yeah. Once people start shooting at me."

"That's part of it. The danger, the anger." He looked me in the eye. "Combat does things to a person. Don't forget what you're fighting against. And don't forget that if things had gone only a little different, we wouldn't have been able to leave and both of us would have ended up in the German Army."

I shook my head. "No way. I wouldn't have ever joined the Nazis."

"You wouldn't have had a choice."

"I would have run away."

"Oh? Where would you have run?"

I thought about it. "I don't know. Switzerland. Anywhere."

"And what if running away would have endangered your family?"

I ran my fingers along the edge of the bedspread and thought about my sisters and my mom, about my dad and the way my friends in Frankfurt had stopped talking to me after his arrest. Being a social outcast had been hard, but everything I'd heard told me Germany was even worse now. "I guess I don't know."

Bastien put his hand on my shoulder. "You're lucky you didn't have to make that choice. The men on the other side did. Defeat them, but don't judge them."

I nodded.

"There are a lot of things you won't be able to control. I want you to come home, Lukas. But that's in God's hands, not mine, not yours. More than that, I want you to come home clean. You can't control what will happen to your body, but you can control what will happen to your soul. I've seen a lot of soldiers decide they don't want to die a virgin. And I've seen a lot of hungry women in Europe with no way to earn a living and nothing to sell except their bodies. You'll be lonely, and you'll have the money. Don't give in to temptation."

"You're acting like I'm going into hell or something."

"War *is* hell, Lukas. Anyone who tells you otherwise is either ignorant or seeking political office."

I rolled my eyes. "You think I'm going to go whoring as soon as I ship off to a base somewhere?"

"I certainly hope you won't, but if you commit now to keeping yourself clean, it will be easier to say no when the offer comes along."

I leaned forward and counted to ten so I wouldn't say anything too awful. I didn't want to yell at him on our last day together. "Are you done now?"

Bastien sighed. "If you want me to be." He gathered up his crutches and stood. "Lukas . . . I'm not trying to talk down to you or suggest you're weak. You're a good kid, and I'm proud of how you've turned out so far. I've just seen a lot of good kids grow up too fast and grow up the wrong way when they're shipped overseas and put through hell and given chance after chance to do something wrong. I have a feeling you're going to see things no one should ever have to see and experience things no one should ever have to experience. And I want you to come back a good man in spite of it." He shuffled to the door.

"Bastien?"

He paused.

I didn't like what he was telling me, but I knew he was trying to help, so I swallowed back my injured pride. "Thanks."

* * *

I wasn't the only one headed off to war when Mom and Bastien took me to the bus stop the next morning. A skinny, balding guy a few yards away hugged a little girl, maybe three years old, while a woman who was probably his wife held a baby and wiped away tears. Beyond them, a kid about my age said good-bye to a middle-aged couple.

"Do you have everything on the list?" Mom asked.

"Yeah." I nudged my bag with the end of my shoe. Most of my stuff was still at home, but I'd left the room clean and my things packed into a trunk so they'd be easy to transport if Mom moved while I was gone. Bastien and Gracie still couldn't find an apartment, so the move was postponed, but Mom started work at the bakery next week.

Mom held out her arms, and I gave her a hug. "Love you, Mom."

She kept holding on, even after I relaxed my arms. She sniffed, and I realized she was crying and didn't want me to see.

"I will pray for you always." Her voice was a little muffled in my shirt, but I picked out the words. "And I will write to you often. Do your best to come back to me."

"I will, Mom. I promise."

She pulled away, blinking rapidly. I thought about telling her not to cry, but I doubted that would make saying good-bye any easier. I couldn't tell her not to feel.

Bastien balanced with his crutches while he stepped forward to wrap an arm around me. He was wearing his prosthesis again for the first time since our sparring accident.

"Take good care of Mom for me. And Gracie."

"I will," he said, hugging me tighter. "You take care too. You won't be able to stay as innocent as you are right now, but try to stay just as good."

He was overdoing it with the sin and temptation advice, but I held my tongue. I didn't want to say good-bye—maybe permanently—on a bad note.

"And there's a surprise for you." Bastien looked over my shoulder. "Right on time."

I turned around and spotted Belle.

"What are you doing here?" I asked, pulling her close and looking around to make sure her dad wasn't nearby. "I thought you were grounded."

She laughed. "Gracie stopped by and said you were leaving today, so I told my dad you left yesterday."

That made Gracie the best sister-in-law in the entire world. "You lied to your dad?"

"I'll apologize later."

I did my best to imitate the high-pitched drawl of our Sunday School teacher. "Now, Belle, you know what a slippery slope you tread when you first begin the path of deceit."

Belle's smile grew wider. "Well, if you're going to lecture me, I'll go start my penance now." She shrugged and turned around like she was leaving.

I grabbed her wrist and tugged her back. "You know I'm just teasing."

"You know I'm just teasing back." She laughed again and put her hand on my arm. Then she dug in her purse and pulled out a handful of envelopes. "I read somewhere that you can't get mail until you're assigned a unit, so I wrote some letters for you. One for each day the first week. Don't open them early. And I expect you to write back on a regular basis."

I took the envelopes from her. The first one said *Tuesday* in Belle's heavily slanted cursive. "Thanks, Belle." I gave her another hug. My mom and Bastien had backed up to give us some space, but the bus stop was too crowded for real privacy. "You know what I wish?"

"What?"

"I wish I would have sneaked out last night so I could have given you a proper kiss without anyone watching."

Belle glanced at my mouth, and the skin around her freckles turned pink. With some girls, their whole face turned red when they blushed, but with Belle, it was just her cheeks, and it was beautiful. "Well, I guess now you'll have to come back safe and sound and give it to me when the war's over."

I wasn't going to get on the bus without kissing her, so I leaned in and met her lips. They were soft and warm, and I wanted to spend an hour or two exploring them, but I had to be content with a second or two.

The bus pulled up and came to a stop. I said my last good-byes to my girl, my mom, and my brother before I climbed on. I got a window seat on the right side and watched them until the bus turned a corner. Then they disappeared: Mom with a handkerchief next to her eyes, Bastien leaning on his crutches, and Belle waving her sun-kissed arm at me. I tried not to think about how I might never see them again. My eyes stung just a bit, so I blinked a few times and cleared my throat. I took a deep breath and reminded myself how long I'd been looking forward to this day.

Leaving was hard.

Staying would have been harder.

* * *

Dear Belle,

You should be proud of me. I only opened one of your letters today. Although, to be honest, the temptation to open more stopped after the bus ride. Since arriving at Fort Meade, we've been too busy to read anything longer than our serial number (I've got mine almost memorized). The afternoon was a blur of aptitude tests, orientation films, and pinpricks for blood typing and immunizations. They had us strip from the waist up and gave us shots for smallpox, cholera, yellow fever, tetanus, typhus, typhoid, and probably a few other diseases too. If your dad gets this letter instead of you, he can be pleased that I had blood streaming down both arms by the time they finished. I'm sore, but it wasn't as bad as rock salt.

I'm now the owner of a large olive-drab and khaki wardrobe and a $10,000 life insurance policy. I still haven't seen the airborne recruiter, but hopefully tomorrow. Sorry this is a short letter—lights out in five minutes. Say hi to your cow for me.

Luke

* * *

On the afternoon of my second day at the Fort George G. Meade Army Reception Center, I finally found the recruiter for the airborne service.

"I'm interested in jump school," I told him.

"That's great. We aren't taking too many this week, but have a seat. Maybe we can use you." He set his pen down and motioned me to a chair on the other side of his desk. "Airborne training is among the toughest in the world. Are you ready for that?"

"Yes, sir!"

"That's what I like to hear. How old are you?"

"Eighteen, sir." I handed him my paperwork, and he set it on the desk.

"Schooling?"

"Just finished high school, a little over a month ago."

He nodded. "What have you been up to since then?"

"I've been working about fifty hours a week on a farm."

"That's a solid work week."

I shrugged. "I had a paper route too. I did fewer hours on the farm during school, especially over sports season, but Mr. Thompson needed a lot of extra help the last month."

"Well, you seem athletic and motivated. That's what we like to see in paratroops."

"Thank you, sir." I didn't care how hard training would be or how scary it might be to leap from an airplane for the first time. I was on my way to Camp Toccoa for basic and then Fort Benning for jump school. I was going to be a paratrooper.

The recruiter pulled out a form and started asking more questions. "Have you ever broken any bones?"

"Yeah. My arm when I was twelve, and my leg when I was fourteen."

The recruiter frowned. "We don't normally accept volunteers with a history of breaks."

"But the last one was over four years ago!" I didn't want the final bit of my dream snatched away. I couldn't fly a plane, but I could at least fly into battle, couldn't I?

"If your bones are prone to breakage, you might not make it through jump school. Or worse, you'll make it through jump school and break something when you land behind lines. We can't drop a hospital out of a C-47. If you broke a bone, you'd be a liability to your squad." He glanced at my paperwork and handed it back to me, an apologetic look on his face. "And we can't take recruits who need glasses either. They're too likely to get smashed on the jump."

I took my paperwork and stood, disappointment so thick I almost choked on it. Why hadn't anyone warned me about how picky the airborne service was? Or how picky the air corps was? I was just a poor immigrant with average grades, but I thought that wouldn't matter in America. I could be a soldier—a good one—if someone would just give me the chance.

I didn't joke with the other men as I waited in line to be classified. Snippets of interviews rolled past my ears. One guy had been a salesman at a men's clothing store for five years. The interviewer recommended he be assigned to a supply company. The guy who'd been in line right in front of me had worked at a car shop. The army classifier recommended he go into armor.

When it was my turn, the man looked over my paperwork and the results of my Army General Classification Test. I'd never been good at tests. I could know everything the night before while studying with Belle, but I'd forget half of it when the paper landed on my desk. My score wasn't great. It wasn't awful either. Just average.

My Soldier's Qualification Card was about average too. I could speak German, and I'd finished high school. That counted for something. So did my participation in sports. But on the occupation side of the card, I doubted my paper route or farm work were very impressive. And I had no previous military experience. Just Bastien teaching me how to sneak up on sentries and how to whack people with the edge of my hand. My brother had done what he could, but he couldn't fix my eyesight or erase my medical history.

The army classifier asked a few questions, then wrote down *infantry*. There would be no jump boots. No elite unit. Certainly no airplanes. Just the infantry, with a bunch of other average, unimpressive draftees.

I'd told the recruiters at the induction station that I wanted to serve my country where I was needed. I had meant it. But I hadn't expected to end up as ordinary cannon fodder.

PART TWO: SOLDIER
AUTUMN 1944
EUROPEAN THEATER OF OPERATIONS

CHAPTER 8

I GRIPPED THE CARGO NET with both hands as one of my feet slipped off the soggy rope. I'd climbed plenty of cargo ropes during training, but they'd been dry and stationary. A wet one attached to a troop ship bobbing up and down on the English Channel was more challenging, and the weight of all my gear didn't help.

"Watch it, kid!"

I glanced at the soldier whose hand I'd almost stepped on. "Sorry!" I said. He'd called me a kid, but he didn't look much older than I was.

"Don't mind that sad sack," the guy above me said as the net lurched up and down again. "He woke up on the wrong side of the bed this morning."

The sad sack huffed. "No. I woke up in a fine bed this morning, with clean sheets. And then I had a hot shower and a hot breakfast and a friendly 'Good morning' from a pretty little nurse. Wasn't nothing wrong with this morning. The problem is tomorrow morning and the next morning and the morning after that when I'll wake up in a foxhole with a puddle in the bottom and nothing but K rations for breakfast. And the only greeting I'll get will be from German artillery and greenhorn buck privates like four-eyes here."

I shrugged away his words. I'd run into plenty of complainers since joining the army, and I'd learned to ignore it when people talked about my glasses. I'd made "expert" on the shooting range, so obviously my eyesight wasn't hampering me too much. I crawled the rest of the way down the cargo net from the troop transport to the landing craft, clinging to the slippery ropes through each rise and fall of the waves and each spray of late November seawater. The frames of my P3 glasses had slid down my nose, so I pushed them back into position when I had a free hand. I spotted an empty seat and hauled my gear toward it.

The landing craft bucked as the water swelled and ebbed. A few nearby gulls squawked as if to warn us that a ride in a Higgins boat was a bad idea, but I didn't have much of a choice. There wasn't enough harbor space in Cherbourg to unload us, so we were taking landing craft to the beach. My stomach lurched with the boat. By the time thirty of us had piled in, the guy next to me was heaving out his guts into his helmet. I looked away so my insides wouldn't copy his.

The cranky veteran from the cargo net chuckled. "The Channel's calm today. Don't know what your stomach's complaining about."

The guy next to me emptied his helmet over the side of the Higgins boat and wrinkled his freckled nose at the inside of his helmet.

"Just wait a minute or two," the sad sack said. "There'll be enough water in the bottom of the boat to rinse it out."

"I take it you've been on one of these before?" I asked.

He had smiled while talking to the seasick guy next to me, but the humor disappeared from his face when he turned to me. "That's right, four-eyes."

"I've got a name," I said.

"I'm sure you do, private." He leaned his head back and tilted his helmet forward. I doubted anyone could sleep on a flat-bottomed boat out on a sea as rough as this, but he did a good job pretending. He was right about the water in the bottom of the boat. Before long, the soldier next to me had scooped out a few helmetfuls to get his helmet mostly clean again.

"I'm Private Winterton," my green-faced neighbor said. "From Oklahoma."

His hand didn't look dirty when he offered it, so I stuck mine out and shook it. "Private Ley. From Virginia."

The sad sack pushed his helmet back to the top of his head. "Virginia? What part?"

"Fairfax."

He grunted.

"Where are you from?" I asked. Along the line, I could see a couple other soldiers barfing into their helmets. My stomach still twisted like a carnival ride, so I focused on my conversation instead of the other passengers.

"Roanoke."

I nodded. We were both from Virginia, but I got the feeling that wouldn't make much of a difference to him.

"What's your name?" Winterton asked.

"Samson."

"So when was the last time you rode one of these things?" Winterton checked his helmet before putting it back on. It was wet with ocean water, but thanks to the sea spray, everyone else's helmet was wet too.

"June 6."

"You were part of D-Day?" I asked. It took effort to keep my mouth from hanging open in awe.

Samson's eyes flickered toward me with slightly less irritation than before. "Yeah."

"What was it like?"

He glanced past me for a few seconds. "Rough. It was rough." He tilted his helmet forward again, signaling an end to the conversation.

Looking at the waves made me dizzy, so I spent the rest of the ride concentrating on the boots of the soldier across from me. About every third crest made it over the side of the boat and showered us with cold saltwater.

Winterton groaned a few times and covered his mouth with his hand, but he managed not to puke again. "If this is a calm day, I'd hate to ride one of these things in a storm," he mumbled.

"How'd you manage the trip across the Atlantic?" I asked. Usually the jostling wasn't as bad on a big troop transport, but we'd sailed through some foul weather.

Winterton grimaced. "Spent most of it wishing a U-boat would put me out of my misery."

Finally, the Higgins boat pulled up to the sand and dropped its ramp. We had to march through a few feet of frigid ocean. I managed to keep my equipment dry, other than the sea spray. My clothes were a different story. Everything from my knees down was soaked, which would make for a miserable march to the rail line. I looked up the shore, where we were headed. Beyond the sand, I could see the tops of buildings, most of them missing a few walls or a roof. The Germans had fought hard to keep Cherbourg within their grasp.

Samson stared up and down the sand, standing stock-still. The beach was busy as we unloaded our supplies and other landing craft brought in more men and equipment, but I got the feeling Samson's mind was in the past, not the present.

* * *

We marched to the Cherbourg train station and rode to a replacement depot outside Rouen, France. Everyone called it a repple depple rather than a replacement depot. We spent a night there in tents. The showers were cold, but the food was hot. I wrote a letter to my mom and told her I missed her and her cooking. The repple depple fare was better than what they'd served us on the troop ship, but that wasn't saying much.

I recognized some of the men from the landing craft and a few from the troop transport, but mostly I was surrounded by strangers. I waited in line for the shower behind someone from Texas and ate breakfast with someone from Wisconsin. We said a few words to each other, but we didn't bother forming friendships. Chances were we'd end up at opposite ends of the front. Some men trained and shipped overseas as a unit. I envied them. I'd been made fun of plenty during training, but I'd also made friends. Now I was a replacement, an anonymous spare part to be plugged in wherever the army needed more manpower.

The repple depple men checked our equipment. Most infantrymen had M1s, but I had a Browning Automatic Rifle. The BAR was heavier to haul around, but it had more firepower than a normal rifle, and I was taller than a lot of the other guys. I could handle the extra weight. Someone reminded us it wasn't too late to buy life insurance. Then they assigned us our units.

A sergeant with a New Jersey accent counted off fifty of us. "All right. All yous guys are off to the 28th Infantry Division, 110th Infantry Regiment. Train leaves in twenty minutes."

Samson was in the group with me. He walked up to the sergeant and took him aside. "There's been a mistake. I'm with the 29th Division. I had to go to the hospital for a while, but I want back in the 116th Infantry Regiment, Company B."

"There's no mistake, private. The 28th needs replacements last week, so collect your things and get on that train."

"Come on, Sarge, I've been training with the men in the 29th since 1940."

New Jersey crossed his arms. "Everybody knows the 29th is really three divisions. One in the field, one in the hospital, and one in the cemetery."

"Yeah, and I just got out of the one in the hospital, and I want back in the 29th in the field."

"Most of the men you joined up with aren't there anymore."

Samson balled one of his hands into a fist. "I don't care if there's only one member of my squad still there. I'm going back to the 29th."

"You'll obey your orders, or you can join the miscreants in the prison cages back there." The sergeant jerked a thumb over his shoulder, not caring that Samson was taller and bigger. "General Cota's moved to the 28th too, huh? It's not the end of the world. They're at a nice, quiet sector in the Ardennes Forest. Take it. Before I have to call a pair of MPs over here."

Samson didn't look happy, but he stopped arguing.

Our transportation was a forty-and-eight boxcar made for eight horses or forty people. They crowded more than forty of us inside. I ended up in line behind Winterton, the seasick guy from the landing craft. I hoped he didn't get train sick.

"My dad told me all about these." He slapped the boxcar as he stepped inside.

"Was he born over here?" I asked.

"Naw. He came over with the AEF as a stevedore."

AEF stood for the American Expeditionary Force during the Great War, but I had no idea what a stevedore was. I debated asking him, but I didn't want to sound like an idiot, so I just nodded.

"My uncle was a marine," Winterton said. "Saw lots of action. Never talks about it. But I guess being a dock worker wasn't as traumatic, so my dad tells his stories whenever he has the chance. Made it sound like an adventure."

I smiled, wondering if he'd been able to tell I didn't know what a stevedore was. "I guess your dad did lots of ship-to-train stuff?"

"Yeah. But he didn't have to ride in them all that often." Winterton wrinkled his nose as he glanced around the dim boxcar. It smelled like the locker room after football practice on a humid summer day.

I thought about mentioning my dad's Great War service, but since he and Winterton's uncle might have been shooting at each other, I settled onto the straw-lined floor of the boxcar without saying anything.

I assumed the straw had been added so we could sleep, but between a nearby soldier's knee digging into my back and another man's helmet pushing straw in my face whenever he moved, I didn't get much rest. The sound of Winterton heaving into his helmet didn't help.

I was grateful to trade the train for a Deuce and a Half truck for the final leg of our journey. The truck rolled through France. The French ignored us. We passed into Belgium. The Belgians waved to us. A few women even brought us pastries when we stopped in a village and got out to stretch our legs. It grew dark, and I drifted off to sleep. I woke when we drove into

Luxembourg. The driver turned south, and I had a view of the eastern horizon out the back of the truck. It looked like a brewing thunderstorm. Low rumbling sounded, and lights flashed. But the light wasn't the sharp zigzag of lightning. It was more of a round flash. Artillery.

I glanced at the soldiers in the back of the truck with me. Most were asleep, but the handful who were awake looked young and scared, and I probably looked just like them.

* * *

The trucks unloaded us in the middle of some village in Luxembourg. By that time, my fingers were numb, and so was most of my face. It was too dark to see much, but my nose picked out the sharp smell of spent explosives and the fresh scent of evergreen trees. A sergeant herded us into a barn for cold rations and a few hours of sleep. There were no longer any animals inside, but their odor lingered. It reminded me of Belle's barn, and I was surprised at how much I missed her and everyone else back in Fairfax.

A stove burned in the middle of the barn, but the wind blew through the building's wooden beams and snatched most of the heat away. When I put on every single item of clothing I'd been issued, I stopped shivering. I wrapped a blanket around me and tried to sleep on a pile of hay, but every boom in the distance, every airborne buzz jerked me wide awake. There wasn't enough light to read my pocket-sized Book of Mormon or my letters, so I watched the glow from the stove play along the barn's roof and listened to a bunch of men snoring.

It was still dark when a sergeant roused us and took us to the company command post located in a stone house. Inside the CP, someone pointed out Captain Wood, our company commander. He was tall and reminded me a little of John Wayne, but I was used to seeing John Wayne in a cowboy hat, and Wood wore a helmet. His body looked relaxed as he spoke to a sergeant, but he had dark patches under his eyes, noticeable even in the dim light.

I studied a set of maps stuck to the wall of what had once been some family's living room. The 110th was in the northern half of Luxembourg, stretched along fifteen miles of the Our River from Marnach to Bastendorf, two towns I'd never heard of. It seemed like a lot of ground for one regiment of roughly 3,200 men to cover. My new company had about three of those miles along the main line of resistance. The river was in front, and a couple miles back was the highway, labeled Skyline Drive.

"Why are we spread so thin?" Samson asked.

Captain Wood replied. He may have looked like John Wayne, but when he spoke he lacked Wayne's deep, confident timbre. Wood's voice reminded me of a teenager's as he squeaked half the words out. "The Germans are busy licking their wounds behind the Siegfried Line, and we're trying to rebuild after the Hürtgen. Ike's gambling that nothing much will happen through here."

Samson grunted. "Ike's betting. And we're the chips."

"So far it's been quiet," Wood said. "Your squad leaders will fill you in."

A few uniformed men filed through the back door, crowding the small house. They all looked filthy enough to be coal miners.

Wood waved over a short sergeant covered in grime. "Martinez, we finally got some new men for you. How's Lieutenant Call?"

The sergeant looked at the line of replacements and walked into the kitchen where he and Captain Wood could talk without the rest of us over-hearing. I wondered what that meant about Lieutenant Call.

When they emerged, Martinez walked along the line of replacements and stopped in front of me. His attention was mostly on my BAR. "You any good with that, soldier?" He said *esoldier* instead of *soldier*, so I assumed Spanish was his first language.

"I qualified as an expert marksman, Sergeant."

He nodded. "Good. We could use a little more firepower in our squad." He pointed to three other soldiers. "You, you, and you, follow me." He glanced back at me. "You too."

I checked to see who else he'd grabbed. Samson, Winterton, and a baby-faced private named Broyles, whose snores the night before had sounded like a tank engine. We followed him through the snow, our boots crunching the ice and our breaths coming out in visible puffs. It was almost December. I'd gotten used to the mild Virginia weather, and I'd forgotten how cold it got in Germany. We weren't quite in Germany—that was across the river. But the extra mile or so to the west didn't make the wind any softer. I hunched my shoulders to keep the gusts from blowing down my neck.

Martinez checked to make sure we were all behind him. "During the day, we man outposts along the river. The rest of the squad should be there already. Most nights, we pull back to a barn on the other side of the village from the CP, so you'll get to sleep indoors. It's been mostly quiet lately, but don't get sloppy. They send patrols out, and so do we. And they've got artillery over there too."

After about a half mile of trudging through the snow, we approached a crest, and Martinez crouched to the ground. "Once we cross this ridge, Jerry can see us, or he can when the sun rises. Our platoon's spread along the river. Our squad's on the far right. I guess you're all fresh from the States?"

Samson spoke up. "I was with the 29th Division. Landed on Omaha Beach and fought through Normandy until a piece of shrapnel came over a hedgerow and nicked my left kidney."

Martinez seemed relieved. "Good. 'Cause right now our squad's down to five men plus me, and two of them arrived last week. Anyone else been in combat before?"

Winterton, Broyles, and I shook our heads. While Samson had been liberating France, I'd been taking high school finals.

Martinez looked at the eastern horizon. "We better get going. Keep five paces apart, and don't bunch up. Samson, you bring up the rear. We'll check in at platoon CP first."

I stayed hunched over, imitating Sergeant Martinez as I followed him over the rise. Stretched out below was a field of white spotted with clumps of trees. It looked like some of the trees had been leveled by artillery or men wanting a clear line of fire, but overall, Luxembourg reminded me a lot of Germany.

The platoon's daytime command post was a foxhole near the center of a clearing, disguised with brush and snowdrifts. A skinny soldier noticed us first. "Hiya, Sarge. Those your new guys?"

"That's right, Dalton. Is Lieutenant Call around?"

Dalton nodded. "Yeah, over with Armstrong's squad. Want me to get him?"

"Sí."

Dalton scrambled from the foxhole and ran off.

"At ease," Martinez said.

That was harder than it sounded on a cold, wet morning that chilled my skin and made my muscles bunch. Broyles sat on a log, and I joined him, resting my BAR across my legs. Martinez paced along a dip in the ground and kept looking east, where the sky gradually changed from black to gray.

Eventually a lanky man with a cleft chin came back with Dalton.

Martinez joined the two of them and pointed out a few indentations in the snow. "I'd like to get a BAR man on the edge of our line. Probably put him with Higham. Split up Krandle and O'Brien and pair them with those two." Martinez pointed to Broyles and Winterton. "I'll have Luzzatto join me. He's a little jumpy still. And put that guy, Samson," Martinez pointed, "with Roland. Roland's the buck private who came up with you last week."

Lieutenant Call studied us each in turn, the thumb and pointer finger of his right hand holding his chin and his left hand stuck on his hip. "I'll have to look at the map, of course." His voice sounded like a radio broadcaster. "Dalton, bring me my maps."

"Yes, sir." Dalton jumped into the foxhole and emerged with a leather case.

Call opened it with a flourish, and the maps spilled out across the snow.

Martinez gathered them up and handed one to Call. "I think this is the one you want, sir."

Call took the offered map and reached for the others too. He spent several minutes on each of them. Samson found a tree stump and sat on it. Winterton yawned and dug a little hole with the toe of his boot. Martinez took out a cigarette.

"Sir?" Martinez broke the silence when he finished his smoke.

"Yes?"

"We've only got about eight hours of daylight. You can switch things up tomorrow if it doesn't work today. But that daylight's coming soon, sir. And these men would be safer at their posts than out in the open."

"Patience, sergeant. Patience."

Martinez's jaw tightened, but he didn't say anything. He looked east again. I followed his gaze. The river was visible now, about forty feet wide, with steep embankments on either side. The sky above it was tinted violet.

"Should we dig in here, sir?" Samson asked. He seemed nervous as his eyes darted from the sky to the river and then to Call. The lieutenant was taking his time, but everyone from the guy back at the repple depple to Sergeant Martinez had said the Ardennes was a ghost front. And if it wasn't, surely Call would pay more attention to the sky, pink now. They didn't let just anyone become an officer. Call had to know what he was doing.

The lieutenant didn't answer.

"Sarge?" Samson asked.

Martinez pointed to a ditch a few yards to the left. He, Samson, and Winterton went there and squatted down. Dalton got back in his foxhole.

I was about to follow Martinez when Call strutted over to the log I sat on and stopped a foot in front of Broyles and me.

He cleared his throat and raised an eyebrow.

If there was one thing I'd learned in training, it was how to salute. Broyles must have had the same thought because we jumped to our feet in unison and saluted.

Call kept us standing there for a few seconds, nodding slightly. "All right, men—"

A thunk sounded, and Call spun around. He swayed like a drunk for an instant, then crashed to the ground. He fell face-first, and his helmet rolled off, turning upside down to reveal a jagged bullet hole.

CHAPTER 9

"GET DOWN!" BROYLES TUGGED ON my wrist and yanked me into the muddy snow.

I gasped for breath. I'd seen dead bodies before, but they'd always been clean, lying in coffins. I'd never seen anyone killed right in front of me. My face felt wet. I wiped my cheek and looked at the cuff of my overcoat. It was spotted with blood.

Martinez said something in Spanish that sounded like a curse. "Dalton, get on the radio to CP. Tell Captain Wood that Lieutenant Call just got himself killed."

"Yes, Sarge."

Martinez swore again. "Sergeant Breckenridge has a what, three-day pass?"

"Yeah," Dalton said.

"So he comes back tomorrow?"

Dalton nodded.

Martinez climbed from the ditch and settled back on his heels, scrunched next to the earth where the bushes would hide him from the German sniper across the river. "Winterton, Broyles, stay here for now." He motioned toward Dalton's foxhole, and the two men ran for it. "Ley, Samson, follow me."

I took another look at Lieutenant Call. A patch of scarlet snow circled what was left of his head. The exit wound was a mess.

"Come on, Ley."

It was hard to breathe, and my hands shook as I grabbed my BAR and followed, imitating Martinez and Samson and keeping low to the ground until we reached a slight indentation in the snow.

"Luzzatto?" When Martinez spoke, two helmeted heads poked out of a well-camouflaged foxhole.

"Yeah?" one asked.

"Gather your stuff. You're sharing a foxhole with me now." Martinez pointed.

"But the sun's up."

"I know. Lieutenant Call got killed. Put us a little behind schedule. Roland, you'll stay here with Private Samson. He's got more experience than both of us combined, so try to learn from him."

"Sure, Sarge."

Private Luzzatto climbed from the foxhole, a helmet on his head, a rifle over his shoulder, and a bag gripped in his hand. My eyes fixed on his helmet, remembering how easily the sniper's bullet had pierced Call's. Samson took Luzzatto's place while he ran to another foxhole about fifty yards away.

"So, uh, who's in charge up at platoon now?" Roland asked.

"Breckenridge is back tomorrow, and Wood will figure something out in the meantime. For now, just keep an eye on them." Martinez pointed across the river.

"Well, that's another ninety-day wonder who didn't even last nine days." Roland shook his head and moved over to make room for Samson.

"Come on, Ley," Martinez said.

I jogged along behind him, not wanting to be out in the open where the Germans could see me. They'd drilled that into our heads pretty well during training. Take cover, and stay out of sight. I'd been eager to see action, but a sniper wasn't exactly what I was looking for. How was I supposed to fight someone I couldn't see? I hadn't expected death to be like that—taking an unsuspecting officer midsentence, without any warning.

I kept thinking about Call. He was new. He was dead. I was new too, and that bullet hadn't been too far away. The sniper could have easily had my head in the crosshairs.

"Ley, I got a tip for you."

"Yeah?"

"Save your salutes for the parade ground. Out here it just tells the snipers who to aim for."

I was so shocked that I almost stopped running. Call was dead because I'd shown the sniper who to shoot? My first hour in combat, and I'd gotten my officer killed. "I didn't know . . . I thought he wanted us to salute."

"He probably did. He hadn't been here long enough to figure it out, and he wasn't interested in anyone helping him along."

"He's dead because of me?" My throat felt dry, and it took extra effort to keep my legs moving.

"No. It's his fault. He thought he knew everything before he got here. If he'd had half a brain or an ounce of humility, he'd still be alive. It's not your fault. But don't go around saluting me or anyone else."

When we arrived, the top of the foxhole was half hidden under a pile of evergreen branches.

"Higham?"

A wide man with a scraggly beard and a sooty face pushed aside the greenery. "Yeah, Sarge?"

"This is Private Ley. He's new. I want a little more firepower over here." Martinez pointed to my BAR. "And Call's dead, just so you know."

"Huh." Higham gazed over toward platoon CP. "Well, maybe they'll send someone better. They'd have to dig pretty hard to find someone worse."

Martinez cleared his throat. "I'll pretend I didn't hear that. I'll check in at nightfall when we pull back."

"Careful, Sarge. I'd hate for you to get caught by a sniper."

"*Sí*, me too." Martinez waved me toward the foxhole and disappeared.

The hole was about five feet deep, with steep sides dusted in frost. A thin puddle covered the bottom.

Higham must have noticed my gaze as I climbed down. "If it gets too deep, just scoop it out with your helmet."

"What's this?" I pointed to a set of stacked C ration cans with a flame that produced a plume of thick, black smoke.

"It's a stove. Look, I was on guard duty all night. I'm going to sleep. Wake me if anything changes." Higham pulled a blanket over his shoulders, leaned against the dirt wall of the foxhole, and started snoring.

I stared at him. How could he fall asleep with his lieutenant lying dead in the snow and a new soldier sharing his foxhole? I had questions for him. "Private Higham?" He didn't move, so I prodded the bottom of his boot.

He snapped awake. "What?"

"I just got here. You've got to tell me what to do."

Higham rolled his eyes. "Keep your eyes open. If you see any krauts, wake me up. Otherwise, let me sleep." He tilted his head back and was soon snoring even louder than before.

Between the noise coming from my foxhole buddy and the memory of Lieutenant Call getting shot in the head, I didn't think I'd have any trouble staying awake. I shivered as a misty rain began to fall and frigid water crept through my boots and into my socks. I couldn't see anyone across the river. If I hadn't just walked past them, I wouldn't have been able to pick out my squad's other foxholes either. Even with the sun up, the day remained gray and depressing, kind of like the slop they'd fed us for breakfast on the troop transport.

My war wasn't going as planned, not at all. I was supposed to be a pilot. At the very least, I was supposed to be a paratrooper or a ranger. I was supposed to be led by a good officer and have a foxhole buddy who actually cared if I got shot. I looked toward the river, toward the enemy. Private Higham was two feet away, but I'd never felt so alone.

* * *

Higham didn't say a single word to me the rest of the day. He woke midafternoon but only shrugged or grunted when I asked him questions. He sharpened his bayonet—twice—even though I hadn't seen him use it.

I'd heard from Belle and my family regularly since enlistment, but it would take awhile for their next letters to catch up to me. I pulled out the last one Belle had written before I'd shipped overseas.

Do you remember the time you dug up all that frozen grass for my aunt and took out a few trees so she could have a bigger victory garden? You worked from sunup to sundown, and Aunt Edith was impressed. She told me, "Your daddy might not like that boy, but my sister would, and I sure do." Then she bought us tickets to go see The Song of Bernadette, *and you slept through most of it. Was it the yardwork or the story that put you to sleep? I guess we should have waited for* Destination Tokyo *instead. I doubt you would have slept through that one. But I kind of liked watching you sleep. I probably shouldn't admit that, and I bet if I looked in the mirror right now I'd be blushing.*

I glanced up at Higham. He stared across the river and didn't seem to notice my gaze. I thought of Belle and how much I missed those blushes. More than that, I missed being with people who cared about me. Out here, I was surrounded by strangers.

* * *

After dark, my squad pulled back to the village to stay in a barn with a big manure pile just outside of it. The other two squads in our platoon were in nearby homes, and the rest of Wood's company was spread throughout the village. We had K rations for supper, and the biscuits all tasted a little like the Wrigley's Spearmint gum that had been beside them in the box.

Martinez sent Samson on outpost duty, and the rest of the squad either burrowed into blankets or sat around and smoked.

"Sarge?" I asked.

"*Sí?*"

"Why do we pull back at night?"

"You complaining about sleeping inside?"

I wasn't sure a barn counted as sleeping indoors, but I kept that to myself. "No, but what if the Germans attack?"

Martinez stubbed out his cigarette. "Well, if Jerry gets to causing trouble, he might raid a line of strung-out foxholes, but he's not going to raid a village held by a whole company. And just in case the krauts do try something as stupid as raiding a village, I've got men on outpost duty at night to warn the rest of us."

"What about a bigger attack?"

"If they tried a real attack, we're too thin to stop them on the line. We can hold longer as a company. But don't worry about that. They'll send out patrols, and they might even launch a raid. But nothing big is coming through here. I don't think the Nazis have anything big left."

A buzzing sounded and grew louder.

"What's that?" Winterton asked. He walked to the barn's doorway and pointed at a blur of light crossing the sky.

"V-1 rocket," Martinez said. "I guess they do have something left—those—but they're probably aimed at Antwerp or Brussels, so we don't have to worry about them."

I joined Winterton outside and watched the V-1. The sky had cleared, making the night colder, but the bright display of stars made up for the temperature drop.

"Doesn't look so different from back home, does it?" Winterton's narrow face was tilted upward, scanning the sky.

"Guess not, but it's a lot colder than Virginia." I pulled the collar of my greatcoat up to give a few more inches of my neck protection from the chill.

Winterton chuckled. "We had winters like this in Oklahoma. Pennsylvania too." He folded his arms across his chest and pulled his lips into a tight, crooked line. I wondered if he missed his home as much as I missed mine, but I didn't think that was the type of question a good soldier asked other members of his squad.

"How's your foxhole?" I asked.

"Wet and cold. Yours?"

"About the same. Guess that's the infantry for you." I shivered. "I never planned on being a foot soldier. I always wanted to be a pilot."

"Yeah? Me neither." Winterton stamped his feet. "Engineering. That was my goal."

Martinez pushed the barn door open. "You two should get some sleep. Winterton, you're on outpost duty later."

I stayed in the doorway another minute after Winterton left, wondering what I'd gotten myself into. A bunch of Nazis were across the river, and they wouldn't think twice about killing me. I shivered and headed back in.

I washed my face with icy well water and brushed my teeth with chalky army tooth powder. I read a dozen verses in my scriptures about the army of Helaman and how they thought more about the liberty of their fathers than they did about their own lives. My dad was dead, like a lot of their dads had been. And my mom was a lot like their mothers—full of faith. But I had a feeling that if they'd been in foxholes, Helaman's warriors wouldn't have ignored the comrade next to them. They'd been an all-volunteer army, and I envied their unity.

I stretched out on the hay and tried to ignore Broyle's snores, but my mind wouldn't settle down. Everything I'd heard so far said we were in a quiet sector. Maybe we were. But a lake with a thin coat of ice was quiet too until the ice ripped apart.

* * *

Instead of counting sheep, I fell asleep counting the sound of V-1s streaking through the air toward Belgium. I woke when Martinez lit a lantern the next morning. But I didn't really move until Winterton slammed his bayonet into the ground a foot away from my head.

I shot to my feet. "What are you doing?" I'd heard about combat driving men crazy, but Winterton had seemed sane the night before.

He twisted the end of his rifle, freeing the bayonet, then lifted it from the straw to reveal a dead rat splayed on the end. "That's number three."

O'Brien rolled over. "Knock it off, and go to sleep."

"But rats spread disease," Winterton said. "We should get rid of them."

O'Brien shook his head. "Yeah, good luck. Stop waking people up when you come back from OP." He tilted his head back and closed his eyes.

"It's time to get up anyway," Martinez said.

I rubbed a kink from my neck. Our creaky barn made the barracks at basic training seem like a luxury hotel. A rat scurried across a beam a few feet over my head. "You missed one," I said to Winterton.

His light brown eyes followed the pest. He must have had quick reflexes to skewer three, but that one was out of his reach.

When it was breakfast time, I passed on the hot coffee and settled for cold water. Then it was time to man our positions along the river.

Other than telling me when to sleep and when to stand watch, Higham only spoke ten words total to me over the next three days. Remembering his reaction to Call's death, I wondered what he'd do if I got it. Probably shrug and push my body out of the foxhole. Maybe he'd feel a little pity, like the type of regret he'd feel if his rifle broke. *Shame about that rifle. Guess I'll have to get a different one. Shame about that new kid. Guess CP will have to send up more fresh cannon fodder.*

I was desperate to talk to someone who would listen, so I took out a piece of paper and started a letter.

Dear Bastien,

You were right about how the army works. I believed you when you said infantry soldiers were interchangeable cogs, but I thought you meant at a bigger level—division, battalion, maybe even company. I'd counted on a little more warmth from my own squad. I stuck to my standards in training, and I still made friends. But out here, I feel like a leper. It's cold all the time and wet. I shovel out the bottom of the foxhole with my helmet, but I never get it all, and the water seeps through my boots and leaves my feet wet all day long. They never stop aching, not even at night when we pull back to the barn.

I'm dirty too. The barn has an almost-frozen well nearby, but by the end of the day, I'm too tired and too cold to scrub much more than my hands and face. I don't have any clean clothes to put on anyway because I wear all my clothes all the time to keep from freezing. I tried shaving once, but I nicked the top of all my goose bumps, so I stopped doing that. I can't believe I used to give you a hard time when Mom told you to give me a bath. If you drew a warm bath for me out here, I wouldn't hide or run away, and you wouldn't have to bribe me with candy or shoulder rides. I'd do all your chores for a month as payment and know I was getting the better end of the deal.

I paused and looked through what I'd written. I didn't think I was allowed to say anything about the squad's barn. And I didn't want a censor reading what I'd written or, maybe worse, my mom. Would Bastien tell her

I was miserable? I didn't want her to worry, so I waited until Higham's back was turned and burned the letter on his makeshift stove. I thought about starting a new one, but writing made my hands cold.

When Higham told me to, I took my turn on watch, staring east across the river for any German troops foolish enough to let themselves be seen. It reminded me of what I'd read about the Great War, except I was in a foxhole instead of a trench, and Mr. Thompson never mentioned getting the silent treatment from other soldiers on the line.

If my dad had been in this part of Europe, he would have faced west instead of east, but I didn't know which campaigns he'd been involved in or even if he'd been in the infantry. The man I remembered from my childhood had danced in the kitchen with my mom and read bedtime stories to my sisters and me with different voices for each character. But I didn't know whether he'd liked the Kaiser or hated him, if he'd been eager to go to war or reluctant. It wasn't something you asked when you were nine.

When Higham took over, I began another letter, and I tried to keep it cheerful.

Dear Mom,

It's real pretty here, almost like a Christmas card. The food isn't as good as yours, but I didn't expect it would be. I'm with the 28th Division. They started off as a National Guard unit from Pennsylvania, but there's been enough turnover that I've met people from all over the US. They landed in France in July, and they've been busy ever since. They landed in France back in 1918 too and were called the Iron Division because they fought so well at Chateau-Thierry. It got me wondering about Dad. Did he tell you what it was like when he went to war? Did he write to you about it?

I put my letter away, planning to finish later. Maybe Winterton would tell me more about the history of the 28th Division and where the other nicknames like the Keystone Division and the Bloody Bucket had come from. I doubted my mom cared, but it gave me something to write about that wasn't as depressing as sitting in a freezing foxhole.

The high-pitched sound of Higham sharpening his bayonet again grated on my ears. Could the Germans hear it across the river? If he kept it up, they might aim a mortar at him just to have some quiet.

Around noon, I ate chipped beef on toast. No one called it chipped beef on toast. It was called SOS because the toast looked like a shingle and the beef looked like something even less appetizing, but it was one of the words Bastien told me not to say. It was a far cry from home cooking, but at least it was warm, thanks to Higham's stove and the wax-coated boxes the food came in, perfect for burning. When he ran out of K ration boxes and C ration fuel tabs, Higham burned gasoline. It left us coated in a greasy layer of black and tickled my throat, but it also meant I could defrost my fingers and heat up my food, so I didn't complain. Like the rest of the front-line men, I probably resembled a coal miner.

Higham stood with his head barely poking over the top of the foxhole. A mound of dirt was at the back of the hole, so it was unlikely the Jerries across the river would see his outline. "You ever gonna smoke those?" He pointed at the cigarettes that had come with my rations.

I was used to being ignored. Higham's voice startled me, and a bit of the chipped beef fell off the shingle and landed on my pants. My uniform was filthy, but I picked up the food and ate it anyway. Back home, my mom would have told me to take my pants off and rinse out the spot before it stained. Out here, a little food on my pants wasn't a big deal. It was less disturbing than the spray of Call's blood still staining my cuff. I grabbed the pack of Pall Malls and tossed them to Higham. "No." Even though I didn't smoke, I usually kept cigarettes for trading. Right then, exchanging them for an acknowledgment that I existed was enough.

"Thanks."

"I'll trade you my coffee for your bouillon cubes," I said. Most of our water tasted like chlorine or soda ash, and the bouillon covered it up.

Higham nodded his agreement. "You're awfully picky, ain't ya?"

Was he actually going to have a conversation with me?

"Where're you from?" he asked.

"Virginia. Fairfax. You?"

"Philly."

"You been out here long?"

He shrugged. "Long enough to figure a few things out."

"Like what?"

"Things like don't get attached to the new guy 'cause he'll probably be dead in a day or two. But they've been mostly quiet the last few days, and I ain't complaining. And you ain't dead yet, so maybe you'll stick around awhile."

I certainly hoped I was going to stick around awhile. But I wouldn't call it quiet. Both sides fired off a few rounds of artillery from time to time, and rarely an hour passed without the sound of small arms. Not even the night was calm, its darkness interrupted by German flares. "You married?"

I'd noticed a ring on his left hand. It had taken me a day to see it because it was as grimy as the rest of his skin.

"Yeah."

"How long?"

"Two years. Half that time I've been overseas."

I almost asked if he missed his wife, but that sounded too personal.

"I have a kid too," he said. "A son. Haven't met him yet. He'll turn one in January."

"Do you have a picture?"

He pulled one from his pocket and handed it to me. A woman with curly dark hair sat on a couch in front of floral curtains. She faced the camera with a lipstick-enhanced smile. A chubby baby sat on her lap with a crop of fair hair and his mouth open in an *O*. Half the couch was empty, a stark reminder that part of the family was gone.

I handed the photo back. "She's pretty. And your son looks healthy."

Half of Higham's mouth pulled up. "Yeah. She's something special. We grew up a few blocks apart. She went steady with my best friend for a couple years. Then he got distracted by some other broad, and I took full advantage of my status as the shoulder to cry on. How 'bout you? You married?"

"No. I just finished high school this spring. I've got a girl though."

"You gotta picture?"

I frowned. "No. Next time I write I'll ask for one." A photo couldn't do justice to how her eyes sparkled or the way her smile put me at ease, but it would be better than nothing.

"All right, private. I'm gonna teach you everything I know."

Had I finally passed some sort of test?

Higham looked at my boots. "First off, change your socks every morning."

"That's your big tip on combat—change my socks?"

"If you can't use your feet, you can't advance, you can't retreat, you can't evade. You're useless."

"Okay." I had an extra pair. "I'll change my socks every morning."

"I keep my spare pair around my neck. Not the most pleasant place for wet socks, but they dry there better than anywhere else. Starting today, we're giving each other foot rubs every morning and every night to make sure the circulation is good."

I wrinkled my nose in disgust. I'd seen Higham rubbing his own feet, and I'd seen how gross his toes looked. But nearly everything about sitting in a foxhole was dirty and smelly and uncivilized, from washing with a helmet full of melted, muddy snow to using a C ration can as a chamber pot.

"Another thing. I've noticed most replacements die in groups 'cause they bunch up and make a perfect target for incoming mail. So spread out."

"Incoming mail?"

"Artillery fire from the other side."

I'd been told not to bunch up before, but I'd also felt the instinct to move next to someone when I saw Call killed, so I was grateful for the reminder.

"If you're somewhere Jerry might hear you, don't cough."

"That's easier said than done."

Higham balled his hand into a fist and pressed it to his neck. "This usually works. Push on your Adam's apple."

I decided to try it out the next time smoke from the C ration stove started itching my throat.

"Sometimes Jerry fires his tracers high, so you think it's safe to crawl under them. Then they take the tracers out and fire low. Don't trust kraut tracers."

"All right."

"And keep your weapon clean. Don't matter how dirty you get, least not while it's cold enough to keep the smell down. But don't let your rifle get fouled."

Bastien had told me something similar, so I cleaned my BAR every day.

He pointed to my cheeks. "Either grow a beard or shave. That scruff won't do much good keeping you warm, but it will keep a gas mask from sealing."

I'd never grown a beard before. I wasn't sure I could. "Do you think they'll use gas on us?"

Higham shrugged. "They haven't yet. But when we cross that river, we'll be in Germany, so who knows. They gotta be getting desperate."

I stood and followed his gaze across the river. Germany. I considered myself 100 percent American, but I still had cousins over there. I still remembered living over there. I hoped I wasn't going to die over there.

CHAPTER 10

HIGHAM DID HIS BEST TO turn me into a combat veteran over the next several days, and I was grateful to have a mentor. When we were told to go across a ridge for hot chow, I made sure I was yards away from any of the other men while we ate, in case a German artillery spotter had infiltrated our lines and was searching for a nice bunched-up target. I cleaned my BAR every day, even when I looked like I'd rolled in the mud. And I rubbed Higham's smelly, hairy feet with the chipped, yellow toenails twice a day and accepted a foot rub from him in exchange.

A few days into December, Martinez greeted Higham and me when we pulled back to the barn after nightfall. "We're supposed to patrol by the river tonight. Higham, you'll stay here and divvy up guard duty with Luzzatto, Krandle, and Broyles. I'm taking Samson, Roland, Winterton, O'Brien, and Ley." He nodded toward me. "I want you with us in case we need something bigger than a rifle."

"What time?" I asked.

"0100 hours."

That meant I could have three or four hours of sleep. Martinez moved on, and I turned to Higham. "Any advice?"

"Yeah. Don't be seen. Don't be heard. Bring enough firepower to blow Jerry away if they send a patrol out at the same time." Higham wished me luck and headed for outpost duty.

I cleaned and oiled my BAR for the second time that day. The sharp scent of gun oil coated my nostrils when I finished. I found a comfortable spot in the straw, and before I knew it, Higham was shaking me awake. I stood and stretched.

"Jump up and down a few times," Higham suggested.

"I'm awake."

"Yeah. But if you have to run, will you jingle?"

I jumped. I didn't hear anything clinking, but I went through my pockets anyway. In the left one, I had some coins and a P-38 can opener. I left the coins in the barn. I wasn't sure they'd be there when I got back, but they weren't worth much, and having one clink at the wrong time might be fatal. Thinking back to Bastien's lessons, I checked my clothes for pieces that might catch on something and refastened my leggings.

"Listen to your nose, kid," Higham said.

"Huh?" I normally listened with my ears, not my nose.

"The Germans smell different. That mix of leather and sweat. They're dirty, like us, but their tobacco's different, and so's their bread."

I nodded, hoping I'd know what he meant when I smelled it.

When Martinez gathered the patrol, I was ready. Nervous but ready. The anticipation was almost like what I'd felt before a football game against a rival team, but the stakes were much, much higher. Everyone said we were in a calm section of the line, but even a quiet section could deliver death.

As we gathered for the briefing, Samson took one look at me and huffed. "Why are we bringing the blind kid?"

"I'm not blind." My voice was louder than it needed to be, so I lowered it. "My glasses make my vision almost normal."

"You're still a greenhorn."

I thought about telling him I'd learned a few tricks from my brother the spy, but Bastien had told me not to talk about his past. Besides, having practiced a few moves from the Shanghai riot squad in the safety of my backyard didn't make me any less of a greenhorn. "I speak German. That might come in handy."

"You speak German?" Martinez said it like it was an accusation. "Why didn't you say something before now?"

"No one asked."

"Got any other hidden talents?" he asked.

"I was good at football and basketball. And I had a crash course on unconventional hand-to-hand combat."

Samson folded his beefy arms across his chest. "Last I checked, we weren't going on patrol to have a conversation with the krauts."

"That will be all, Private Samson," Martinez broke in. "This is just a routine patrol to make sure Jerry isn't crossing the river in the dark to get artillery targets or plant mines. Perfect time to give the new guys some practice."

I wondered what I'd done to make Samson hate me so much. It had to be more than my glasses. Was he still mad that I'd almost stepped on his hand in the English Channel? I tried to shrug it off as we left the village. Bastien had said to ignore people when they called me a sissy, and this wasn't much different. Maybe I could work it into a funny story for my next letter to Belle. It didn't seem fair that I might make her laugh and not be there to watch it, but she did the same thing for me most letters, so I could try to return the favor.

Six of us headed to the river. We stayed far enough apart that a single artillery burst wouldn't wipe us out but close enough that we could see the person in front of us. Martinez assigned me to the middle, either because I was inexperienced or because I had the most powerful weapon. I wasn't sure which. Roland led. Martinez was second. Winterton and O'Brien were behind me. Samson brought up the rear.

The sounds of the swollen Our River cut through the otherwise quiet night, and every once in a while a mound of snow would slide from a tree branch and fall to the earth with a soft thunk. Or was the sound an enemy scout? My eyes kept a constant scan of the shadows surrounding us, but a bush and a hunched-up soldier looked about the same in the dark.

A German flare burst above us, and we dropped to the dirt as it bathed the ground in a sickly white glow. I banged my elbow on the way down. The flare burned for several minutes, long enough for moisture to seep through my clothes to my knees, thighs, and forearms. Goose bumps formed on my skin, and I had to clench my jaw shut to keep my teeth from chattering. I'd spent hours watching the ground near the river, but it looked different by flare light, sinister and shifting.

When the light burned out, Martinez signaled us back to our feet, and we moved forward. The trees grew thicker, and the dips in the snowy ground grew larger, enough to hide us if another flare went off. I hoped that meant we wouldn't have to lie in the freezing mud again. I moved quietly, the way Bastien had taught me—stepping with the outside of my foot first and then rolling in.

I shivered in the cold, trying to ease the tension in my shoulders. The Germans had been retreating at various speeds since June. If I were them, I'd be building up defenses along the Siegfried Line, not wandering around on our side of the river. I tried to convince myself that our orders were routine, nothing dangerous, but the tight ball that had once been my stomach wouldn't relax, especially when I heard a twig snap.

Roland paused and lifted a hand to signal us to stop. Martinez raised his hand next, and I passed the signal along. I held my breath. The noise could have come from an animal, except most animals had been smart enough to evacuate the war zone. Sometimes we ran patrols to make contact with the company in the village to the south of us, but that wasn't our assignment tonight. If there were other men out here, they were probably hostile.

The silence stretched out as we waited, straining to hear. Eventually Roland turned back to Martinez, who nodded, and we moved forward again. Something seemed to move in the undergrowth. I stopped, staring into the grove of trees as the clouds moved across the moon. Had something more solid than a shadow changed positions, or was I just jumpy?

We advanced only a few yards before Roland crouched to the ground and signaled us to wait again.

Then a German call sounded. "Halt!"

The Germans were out here after all, and we'd run right into them. A chill of fear tightened around my lungs.

Martinez wiggled a finger at me. I took a deep breath and drew level with him, staying low and hoping none of the krauts could see me. "Can you talk to them?" he whispered.

"What are you doing over here?" I hoped my German was still good enough to pass as a native. I switched my BAR's lever from safe to full auto and tried to pick out targets in the darkness. I could see two shadows, but I was certain there were more.

"Patrol. You?" The German's voice was a low croak.

"We're finding artillery targets. No one told us anyone else would be out here." As I spoke, Martinez motioned Winterton and O'Brien to sneak around to the side of the Germans.

"Typical," the other soldier said. "No one told us about you either."

"Keep him talking," Martinez whispered.

"How big's your group?" I asked. "We found a company command post. The guards are asleep. We could raid it."

"Ten."

I flashed five fingers twice to show Martinez the number.

"But we've been told not to stir up trouble," the German continued. "Didn't you get that order? Which unit are you with?"

The game was up. I didn't know if Winterton and O'Brien were in position or not, and I had no idea where Samson was. Roland was nearest the enemy patrol, and he'd removed his helmet so the shape wouldn't give away the fact that he was American. "Are we ready?" I whispered to Martinez. Then louder and in German, I said, "Field artillery." It was too vague and had been too long in coming.

A grenade exploded behind the man I'd been talking to, and he pitched forward into the snow. The light blinded me for a moment, but it also highlighted the silhouettes of several other men with coal-scuttle helmets, all of them scattering into the nearby trees. Martinez fired, and I yanked the stock of my BAR into my shoulder and joined him. The flash of tracer rounds broke the darkness, and the sounds of gunfire and men shouting shattered the silence. Some of the Germans were slow to react, but soon the enemy returned fire in force.

Men groaned ahead of me and yelled off to the side of me. In the dark, it was hard to tell who was friend and who was foe. Martinez stayed nearby, but after the initial burst, I couldn't see anyone else. Branches snapped, and feet stomped as the remnants of the German patrol fled. My pulse raced, and I gasped for air as I searched for targets. I shoved a new twenty-round magazine into my BAR and aimed where the enemy had been; they were either dead, or they'd run off. Bursts of bullets tore through the air, first off to the left, then off to the right. The firefight wasn't over, but it had moved.

"Ley!" Martinez motioned me toward the river.

I tried to say "Yes, Sarge," but the words stuck in my throat. I crept toward the water, staying near the trees so I wouldn't be in the open. It would have been easy to climb one of the pines and hide until the firing stopped, but I forced myself to keep moving. Toward the river. Toward the enemy.

A flash of moonlight reflected off a coal-scuttle helmet ten yards ahead of me. I aimed and fired. The figure cried out and dropped. The sound was pitiful enough to make my jaw tremble. I clenched my teeth and ran toward the sound of a German rifle echoing through the trees.

Another German soldier was nearby, but I couldn't see him. American M1 fire sounded in the distance, probably on the other side of the skirmish. My hands shook, and it took effort to breathe normally. I'd never been so scared before, not when Lieutenant Call was shot, not when our convoy saw a U-boat in the middle of the Atlantic, not when Bastien told me Dad was dead. Remembering Bastien's advice, I slowed down and controlled my steps. I wanted to hear the enemy before he heard me.

I was nearly to the river when I found him. Solid body, average height, field gray uniform, Mauser carbine aimed at the ground a few feet ahead of him. He stepped carefully, like he was stalking someone, and his footsteps made no sound. Branches from a pine tree blocked my shot, so I stepped to the side and saw the German's prey: Winterton. The lanky college kid wasn't exactly loud, but I could hear the snow crunch beneath his feet. He was neither woodsman nor experienced soldier, and those facts were almost the end of him. The German slowly raised his weapon.

I still wasn't in position to shoot. "Winterton, drop!" I crashed through a bush and fired at the kraut. In my hurry, I missed. He ducked into a ditch before I could adjust my aim.

"Ley?" Winterton called.

"Yeah?"

"Can you see him?"

"No. But I know where he is."

"I can't see him either. Ask if he'll surrender."

I took a deep breath before bellowing in German, "Put your rifle down and your hands up and we won't shoot you." Nothing happened. Maybe he'd understood my conversation with Winterton and knew we couldn't get him unless we moved, which might open up a shot for him. "You have five seconds before we fire."

He took four seconds to think it over. "Komerade! Komerade! Don't shoot!" He lifted his rifle, holding it by the barrel, and then set it down. He stood slowly, his hands above his head. I covered him while Winterton frisked him.

"Do you think it's over?" Winterton asked as he and the prisoner drew level with me.

I hadn't heard any shots since I'd warned Winterton, but that didn't mean there weren't more German soldiers out there silently stalking my squad or trying to sneak back to the east side of the river. "I don't know."

I took the lead, scouting ahead for each tense yard to make sure there weren't more krauts lingering in the trees as we headed to where I'd last seen Martinez. I checked behind me every few steps, but our prisoner behaved himself, especially with Winterton's rifle pointed at him.

I found Martinez first, hunched over a body. As I drew closer, I recognized Roland writhing on the ground. He'd been closest to the enemy when the firing had begun. He wasn't dead, but he clutched a wet spot along his abdomen.

Martinez dug for his first-aid kit but glanced up long enough to see us. "You seen Samson or O'Brien?"

"No."

Martinez put a bandage on Roland's wound. "Are you hit anywhere else?" he asked Roland.

Roland's reply was more of a whimper than an answer, but he shook his head no.

"Ley, do a body count. See if we got all ten of them. And see if you can find O'Brien and Samson," Martinez said. "Winterton, keep an eye on that prisoner."

Three German bodies were visible within a few steps. Two of the corpses had been torn apart by the grenade. Blood and gore stained the snow. Roland groaned behind me as I found the fourth German corpse. Twenty yards farther, I found number five half hidden under some bushes. Add in the one I'd shot and the one I'd helped capture, and I was up to seven.

A shadow moved to my left, and I jerked my BAR around.

"Easy, four-eyes." Samson pushed a German soldier to the ground in front of him. The prisoner had his hands up. He was missing his helmet, and his eyes were wide with fear. "Ask this kraut what he's doing over here."

"How many of you were there?" I asked instead, in case the one I'd been talking to had lied.

"Ten." The man's voice trembled. He seemed more a boy than a man. "Please don't shoot me."

"Did you see any others?" I asked Samson.

"I saw two run off."

"Do you think they'll counterattack?" I looked around, wondering if they were hiding behind a tree, their rifles aimed at us.

"I don't think so." Samson kicked his prisoner's boots. "If they're all like their buddy here, they'll keep running until an officer stops them."

After watching that other soldier sneak up on Winterton, I wasn't sure I agreed with him. "Have you seen O'Brien?"

"Nope."

I watched the prisoner. He was still whispering, pleading for mercy. I hadn't expected to feel sorry for a Nazi, but he looked about thirteen. I tuned him out. If Samson wanted to shoot him, he would have already done it. I had three more people to find.

I walked another two minutes before I heard a crunch of snow followed by a low moan. With my eyes to the ground, I caught a trail—torn-up snow, broken shrubs, and blood. Boots appeared next, sticking out from under a bush.

"Come out with your hands up." In English, that would have sounded a lot like something from Hollywood, but in German, it did the job.

The German patrolman slithered into the open. He'd unbuttoned his coat, probably to examine his wound, a gaping hole in his gut. "Wasser," he pleaded. *Water.*

I kept my BAR on him as I got out my canteen, but he was too injured to be dangerous, so I came close enough to hand it to him. He kept one hand over his torn innards and reached with the other. His hand trembled, so I bent down and held it for him.

"Danke." *Thank you.*

I reached for my first-aid kit and pulled out a pack of sulfa powder and a bandage. But I didn't use them. When I looked at the soldier again, his eyes and mouth hung open, and his hand had slipped from his wound. I pulled off a glove and checked his pulse, but I couldn't feel it in his wrist. I moved my fingers to his neck, but I couldn't find it there either. I held my hand near his nose and mouth to see if I felt him breathing. Nothing. Another glance at his wound, and I lost what was left of that evening's K rations. A tree blocked the moonlight, so I couldn't even see the man's intestines that well; it wasn't the sight of the wound that made me vomit. It was more the knowledge that the soldier at my feet and six of his buddies had been alive ten minutes ago.

I took a few deep breaths and told myself to focus. I still needed to find one more enemy and one more squad mate. Where had O'Brien gone? Had he chased a kraut to the river? I'd overheard a few of his hunting stories. He'd tracked deer and elk since he was a boy. Now that he was in Luxembourg, did he hunt enemy soldiers? Or was he bleeding somewhere in the snow? Dead? Captured?

I moved forward, along the path our patrol would have taken us. I assumed it was roughly the same path the German patrol had come up, maybe the way its last member had retreated. I didn't like being alone in the dark, vulnerable if another patrol came along or if the last German soldier hid among the trees. The hoot of an owl or the baaing of a sheep would have made the night seem less dangerous, but other than the river, the silence was complete. I looped back, away from the river, thinking I might find someone closer to the village.

Footsteps came toward me, steady as they crushed snow and cracked twigs. I hid behind an enormous pine in case it was the enemy.

O'Brien walked into view, the end of his rifle prodding the last German soldier.

"O'Brien!" I called.

He stopped abruptly, so startled that he nearly dropped his rifle.

His prisoner must have felt the change in pressure on his back. He spun around, tore O'Brien's rifle from his hands, and used it to beat O'Brien's head.

O'Brien grunted and tumbled to the ground. The prisoner whipped the rifle around toward me, but my fingers squeezed the trigger on my BAR before he could aim. He fell next to O'Brien.

I dropped to my knees to check on my squad mate. Blood dripped from a six-inch gash across O'Brien's cheek, but he was still conscious.

"What were you thinking, jumping out at me like that?" he yelled. "You almost got me killed!"

"I didn't know if it was you or a kraut—what was I supposed to do?"

O'Brien swore and pushed himself to his feet. He felt his cheek and swore again at the blood.

"I'm sorry," I said. "Do you need a bandage?"

"I don't know yet. Is he dead?" O'Brien pointed to the German soldier.

I'd shot him in the chest, so I was fairly certain of what I'd find, but I looked anyway. "Dead."

O'Brien checked his cheek again. "Where's everyone else?"

"Back where it started."

I led the way. O'Brien was quiet. That was better than him bawling me out, but only a little.

Sitting out the war wasn't an alternative I could live with, but I hadn't expected combat to be like this. I'd thought there would be more time to think, that I'd have more control over what happened, but the battle had been chaotic, and I'd been terrified the entire time. Part of me worried that I'd throw up again. My muscles ached, not only from exertion but also from the stress of being so tense for so long. But I couldn't relax yet. Another kraut patrol might be out there.

Roland was still alive when we got back, with Winterton huddled on one side and Martinez on the other.

"Where's Samson?" I asked, suddenly afraid the pathetic prisoner had been putting on a show to lull Samson into being careless, just like O'Brien's prisoner had.

"I sent him to take the prisoners back and get a medic," Martinez said. "Did you count the bodies?"

"Yeah, they're all dead or captured now."

Martinez waved me toward the river. "Stand guard over there in case another patrol's out. O'Brien, you do the same over there." Martinez pointed in the opposite direction.

I obeyed, going to a mound of dirt and brush that would be easy to defend if another patrol came along or if they'd lied about their numbers. I had a better view of the river from my new spot, but I was still close enough to hear the others.

"Where are you from, Roland?" Winterton asked.

"Easton, Pennsylvania," was the muffled reply.

"Oh yeah? I went to Lafayette University for about a year. Until the army ended the ASTP. Nice town."

"My dad works at Lafayette."

"Is he a professor? Maybe I took one of his classes."

Roland gave a short chuckle. "No, he's a janitor."

"What did he say when you joined up?"

"He was real proud." Roland's voice was getting weaker and weaker. I glanced back. Martinez added another bandage to Roland's abdomen. Winterton held one of his hands.

"I bet he'd be proud of you now too. You handled that German patrol real well." Winterton kept talking to him, even though Roland's answers grew softer and shorter. Winterton spoke about Easton, asked about Roland's family, and did it all with a calm, kind voice. It made my conversation with the dying German seem clumsy. Winterton was a greenhorn too, but he was a long way ahead of me when it came to compassion.

"I'm thirsty," Roland said.

"We can't give you anything," Martinez said. "No water for stomach wounds. It might kill you."

Winterton kept Roland distracted, but I didn't hear any more of the conversation.

I'd killed that wounded German by offering him my canteen, as sure as if I'd put a bullet through his head.

CHAPTER 11

MY FEET FELT HEAVY, AND the night felt particularly black as we shuffled back to the barn. I'd survived my first firefight, but I'd also killed. On top of that, I'd nearly gotten O'Brien shot, and I'd finished off a wounded man. In my head, I composed part of a letter, one I knew I'd never write. *Did you ever kill anyone, Bastien? I shot and killed at least two men tonight, probably more. Both of them were trying to shoot back, so it was justified, but it's hard to wrap my head around it. Another one was wounded. I didn't shoot him, and I didn't mean to kill him, but I did when I gave him my canteen.*

I sat in front of the stove and tried to warm up. I shook with cold, or at least that's what I told myself. Someone from the supply company brought up coffee and hotcakes, but I wasn't hungry. Deep down I knew drinking something warm wouldn't stop the shaking, even if I hadn't been raised to avoid coffee. I flipped through a copy of *The Stars and Stripes*, but I couldn't focus on the newsprint.

Krandle went to relieve Higham from his second stretch of guard duty, and Higham actually looked happy to see me when he got back. "How'd it go, kid?"

I shrugged.

Higham sat between Winterton and me. "That bad, huh?"

"Roland got shot," Winterton said. "It looked pretty serious."

"What happened?" Higham held his hands out next to the stove.

I let Winterton fill him in. "We ran into a German patrol. Ley talked to them long enough for us to sneak around so we could attack from two sides at once. We killed eight, captured two."

"What were our casualties, other than Roland?" Higham asked.

I glanced at O'Brien, who was getting a coffee refill. A white bandage covered part of his cheek. "I startled O'Brien, and his prisoner stole his rifle and knocked him in the face."

Higham followed my gaze. "He don't look too bad now."

"I almost got him killed."

"O'Brien should know better than to be surprised. Anyway, I'd say we won that skirmish." Higham seemed satisfied. "Shame about Roland, but I think there's a regulation against dying at an aid station. If he got that far, he should be all right. Some days I wouldn't mind catching a million-dollar wound like that myself."

A million-dollar wound. Something that took a soldier out of combat without killing him or leaving him permanently crippled. I wasn't sure Roland's wound counted—it seemed a little too serious.

Higham took his helmet off, and his greasy blond hair stuck out at funny angles. He squinted at me. "What's eating you? Sounds like you were pretty important in the little firefight."

I took my time answering. "I think I killed one of the Germans."

Winterton cleared his throat. "Ley, it's war. It's okay to kill them when they're trying to kill us."

I shook my head. "No. One of them was injured. Stomach wound. He wasn't trying to kill anyone anymore. He was just trying to keep his guts out of the mud. He asked for some water, and I gave it to him. I didn't know it would kill him."

"Didn't they mention that in training?" Higham asked.

"If they did, I forgot."

"He might have died anyway," Winterton said.

"Maybe, maybe not." I squeezed my eyes shut, wishing I could squeeze the memory away. "I was just trying to be decent, and then he up and died on me before I could find my first-aid kit."

"You didn't kill him." I expected Winterton to blame it on Hitler or circumstances or the grenade shrapnel that had sliced open the soldier's intestines, but he looked at Higham and then looked at me and said, "Water wouldn't have finished him off that fast."

Higham nodded. "That's right. He must have been about to die anyway." He slapped me on the back. "Have some food while it's hot. You like hotcakes, don't ya?"

"Yeah," I said. Higham left the stove's warmth to get some for me. They were covered with sweet syrup, and as they settled in my stomach, I realized how hungry I'd been. Relief that I hadn't killed the injured German was even more comforting than the food.

"Do you think Roland will live?" I asked.

Winterton shrugged. "Probably. He might not be back here until spring. That could be a good thing."

"I think you helped him, talking about his hometown. But what's the ASTP?"

Higham chuckled. "All safe till peace, right?"

"That's what my mom thought." Winterton smiled wistfully. "Army Special Training Program. The army sent me to college to study engineering. But then they needed replacements this year instead of engineers in two or three years, so they cut the program and sent me to the infantry."

"Did you like college?" I asked.

"Yeah. Course, we were taking double class loads and had to fit in training too. I wouldn't mind going back after the war. It would be nice to have a normal schedule and be able to take a girl for an evening on the town without having to get back before lights out."

"Yeah, yeah." Higham waved a hand at Winterton. "Poor college kids. Having to juggle homework and a bunch of fawning coeds."

Winterton smirked and started singing. "Take down your service flag, mother, your son's in the ASTP. And if ever a German I see, I'll take out my trusty old slide rule and square root the Sine of B."

"What's the Sine of B?" Higham asked.

"Trigonometry stuff." I made a face. I wouldn't have passed trig if it hadn't been for Belle's tutoring. "You good at stuff like that?" I asked Winterton.

He shrugged. "Good enough to stay in the program while it lasted."

I yawned. My feet were finally warm, and I was about to go lie down when a corporal came in with mail. Some of the envelopes were for me. Even better, one was from Belle, and inside was a picture. She couldn't have gotten my letter asking for a photo yet. Somehow she'd known to send it anyway.

She worked for Western Union now, in the big Washington, DC, office. I read all about the latest movie she'd seen and about how irritated she was when some of her coworkers cheated on rationing and then bragged about it. Toward the end of the letter she said,

My letters are probably boring you. Sometimes work is great—I see telegrams announcing births or engagements. But more often I see telegrams from the War Department. Soldiers, sailors, marines, or airmen: missing, dead, or captured. It's sad, and it gets to me sometimes—all those families with heartbreak, all those men with such huge challenges ahead. But I can't forget what you told me about living under Hitler, so this is a war we have to fight. Unfortunately, complaining about people who use the black market won't shut it down. And wishing away bad news won't make it disappear. But I have an idea. I'm going to start a story. You add something and send it back to me, and then I'll add more, and we'll see how far we get.

Once upon a time, there was a brave knight who wanted more than anything to embark on a quest to slay a dragon. The knight wasn't foolhardy or vain, nor was he seeking fame or fortune, but the dragon was very, very bad and the knight was very, very good, so seeking to vanquish the dragon was the knight's inevitable task.

No knight could slay a dragon without preparation, so the knight diligently learned all he could of the dragon's weaknesses. He listened to others who had fought dragons and grew skilled with his sword and his lance. He knew quests required strength and stamina, so he honed his body until it was powerful and able to endure repeated hardship. After an intense period of training, the knight began his quest.

First, he crossed a great sea. The blue water shimmered in the sun and reminded him of carefree summer days. He wanted others to enjoy days like the ones he remembered, warm and wholesome and relaxing . . . and now threatened by the dragon. Then the knight crossed green hills and wooded vales, picturesque hamlets and bucolic farms. He knew the lands he crossed were threatened by the dragon, and he was driven to protect them.

As the knight traveled, he gathered allies in his crusade to rid the world of the horrible monster.

Okay, Luke, your turn now.

I chuckled at Belle's story and put it away to reply to later. I read my other letters: two from Bastien, two from Mom, and one from Hannah. That night, I didn't dream about dying German soldiers. I dreamed about dragons.

* * *

On December 10, our company shifted positions. It wasn't much of a move. We were still in Luxembourg, but we had a slightly different view of the Our River. We still spent the days in freezing foxholes, but instead of a barn at night, we slept in a cellar. The village was mostly evacuated. We scrounged mattresses from nearby homes and pulled them below ground with us.

Stocked with sheets and pillows, we went to sleep each night feeling like royalty.

After two nights in our new area, Higham came in from outpost duty with a puzzled expression.

"What happened?" I asked.

"They're making a lot of noise over there."

"What did you hear?" Martinez asked.

"Engines. Lots of 'em. More than a few trucks bringing in chow or an ambulance coming in to evacuate the wounded."

Martinez headed for the door. "Are they still making noise?"

"It stopped about a half hour ago."

Martinez paused. "Supply convoy? Armor?"

"Maybe armor. Maybe motorcycle couriers—but lots of it, whatever it is."

A frown crept across Martinez's face. "We need to tell Breckenridge. Come with me."

They returned a half hour later. By then, everyone was awake and most of us were on the main level of the house, heating our K rations in the kitchen. Winterton was telling me about the dust storms in Oklahoma, and O'Brien was listening in, which I hoped meant he wasn't still angry that I'd startled him at the end of our last patrol.

Higham walked over and sat on the table because the chairs were all broken or occupied. "Me and my big mouth," he whispered.

I glanced at Martinez, then back at Higham. "What?"

"Breckenridge had us report to Wood. I earned our squad a patrol."

O'Brien and Winterton groaned. Samson chucked an empty K ration box at Higham's helmet.

Martinez held up his hands. "Wood said we were going on patrol tonight anyway. This just made it certain and changed its purpose."

Samson huffed. "No offense, Sarge, but a patrol to contact friendly forces the next company over is a lot easier than poking around the German lines."

"*Sí.*" Martinez sighed. "But orders are orders, and if Jerry's up to something, we need to know. Higham, Samson, Winterton, and Luzzatto, you'll come with me tonight."

Samson chewed on his bottom lip for a few seconds, staring at me. Then he turned to Martinez. "Seeing as how four-eyes speaks German, do you think we should bring him along too? Just in case? He did all right on the last patrol."

Coming from Samson, that was high praise. I wasn't eager to sneak up to the German line after dark, but I was willing to help my squad.

Martinez nodded. "Fine. Luzzatto, Krandle, Broyles, and O'Brien stay. Everyone else comes. In the meantime, we've got about thirty minutes to get in our foxholes."

I shoveled in the last of my chopped ham and eggs before tossing the empty can in the trash. The K ration version didn't taste much like the real thing, but I always ate it all anyway.

I grabbed my gear and followed Higham out into the cold morning. The chill bit into my nose and snaked down the back of my neck. "I wonder how long it would take my mom to knit a scarf and send it over here."

Higham chuckled. "Might be spring before it arrives if she's anything like my mom."

"No, she's quick with her knitting needles." I tightened my shoulders to keep from shivering. "But even if she mailed it today, I might turn into an icicle before it got here."

"I have a friend working in a supply company. Gotta letter from him last week. He asked me how I like the new boots. They've got rubber bottoms so they don't soak up water. Better insulation. Everyone in his unit has 'em. I told him all of us living in freezing mud up on the main line of resistance have the old kind."

I glanced at my leather combat boots. When the snow thawed, the leather soaked up the moisture, and it took forever to dry. If I took them off when it was cold, the soggy leather froze solid, and I couldn't get my feet back inside. "Rear-echelon jerks."

"They get all the best cigarette brands too. Not that you'd know anything about that."

Our grousing finished as we reached our foxhole. It looked undisturbed. Higham lighted his C ration stove, sharpened his bayonet, and then settled in for a nap. By the time he woke, I'd thought of what to write to Belle.

First off, the water the knight crossed wasn't really blue. It was more gray and churning. And most of the hamlets had been partially destroyed by the dragon, so they weren't that impressive to look at. The knight thought the water was kind of ominous and the villages were kind of sad.

The knight didn't get along too well with his allies at the beginning. The other fellows had seen lots of people come to battle the dragon. And most of them ended up dead. So they ignored the new warrior. Then one day the new guy finally did something right, and then he made some friends.

The dragon sat there and watched the knight and his buddies. Sometimes he blew fire at them. Sometimes the knights threw spears at him. Everyone was miserable, but the dragon wasn't going to roll over and die, and the knights weren't going to give up. So they stayed there. Sometimes they were bored, sometimes they were cold, and always they were a little scared.

Meanwhile, the knight's lady fair was back in the kingdom. All the nearby knights and squires sought her out day and night. She found it annoying and started carrying around a club so she could beat back anyone who got to bothering her too bad. She missed her *knight, the one who had gone to slay the dragon. Just about every day she cried because she missed him so much.*

The knight missed his lady. He was glad when she sent tokens and letters and stuff, but he didn't cry, because knights don't cry.

"Who you writing? That girl of yours?"

I looked up to see Higham watching me. "Yeah."

"Figured. You got a goofy grin on your face." Higham lit a cigarette and turned back to the German lines.

I went back to my letter, determined to keep a straight face.

Belle, don't ever worry about boring me. I'll reread your letters over and over again no matter what they say. Next time you have a few free minutes, will you sneak over to my house and give my mom a hug for me? And let me know how Bastien's leg is? I asked him in a letter not too long ago, but he'll probably write back and say "It's fine" without any details.

It took longer than I thought it would to settle in with my squad. Things are better now, except the weather. It warmed up a little, but that just made some of the snow melt and now everything is muddy. And it still gets plenty cold at night.

I shivered, remembering my last stint on outpost duty. It had been pitch black and freezing, and I'd been all alone, listening and watching for a German attack. Each assignment was three hours of misery, stretched to feel like it was much, much longer.

I miss you, Belle. I miss my family too. But I'm doing okay. These hard times will lead to peace and freedom eventually.

* * *

That night I tried to hide my jitters while we waited for our patrol. Wood wanted us to cross the river and get a good look at what the krauts were up to. It wasn't a very big river. In the summer, people probably waded across it with scarcely a second thought, but all the rain and melted snow had turned it into a rapid, icy surge. Our orders were to plunge through it in the dark, in winter, and when we got across, we would face armed enemy soldiers.

"You cleaning that *again*?" Higham asked as I stripped down my BAR.

"Yeah." It gave me something useful to do, even if I'd already cleaned it a few times that day.

Higham sat and started sharpening his bayonet.

"You sharpening that *again*?" I asked.

He smiled. "You betcha."

Maybe he needed something to do as badly as I did. When he finished, he cleaned his rifle.

"What'd that sugar report say?" I asked. He'd received a letter from his wife that evening when we'd pulled back to the barn. I'd gotten mail too, Belle complaining about how long the bus rides to DC took and Bastien asking a bunch of questions about what I was doing on and off duty.

Higham grinned. "My son's walking. Getting into everything. My wife said she's trying to teach him to say 'Dada' when she shows him my picture."

"Does he say it yet?"

"Naw. But she thinks he will soon." Higham's hands paused while wiping down the trigger assembly. "I'm missing out on a lot. First smile, first laugh, first step, first word. Nights like this, I wonder if I'll ever see him."

"Sure you will. Right in time for his first big tantrum."

Higham laughed.

Winterton sat next to us to field strip his M1. He moved more quickly than Higham or me. Maybe he was cleaning his weapon to make sure it was clean instead of cleaning his weapon to keep his mind off what came next.

The company kitchen brought in real food instead of C rations. The spaghetti wasn't as good as Gracie's, but it beat K rations hands down. We all got big servings because the quartermasters hadn't taken into account that Call, Roland, and a couple guys from another squad were gone. We were supposed to get a new lieutenant soon, but Sergeant Breckenridge, the acting platoon leader, had been with the company since they landed in France, and most of us weren't eager to risk another green lieutenant like Call who didn't listen to his noncoms.

When it was time, Martinez led us outside. The night was crisp and cold, with a bite that made my skin tingle before leaving it with a numb ache. Samson took point, and the rest of us strung along, staying several yards apart. I followed Samson as we left the village and crept into the open. Martinez was behind me. Winterton and Higham took parallel paths, Winterton to the left and Higham to the right. Most of the snow had melted, and I missed it for the night patrols. The snow reflected the moonlight. The frozen mud absorbed it, making the night darker. I didn't want to think about how many German soldiers might be hidden in the dark, but thinking about the enemy was my job.

A whoosh sounded, and I nearly dove to the ground. I relaxed when I heard the hoot and smiled when I heard Samson cursing the owl. I wasn't the only person who'd been startled. I didn't know what an owl was doing out here. Even in our so-called quiet sector, there was enough noise to clear out most animals. I could count on one hand the number I'd seen from my foxhole. In town it was different—there were always rats—but most of the wildlife in the woods had fled.

We made good time to the river. I wasn't looking forward to crossing the freezing torrent. Sure, battalion needed to know what the Germans were up to, but we wouldn't see much in the dark. Better for battalion or division to send up one of the little Piper Cubs and have them take a few pictures. Except the weather had been bad enough to ground most airplanes. In training, they'd told us how great it was to have air superiority, but it didn't do us much good if the clouds and the wind didn't cooperate.

Samson slowed, and I could make out the rustle of the river. I came level with him but stayed a few yards away. Martinez drew up on the other side of me, keeping the normal spacing.

Almost immediately I caught bits of German words from across the river.

Martinez waved me closer. "What are they saying?" he whispered.

I strained my ears, focusing on the enemy's conversation and trying to block out the water. "Joking about someone they call the little Graf. That's like a count. Probably one of their officers." I listened longer, and the banter made me tense with worry. "And now they're joking about all the American rations they'll soon be enjoying."

Martinez turned to Winterton, who was only a few feet away. "Are they doing what I think they're doing?" Martinez asked.

"Looks like they're building a bridge to me." Winterton must have come to that conclusion before he was asked because he whispered his answer immediately.

I'd been focused on listening rather than watching. I'd noticed the wood they were hauling, but nothing showed above the water. "I don't see a bridge."

"They're building it under the water level," Winterton said softly. "Probably so our airplanes won't notice."

"What good is a bridge covered in water?" I looked back at the joking Jerries.

"It's probably only a foot under."

I nodded. If I had the choice of crossing the river on a slightly submerged bridge or fording the river without one, I'd take the wet boots and the bridge and pass on getting a lot more of me soaked. And a bridge, even a sunken one, would be good for other things too. "Armor?"

Martinez nodded. "Armor. Trucks. Artillery. They're up to something. I'd say a raid, but it's gotta be a little bigger than that or they wouldn't need a bridge."

"So much for a nice stay along a quiet front," Winterton whispered.

We watched the men a few more minutes. Eventually the conversation turned to raunchy jokes and loud laughter.

Martinez motioned Samson and Higham over. "We can't cross here," Martinez said. "Higham, you lead. We'll go south along the river, see what else we find."

A quarter mile to the south, we heard the type of engine noises Higham had reported yesterday. We stayed to observe and listen, but the trees and the nighttime darkness blocked our view, and the engines drowned any conversations coming from Germany. Martinez looked at his watch and motioned for us to head back. We wouldn't have to cross the river after all, and we'd already learned far more than I'd expected we would.

Martinez led us to the company command post in a sturdy stone home standing guard over a narrow crossroad. I followed him inside, and my glasses fogged up, so I took them off and held them. It was worth it to be warm.

Wood spoke with a civilian. I hadn't seen many civilians in the last few weeks. To make it even more strange, it was a woman.

"More men than I could count; more tanks than I could count." The lady spoke English, but it sounded like she had to think of each word before she said it.

"What type of troops?" Wood asked.

"All ages. Young, old, and what you would expect for soldiers."

Wood crossed his arms. "And why were you on the other side of the river?"

"My cousin lives there. I haven't seen her for months, and I was worried. But as soon as I crossed the river, the Germans brought me to one of their officers and asked me about the Americans."

"What did you tell them?"

"I told them I lived on their side of the river, that I had come to this side for only a day to visit a relative. They asked me over and over again, but I always said the same thing."

My glasses were clear, so I put them back on. The woman was older than I'd thought at first—probably my mom's age.

"Eventually they let me go," she said. "I still haven't seen my cousin, but I don't want to be here when they attack. I have seen that before, in 1940 and in 1914."

"Did you hear when they'd attack?"

"No."

"Did they say where they'd attack?"

"No."

Wood nodded. He motioned for Sergeant Anders, the company communications sergeant. "I think battalion needs to hear this. Will you take her there? Tonight?"

Anders nodded. "Yes, sir."

Martinez cleared his throat. "I'd like to add my report, sir, before you inform battalion."

"Did you make it across the river?"

"No, sir, but the Germans will make it across easily when the time comes." Martinez explained about the bridge and the noises we'd heard. Winterton answered questions about the construction project. However long he'd been in college, he'd learned enough about engineering to impress Wood.

When we left, I walked beside Martinez. Back in the States, if someone printed a map of our division, they'd probably show a line running roughly north to southeast along the German border. But that wouldn't be accurate. It wasn't a line. It was more like a series of dots, little bits of men scattered about, facing the Siegfried Line. Not only was this supposed to be a quiet sector, but it *needed* to be a quiet sector because we were spread thinner than a civilian's butter ration. "Sarge, what are we going to do if the Germans come through here with more than a company or two?"

Martinez looked back at company CP, then east. The sky had been black when we'd arrived, but now parts were lightening to gray. "We're going to hope we're wrong. And we're going to hope someone at division finds more men or sends the air force up to knock out that bridge. And we're going to make sure our defenses are as strong as they can be. Then we'll have to wait."

CHAPTER 12

OUTPOST DUTY WAS ALWAYS LONELY, cold, and tense. The only things between me and the German Army were my Browning Automatic Rifle and the Our River, and the underwater bridge had changed the river from a real hurdle for the enemy to a mere annoyance. My squad and the rest of the company were nearby, in the village. But the next companies over were miles away.

It was December 16, and I shivered in my position. My arms were sore from all the shoveling we'd done over the past few days. I hoped the Germans weren't going to launch a raid anytime soon, because so far, battalion hadn't sent any reinforcements, but if the Germans came, the bridge would take them right up against Wood's company. My company.

I'd gotten a letter from Bastien the day before.

Lukas, I forgot to tell you another rule: learn which officers you can trust. It takes a different type of man to organize an army in peacetime than it does to lead an army during war, and sometimes the shakeup takes awhile to work out. You'll want to listen to the good ones immediately. Trust their instincts, because sometimes you won't have time to think it through yourself. The bad ones, on the other hand, are as much a danger as the enemy.

Martinez was one of the good ones, even though he was an NCO rather than a commissioned officer. Call had been one of the bad ones. We were still waiting on Call's replacement, but I thought Captain Wood was worth following, even if his squeaky voice reminded me of a thirteen-year-old. I sure hoped I wasn't going to have to follow them anytime soon though. I'd been eager to fight the Germans when I'd joined up, but I'd seen enough over the last few weeks to be content holding the line until spring.

The night was quiet. Too quiet. Usually the krauts launched a few star flares into the darkness, either to check that we weren't attacking or to interrupt our sleep. I didn't trust the sudden stillness.

I glanced at my watch. I was on outpost duty until 0600 hours, and it was 0530. A half hour left. I'd probably have time for a letter when I got back, but I wasn't sure how much I could tell Bastien about my officers when they were the ones censoring my mail.

I stared out toward Germany. I could see only a few trees through the patchy nighttime fog. Maybe I could cut one down on my way back and take it to the barn for a Christmas tree. It might look all right with some bandoleers as garland and some can openers as ornaments.

I shivered and stamped my feet, and then the eastern horizon exploded in a flash of light. German artillery kept us on our toes, but I'd never heard that many field guns fire at once. At least a hundred thin streaks of light arched toward me. My mouth dropped open, and my grip on my BAR slipped. More booms sounded. As the first salvo whistled past me, I did the only thing I could do during a barrage like that. I pulled a pile of branches over my foxhole and huddled at the bottom.

The ground trembled, and the branches above me shook with each hit. I pressed my back into the frozen mud along the sides of the foxhole, wishing I could crawl under the dirt where jagged pieces of artillery wouldn't find me. I pulled my helmet tight on my head and tried to keep breathing. The barrage no doubt signaled a German attack, but anyone out in that much artillery fire would get hit, so I had to wait it out. But waiting was so hard. Every crash rattled me from head to toe and made my insides tighten. I tried to make myself as small as possible so I was less of a target for all the deadly pieces of flying shrapnel. Part of me was glad no one could see me curled up like a baby at the bottom of my foxhole, and part of me wished I weren't alone.

I'd heard of people going crazy during shellings. I'd never doubted it, but now I understood it. If the barrage kept up much longer, I was afraid I'd lose my sanity. I prayed. It wasn't a normal prayer with a formal beginning and end. It was more of a thirty-minute plea for survival.

I couldn't see anything from the bottom of my foxhole. But I heard boom after boom, strike after strike, whistle after whistle, shriek after shriek. I was afraid that when I did look out, all of Luxembourg would be destroyed. How much artillery were the krauts going to fire?

After awhile, the bursts came with less frequency. The sun wasn't supposed to rise until about 0830, but the barrage had lasted a lifetime, so it had to be nearly dawn. I glanced at my watch. It was only 0610.

0610. I was no longer on outpost duty. Once the attack began, I wouldn't stand a chance out in front of the line all by myself. But Martinez had ensured we'd have a good line of defense in the village. There, with the rest of my squad, I could do some real damage to a German raiding party.

Knowing I should go back to my squad was one thing. Working up the courage to climb from my shelter was another. I hesitated, counting the seconds between shell bursts. It reminded me of popping popcorn over a bonfire with Belle and knowing the batch was ready when the time between pops petered out.

I said another prayer, begging for help, and pushed the branches aside. Part of the snow had melted, leaving dark patches along the ground. I expected the sky to be just as dark, but it was like a full moon. The closest full moon was still two weeks away, but light reflected down from the overcast sky, bathing the ground in glow and shadows. Whatever it was, it wasn't normal, and it was going to make getting from my outpost to the village that much more complicated.

A crooked pine tree, knocked by artillery, fell flat into the mud by the river. Then my breath stopped. The woods were moving. Soldiers, visible whenever the fog shifted, crept among what was left of the trees. They had to be German because we didn't have that many men in this sector, not even if we pulled in the company to the north, the company to the south, and the regimental headquarters staff back in Clervaux.

I had to warn the squad, warn the platoon, warn the company. If this was a local raid, it was a big one. I had a feeling it was more than we could stop on our own.

I gripped my BAR and took a deep breath. Roughly fifteen yards behind me was a bush. That was my first target. I turned my back to the marauding Germans, set my weapon down to clamber from the foxhole, then grabbed it and ran in a crouch for the bush. I paused there, then shimmied into a depression and jogged along the bottom with my head down.

German artillery whistled as it passed overhead, but they'd switched to targets farther beyond the line. The firing was more sporadic now, but each shriek made my stomach clench a little harder. German burp guns sounded, and I hoped they weren't aimed at me. I made a lot of noise as I ran, and the unnatural moonlight meant it wasn't dark. Fog was common along the Our River, and wisps of it gathered in the nooks and crevices of the ground. I wished it was thicker. If I could pick out the krauts through the fog, they'd be able to pick me out too.

I heard a burp gun again and saw the flash of a yellow tracer hit the bank of snow I was running toward. I changed direction and darted into a group of trees. My lungs heaved and despite the cold, I felt sticky with sweat. I thought about propping my BAR on its bipod and sending a stream of bullets toward the Germans. They were so thick I couldn't miss, but I needed to warn my squad.

So much for being in a quiet sector.

An open field lay between me and the defenses Martinez had insisted we build. If the Germans saw me, they'd shoot, and if my squad saw me but didn't recognize me, I'd be under fire from both sides. From where I was, I couldn't see the Germans, but one shift in the fog could open up their view. I slung my BAR across my back and crawled.

Most days I spent a lot of effort trying to stay dry, but I forgot all about that as I slithered toward my squad. I avoided one puddle, but the thin layer of ice over another one broke as soon as I put pressure on it, sending up a fissure of water that somehow made it through all five layers of clothing. My skin pulled into goose bumps from the back of my neck all the way down to my ankles.

My ears hurt from all the noise. My fingers were frozen in my gloves. And I was afraid any moment the sky would grow even brighter or a gust of wind would roll the fog back and expose my position.

"Ley, is that you?"

I recognized Higham's voice and breathed a little easier. "Yeah!"

"Get over here!"

That was easier said than done. I was fifty yards away, but now I didn't have to worry about my own squad hitting me. I couldn't see any Germans behind me. I prayed that meant they couldn't see me either. I pushed myself to my feet and sprinted for the slit trench I'd help dig the night before. Tracers whizzed past me for the final few yards.

When I dove inside, I almost landed on Winterton. Martinez was right behind him, one ear pressed into a field telephone.

"Sarge, there are a couple German companies between us and the river," I reported.

Higham huffed softly behind me. "We've noticed."

I turned to ask if they'd seen anything else, but the orange glow behind him changed my question. "That isn't what I think it is, is it?"

Higham glanced over his shoulder. "Our house. Direct hit."

"Was anyone inside?"

"In the basement. No casualties, but most of our equipment is gone. So's your breakfast."

I wasn't hungry anyway, not with the woods packed full of German soldiers.

Martinez covered the phone's mouthpiece with his hand and pointed to my BAR. "Take out your tracers."

I nodded and started stripping them from the magazine. "Why are we taking out the tracers?"

Winterton stooped to help. "So they can't see where we're shooting from."

"Is anyone sending reinforcements?" I asked.

"They're working on it, but it might take awhile. Prepare for a rough morning."

"Do you know what that light is?"

"Searchlights," Higham said. "Bouncing off the clouds."

"Why?" I asked. "We can see them when the fog cooperates."

"When the krauts make mistakes, you don't ask why. Just take advantage of the situation while you can, 'cause they'll fix it soon." Higham turned to Martinez. "Should we go at it yet?"

Martinez shook his head. "Other units are reporting problems too, so it might be awhile before help arrives. We can't waste bullets. Wait till you can't miss."

Winterton propped his M1 up on a sandbag. Samson did the same thing on the other side of Higham.

Martinez held his hand out for silence and spoke into the field telephone. "Have you got battalion on the radio yet?" There was a pause. "What about division?" Another pause. "*Sí,* it sounded like artillery fire to the north and south of us too, but it's hard to tell when we're being hit this hard. No, no casualties for our squad, but most of our ammo went up with the house. Rations too. *Sí,* Armstrong's squad is in position on our left . . ." Martinez stared at the phone. "Hello? Hello?" He tossed the phone aside with a murmur, probably a curse, but it was in Spanish, so I wasn't sure. "Fire when they get past that ditch. Don't miss, 'cause we might be here awhile before we get help."

I watched the Germans approach through the artificial moonlight. They weren't running right at us, but they weren't being as stealthy as I would have expected. That gave me hope. We were outnumbered, but we were outnumbered by second-rate troops rather than a crack division. They passed the ditch, and we started firing. The krauts were packed so tight that they fell in rows, the way Mr. Thompson's hay crop did at harvest time. German artillery had been on target, but their infantry was less impressive.

Everything was a roar: the field guns, the rifle fire, the BAR fire. We shot round after round. We received round after round too, but there was no organized effort to locate and neutralize us. Either they weren't trained well enough to surround us and take us out, or they were leaving us for someone else.

When the shots from our squad lulled, I could hear Armstrong's squad to the north. Both sides were firing artillery, on and off. Martinez probably would have called some down on the field in front of us if the telephone had been working.

German artillery never completely let up. Most of the shells hit beyond us, but each whistle still made me want to cower in the bottom of our slit trench. Just before dawn, German artillery started working overtime. The noise was almost continuous, and the ground shook so much that I worried Winterton would get seasick.

Martinez squeezed past Winterton. "Ley, we need more ammo. Could use a radio or something too. You and Higham run over to company CP and find out what's going on."

I nodded. The sun had crept over the horizon, lighting the clouds in the east. I'd be visible, but most of the Germans in the field in front of us were hurt or dead. Between artillery blasts, I could hear the cries of the wounded.

"Good luck," Winterton said. He slapped my shoulder as I followed Higham out of the trench.

"Got any advice for what to do in a situation like this?" I asked Higham once we'd made it across the first stretch of open ground.

"Pray."

"Already have."

"Do you think it will work?"

I was saved from having to admit I didn't know by a shriek and a blast that was close enough to knock us off our feet. I felt something hot and sharp in the back of my left arm and shouted in pain. I probed it with my right hand, and my glove came away warm and sticky.

"Can you walk?" Higham asked.

I wanted to lie down, but that was foolish during an artillery barrage, and there wasn't anything wrong with my legs other than the cold. "Yeah."

"How bad is it?" Higham took a look at it, but I guess he couldn't tell.

"I don't know." It hurt worse than the rock salt in Belle's daddy's shotgun, but I could still move my arm and my fingers. And I could still walk.

Company CP was a hive of activity when we arrived. Sergeant Anders, the communications officer, was glued to a radio, tapping out Morse code as Wood took reports and gave orders to members of all the other squads in the company. Higham found a medic and sent him over to me.

"Let's see it." The man had a round face, brown eyes, and a Red Cross brassard on his arm. He helped me out of a few layers of clothing so he could get at it better. I bit my lips to keep from screaming when he yanked a piece of shrapnel from my arm.

"You could probably use stitches, but it's not too deep."

I was afraid if I opened my mouth, something I'd regret would come out—either a cuss word or a baby-like whimper. So I didn't answer him.

He sprinkled some powder on the wound and wrapped it. "That should hold for now. Someone back in Clervaux can give you stitches, but it'll be hard to get there until this clears up." He glanced at the commotion surrounding Wood. "And that might be awhile. All our platoons are reporting krauts. B Company and K Company are saying the same thing. Orders are to hold in place."

If B and K Companies were under attack too, they wouldn't be able to come to our aid. Our closest help was tied up, and the woods were swarming with Nazis.

I flexed my arm and tried not to wince. "My squad needs ammunition. I better get some and take it back."

"Yeah, your squad and all the others." The medic turned as someone handed him two mugs of coffee. I accepted one when he offered—it made a good hand warmer.

Higham squatted down next to me. "How bad it is?"

"Nothing that can't wait awhile." I handed him the coffee, even though I wouldn't have minded holding it a little longer. My fingers were just warm enough to hurt. Higham had a radio strapped to his back. "Did you get any ammo?"

He motioned to a wooden box by the door. "A little." He sipped the coffee and made a face. Either it wasn't very good, or it wasn't very hot. "As much as I'd rather be here, we better get back."

I shrugged on my jacket and greatcoat and pushed myself to my feet. I could think of a lot of places I'd rather be. I pictured my mom baking something sweet, Belle laughing at one of my jokes, and Bastien and Gracie snuggling next to each other on the sofa. It all seemed a world and a lifetime away.

We each grabbed one end of the wooden ammo box. It was one of the better boxes, with rope handles, but it was lighter than I'd expected.

Higham shrugged. "They couldn't give us the whole box."

That would make an easier trip back, but it also meant we wouldn't be able to hold out as long. I wasn't sure how many casualties it would take to convince the Germans to call off the attack. Would the bullets shifting along the bottom of the box be enough?

"How's the arm really?" Higham asked when we were outside.

"It hurts. A lot."

"Maybe you should head for the aid station. I've got a feeling today's gonna get ugly. Could be your ticket outta here."

I grunted. The day was already ugly, but I hoped he was wrong about it getting worse. The Germans couldn't attack indefinitely, could they? I hadn't seen any armor yet, and we could hold off the infantry for a long time. Maybe their underwater bridge wasn't strong enough for trucks or tanks. "It's just a deep cut." A deep cut that throbbed. Except when I flexed my arm, and then the pain turned sharper than Higham's freshly honed bayonet.

We hunched over and shuffled as fast as we could on the slippery ground. The German artillery barrage continued without a lull. Some shells whistled as they flew past us, and others swished as they hit nearby. Small arms sounded from every direction, but it wasn't until our squad's flaming former headquarters came into view that the sound of German burp guns seemed aimed at us.

Higham grunted, and I felt the weight of the ammo box shift as he released his end of it.

"Higham!" I dropped the box and huddled next to him. "Where're you hit?"

His only response was a gurgle as blood shot from a hole in his neck. I slapped my hand there to stop the bleeding, but it was like trying to dam the Our River with a canteen. I didn't even have time to grab a bandage. Higham's eyes and mouth opened wide, and then his head slumped back, and the blood changed from a rhythmic gush to a trickle. All I could think about was the fat-cheeked baby in Higham's picture, the little boy who was never going to meet his father.

My throat felt tight, and a few tears leaked from my eyes, warming my skin for an instant before turning cold. My hands were covered in blood, and they too grew cold. Just like that, Higham was dead.

CHAPTER 13

THE BURP GUNS FELL SILENT, probably because I was on the ground and out of sight. The calm was brief. Another burst from an automatic weapon brought me back to the battlefield. I needed to get the radio and ammo forward, but it felt wrong to leave Higham lying there. Even though I knew he was dead, I checked again, hoping it had all been a mistake. It hadn't been.

I unthreaded his arms from the backpack radio. The radio was heavy, Higham's body was awkward, and the cut in my arm protested with each movement. I yanked the pack out from under him and slid it onto my back. The edges dug into my skin. I crawled forward, dragging the ammo box with me. We'd worry about burial duty after we beat off the raid.

The fog was thinning, but the air was thick with smoke from artillery shells and the fires they'd caused. The crisp smell of winter pine was overpowered by the sharp scent of spent gunpowder. Cordite, someone had told me. It took effort to keep my lips from quivering when I remembered it had been Higham.

When I scrambled back to my squad's trench, Martinez put a hand on my shoulder. "What happened to you?"

I looked down at my uniform. Blood covered my hands, forearms, elbows, and most of my chest. "Higham's dead."

Martinez didn't say anything for a few seconds as he processed what I'd said. "Where?"

I pointed. "On our way back. I . . . I couldn't get him and everything else." I lifted the ammo box, and Broyles took it from me. His slightly opened mouth, with his lips curved down and his eyes pinched with pain, made me think he'd heard the news. He broke open the box and handed out M1 ammo.

Martinez helped me with the radio. He pointed to my bandaged arm. "You injured?"

"Little piece of shrapnel on the way there." And even though it still hurt, I was alive and standing. Had some kraut aimed their burp gun at a slightly different angle, I'd be lying dead in the mud, either instead of or next to Higham.

"You can fight?"

I nodded.

"What's going on at headquarters?"

"I was getting this patched up when Higham spoke to Wood. The medic said everyone was saying the same thing, our company and B and K companies too. Jerries everywhere, not enough ammo. We're supposed to hold in place for now." I'd thought I was firmly in control of my emotions, but my voice shook a little when I spoke.

Martinez watched the field in front of us as he thought. The German attack seemed to have stopped, for now, and the artillery had gone from a continuous howl to an occasional roar. "If we're holding here, we better get organized. Samson?"

"Yeah, Sarge?"

"Take O'Brien—head for that foxhole between us and Armstrong's squad. We don't want any of those krauts coming through the gap."

"Sure, Sarge."

"Winterton, you and Broyles go up to that house and keep the Jerries from coming around on our right flank."

That left Martinez, Krandle, Luzzatto, and me to man our slit trench. I laid down a thick stream of cover fire as first Samson and O'Brien, then Winterton and Broyles ran to their new posts. Only when they made it did I realize how nervous I'd been and how tight my muscles had clenched. Krandle worked with the radio and finally got a connection with company CP. They couldn't do much to help us, but being able to talk to them made us feel less alone.

The Germans organized another attack. They still acted like second-class soldiers, charging us in a mob that was easier and easier to see as the sun lifted over the horizon and cut through the fog. When they came too close, we lobbed grenades at them. We slaughtered them each time they approached, but they kept coming. And our ammo supply kept getting lower and lower.

All morning, the Germans attacked. Each wave came a little closer to us before their ranks disintegrated. I was exhausted each time the attack lulled, but the relative calm never lasted.

Martinez had been trying to get an artillery unit on the radio for an hour. It finally went through. "The field in front of us is crawling with krauts . . . How long do you think that will take?" Martinez grunted and passed the handset back to Krandle. "They can't shoot now 'cause they're surrounded, and if they put their rifles down long enough to send some shells this way, they'll be overrun."

A group of Germans crawled up a draw and huddled next to the ground. We shot at them until half were lying bleeding in the snow and the other half retreated. As they disappeared back into the trees, Krandle gave the handset to Martinez. "It's Wood."

Martinez listened for a long time. "We lost Higham on his way back with supplies . . . He's dead . . . Ley's wounded but still fighting. The rest of us are low on ammo, but no other casualties." A few seconds passed. "Yes, sir." Martinez handed the phone to Krandle and turned to the rest of us. "Wood finally got a hold of battalion. Jerry's attacking everywhere. Wood's trying to get reinforcements, but so far, nothing. The other companies are busy with attacks in their areas, so they can't send anyone to help. We're supposed to form a roadblock in the village square."

"By ourselves?" Luzzatto asked.

"No. All of first platoon. But Breckenridge is dead, and Wood lost contact with the rest of platoon headquarters. Armstrong's squad was taking a lot of fire when Wood spoke with them. Could take awhile to disengage. Wood's putting second platoon along the main north/south road on both ends of the village, so we just have to stop everything moving west." Martinez glanced at the field ahead of us. It looked calm, but that didn't mean there weren't a hundred German soldiers hidden there. "Cover me while I tell the others. When I signal, Luzzatto and Krandle lead the way. Go as far as that house." Martinez pointed to a two-story stone home. "Hold up there and cover the rest of us while we pull out. Krandle, you take the radio. Ley and Luzzatto, divvy up the rest of the supplies."

I kept my BAR aimed ahead of me as Martinez dashed over to Winterton and Broyles. While he briefed them, Krandle, Luzzatto, and I reloaded .3 caliber bullets into magazines, twenty rounds for my BAR and eight rounds for the M1s. The three of us laid down an enfilading sweep of fire as Martinez ran from Winterton's position to Samson's. While he was there, we shoved the bullets that didn't fit in our magazines into our pockets and draped a few bandoleers around our necks.

On a signal from Martinez, Luzzatto and Krandle took off for the village. That left me alone in the trench but only for a few minutes. Martinez slid in just as a German mortar round crashed down a few feet in front of us. The noise drowned out everything else for several long seconds, and a shower of wet earth rained down on us. We looked at each other, but there was no need for words. The shell had been close. Too close.

Once Luzzatto and Krandle were in place, Martinez signaled, and Broyles and Winterton scrambled from their spot on our right flank to where Luzzatto and Krandle waited, then beyond. They disappeared from sight, and another German mortar shell exploded, this time a few feet behind our trench. It knocked Martinez and me to the bottom, and I banged my injured arm and let loose a cry of pain.

"Ley?"

"I'm okay. You?"

"*Sí*. But I'm betting the next one will be a direct hit."

Martinez waved to Samson and O'Brien. They fell back next. The second they disappeared into the village, Martinez and I jumped from our trench and ran after them. We were trying to avoid rifle fire, but even more than that, we were trying to outrun that mortar.

We turned the corner past Luzzatto's position and slammed our backs to the wall, weapons ready as we gulped for breath.

"We left Higham's body," I said.

"We'll come back for it. If we can."

That was the best we could do, and I had the feeling he'd understand. "What do we do next?"

"We set up that roadblock. Because if they want to beat us, they'll have to throw in some armor. And if they want armor, they'll have to take the roads. The ground's too mushy, and there're too many trees to go cross country."

I thought of the maps I'd seen at headquarters and all the roads that went through Bastogne. "You think they're trying to get Bastogne?"

"*Sí*. Can't get out of the Ardennes without it."

That made our mission simple, but I had one huge, nagging concern. "Sarge, I'm guessing a lot of krauts snuck past us in the dark. We can hold the road, but what happens when the infantry surrounds us?"

One corner of his lips twitched, and he looked away. "That's Wood's problem. We have to hope he figures it out." An artillery shell whistled overhead and slammed into something on the other side of the village. "And that he figures it out quick." He stuck two fingers in his mouth and whistled.

Luzzatto and Krandle ran around the corner.

"There's a group moving up right behind us, Sarge, just reached our old positions," Luzzatto said.

Martinez nodded. "Right, don't engage them unless you have to. Ley and I will go forward. Cover us. When we get to Winterton and Broyles, you follow. Ready, Ley?"

I nodded, even though the thought of running across the open road and past six houses that might be hiding German snipers wasn't pleasant. It made my heart hammer as loudly as the band at my high school football games.

Martinez darted across the road, and I followed. Artillery explosions and small-arms fire still punctuated the cloudy, gray sky, but I didn't think Jerry saw us. When we reached Winterton and Broyles, they were sheltered behind a little stone wall.

"We're rolling up. Cover us, then cover Luzzatto and Krandle from where they are up to where Samson and O'Brien are. They'll cover you, and you keep on coming to the town square."

Winterton nodded, keeping his eyes on Luzzatto and Krandle's position.

"Got any extra ammo?" Broyles asked.

I handed him a bandoleer.

"Thanks."

Martinez slapped my good arm. "Ready?"

I nodded and followed him again. This time we didn't have to cross a street, but we still had to pass a half dozen three-story houses before we made it to Samson and O'Brien. Martinez told them what to do, then we took off again, trying to get to where Wood wanted the roadblock.

The church steeple came into view, and Martinez slowed from a hunched-over run to a more cautious jog. We passed a tavern on the southeast side of the square, and he stopped completely, probably trying to figure out the best place to set up our checkpoint. He pointed to the church on the opposite corner. "We can post someone there and call in artillery fire if the arty boys beat back the Germans."

He motioned to the northeast side of the street at a two-story house with large windows on the upper level. "I think that's our new squad headquarters. It's got a better view than the tavern. Armstrong's supposed to take the church."

I nodded.

Martinez's eyes never stopped moving, on the lookout for roving German soldiers. "Luzzatto and Krandle should be here any minute. I want you to check the church. I don't think Armstrong's there yet, but let's make sure there aren't any Germans there either."

Rather than running from the southeast to the northwest corner, I darted first across one road, then across the other. The churchyard was calm. Even the boom of field guns seemed softer there. I'd always liked churches. There weren't enough Mormons around Fairfax to justify a real church, nor had we had a dedicated building in Frankfurt. We'd met mostly in member's houses. The village church wasn't as large as others I'd seen, but it was still beautiful.

I circled it as quickly and quietly as I could. From the outside, it looked like it had one story with a vaulted ceiling. Except the steeple. That looked like a good place for a sniper, so I hugged the stone wall as I made my rounds. A look through the long, thin windows confirmed my guess about the ceiling, but it was too dark inside to see if any Germans hid between the pews or up in the bell tower.

As I crept around the north side, two men turned the corner. They wore coal-scuttle helmets and field gray uniforms, carried MP 40s, and were only three yards away. I hadn't been expecting anyone, and my reaction was slow, but they were surprised too. I brought my BAR up and fired before either of them reached their triggers.

They weren't the first people I'd shot. But they were the first people I'd shot that close in daylight. If I'd had a bayonet, I could have used it. Killing them had been necessary, but it was sickening to see how much damage a string of .3 caliber bullets could cause to a human body.

Both men looked young, younger than me. Had my family stayed in Germany, would I already have a couple years of war under my belt? Given the chance, would either of them have left Germany, or had they been eager to serve their Führer?

Thirty seconds after I shot them, I heard someone running around the church. I aimed in the direction of the sound, hoping my ears were right and it was only one person and not a squad of krauts. When Martinez jogged around the corner, I lowered my weapon and let out my breath. He must have started running when he heard the shots.

"You okay?" he asked.

"Yeah," I said. As okay as a soldier could be in the middle of a German attack.

"See anything, other than them?"

"Not yet."

He glanced at the tavern. "I got to get back. Check inside. I'll send someone over to help soon."

"Yeah, okay."

Martinez darted off. My eyes swept from left to right, on the lookout for more German troops. How many hid in the village? Every tree, every fence, every house was a potential ambush. Each crack of a rifle and each boom of artillery made my fight or flight instinct flare, even when I could tell it was far away. I was tense and jumpy as I ended my circuit at the church's front entrance. The tall door was locked, but I had to check inside. One of the nearby windows was marred with a bullet hole. I felt better about breaking a church's already damaged window than its front door, so I used my rifle butt to clear out the rest of the glass and climbed through.

The sound of my boots echoed through the church. I slowed, making an effort to step silently. A kraut soldier might be behind a tapestry or under a bench. I made it up one side of the pews and around the rostrum and choir seats without getting my head blown off. The church wasn't any warmer than it was outside, but before starting on the next row of pews I paused to wipe away the sweat that lined my forehead. How long could my body function under this much tension? I took a few deep breaths and focused on the way the light shone through the tall windows, creating columns of brightness that lanced the shadows.

I said a silent prayer for courage and stamina, then continued my search. I was halfway down the other side of the church when the back door burst in. I hit the ground and crawled to the edge of a pew. Highlighted in the door was a soldier. The helmet was American.

"Hello?" the man hollered.

"Yeah?"

He must not have expected anyone to answer because he ducked to the floor and whipped his rifle around. "Who's there?"

"Part of Martinez's squad. Who's asking?"

He let the dangerous end of his rifle point to the ceiling. "Armstrong's squad. What's left of it."

I stood and walked over to him. I didn't know his name, but he looked familiar. "Rough morning so far, huh?"

He huffed. "Yeah. We've already lost half our squad. We'll take it from here."

I left the church to him and his three buddies waiting outside. On the way back to Martinez, I stopped at the bodies of the German soldiers I'd shot and gathered up their machine pistols and extra ammunition. One of the boys had a thick piece of bread in his pocket, and I took that too.

As I joined Martinez, Krandle came from the house across the street to make his report. "It's clear."

"So's the church," I said. "Clear of Germans, anyway. Four of Armstrong's men are there. He's not."

"Are the others coming?" Martinez asked.

"That's all that's left."

Martinez looked doubly unhappy. He and Armstrong were friends. And he'd probably been counting on more than four men to help hold the crossroads. He adjusted his plans and pointed to a window on the top floor of the house Krandle had checked. "Ley, I want you up there. Tell Luzzatto to take the bottom floor where he can cover the back exit."

I nodded and headed over. A crash sounded from the back of the house. I jumped and swung my BAR around. Luzzatto was in the kitchen, staring at what must have been a serving bowl or a platter.

"I didn't mean to drop it," he said. "I was just seeing if there was any food."

"Find any?"

He shook his head. "I feel bad for the people who live here. They won't have much to come back to."

I glanced around the kitchen. Dust coated the furniture, and shards of whatever Luzzatto had dropped spread across the floor. The home looked abandoned. It smelled that way too. I took the bread from my pocket and ripped a chunk off. I handed Luzzatto the rest. "Martinez said to cover the bottom floor, back exit."

I climbed the stairs and went to my assigned position in a bedroom facing the street. The blankets were on the floor, and the sheets were gone. I could guess where. The army hadn't given us winter gear. Some of the other squads had taken white sheets and made them into ponchos so they could blend in with the snow. I didn't blame the soldiers; they were just trying to live a little longer. But when the civilians came home, their bedding would be gone. Something told me lost sheets wouldn't be the only thing wrong with their house by the time we were done with our roadblock. And if the Germans drove us out, the civilians would be missing not only their linens but their liberty too.

The window screeched as I opened it. Firing through the glass might throw off my aim, and if someone shot back, I didn't want shattered window pane flying at me along with the bullets. I moved a dresser to shield more of the opening and spread my ammo magazines in front of me, where I could grab them when needed. I settled in, wrapping one of the blankets loosely around my shoulders because I was cold. I wanted to snuggle in more, but I needed to keep my hands free. Across the street, Martinez kept watch from a ground-level window.

It took longer than I'd expected, but eventually Samson and O'Brien joined us. It should have been Winterton and Broyles. I could tell by Martinez's expression that something was wrong. He crossed the street, and before long, I heard his footsteps on the stairs.

"Samson and O'Brien saw a bunch of Germans attacking Winterton and Broyles. They disappeared."

Martinez's words sent icicles down my spine. Our squad had included nine men that morning. Now we were down to six, but there wasn't time to grieve. "Do you still want me here?"

"*Sí*. For now. I'll have the others haul out furniture and block off the road. Cover us."

I nodded.

"Samson and O'Brien will be with me across the street. Luzzatto and Krandle will be here, downstairs. Armstrong's men in the church. If things go according to plan."

I had a feeling things wouldn't go according to plan, but I was sure Martinez already knew that.

"Wood said we might get a few friendly tanks. Probably go to another platoon's checkpoint first, so we might not see 'em, even if they make it. Krauts might push out some armor too. If it's on wheels, it needs to stop for our checkpoint. If it looks like it isn't slowing down, go ahead and shoot."

"Do we have anything besides rifles?" .3 caliber bullets wouldn't do much to a tank, and the Germans had a bridge. Enemy armor had to be on its way.

"A few grenades. Once we're set up, I'll send someone to company CP. Maybe they have a few bazookas."

Martinez went back downstairs. The others piled furniture around the front doors. I was glad I wasn't helping, because my arm still ached. They narrowed the road too so vehicles would be forced to slow down, but what we really needed were sandbags and a few friendly tank destroyers.

CHAPTER 14

THE FIRST ENEMY TROOPS ARRIVED as Samson and O'Brien hauled a china hutch onto the road. The afternoon wore on in a cold, bitter series of German thrusts. There was rarely more than a minute or two reprieve before the next group tried to take the road from us. I switched my BAR to the slower rate of fire so I'd have better aim. Heads covered by coal-scuttle helmets kept creeping along the houses, keeping me busy through three ammo magazines.

Then, after hours of us driving off advancing krauts, they stopped. Small-arms fire and the occasional artillery burst still sounded, but it was in the distance. Our street was calm. I looked at my watch. Three thirty. All was quiet. The streets were deserted. Had they given up?

The rip of a burp gun at the back of the house destroyed the lull. I bolted for the stairs, and only training kept me from sprinting down them. Tracers flew across the home's ground level. I picked out Luzzatto hunched behind a sofa and followed his aim to a group of krauts pouring through a back window.

I fired until my magazine was empty, then switched and emptied a second one before the Jerries gave up. As I caught my breath, I inspected the bodies just inside the window. They were all dead. But there were plenty of live Germans coming across the river.

"You all right?" I asked Luzzatto.

He nodded. "Krandle's hit but not bad. I can patch it up."

I went back to my post, wondering when and where the next emergency would strike.

It hit the church. I couldn't see the building, just the grounds in front, so I couldn't offer supporting fire. Only four men defended it, maybe fewer, and it sounded like they were taking a beating.

Martinez sprinted across the road, and I heard the downstairs door slam shut.

"Ley!"

I ran to the stairs. "Yeah."

"Come down here a minute."

I obeyed.

Martinez had already gathered Krandle and Luzzatto. Krandle's shoulder was wrapped in a cloth that had probably started out white but was now stained red. "I've been on the radio with CP. The tanks got held up at the edge of town. Krauts disabled half of 'em. Wood's trying to get more for backup, and he's still working with the artillery, but they had to pull their guns back, and now they're out of range. We don't have enough people to hold all three corners, not with the way the krauts keep attacking. Wood wants us to keep the church because we'll need the steeple if the field guns make it back into position."

"Yeah, but the road's more narrow over here," Luzzatto said.

"I know. But if we keep the church, it will be harder for them to sneak up on us. And that's what Wood wants, the tavern and the church. I don't have contact with Armstrong's men, but they must be alive, or the Germans wouldn't be shooting at 'em. Ley and Luzzatto will reinforce the church. Krandle will transfer to the tavern."

Bullets had been flying all day, but a new series of them raked the front of the house, shattering what was left of the windows and making us hit the ground. Martinez crawled to a window and fired back. I went to a different window and peeked over the rim. The Germans had set up a machine gun on the roof of the shop next to the tavern, where they could shoot right down into us. Anyone who left the house would be dead.

I ran up the stairs, thinking I'd have a better angle from the second story. I had to admire the two soldiers who had dragged a twenty-five pound MG 42, plus an ammo belt, onto a slippery slanted roof. But admiration didn't make me hesitate. I took careful aim, shot, and watched one of them slide off the roof into the narrow space between the shop and the tavern. My second shot hit home too, and the coal-scuttle helmet slumped forward on the eaves of the house.

When I returned downstairs, Martinez gave me a weary smile. "Nice job, Ley. Cover us while we cross to the tavern, then we'll cover you to the church. Krandle, you ready?"

Krandle nodded. Then we all froze. The noise was soft at first, scarcely more than a rumble. Gradually it became unmistakable. Armor. If our armor had somehow made it through, then our roadblock was saved. We wouldn't have to abandon the house, and we'd be able to hold the road a lot longer. But if it was German armor, we were in deep trouble.

"Is it ours?" Krandle asked.

Martinez listened another few seconds. "Can't tell yet."

I risked a glance out the window and saw it turn onto the street we were blocking. I wanted to see a white star, but the black cross outlined in white made it absolutely clear. "It's German."

Luzzatto stuck a cigarette in his mouth. When he tried to light it, his hands shook.

We didn't have any antitank weapons. I wasn't sure how we could stop a tank with M1s and a BAR. But we were supposed to hold the road. One tank getting past us might not roll up the whole division, but if German tanks were crossing the Our River on an underwater bridge, we had to stop them.

"I've got to report this to Wood," Martinez said. "Cover me."

"What do we do?" Krandle asked.

"Hold here. I'll be back after I talk to Wood."

Running across the road in front of a panther took guts, but Martinez didn't hesitate. Maybe that was why he made it before the infantry milling around the tank got any shots off.

"Sure he'll be back," Krandle said. "If he's still alive."

A cold, empty feeling consumed me. I was tempted to flee out the back door, but I couldn't desert my squad. I stumbled back to the upper story and picked off infantrymen as the tank drew closer and closer and closer. They had to know both buildings were occupied, so I waited to see which way the turret would turn. The tavern, or the house?

I'd never fully understood terror until I saw the turret of a tank turn toward me. The barrel rose until it was pointed directly at my chest. I scrambled back into the hallway, and then the roar came, and I was engulfed in smoke and the roof came crashing down all around me.

* * *

Everything was black. I wasn't sure I was still alive. I couldn't see anything. I couldn't hear anything. But I felt plenty. Everything hurt.

I'd lost my helmet, and something gritty and itchy covered my hair. I didn't know where my BAR was, but something heavy pinned my chest to the floor, and something else crushed my thighs and poked my legs. I finally yanked a hand free. My glove was missing. When I reached for my face, powdered plaster fell away from my fingers, and jagged pieces of my glasses cut into my palm. Something was wet, but I wasn't sure if it was blood or water. I sneezed, which made the heavy object on my chest dig in even more. One side of my glasses still hung on my ear, but I could feel the empty rim on the left side and the cracked glass on the right.

I wriggled and squirmed and managed to slide a couple inches. The effort left me gasping, and my mouth was soon coated in dust and smoke. Debris cut into my hands and scratched my back and face. I shifted again and finally saw something other than darkness. The sky, hazy with smoke, was visible between a few naked beams. That meant most of the roof was on top of me. I pulled off my useless glasses and let them fall into the rubble.

My hearing returned. The crackle of rifle fire surrounded me, along with the rip of machine guns and deeper explosions of something bigger. My squad didn't have machine guns or mortars. All the big stuff had to be from the krauts.

I kept struggling to get free of the wreckage. A fire burned nearby, but it seemed to be dying rather than spreading. In normal times, I would have hollered for help, but the Germans would shoot me before they helped me, and noise from the firefight told me my squad was preoccupied. I pushed a splintered board off my hips and finally scrambled free, then dug around and found my helmet. It had probably saved my life, but now it was bent too badly to fit on my head. I couldn't find my BAR or my right glove.

I wasn't sure how steady the floor was, so I crept to the edge of the house, keeping my distance from the fire and checking the boards with my hands before crawling forward. The tank had moved to the church, which was missing its steeple. As I watched, two Americans came from the church with their hands over their heads. I assumed that meant the others were either wounded too badly to walk or dead.

German infantry moved with caution up and down the street. One fell, so someone in my squad was still alive to shoot.

Small-arms fire was constant, so I didn't pay attention to any specific shots. But when I looked over at the church again, the two Americans who had surrendered were lying dead on the ground. I hadn't seen it happen, but I was pretty sure they'd been executed.

I shouldn't have been surprised. I'd lived in Germany, and I'd seen what the Nazis were capable of, been reminded of it every time I'd woken up to a home with no father. Yet for some reason, I was startled and sickened. This was war. People were dying all around me. But shooting unarmed prisoners took away the last remnants of decency. I wasn't fighting soldiers anymore. I was fighting butchers.

Bastien's first rule was to get a weapon. I wanted my BAR back, but the roof was on fire, and I didn't have a spare hour to search for my gun. I picked up a two-foot-long piece of wood instead. It wasn't much, but it would do until I found something better. I'd left the German machine pistols downstairs. Maybe they were still there.

I couldn't find the stairs at first. The top floor was a pile of ruined masonry and splintered wood, and nothing was where it had been before the tank had blasted a shell through the walls. I closed my eyes for an instant and pictured the floor plan. The stairwell was roughly in the center. I crawled around and used my board to poke through rubble until it finally went down farther than my knees. I dug until I uncovered one stair, then two, then three. That made enough of an opening for me to slither through.

The heavy debris hadn't made it past the top half of the stairs. But bullet holes punctured the walls, and chunks of plaster had fallen from the ceiling and crashed all over the floor and the furniture.

I found Luzzatto and Krandle in front of the windows facing the main street. Krandle lay on his back, his face fixed in a permanent grimace of pain and terror. Three bullet holes marred his chest, surrounded by circles of blood. Other holes were there too, but they hadn't bled much. He'd probably been dead when the last ones had hit. Luzzatto was slumped over the windowsill, half his body hanging outside the house. I pulled him back and discovered a hole in his forehead.

First Higham, then Winterton and Broyles, the two survivors of Armstrong's squad, and now Luzzatto and Krandle. Was everybody dead except me?

The battle outside still sounded in my ears, so someone was fighting the Germans, and I needed to find them. I took Krandle's M1 and checked the magazine. Empty. He had an extra in his pocket. So did Luzzatto. I had a rifle and sixteen shots.

I peeked out the window. There were plenty of German infantrymen to shoot at. Most were smart enough to stick near the houses, but a couple were in the open where I'd be able to pick them off. But I hesitated. I had only sixteen rounds. I wasn't bad with an M1, but I was missing my glasses, and even if I hit an enemy soldier with each squeeze of the trigger, there were more than sixteen of them. And as soon as I fired, they'd know I was here.

A hail of bullets exploded from the house across the street, aimed at the krauts. Most of them dropped to the ground or darted inside a building. Samson appeared in the doorway an instant later, a body slung over his shoulder. As he ran into the street, I spotted Martinez providing cover fire from the window. I joined in, hitting three Jerries by the time Samson arrived.

Samson grunted and laid an unconscious O'Brien on the floor. He joined me at the window. "The moment he runs out, we lay down cover fire. Got it?"

"Yeah."

Martinez darted out a second later. I fired at the Germans on his left, and Samson fired at the Germans on his right. Martinez was three-fourths of the way across when he pitched forward. Samson was up in an instant. He ran out, grabbed Martinez, and pulled him inside.

They both sat in the doorway for a few seconds, breathing hard. The Germans outside were firing in our direction, but they'd taken shelter where I couldn't see them.

"Thanks, Samson. I owe you." Martinez pushed himself to his feet and limped toward the back of the house. "Glad to see you, Ley. I thought you were dead."

"Yeah, so did I." Despite my best attempt at bravado, my voice cracked. I blamed it on all the plaster I'd inhaled.

"We've got to get moving before we're overrun," Martinez said.

"Don't you need a bandage or something?" I asked.

"No time." Martinez winced as he put weight on his foot. "Wood wants us to meet him at an observation post about a mile west of the village. He's going there with the headquarters staff, kitchen crew, everyone he can scrounge up. We'll hold the road there." Martinez poked his head out a back window. "Looks clear so far. Let's go before that changes. Samson, you'll have to contact the men in the church."

"They're all dead," I said.

"You sure?" Martinez asked.

"Two of them surrendered. The Germans shot 'em."

Samson swore as he picked up O'Brien. "Another reason for us to get outta here. Sounds like this ain't the type of unit we wanna surrender to."

Martinez led the way through the backyard and into the garden and back door of another home. I brought up the rear, checking behind us every few steps, praying a burp gun wasn't about to cut us into pieces.

It was strange how one street could be engulfed in a battle and the next street over could be calm. Samson put O'Brien down, and Martinez and I looked out the home's windows. It seemed quiet.

"How hard will they search for us?" I asked.

"I don't know. They seem in a hurry to take the town and move on." Martinez pulled up the leg of his pants and Samson bent down to bandage his wound.

"What happened to O'Brien?"

"Head injury. Bullet ran along the inside of his helmet." Samson finished with Martinez and checked on O'Brien. "What happened to you? Looks like a cat clawed your face."

"The roof fell in on me." With Samson's reminder, my whole body seemed to wake up. Every single muscle was bruised, and most of my skin felt like someone had taken sandpaper to it.

"Where're your glasses?"

"Broken and cracked."

Samson grunted. "Guess I can't call you four-eyes anymore. Any of your bones broken or cracked?"

"Don't think so."

Martinez kept watch at the window. "The sun sets in about an hour. Ley, check the cellar. Maybe we can hole up here until dark."

I found a lantern and matches in the kitchen. I searched for food too, but there wasn't any. I glanced at Samson keeping watch in the back and Martinez in the front before going down the creaky wooden stairs.

The low-ceilinged cellar was bitterly cold, but at least it was dry. Barrels lined one of the walls, and my mouth watered. I hadn't eaten since supper the night before. I felt my pocket—the scrap of bread from the dead German was still inside, but split three ways, it wouldn't do much to check my hunger. The first three barrels were empty. I shined the lantern into the fourth and final one. Inside were two small potatoes. I checked behind the other odds and ends in the basement: a bucket, a broken bed frame, a bin of coal, a pile of wooden boards.

I went back up. "The cellar's clear."

Samson and I carried O'Brien down the steps. We turned the lantern down low and divided the strip of bread and the two raw potatoes. Then we waited under the stairs. I sat with my back against the cold wall and could barely even hear the gunfire. It wasn't late, but it had been a rough day. I yawned and leaned my head back.

I jerked awake when a crash sounded directly over my head.

CHAPTER 15

SAMSON DOVE FOR THE LANTERN and smothered the light. Another crash from above broke through the darkness. There were at least two sets of feet above us. I looked up, even though I couldn't see anything.

The basement door creaked open, and a beam of light shone down the stairs. It lit the empty barrels first and then the packed dirt floor. Whoever it was would have to come down the steps before he could shine the light on us, and soon footsteps thumped on the stairs. I grabbed Krandle's rifle, but firing it would alert whoever else was upstairs, maybe whoever was outside too. A basement gave us good shelter from artillery fire, but it was a bad place for a shootout. We were trapped.

The soldier reached the bottom step. The beam of his flashlight moved in an arc toward our hiding place. "Hello?" he called in German.

My helmet was gone, and my uniform was covered in so much grime that even in broad daylight it would take close inspection to see it was olive drab instead of field gray. If I said nothing, we would be in a firefight. I didn't doubt that we'd kill the man in front of us, but I also didn't doubt that we'd lose when the rest of the German Army heard our shots. I set my obviously American rifle on the floor and answered in the tongue of my birth. "What do you want?"

The beam jerked in surprise. "What are you doing down here?"

I walked toward the kraut and put my hand up to shield my eyes. I hoped he would focus on me, not on Samson, Martinez, and the still unconscious O'Brien. "I've been up since before sunrise, and I'm wounded. I'm resting."

The German soldier huffed. "Resting? I say you're deserting."

I pointed to my arm and hoped he could see the scratches on my face. "I'm not a deserter. But I am wounded."

"Don't you know we have a strict time line? We're supposed to cross the Clerf tonight and be in Bastogne tomorrow. Upstairs with you, and I'll check that wound of yours. We can't neglect our duty to the Führer and the Fatherland over a little scratch."

I hung my head as I walked past him and sized him up. He relied on military authority to get me to obey, so his rifle wasn't aimed at me. It was in his left hand. His dominant hand? Or was the flashlight in his good hand? As I stepped up the stairs, he followed.

I thought back to Bastien's lessons and took a deep breath. I spun around and chopped my right hand into the front of his neck. It made his face come forward, and he dropped the flashlight. I grabbed his collar and yanked his head into my knee. As he crumpled to the floor, I grabbed his rifle and knocked the back of his head with it. He slid down the stairs as the flashlight's beam spun out of control. Once he reached the bottom, he didn't move.

"Feldwebel Schmidt?" A voice called from the top of the stairs.

I thought about imitating Schmidt's voice, but I wasn't sure I could get mine that deep. I tiptoed down the steps and pulled Schmidt under the staircase, where his buddy wouldn't see him. The other German's footsteps echoed down the stairway, and his flashlight beam bounced along the walls. I crept back to the side of the stairs, just out of the flashlight's beam. I sensed more than heard Samson draw next to me.

"Feldwebel?" The soldier reached the bottom of the stairs and turned his light.

The instant before it shone on Martinez, I thrust the end of Schmidt's bayoneted rifle into the other soldier's jaw. It was an ugly way to die, but a bullet would have been too noisy.

Samson grabbed the flashlight and made sure both soldiers were dead. "You're tougher than I thought, four-eyes."

I didn't feel tough. I felt brutish and desperate and scared and exhausted. "There might be more of them up there."

"Of course there are more of them up there. They're trying to break through the Ardennes Forest."

"I meant inside."

Samson headed up the stairs. I wanted to sit down and cry or lie down and sleep or dig a hole and crawl inside and hide for a year or two. But I followed Samson. Martinez limped along behind me.

Samson switched the flashlight off before he opened the door. He stepped to the left. I went to the right. The last light of day shone through the windows, revealing an empty house.

The same wasn't true of the street outside. From the window, I watched a two-man patrol enter the house across the street. An officer stood in the center of the road, directing what I assumed were several teams.

"How do we get past them?" I asked as Martinez peered out a window. "They're going to notice that Schmidt and that other soldier came in here but aren't coming back out."

Martinez eased himself away from the window and grimaced at his leg. "Did he say anything useful?"

"Just that they're on a tight timetable. Supposed to cross the Clerf River tonight, be in Bastogne tomorrow."

Martinez raised an eyebrow. "That's ambitious."

"How big do you suppose this attack of theirs is?" Samson asked.

Martinez shrugged. "Big enough that some intelligence officer's head is gonna roll somewhere up the chain of command, and big enough that we're gonna have trouble getting around it. If we can get to Wood, maybe he'll have more information." Martinez lurched to the back windows. "If we go out the back, maybe we can wait the search out and get around them in the dark."

"There are two German helmets in the basement." Samson took his knife and popped the pins from the hinges on the basement door. "Soon it will be dark enough that we won't need nothing else to blend in."

I helped Samson lower the heavy wooden door. "What's with the door?" We'd snagged plenty of doors to cover our foxholes, but I was pretty sure someone would notice if we dug a foxhole in the back garden.

"Makeshift litter. I don't think I can carry O'Brien all the way to the observation post by myself."

"I'll keep an eye on things up here while you two get O'Brien." Martinez rubbed his eyes. "Grab those kraut helmets too."

We brought up O'Brien, the German helmets, the German greatcoats, and the German weapons. None of us had much ammo; our lives might depend on our enemy's rifles. We ripped a tablecloth up and used the torn strips to strap O'Brien to the door, then covered him and our remaining American helmets with the German coats. Martinez and I wore the kraut helmets.

Martinez led us out the back door, and Samson and I followed behind, carrying O'Brien on the basement door.

The streets were noisy. Nearby engines and distant small-arms fire punctuated the approaching darkness, and the German officer barked out orders on the other side of the house. The artillery was tame compared to this morning, but it still shrieked by every minute or so.

O'Brien was shorter than I was and on the lean side. But he wasn't a featherweight, and the door was solid. The shrapnel cut in my arm burned, and the bruises on my legs protested each step of the way. "How far away is that OP Wood wants us to go to?"

"A mile by jeep," Martinez said. "Maybe less since we're cutting fields."

"Or it might be more because we're trying to avoid krauts." Samson moved one hand to the center of the door and shook out the other.

We didn't go to the house I'd been in with Luzzatto and Krandle. We went to the one beside it, farther from the church. But we passed the house I'd been in. The tank had destroyed three-quarters of the roof, and the remaining beams stuck out like the fingers of a shriveled hand.

Martinez followed my gaze. "Hard to believe you crawled out of that alive, huh?"

"Yeah. Crazy luck." Or maybe it was my mom's persistent prayers.

* * *

We waited an hour, checking O'Brien's vital signs every few minutes and hoping the Germans had already searched the house and wouldn't come back to search it again. When the darkness was total, we crept out. I'd swiped O'Brien's right glove to replace the one I'd lost and wrapped a dish towel around his hand. Martinez and I held the front corners of the door. Samson took the back.

There were German soldiers outside, especially along the main road, but we took side streets on our way from the village and then open farm fields and forests. A few krauts saw us, but our helmets had the right profile, and none of them wanted to be the fourth man on the stretcher party, so they didn't bother us.

We spent a lot of time stumbling around in the dark. My fingers, clinging to the heavy door, were numb within minutes, even in gloves. The day had been cold to start with, and the temperature plummeted with the sun's disappearance. We couldn't go too far from the main road, or we wouldn't be able to find the OP. But we didn't dare get too close to it either, or we might blunder our way into the German Army. The ground was bumpy, and my feet were tired, so time after time, I nearly tripped on an unseen root or a mound of mud that had frozen solid. O'Brien seemed to get heavier with each step, and every part of my body ached, especially my arm. Eventually we took the kraut helmets off, which helped with the weight, but then the wind cut even deeper into my scalp.

"Halt!"

Martinez, Samson, and I paused. The command had been in English, but I couldn't see the speaker.

"Yeah?" Martinez asked.

"Who are you?" The voice sounded American.

"What's left of first platoon. Looking for Wood's CP. Did we make it?" Martinez shifted his hands around on the stretcher. I wondered if his arms were as sore as mine.

"What are your names?"

"Staff Sergeant Martinez, Private First Class Samson, and Private Ley. Come on, where's Wood?"

I could make the sentry out now. His rifle was pointed at my head. Martinez's Spanish accent didn't sound German to me, but the guard was jumpy and suspicious. If Bastien had been here, the guard probably would have shot him for his pronunciation.

"First you have to answer a few questions. What's the capital of Washington State?"

"Seattle?" Samson asked.

The guard turned his rifle from me to Samson. "No."

"Tacoma?" I asked. The rifle swung back to point at me. "Give us a different state, then."

"California."

"Sacramento," Martinez said.

"All right." The sentry nodded. "Who's Mickey Mouse's wife?"

"Minnie," I said. "Are they married?"

"I don't know. Look, one of the other companies reported some krauts pretending to be Americans, and I don't recognize you, so I got to be careful. Who won the last world series?"

"St. Louis," I said.

"Browns or the Cardinals?"

I couldn't remember. I figured Martinez had been fighting then and Samson had been in a hospital—a hospital in Britain—so I wasn't sure either of them would know. "Look, these two were overseas, so they probably didn't hear about it. And I was in training, and we were out on practice maneuvers. No one really cared anyway because all the good players have been drafted. But we're tired 'cause we've been fighting all day, and we've got a wounded man with us, and my arms are about to fall off. So can you let us past, please?"

The sentry finally lowered his weapon. "Wood's back there." He pointed over his shoulder. "That first stone house."

"You're in Wood's company?" Martinez asked.

"Yeah."

"For how long?"

"Three days. Four now."

That explained why he didn't recognize us.

A few minutes later, we stumbled into another sentry outside a large two-story home. He recognized Martinez, so he let us in. It wasn't warm inside, but at least we were sheltered from the wind. We set the door down as Wood walked over to us. I recognized Sergeant Anders working on a radio. A couple other men were scattered around the room. That was it.

"Dalton, go get Lance," Wood said.

The skinny soldier I'd first seen the day Call had been shot disappeared down a set of stairs. He came back with the medic who'd wrapped my arm that morning. The medic's uniform had been relatively clean then. Now it was coated in blood, and he looked as though he'd aged in years instead of hours. He gave me a nod of recognition before crouching next to O'Brien.

"He's dead."

"What?" Samson knelt too. "I just checked on him a half hour ago."

Martinez looked haggard, as if this last death was one too many. For me, it was one final failure. We hadn't stopped the Germans, hadn't held the road, hadn't buried Higham, hadn't saved the last of Armstrong's squad, hadn't kept O'Brien alive. And as I saw the weary faces and slumped shoulders of Wood and his headquarters staff, victory still seemed as hard to grasp as that morning's fog.

"Try to catch a few hours of sleep, Ley, Samson," Martinez said. "I'll report, then join you."

Samson nodded and took a final glance at O'Brien before going to the stairs. "You'd think he would have had the decency to die before I hauled him halfway across Luxembourg."

CHAPTER 16

I DRIFTED OFF, DESPITE MY aching arm and the freezing basement. It felt like five minutes later that someone shook me awake.

"Ley?" Martinez was at my elbow.

"Yeah?"

"Time for guard duty. I wish I could let you rest, but just about everyone else is wounded too, or they're on duty now and haven't slept a wink since the attack started."

I glanced around the basement. A lantern showed the outlines of about a dozen soldiers, most of them sleeping soundly. And I noticed some civilians: an old woman, a middle-aged couple, and three kids. "Civilians are here?"

"Sí. This wasn't the front line until yesterday afternoon."

"What time is it?"

"Two o'clock."

I'd been asleep for three hours, but if anything, I felt more tired than I'd been when I'd lain down. My arm had stiffened, and as I flexed it, the pain resurfaced, strong and intense.

Martinez rubbed a hand over his face.

"How's your leg?" I asked.

"Bandaged. It'll hold."

"Did you sleep?"

He nodded. "About an hour. I don't think there's time for more than that. It's gonna be another long day."

On the ground floor, Wood bent over a map, his fingers tapping along the edge of the table. A few pairs of soldiers surrounded him, probably ready to go out on guard duty just like Martinez and I. As we approached, the captain looked up with bloodshot eyes.

"Any good news?" Martinez asked.

A slight smile pulled at the end of Wood's lips. "Maybe. Battalion HQ said division might find more armor for us. A couple Shermans. Maybe a few tank destroyers. We've only got one tank left from the platoon they sent yesterday. And I wouldn't call it good news, but another company captured a German map, so we know their plans. Jerry's trying to make it to Antwerp, and the whole 5th Panzer Army is coming right through here. We're outnumbered about ten to one."

"Is division sending any infantry with that possible armor?" Martinez asked.

Wood pointed to the map. "Standard army doctrine in a situation like this is to hold the shoulders of the breakthrough to keep the gap from getting any wider. I'm not sure how big the attack is. If the captured map is right, it's along most of the army group. Word from division is it's all across the 28th's front, but communications are spotty, so they can't confirm what's going on anywhere else. However big it is, priority will go to the northern and southern ends. Probably Bastogne and St. Vith too because of all the roads that pass through there. Unfortunately, we seem to be in the middle of the breakthrough. Even if that German map is wrong, it will take a few days before they can reinforce us, maybe more, and I'm not sure we can last that long."

"Fighting withdrawal to Bastogne?" A sergeant from second platoon adjusted the strap on his rifle. His hands shook.

Wood frowned. "No. Our orders are to hold at all costs."

"Have you seen how many men they have? And how much armor?"

"I know. But if they cut through us and gain control of the roads that pass through Bastogne before Ike can bring more troops in, the center of our whole army will collapse." Wood studied the map, then studied his men. "I'm sorry. We can't stop them, but we've got to slow them down."

I could see it on the map, the little Belgian town in the center of our army group. Seven roads ran through Bastogne. I understood why we had to keep the Germans from capturing it, but I still felt like I was in the wrong place at the wrong time.

One of the other soldiers swore. Another glared at the map. A third burst out, "We're just supposed to die?"

"Hold as long as you can. If a position becomes untenable, fall back and hold again. Keep doing that as long as you can. I'm sorry it's come to this. You deserve better, all of you. Make them pay for every yard."

My throat was dry, and I was dizzy as I realized this was probably my last day on earth. I'd promised to serve my country however I was needed, even as cannon fodder, but I'd never expected to be overwhelmed like this, without enough ammo, without support, and with no chance of winning.

Sergeant Anders strolled to the table. If he was scared, he hid it well. "We've got enough K rations for one per every two soldiers. And one emergency ration each."

I shared a dinner ration with Martinez, even though I would have preferred a breakfast meal. We split the biscuits, canned meat, and cheese. Martinez took the cigarettes, and I took the gum and the orange drink powder. We both stuck our D rations in our pockets. The four-ounce bar was high in calories and wouldn't melt from body heat, but despite being made of chocolate, it was bitter and almost impossible to bite into. I usually ate it by peeling bits off with my knife. During training, someone said the military specifically asked the Hershey Company to make it unappetizing enough that soldiers wouldn't eat it just to satisfy a sugar craving. I'd have liked to make whoever came up with that idea live on nothing but D rations for a few weeks and see how he felt about it after that.

Anders divided the ammunition next. Martinez grabbed a bazooka and headed outside. I grabbed a rocket and a few clips of rifle ammo and followed him.

"So what's the plan?" I asked.

"You heard Wood." Martinez limped along beside me. "Take out as many Germans as we can before we run out of bullets. Or run out of luck."

"Yeah, but where?"

Martinez pointed ahead, slightly back the way we'd come a few hours before. "Up along the road. We're supposed to watch for incoming armor. Hit it with this." He shifted the bazooka.

"Then what? Anders only gave us one rocket."

"There's a friendly tank out there somewhere." Martinez pointed west, or at least I thought it was west. It was hard to tell in the dark. "There are a couple mortar crews along the road too."

"Do they have any mortars?" If their supplies were anything like ours, they wouldn't be able to hold out for long either.

"*Sí.* A couple. Wood's trying to raise the Long Toms. See if they were overrun or not. If they're still around, he'll call in artillery."

"And if they were overrun?" I hated sounding like a sad sack, but so far, it seemed like we'd be lucky to last the morning. I wanted something that would help us win.

"About the time you went to sleep, Wood sent Dalton in a jeep to try to get more ammo. Don't know if he'll make it or not, but he might. If not, we do what we can against the infantry and hope somebody up ahead slows down the armor. Shooting off their escorts will make them an easier target for whoever's farther west." Martinez stopped walking and turned toward me. "Look, Ley, you've done a good job so far. We've been asked to do a hard thing. I need you to be just as dependable today as you were yesterday."

I nodded. I didn't like our situation, but I'd do my best. If I was going to die anyway, I might as well die holding out like Davy Crockett at the Alamo. Belle had lent me a book about him a year ago. Belle. I'd never find out what happened next in that story we'd started writing together. Worse, I'd never get to give her that kiss I owed her.

We took over a foxhole from a pair of soldiers who'd been watching the road while we'd slept. I didn't recognize them; they must have been from a different platoon. While they went back for their meager rations and a few hours of sleep, Martinez and I dug around the foxhole, repairing a side that had caved in and making it a little deeper. Someone had blocked the road with a few chopped-down trees. I checked the barricade to make sure it was secure. It might slow a tank, but I didn't think it would stop one.

Then we waited. The krauts had to be just as tired as I was because they'd been fighting just as long. I remembered some of the German soldiers I'd seen in Frankfurt before my family had left. They had seemed polished, disciplined, tough enough to attack for three days straight. The men in newsreels looked a lot like that too, but most of the soldiers from yesterday hadn't. If they were resting, we had more time. If they weren't, they'd be weary enough to make mistakes.

It hadn't been warm at the outpost, but it was freezing outside. I stomped my feet and rubbed my gloves together, but it didn't do much good. "Brrr."

"*Sí*, I wouldn't mind being back in California about now, for a couple of reasons." Martinez had his gloved hands tucked in his armpits, and his shoulders were hunched up to keep his neck warm.

"When I went in for my induction exam, a recruiter tried to talk me into joining the Marines. If I would have listened to him, I might be on some island in the South Pacific right now." I imagined the heat, and my arms almost stopped shaking from the cold. Almost.

"Wonder what's worse, shooting at krauts in the snow or shooting at Japs in the heat?"

I shivered and stomped my feet again. "Right now, that hot sand sounds pretty good."

"It's not always sand. Sometimes it's just a hunk of coral. And there are lots of bugs; that's what I hear."

"It probably smells better in Luxembourg."

Martinez snickered. "For now. Wait till spring."

I thought about all the dead bodies in the field between the Our River and the village we'd held until yesterday. And I thought of them in the sweltering heat. Add in a few latrines and the result would be stomach-churning.

For now, it was foggy again. Cloudy again too. I couldn't tell the exact moment the sun came over the horizon. The sky gradually changed from black to charcoal to battleship gray. I cursed the clouds. I would have welcomed a little help from the air corps. I might have even forgotten about how jealous I was that they got to fly and I didn't. But if the sky was cloudy, the air corps would be grounded. We were on our own. Again.

It was Sunday, but I doubted I'd be doing anything religious, except maybe meeting God. It would be Christmas Eve in a week. Christmas carols played in my mind, all about peace on earth and silent nights. It wouldn't be that type of Christmas, not in Luxembourg, not in Belgium.

I tensed when we saw the first German troops creeping along either side of the road.

"Should we shoot?" I asked. They might not see us in the fog, but they'd know we were there the second one of us squeezed the trigger.

A low rumble sounded. Armor. Martinez nodded. "*Sí*, 'cause the more we shoot before that tank arrives, the better. Shoot when you're sure you'll hit. And don't forget you're missing your glasses."

I propped my M1 on the ground in front of me and focused in on the nearest German soldier. I didn't need a reminder that my glasses were gone. The difference in my vision was noticeable, especially in the fog. How had I caught so many footballs in high school without glasses? "I'm ready," I whispered. "Got the first guy lined up in my sights."

"Go back two men. I think that's the squad leader."

I aimed as directed. "Now?" As soon as we fired, the enemy would dive to the ground and try to take us out. We couldn't waste our first shots.

"Now."

I opened up on the string of soldiers and saw several of them fall. Martinez fired beside me. Over the rifle fire, the roar and click of the tank got closer and louder.

The German troops fell back into the fog, where I couldn't see them. Martinez grabbed the bazooka and ran out onto the road. "Come on."

I didn't want to face an enemy tank again, but I couldn't let Martinez down. I followed him into the middle of the road. The giant tank's outline was blurred in the fog, making it seem more like a shadow at first. That didn't make it any less terrifying. I loaded the bazooka with shaking hands. Martinez fired. It hit right in the middle of the tank's front armor. And it bounced off.

Martinez swore in Spanish, and both of us scrambled off the road. German bullets tore into the ground around our feet. We dove into our foxhole, and I wondered if the tank would come after us.

"Is it time to withdraw yet?" I asked.

Martinez peeked over the top of the foxhole and shot at a few more krauts. "No, it's continuing forward."

That was bad for whoever was farther west, but I was glad it wasn't charging our foxhole. The relief was short lived because I soon heard another engine. Another vehicle was on its way.

The back of the first tank disappeared, and a second loomed through the mist. I saw something out of the corner of my eye and turned. German troops were sneaking around behind us. I sent three shots their way, emptying my M1. I loaded my last magazine and kept firing. A burst of bullets tore into the dirt behind me, and Martinez yanked me to the bottom of the foxhole.

When the firing stopped, I peeked over the top of the hole and immediately dove back down. The tank was coming right at us. They wouldn't even have to shoot. They could just roll back and forth across the top of the foxhole and bury us alive. German infantry was everywhere, so running away was just as dangerous.

A bright flash and a loud boom filled the air. It sucked the oxygen from our foxhole and when I gulped for breath, it tasted like smoke. Martinez coughed, then peered out the top of the foxhole. I expected the tank tread to run into his face any instant, but he waved me up.

Hesitantly, I straightened. The tank, four yards away, was a flaming ball of fire.

"Did Wood get the artillery?" I asked.

"I don't know. But I'm almost out of ammo."

"Me too."

Martinez took a shot at another kraut soldier. "Time to withdraw. Break back toward Wood's post. Fire from the hip and run for all you're worth because Jerry's all over the road."

I nodded.

"Now!"

We scrambled from the foxhole and sprinted into the woods. There were targets everywhere, but I fired only at the closest krauts. Martinez and I made it over a slight rise, and then we were safe from the tanks. Martinez slowed, and I followed his lead, trading speed for caution.

"Do you think Dalton made it back with more ammo?" I asked. I was down to three or four bullets. I'd tried to count as I shot, but I'd lost track.

Martinez shrugged. We came over a small ridge, and the road curved back into view. Samson and another soldier hid behind a nearby clump of trees. Samson had an empty rocket launcher balanced on one shoulder.

"You guys the ones who took out that tank?" Martinez asked.

Samson nodded.

"Thanks. It was about to take us out." Martinez looked toward the road. "Got any extra rifle ammo?"

"No," Samson said. "And I just came from HQ. They don't got much either. And we're down to two bazooka shells."

While Samson and the other soldier aimed for and hit another tank, Martinez used Samson's rifle to pick off infantry, and I scrounged weapons and ammo from dead German soldiers strewn among the trees. I was so focused on finding more weapons without getting shot that I didn't realize a German tank had left the road until it plowed over a sapling and roared toward the other three men. They scattered, but the tank fired before they could get far.

When the smoke cleared, everyone lay motionless. The tank turned back for the road, confident it had destroyed its target. I felt sick. I wanted to run away, but more than that, I wanted to see if my friends were alive.

It seemed like an entire army group was moving down that road. The fog was thinner now, and I saw a long line of German troops. Other teams would harass them as they moved forward, but they were rolling us up, first with the foxhole Martinez and I had held, then with the bazooka crew. There were only a handful of men between the German Army and company headquarters, and only a handful of men at the stone house to slow them. Our entire company was being swallowed.

Armed with a German burp gun, I crawled forward. Martinez was unconscious, but he was alive. I almost sobbed in relief. Samson was alive too, just starting to wake up as I came up to him. The third man was dead. Half his body was missing.

"Are you all right?" I asked Samson.

He looked at me and felt his ears. "What?"

"Are you okay?"

He felt his ears again. "I can't hear anything." His voice came out as a whisper.

I pointed to Martinez. He had what looked like a bloody nose, but I didn't see anything else bleeding. The bandage on his leg was still secure. Maybe he'd just knocked his head. Samson helped me drag him farther from the road. We kept our distance from the Germans, trying to make our way back to the house. The trees helped, and so did the remnants of fog. I still heard plenty of small-arms fire, and I was terrified it was aimed at me. We dashed over a hill, and I breathed a sigh of relief. For the first time in about an hour, I couldn't see any Germans.

Samson shook his head again. "I think my hearing's coming back, at least in one ear."

Martinez mumbled something in raspy Spanish, but his eyes stayed shut.

"Do you understand him?" I asked.

Samson shook his head. "Sounds like he's praying or something."

A bullet cut through a branch half a foot to my left. I looked over my shoulder and saw six German soldiers cresting the ridge behind us. "Run!"

We bolted, still supporting Martinez between us. The Germans chased us. I was tempted to drop Martinez, but I knew he'd have carried me if our roles were reversed. And we were nearly to another hill. Once we passed it, we'd be out of sight, at least for a few seconds.

When we ran over the hill, Samson threw Martinez over his shoulder in a fireman's lift, and I covered him while he moved into the thicker woods. Part of the kraut patrol followed and spotted us, but I dropped two with the burp gun, and the others dove for the ground. I ran after Samson, and no one trailed us.

I checked the path ahead as we wound through the trees. I was grateful for the pines that kept us hidden, but their full boughs could just as easily conceal a kraut, so each yard forward was tense and uncertain, like walking through a minefield.

We were far enough from the road that I worried we'd get lost, but before long, the sound of a firefight rang out like a beacon calling us back into action.

"You want to trade?" I asked Samson.

Samson grunted. "Yeah." He laid Martinez across my back and took the burp gun from me.

Martinez was shorter than I was, but he was heavy. I was glad when the stone house came into view because it meant we were almost there. But the German troops surrounding it and the tank rolling up to the front door wiped out my relief. Something whistled through the air and swished into the road in front of the house. It exploded on impact, damaging the tank and making the infantry scatter. A few seconds later, about a dozen more shells saturated the road, finishing off the tank. The barrage probably took out a few enemy infantry too, but the smoke made it hard to tell.

"That's ours, right?" I asked.

"Yeah. About time the artillery started pulling their weight. Let's get inside while we can."

Samson led the way, and I ran after him. By the time we reached the back door, my lungs were heaving. I let Martinez slide to the ground. Another soldier hollered down the stairs, and the civilian man and one of the older kids came up and took Martinez down to the basement.

I was ready to collapse, but Wood handed me a rifle. "Take the front window."

I checked the M1 magazine. It was full. The fight wasn't over yet.

CHAPTER 17

FROM MY POSITION AT THE window, I watched an enemy tank charge forward. With everyone else in the house, I cheered when a friendly artillery salvo destroyed it. Sergeant Anders, on the field radio, told the artillery they'd scored another tank.

I spent an hour at the window watching for German soldiers and shooting them when they got too close. Samson was one window over, and a soldier I didn't know manned another. The home was two stories high, and shots came from the upper level too. We'd been ordered to hold the road, and now that we had artillery support, we were doing it. Scarcely any infantry got past us, and none of the tanks did. I was starving, so between shots, I broke off pieces of my D ration and drained my canteen.

Sergeant Anders finished with the radio and said a few words to Wood, who then joined us at the front of the house.

I prayed our John Wayne look-a-like had good news. He didn't. "The artillery's under attack and out of shells. That was probably the last they can give us."

I looked from Wood to Samson, then out onto the bleak, broken road. I wasn't sure how many wounded men were in the basement, but I assumed none of them could fight. The medic was down there with them, a few civilians too. There were three men upstairs. Three men downstairs, plus Wood and Anders. That made eight of us, maybe nine if the medic took off his Red Cross brassards and picked up a rifle. Our company had been whittled down to less than a squad, with no artillery support and no armor. There was no more food, and not much ammo.

Outside, a few Germans crept closer. Samson got one, and I got the other, but more were on their way.

The house was under siege, and we were on our own.

For the next hour, the fighting fell into a pattern. The Germans advanced. We shot at them until they gave up. The artillery had taken out all the tanks, for now, but as soon as the krauts got more armor, they'd blow the house to pieces. We were armed with rifles and one machine gun set up in a window on the top floor. But the machine gun ammo was just as depleted as the rifle ammo, so it wouldn't do us much good for long.

As the afternoon wore on, the soldier to my right got hit. So did one of the men upstairs. Lance, the medic, came up from the basement, took off his Red Crosses, and fired at the enemy. The Germans hadn't mounted an organized attempt to take the house—yet—but they kept steady pressure on us.

We couldn't hold much longer. I wanted to ask Wood when we could head for Clervaux or Bastogne. Maybe they'd have ammo there. But Wood stayed calm throughout the fight. It was hard to ask about running away when he was living up to his John Wayne–like appearance. I'd yet to see him retreat in one of his movies. Usually the cavalry rode up and saved the day. I didn't think horsemen would do us much good, and the sky was too cloudy for airplanes, but a few tank platoons would have done the trick nicely.

If I were honest with myself, it seemed a lot more likely that we'd all die.

I wasn't eager for death, but part of me was curious. Would my dad be there waiting for me? Would I finally meet the brother who had died before I was born? Would Higham give me a hard time about not burying him?

"You're looking awfully thoughtful over there, kid." Samson switched magazines. The one he put in was his last.

"Just thinking about my dad. He died when I was ten. I might see him again soon."

"You sure?"

"That we're going to die?" I shrugged. "If I was sure, I wouldn't be saving the last two squares of my D ration. Maybe when we run out of ammo, we can sneak out the back door, grab some German uniforms, and blend in long enough to get away from the shooting."

"No, that ain't what I meant. Are you sure there's something after we die? That if some kraut knocked one right between your eyes, you'd really see your dad?"

I'd questioned a lot of things in my nearly nineteen years. But I'd never questioned that. "Yeah, I'm sure."

Samson was quiet for a few seconds. "I hope you're right. Either way, I've got a feeling we'll know for certain before much longer."

Minutes later, the Germans organized a full attack, launching one group from the road and sending another around the back of the house. Bullets flew everywhere, slamming into the boards around the windows and knocking out the few shards of glass that still clung to the frame.

Wood had taken over one of the front windows. "Ley, cover the back."

I ran through the house to my new position. I was down to my last magazine, so even though I saw plenty of targets from the back door, I held my fire for all but the closest.

My plan to sneak back to the American lines no longer seemed possible. There were too many enemy troops. In the dark, we might have a chance, but it was only midafternoon. Anders ran down to the basement and asked for weapons. He came back with a pistol.

A bold German officer tried to lead a dozen kraut soldiers to the barn. If they made it there, they could approach within twenty feet of our house without exposing themselves to fire. I took out one, and the rest fell back, but I had a feeling it wouldn't be long before they tried again. Sure enough, maybe three minutes later, they crept forward. I took out two, but they kept coming.

The click of my empty ammo magazine echoed around the room. I searched for more, but all the ammo boxes by the radio were empty. Then I looked more closely around the house. Sergeant Anders lay facedown in front of a window, completely still. Captain Wood lay faceup only a few yards away. Blood stained his chest and ran from his mouth, and his eyes stared straight at the ceiling. I checked their weapons. The pistol Anders had taken from the basement had one bullet left. Wood had a knife. That was it.

"Check upstairs, kid," Samson said as he aimed out the window and sent another bullet toward the Germans. He was the only other person on the ground floor still alive.

I ran up the narrow staircase. Lance, the medic, was in a corner, trying to bandage his own arm. I tied the bandage over the blood for him.

"Thanks."

"Anyone else up here still?"

"Dead bodies. And Corporal Koslow in there." With his good hand, Lance pointed to the nearest bedroom.

Koslow huddled at the window and fired. He must have heard my footsteps because he jerked around. "Do you have any ammo?"

I held up the pistol. "One shot."

He dropped his rifle and reached for the pistol. He aimed and shot, but I couldn't tell if he hit anything. He swore. "That tank's gonna blow us all to kingdom come."

I'd been dreading this moment. German armor had arrived. And any second they would destroy the house and everyone inside.

Maybe the Germans noticed that we weren't shooting back as much as before. One hollered at us to surrender. He even spoke English. "If after two minutes you have not give up, we are to destroy you."

We had fought so hard for so long. We couldn't surrender now, could we?

I wasn't sure what to do. In two minutes, the tank would fire shell after shell into the house, and we had nothing to hit back with. The Germans held the barn and the road. They'd pick us off one by one if we tried to run.

Koslow sneaked back from the window. "I guess we better talk to Wood."

"Wood's dead."

Koslow bit his lip. He looked at me, then headed for the stairs. I helped Lance down, and we caught up to Koslow and Samson in the front room.

"Well, Corporal, you're the ranking man," Samson said.

"Me?" Koslow's mouth hung wide. "I was in charge of a mess hall. I'm not a front-line soldier."

"You got any ammo?" I asked Samson.

"Less than a clip. You?"

"All out."

Samson looked at Koslow, at Lance, and at me. "Out the back way?"

I shook my head. "They've got us surrounded."

The German yelled again, "Kameraden, time is almost up."

"I think you better go talk to him, Ley." For the first time that I could remember, Samson looked scared. The skin around his eyes was pinched, and after he spoke, he clamped his jaw shut, probably to hide the trembling in his bottom lip.

I crept to the window that Samson had manned, not quite believing what I was about to say. "We're ready to surrender," I called out in German.

"Throw your weapons outside and come out with your hands up."

I translated the order.

Samson checked the magazine of his M1. "Only two bullets left anyway."

It made the most sense for me to go first. I hadn't been warm for at least two days, but the thought of walking outside in the open made my skin slick with sweat. What if they simply shot us? Prisoners taken by the Germans disappeared all the time. It had happened to my dad eight years ago. It had happened to the men from Armstrong's squad who had surrendered in the church. Was that what would happen to us?

Samson tossed his M1 out the window. I followed his example. As Samson gathered the other weapons, I opened the front door. With hands raised above my head, I walked through the doorway and into the yard. The bodies of dead soldiers, most of them krauts, were strewn along what was left of a row of trees. More were piled near a half-frozen puddle partway to the barn. Twenty live German soldiers still stood, all of them armed, and every single weapon was aimed at me. A Panther tank rumbled behind them.

One of the Germans strode toward me as soon as I cleared the house. He was shorter than I was by a few inches, and his pale, close-set eyes looked at me with contempt. He grabbed my coat and yanked me forward, then gave me a rough pat-down. He took my canteen, shook it, and tossed it to the side. I watched it go. It was only five yards away. If I kept my eye on it, maybe I could retrieve it because I had a feeling I was going to want it if I lived long enough to be thirsty again. He took my watch and put it on his own wrist. It joined three others. He took my gloves too, and the exposed skin instantly stung.

Then he started with my pockets. He stole the last of my D ration chocolate bar. Several times over the last few hours I'd wanted to finish it off, but I'd saved it, thinking I'd want it more in a few hours. It made me furious, but a glance at the thief's armed comrades kept my temper in check. Next he took everything out of my pockets: can opener, spare socks, stick of gum, an extra shoelace, my Book of Mormon. He kept the gum and can opener and dumped the rest on the ground. If he didn't want it, I didn't know why I couldn't keep it. I wasn't sure what was ahead, but anything I could take with me seemed to increase my chance of survival—by trade, if nothing else.

Samson and Koslow came out, and German soldiers went through their pockets too. An officer ordered a group inside to search the house.

The soldier frisking me told me to unfasten my greatcoat. I obeyed, shivering as I undid the buttons. He was close enough that several of the moves Bastien had taught me would have landed him in the snow, dead, before he could react. But since he wasn't the only soldier around, I held still. Bastien never taught me how to disarm an entire army.

He found Belle's photo and let it fall to the ground.

"Hey!" I bent down to get my picture. Before my fingers grasped it, the kraut yelled and slammed the butt of his rifle into the back of my neck. I dropped into the mix of mud and snow. He hit me again on the shoulder. I gritted my teeth and nearly tackled him, but through the fog of pain, I heard a voice.

"Stay down, kid." It was Samson. "Don't move, and he'll stop."

If he'd called me four-eyes, I probably would have ignored him. But I held still, trusting Samson that submission was the key to living through the next few minutes.

For me, the battle with weapons was over.

The battle for survival was only getting started.

PART THREE: POW
WINTER AND SPRING 1944–1945
GERMANY

CHAPTER 18

A PAIR OF ANGRY GUARDS shoved us onto the road and sent us back toward the Our River. The wounded were still inside, as were the civilians, so I didn't see what happened to Martinez or any of the others in the basement. I didn't hear any pistols discharge. I hoped that meant they weren't executing the injured, but I wasn't sure I'd be able to hear it if they were.

As we left, an officer bawled out his men for letting a handful of soldiers hold them up all morning.

"What's he saying?" Samson asked.

I opened my mouth to answer, but one of the guards yelled at us to be quiet and lifted the butt of his rifle like he was going to pummel me with it if I spoke. I kept my mouth shut. I should have felt satisfaction that we'd slowed the enemy, but I was overwhelmed with other, more powerful emotions, like terror that a kraut guard was going to shoot me in the back of the head or stick his bayonet through my ribs.

After awhile, one of the guards turned back, leaving a single man to guard us. I tried to work out how I could disarm him and escape. Maybe Samson, Koslow, and I could sneak through the woods to the next American outpost. Except I had no idea where the next American outpost was. The last update had been from Sergeant Anders when the artillery had pulled back. Who else was retreating as the Germans pushed forward?

An opportunity to disarm the guard never came anyway. We marched along the side of the road with our hands on the back of our necks. Holding my arms up made the shrapnel wound burn with pain, but I didn't dare relax. A steady stream of German traffic went the opposite direction. Wherever the next American outpost was, they were going to be hit hard. Infantry, armor, horse-drawn artillery pieces. We may have slowed down the tip of the German advance, but beyond the tip was a powerful invasion force. I swallowed back the bitter taste of defeat and fear. The war wasn't going to end anytime soon. If the Germans didn't shoot me, I was going to be a prisoner for a long time.

When we arrived at the village we'd fought over the day before, they herded us together with a handful of other American prisoners and forced us to haul around the German wounded. They'd made one of the houses an aid station. Samson and I carried a young German soldier with a slit across his abdomen to the last bed. When we came back, we put a whimpering feldwebel with a hole in his thigh on the ground. Two trips later, we left an unconscious guy with a head wound on the ground outside.

"Should we say something?" I asked. "He'll freeze to death if he stays out here."

Samson shook his head. "They know they've got men outside. I say we keep our heads down. I've half a mind to drop our next patient on his noggin just to make sure he's not fighting us again in a few months."

My fingers were so cold I could barely maneuver them, and after lugging the wounded around, they were covered in blood. Another pair of prisoners plucked the last German wounded from the field. I stuck my hands in my armpits, trying to warm them, but I relaxed for only a second before one of the German guards gave us our next assignment.

"Now bury the dead."

There were more German than American bodies. We put them in separate holes. After the second mass grave, my toes rivaled my fingers for numbness, and the ache in my arm still burned.

"Here." Samson stripped a pair of gloves off a dead German soldier.

I shook my head. "They'll think I stole them, and they'll shoot me."

He found another pair of gloves on the next dead American body we came to. "Take these. He don't need 'em no more, and if you don't have gloves, you're gonna lose a few fingers."

A crazy thought came into my head: I couldn't milk Belle's cow without fingers. It was an odd thing to think when I hadn't milked a cow in months, but I took the gloves. Someone else had already stolen the poor man's overshoes.

A lot of the dead Germans looked too young for war. And a lot of them looked too old for war. Some of them looked calm, some of them looked pained, and some of them looked as if they'd died in terror. Anybody who described war as glorious should have to cart around the wounded and bury the dead. They'd see in each broken body, contorted corpse, and mangled man that war was among the ugliest things humans did to each other. Maybe the only thing uglier would be not fighting and letting a man like Hitler continue his reign unopposed.

I took extra care with the Americans I buried. I hadn't been in the company long enough to know the names of many men outside my squad, but I recognized faces. And I recognized Higham. He wasn't exactly where we'd left him, but he was close. The filthy krauts had stolen his wedding ring, his wrist watch, and his boots. I checked his pocket for the picture of his wife and kid. It was gone, and that theft seemed worse than any of the others.

Samson helped me lower Higham's body into the ground.

"He had a wife and a son."

Samson looked startled for a moment. "I know. Don't think about it now."

I doubted thinking about it later would make it any less disturbing. As I grabbed the next body and felt the tug of pain in my arm, I wondered if he'd been married, if he'd had a couple kids waiting for him to come home. Rows of shattered bodies and frozen faces stretched out in the snow. Most of them would leave behind someone who would mourn. When I thought of them as a group, it was tragic. When I thought of them as individuals with parents and siblings and spouses, it was a long line of broken hearts and changed lives, almost overwhelming in how many people it would affect.

Daylight was fading when we finished. The guards marched us across the river into Germany. It was a different bridge from the one my squad had seen on patrol. This one was a series of farm carts dragged into the water and topped with doors.

When they told us to turn off the main road, I was certain they were taking us into the woods to shoot us. Panic boiled in the pit of my stomach, but instead of executing us, they marched us into an old barn and locked us inside with about fifty other cold, hungry prisoners.

My first night as a captive came and went. I slept a little because I was exhausted, but I spent more time shivering in the cold because there were no stoves or blankets. There wasn't any food either, so each time I woke, my empty stomach reminded me that it hadn't had a real meal in days. Blisters had formed on my hands during burial duty, and a few of them popped and oozed sticky liquid onto my hands and gloves, running into the cuts lining my palms and fingers.

Some of the other men cried. It took effort not to join them.

Over and over again, I replayed what had happened at the house. We had surrendered. I didn't think there had been another choice, other than death, but did that make us cowards? I pictured the way Martinez had hauled his bazooka onto the road to fire at the German tank. No, he wasn't a coward, nor was his squad. But I couldn't shake the feeling that we'd somehow failed everyone: our division, our army, all the people back home.

When a German guard burst through the barn door the next morning brandishing a machine-pistol and yelling loud enough to be heard on the other side of the river, we all struggled to our feet. I felt dizzy when I stood but managed to stay up in spite of the way the barn around me rotated and went out of focus. The guards doled out a drink of water each. Since my canteen was stolen and my helmet smashed, I borrowed Samson's helmet and drank my share from that.

Then we marched. Other groups of prisoners joined us as we passed another barn, a school, and a house missing three of its four walls. I didn't pay much attention to the other men. At first I was too busy taking in the pillboxes and dragon's teeth of the Siegfried Line. The jagged rows looked like miniature pyramids, some knee-high, some waist-high, and some shoulder-high. They were designed to stop tanks, but they were also effective at wearing out captured soldiers.

We left the Siegfried Line behind, and I was painfully aware of how well it would slow down the US Army as they pushed into Germany. We marched on the side of the road because the roads were full of German troops, tanks, and horses moving west. As the full might of the German Army rolled past us, a growing fear that the US wasn't going to win after all started to gnaw away at me.

"Out of the way!" A German soldier riding on the side of a tank swung his rifle around, and the stock struck me in the face. I stumbled back, one hand flying to my nose. The German soldiers laughed as I wobbled around, trying to catch my balance. Then they repeated the whole thing about twenty prisoners back.

Samson had been a few men ahead of me. He turned back, but one of the guards threatened him with his rifle, so he didn't stop.

The same guard poked me with his bayonet. "Get going!" The swine didn't break the skin, but I didn't doubt he would if I gave him an excuse. I wiped a hand across my mouth, smearing the trickle of blood streaming from my nose. Then I followed the boots of the guy ahead of me.

We marched all morning. At noon, we stopped for a few minutes. I collapsed to the muddy ground with the other prisons. The guards ate. One of them tossed a crust of bread into the dirt as he finished, and two of the prisoners nearly strangled each other for it. Had I been closer, I might have dived for it too, but I didn't think there was any way I could have won a wrestling match, not even with food as the prize.

My limbs barely cooperated when the guards ordered us back to our feet. A sharp, rhythmic pain pounded in my head. My hands alternated between tingling numbness and a burning itch. My jaw and nose were swollen from the enemy rifle stock, and my throat ached for water. When the guards weren't looking, I stepped out of line to scoop up some snow. It relieved my thirst, but it also chilled my throat and left me fighting to keep my teeth from chattering. But the worst was my arm. The wound had split open again, and blood soaked the bandage.

I spent the next hour fighting to stay on my feet, my mind turning out scenario after scenario of how I could have done something differently to end up somewhere else, anywhere else. Maybe I should have taken Higham's advice and gone back to Clervaux for stitches. Or maybe Samson and I should have taken Martinez deeper into the woods instead of holing up in the Luxembourg farmhouse with the last of Wood's company. We could've made a break for it when the artillery had withdrawn, before the Germans had surrounded us.

As I stumbled along behind the other prisoners, a rage built in my chest. We'd warned battalion that the Germans were planning something. Why hadn't they listened? Why hadn't they sent in tanks and tank destroyers? Why hadn't they made sure we had enough ammunition and enough artillery support? Why hadn't the air corps bombed the German bridge under the Our River to smithereens?

I slipped and lost my balance. I caught myself with my hands, and the pain in my injured arm exploded. One of the guards was on me immediately, kicking me with his boot and yelling for me to get up. I struggled to my feet and marched a little longer.

The cold crept deeper and deeper into my skin as we pushed farther and farther into Germany. I tripped again and crashed into the cold mud. I stayed there. Even if I had wanted to get up, I wasn't sure I could. But I didn't care anymore. I could hobble along, cold and hungry and struggling to put one foot in front of the other, or I could lie in the ditch off to the side of the road, cold and hungry but without the constant effort of keeping up with the forced march. I'd done the best I could, and I'd failed. Every step into Germany showed me how wrong we'd been. The German Army wasn't dead. They were joking about spending Christmas in Paris, and if the tanks I'd passed were standard all along the front, they just might make it.

A hand gripped my good arm above my elbow and yanked. "Come on, Ley. Get up."

I glanced at my assailant as he dragged me from the mud. It was someone I'd never expected to see again: Winterton.

He was the first good thing I'd seen all day. "Where did you come from?"

His lips pulled into a grimace before relaxing again. "Captured the first day. Joined your column a couple hours ago."

"Broyles too?"

He shook his head. "He didn't make it."

I should have felt something, but I was too numb, too overwhelmed by everything else that had happened the last three days. "Neither did Krandle or Luzzatto. O'Brien died too. We left Martinez in a basement. He was delirious, mumbling in Spanish."

"Come on." Winterton glanced at a German guard heading toward us.

I shuffled along beside him for a few minutes before I ran out of energy again. "I need to rest. I haven't eaten anything bigger than half a K ration since the attack started. My arm's killing me. And my toes are frozen. They've got to do something different for the wounded, right?"

Winterton shook his head. "No, you don't want to be with the wounded."

"Why not?"

"Last night I saw a few members of an American artillery unit. Negro troops. Wounded. Could barely walk."

"And?"

"This morning they were all dead. Looked like they were skewered with a bayonet. I'm not sure if the Jerries killed them because they were wounded or because they were colored, but you don't want to be wounded. Keep walking, Ley. It's your best chance of staying alive."

I kept putting one foot in front of the other, even though every step made my toes feel as though they would snap off. I wasn't sure which artillery group had saved my squad on the second day of the attack, but I thought of them lying dead in the snow, bayoneted to death after they'd been captured. They could have retreated to safety. Instead, they'd held out long enough to help the infantry in front of them, and it looked like their courage had cost them their lives.

I took a better look at Winterton. His face was red from exposure, just like everyone else's, but he didn't look wounded. "Where's your coat?" I asked. He wore his olive drab Eisenhower jacket, but his greatcoat was missing.

"One of the krauts stole it. It's against the Geneva Conventions to deprive a prisoner of needed clothing, but I'm pretty sure the guy taking it would have shot me if I said anything."

"Did the same guy take your overshoes?"

"No. That happened a few hours later."

Seeing Winterton alive made things less gloomy, but soon I was dragging again. He stayed beside me, pulling me back into the column whenever I grew so dizzy I couldn't see straight. "Here, take this." He handed me a chunk of a D ration. I sucked on it, blessing the Hershey Company and their bitter, high-calorie chocolate bar.

"Thanks."

The bit of chocolate made it easier to focus on walking for a while. But all too soon, I was stumbling worse than ever. The wind whipped through my clothes and stung my face. I would have traded just about anything to be in a foxhole with Higham's C ration stove and its greasy black smoke.

"I need to rest," I finally said.

"You've got to keep walking." Winterton grabbed my uninjured arm and tugged when I started slowing down.

"I can't."

"You can do it for another thirty minutes, right?"

I shook my head. "My toes are going to fall off before then. And I don't think I've ever been this hungry before."

"I'd give you food if I had any more, but that was my last piece."

"You gave me your last piece of chocolate?" I was stunned.

Winterton kept shuffling along, pulling me with him. "I figured a piece that small wasn't much good for nourishment. More of a morale booster. Come on, Ley, you can give me another thirty minutes before you pack it in."

I glanced to the side of the road where the line of prisoners hadn't trampled the ground into mud. I wanted to go over there and lie down, even if I got shot for it, but if Winterton had given me his last bite of food, I could give him another thirty minutes. I'd been walking all day. What was another half hour?

Another half hour ended up being misery. The Germans had stolen my watch, so I wasn't sure of the time. I would have guessed two hours, but when I asked Winterton, he kept looking at his watch—somehow none of the krauts had pinched it—and telling me a little longer.

When my legs quaked and I could no longer stand up straight, I stepped out of line.

Winterton dragged me back into the column. "Twenty more minutes, huh?"

"I can barely walk." My tongue was so dry I was surprised he understood me.

"If you stop now, it will be harder to start again. Just keep moving. Twenty more minutes. You can do twenty minutes for someone back home, can't you?"

I was so tired and so cold that dying sounded like a release. The temperature in heaven had to be above freezing, and I didn't think we'd have to march up there, at least not in wet boots. But I thought of my mom and forced myself to walk.

Twenty minutes later, Winterton convinced me to go another fifteen for Belle, then ten for Bastien, and five for my nephew who I still hadn't met. But after that, I could barely keep my tongue in my mouth, my arm ached enough that an amputation sounded nice, and each step forward made my muscles burn. My legs shook so bad that when Winterton took my good arm and slung it over his shoulder so he could help me walk, I worried I'd stir up his motion sickness.

"I can't go any farther," I finally said. "I don't care if they shoot me."

"Just to that house up there."

I squinted in the fading light. I couldn't see it without my glasses. "What house?"

"Trust me, it's there, and you're going to make it. But I'm not feeling so hot myself, so don't make me carry you, huh?"

I shivered as a gust of wind whipped around me. I still couldn't see whatever building Winterton had pointed to, but noise from the men ahead convinced me he wasn't making it up. "All right, to the house."

"Look, Ley, we're going to stick together, and whatever they do to us, we're going to survive it, all right? Don't give up on me."

I thought about the people waiting and praying for me back in the States, and I nodded my agreement.

The guards herded us into a schoolhouse. The classroom we were sent to wasn't heated, but it was sheltered from the wind, and I could lie down while the ends of my fingers and the tip of my nose gradually regained feeling. I was so relieved to be off the road that I almost cried. Winterton checked my arm and reinforced the bandage with a mostly clean handkerchief. I gave him my jacket since his greatcoat had been stolen, and we shoved pages from old textbooks inside our clothes for extra insulation.

Winterton appearing when he had was like an answer to a prayer. I hadn't prayed, but I was sure my mom had and Bastien and my sisters too. I took a few quiet moments to thank God and to apologize for not praying sooner. Now that the day's march was over, it was terrifying to realize how close I'd come to giving up.

One of the guards called for silence and told us there was food. One loaf of bread for every two men and one can of sardines for every four men. I gobbled up most of the food as soon as it was divided, but I saved a piece of bread for later. I didn't trust the krauts to give us breakfast, and having something to snack on during tomorrow's march would help me keep going. But the initial relief at having something in my stomach soon changed to discomfort from eating too quickly.

"I never really liked sardines until today." Winterton grimaced. "But I don't think they like me."

"Yeah. They're swimming around in my gut too. Maybe they were spoiled. Couldn't give them to their own soldiers, so they gave them to us instead."

He stifled a groan and changed positions on the hard floor. "One more way of making us wish we were dead."

"Winterton?"

"Yeah?"

"Thanks for getting me here. I was ready to give up. A couple times."

"Today was rough," he said. "Maybe tomorrow will be easier."

I hoped he was right. I wiped at my nose with my sleeve since I didn't have a handkerchief and something in my sinuses had defrosted along with the rest of my limbs. Belle would have been disgusted. I frowned. Her picture was probably lying in the bottom of a puddle next to my Book of Mormon, soggy and faded and gone forever.

It wasn't late, but I soon drifted off to sleep. When the morning sun shone through the windows and plucked me back to reality, I moaned. I was used to sleeping without a real bed, but my body was worn out beyond anything I'd ever endured before, and the school floor had been extra hard.

The hundred or so other prisoners began stretching and sitting up. I glanced around, hoping to see something for breakfast. It looked like we wouldn't even get bread. My stomach rumbled in protest, and I nibbled on the piece I'd saved from the night before.

A group of three German officers came through the door. They wore army uniforms, so I told myself not to worry, but something about them made me nervous.

Winterton figured it out first. "Ready to be interrogated?"

CHAPTER 19

My nerves went from alert to panicked. I'd heard a thing or two about Nazi interrogations. I couldn't handle torture, not today.

"Ley, calm down," Winterton whispered. "According to the Geneva Conventions, all we have to tell them is our name, rank, and serial number. They might ask a few other questions, but they aren't going to spend much time talking to privates."

I took a deep breath and nodded. It was the army, not the Gestapo. They'd probably ask the type of questions we asked our prisoners: what unit we were from, how long we'd been there, what our plans were, maybe a few questions on morale. All I had to do was play the part of a confused replacement. It wouldn't involve much acting. If I was lucky, it would only last a minute or two.

The guards rounded up a few prisoners at a time and sent them into a hallway. I watched Samson and Koslow go and come back, and by then, Winterton and I had been ordered to our feet.

As we passed Samson, he whispered to us, "Say ya just got here and don't know anything."

We waited in line in the hallway. I wasn't sure if I should act meek and harmless or if I should let my contempt show. When one of the guards pushed me into a smaller classroom and I glanced at the officer sitting behind a desk, I made my decision. I was a prisoner, but I was still a soldier. I wouldn't grovel to a Nazi, no matter what his rank.

"What unit were you with?" The officer's English was better than Bastien's. That surprised me a little, but it made sense. The Germans were organized. They'd make sure an interrogator could understand his prisoner.

"I only arrived a few days before the fighting started. I don't remember."

The officer raised an eyebrow, clearly not impressed. Maybe what had worked for Samson wasn't going to work for me. "Where were you captured?"

"In Luxembourg, I think."

"Where in Luxembourg?"

"Just some house out in the country."

He wrote something on his paper. "Was it a house with a barn out back?"

"Yeah." I doubted that would tell him much. Most of the houses out in the countryside had barns nearby.

"How many were you captured with?"

"I'm not sure."

He gave me that unimpressed look again. "You're not sure?"

"There were wounded in the basement. I don't know how many."

"Your name?"

I hesitated before answering. I didn't want them to know I was born in Germany. It was one thing to be an enemy soldier; it might be something else to be a former countryman now fighting for the other side. But I still had my dog tags on, and it seemed unwise to lie when he could yank on the chain and check what I told him. Ley was a German last name, but it was an English last name too. "Private Ley."

"And you're wounded?"

I glanced at my arm. "Yeah."

"How?"

"Piece of shrapnel."

"Where are you from, Private Ley?"

"Virginia."

"Born there?" His blue eyes stared right at me.

"I've lived there since I was ten."

"I was in Virginia once. Went hiking in the Shenandoah Mountains. Have you ever been there?"

This guy had been to Virginia? "Yeah, I went to Shenandoah a few times." Bastien had taken me camping. We'd slept under the stars and come home covered in mosquito bites, but that hadn't stopped me from begging him to take me again over his next leave.

"Do you want to get back to Virginia?"

I nodded, homesickness crashing over me like the concussion of a mortar shell.

"Then you can start by being more talkative. Which unit were you with?"

"I already told you. I haven't been here long enough to know."

Another German officer interrupted us and switched the conversation to German. "Has he said anything useful?"

"No. I daresay he's lying to me, but he's not very clever. Give me a few more minutes, and I'll trip him up."

When I'd started school in the US, I'd overheard a few teachers say I was stupid. Mom had said it was just the language barrier, and sure enough, my grades had improved each year. But my current interrogator stirred up the exact same feelings of shame and resentment and insignificance.

He turned back to me with a smile and switched to English again. "Tell me what happened when you were captured."

"I'd like to go back with the other prisoners now. I don't have anything useful to tell you. I wasn't smart enough to know what was going on above the squad level, and my squad's all captured or killed."

"You speak German?" he asked.

I opened my mouth to protest, then I realized how effectively I'd blown my secret. He was right. I wasn't very clever. "Yeah," I mumbled.

"Where did you learn German?"

I was afraid if I opened my mouth again, I'd end up in an even deeper hole, so I kept it shut. My Sunday School teacher's warning rang through my head: lying was tricky. It was easier to stick with the truth.

"One of our men reported a German speaker surrendering a house in Luxembourg with a barn out back and a basement full of wounded. He said it was only a private, but his German was excellent."

I still didn't answer.

"Where were you born?"

I looked away. "I'm a US citizen now, so it doesn't matter where I was born."

"Berlin? Hamburg? Munich? Frankfurt?"

I flinched when he said Frankfurt, which was as good as answering. I didn't dare meet his eyes. I sent a plea heavenward that being born in Germany wouldn't equal a quick execution.

"Interesting."

He held me there for a few slow minutes before releasing me. My stomach was strung in a knot and cinched tight as I went back to the other prisoners.

"How'd it go?" Winterton asked.

"He knows I was born in Germany."

Winterton looked to where the guards were taking back another prisoner. "Did they do anything?"

"Not yet." But I was terrified that they would.

* * *

The guards didn't give us any food before pushing us out to the road again, but I was so relieved that the German officer hadn't called me back or separated me from the others that I hardly cared.

But before a quarter mile was up, my feet blistered and my fingers stung from the cold. I wasn't as dizzy as I'd been the day before, but I was just as sore, and my muscles were just as tired. I thought about my family and about the promise I'd made to Winterton. I had to make it, even if I was cold, hungry, and exhausted.

"When I get back to the States, I'm moving to Arizona or California," Winterton mumbled. "Someplace where it doesn't snow."

"Isn't your family in Oklahoma?"

"Yeah. I'll have to start a business and make a lot of money. If I can give them good jobs, they'll come join me."

I thought of my family. One of my brothers-in-law was from Kansas, and the other was from Colorado. When the war ended, I had no idea where my sisters would live. I didn't really know where Bastien and Gracie would live either. But it would be nice for us all to be close.

Thinking of my family was a mistake. I pictured my mom sitting at the kitchen table with her hands covering her mouth as she read the news and fretted. She knew I was on the line. She didn't know where because I wasn't allowed to say, but she'd worry until she heard I was safe.

"What will they tell our families?" I asked.

"They'll send a telegram saying we're missing. Once we get somewhere permanent, we're supposed to get postcards to mail through the Red Cross. But those can take awhile."

"Do you think we've been reported MIA yet?"

Winterton shrugged. "Probably not. Sounds like everything was in chaos."

Maybe that was better. If the telegram arrived late, there would be a shorter stretch between when it came and when the postcard made it through. Bastien had never been reported missing, but I'd seen the way the circles under Mom's eyes grew darker when she didn't hear from him, and I'd overheard a few of her prayers. I didn't want her to go through that again.

The weather was worse than it had been the day before, but the interrogations gave us a later start, so the march wouldn't be as long. German troops and vehicles still passed us, going the opposite direction, but no one bashed my face with their rifle. I had Winterton to walk with, and he'd told me we were going to make it, together, so I never felt like quitting.

As the sun disappeared, we came to a town. It looked like the air corps had hit it a few times. The few civilians still out spat and shook their fists at us. They were all women, old men, or children, and they looked angry enough to kill us as the guards marched us through the town center.

We spent the night in a straw-lined warehouse. They gave us a cup of water and one loaf of bread for every six men.

The next day was more of the same. The blisters on my feet burst, but they didn't hurt for too long because my feet were numb well before noon. When we passed through a town, some kids threw rocks at us, and we didn't get any food when we settled into a barn that night.

The day after, we marched again. They gave us cabbage soup at about noon. I counted three tiny pieces of cabbage in my bowl. I drained my soup, slipped my belt into the next notch, and kept walking.

One night, a few of the guards sang Christmas carols. It was Christmas Eve. They sang "Silent Night" in German, and then a few of the prisoners sang it in English. The guards and the prisoners took turns singing, and the music made things seem a little brighter. I joined in for "O Little Town of Bethlehem," but when someone started "I'll Be Home for Christmas," I didn't feel like singing anymore.

We arrived at a train station on Christmas Day. My battered feet had reached their limit, so the old boxcars looked almost as inviting as Higham's C ration stove. It was dark when we arrived, so there weren't many civilians out, and they did their best to avoid us.

"Maybe the air corps hasn't been over this way yet. They don't look like they want to murder us," I said to Winterton.

"Or maybe they're avoiding the smell."

Our column had grown to several hundred prisoners. None of us had shaved for at least a week, we wore the clothes we were captured in, and even though we weren't eating much, nearly everyone's gut was rebelling against the poor food and dirty drinking water. With no toilet paper and no soap, the column smelled like a latrine.

We were all hungry, so we welcomed the steamed sauerkraut the guards gave us, even if it was cold. They handed us a bit of cheese and half a loaf of bread too. They didn't give us any water, so I found some snow that looked mostly clean and sucked on that.

"Come on! Move it!" The guard nearest me motioned to the boxcars and used the stock of his rifle for extra emphasis.

I'd thought the US Army packed us tightly in the forty-and-eight boxcars we'd taken across France, but the Germans had it down to a science. They put far more than forty of us inside, and when it was full, they shoved in a few more. We were so crowded we couldn't even sit.

"Don't try to escape," a guard said. "We're counting, and if anyone is missing when we arrive, you will all be shot." The door clinked shut, and even though I was on the far end of the boxcar, the sound of the lock clicking closed seemed to echo right through me. I'd been eager to ride, but now I wasn't so sure. It was dark, and despite the mass of prisoners, it was cold. Every time someone moved, men three bodies away had to adjust.

The train lurched forward, making us bump into each other as it took us deeper and deeper into Germany. Farther and farther from freedom.

Winterton pushed past me toward the center of the boxcar. "Excuse me," he said in his most polite tone over and over again. "Listen, if we take turns, I think we can get about a third of us sitting at once. So everyone on the edges, move toward the outside. We'll let the people in the center sit for now."

"Why should they get the first turn?" someone asked. "They've already got more body heat."

"We'll switch in two hours." Winterton's statement left little room for argument. He glanced at his watch and took his place on the edge of the boxcar, next to me.

"They should have made you an officer," I said.

He pursed his lips. "They almost sent me to officer candidate school. The ASTP sounded like a better option. You know, a chance to get a college degree on the government's nickel and learn something I could make a living at when the war's over."

"Then the ASTP ended."

"Yeah. And OCS wasn't an option anymore. They sent me straight to the infantry."

Samson pushed around a few other soldiers to stand next to us. "Ley, you pick up anything about where we're going?"

"No." And that was the worst thing about being on that cold, smelly train. We had no idea how long we'd be in the boxcar and no idea where we'd end up when the train pulled to our final stop.

* * *

The guards kept us locked inside the boxcar for two full days. They opened the door only long enough to dump our latrine pail. It would have been long enough to give us food and water too, but we didn't get any food until the third day of our journey. When the single bucket of watery barley soup was divided among the sixty-five of us smashed inside, it was enough to ease our hunger for about ten minutes. At least they'd let us outside for a bit.

The train stopped from time to time, usually to sit off to the side while other higher-priority trains barreled past. We banged on the siding and yelled through the vent holes, begging for water, for food, for a chance to stretch our legs. The guards shouted back, ordering us to quiet down.

"Someone pass the crap helmet, quick!" a voice called from the middle of the boxcar. One bucket in the corner didn't cut it because most everyone had diarrhea, and we were packed in too tight for quick movement. A helmet got handed around and used as a pail. One of the soldiers near a vent dumped it outside, but plenty spilled, so the stench never went away.

A nagging thirst had been with me since the battle began, and it grew worse with each click of wheel on track. But the freezing weather turned out to have one good side effect. Frost lined the top of the boxcar the way it lined the second-hand freezer in my mom's kitchen. When it was my turn to stand on the edge, I licked what I could reach with my mouth and used my fingers to scrape the crystals above tongue-level.

The train slowed to a stop, and Samson nudged me in the elbow. "Can you talk to the civilians? Ask where we are?" His voice sounded hoarse. I guess he was thirsty too.

A pair of prisoners hoisted me next to the vent, and I strained to see through the wire mesh. People crowded the platform, and they must have known who we were because they threw rocks, raised their fists, and shouted insults. Surveying the nearby rubble, I could guess why. The air corps had hit the area hard. But I recognized the buildings that hadn't been bombed into ruin. There was no need to ask where we were. "Frankfurt am Main."

"Someone told you already?" Samson asked.

"They don't need to tell me. I was born here."

I scrambled down with a mix of emotions. I had a lot of memories of Frankfurt, some good and some bad. We'd left so suddenly, without a chance to tell anyone good-bye. Mom and Bastien had starting planning it when they'd found out Dad was dead and Bastien was due for conscription into the German Army, but they hadn't told my sisters or me. One day, Bastien had met Stefanie and me after school and walked us to this very train station. We'd met up with Mom and Hannah, and then we'd left, with one piece of luggage each. I didn't feel like I was home, but there was still a connection with Frankfurt, a stronger one than I'd expected.

Samson shuffled over to stand beside me. "Can you get someone to sell us food?"

"They look angry enough to lynch us out there." But I let the soldiers lift me back to the vent, and I held up some cigarettes another prisoner handed me. I was surprised Samson hadn't talked the man out of his Camels yet. He'd been so desperate for a cigarette yesterday that when they'd let us off the train for a few minutes, he'd tried to smoke a clump of dead grass. I'd tried to eat a twig, so maybe we weren't so different.

"Bread for cigarettes?" I got a few people's attention. One of the civilians spat in my direction. Another looked like she might take me up on the offer. But the third person who noticed was a guard, and he strode over and hammered his rifle stock into the vent. I jerked back and lost my balance. We were so tightly packed that I didn't tumble far before about six prisoners caught me. But that was the end of our bartering. A few hours later, the train moved on.

We didn't get any food that day.

We didn't get any food the next day either.

The day after, our boxcar of sixty-five soldiers got a total of eight loaves of bread. Winterton made sure we all got equal portions. The bread was old and hard, but I pretended it was one of my mom's rolls or one of Gracie's biscuits. I was dizzy all the time now, and the bread wasn't enough to stop it. The pain in my arm was growing worse too.

"How long are we going to be on this train?" I asked. "We've got to be nearly to Poland by now."

Winterton nodded in sympathy, even though we both knew I was exaggerating. We'd been stuck in the boxcar for days, but most of that time the boxcar hadn't moved.

Eventually we arrived at our destination. I left the train knowing I would be content to never enter a boxcar again, even if I lived to be a hundred. We stumbled from the station, our legs wobbly with cramps, and looked around. It was late afternoon, and everything was covered in snow. The bare landscape was spotted with a few leafless trees. They looked as lifeless as I felt.

German guards lined the route from the station to the camp, where ten-foot-tall posts held up a double barbed-wire fence. On each corner and a few places in between were tall guard towers manned by men with submachine guns. Angry barks filled the air as dogs strained at their leashes. I didn't want to go inside. I glanced around, looking for a way to escape, but we were surrounded by German soldiers, and there was nothing but snow to hide in. The sides of the main gate stretched up to support a porch and a windowed guard shack. Across the front were the words *M. Stammlager IVB.*

CHAPTER 20

THE GUARDS HERDED US INTO an open area inside the wire. The camp sprawled across several compounds, with wire fences surrounding the perimeter and cutting the camp into different sections. I tried to count the number of barracks. I couldn't see them all from where I stood, but I guessed there were about fifty.

A portly German officer strutted in front of us. His jowls shook as he looked us over, his hands on his hips and his feet spread wide, almost like he was bracing himself for a punch. He cleared his throat and began. "Welcome to Stalag Four B. I am Oberstleutnant Schultz, the camp commandant."

The commandant had spoken in German. One of the guards translated, so I heard the same thing twice.

"For you, the war is over," the commandant continued. "This will be your new home for a time, but most of you will not stay long. In accordance with the Geneva Conventions, all enlisted men will work. In the interim, you will be placed in the British section of camp. They will tell you what to expect, but a few rules are paramount. First, do not miss roll call. Second," the commandant motioned to a guard and paused.

The guard marched to the edge of the compound and grabbed a wire strung a foot above ground on the inside of the double fence.

"If you cross the warning wire, you will be shot. If you leave your barracks at night, you will be shot. If you disobey the guards, you will be shot." While the rules were translated, he studied us with narrowed eyes. "Now, all Jewish prisoners will step forward."

I tensed. Most men in the US Army knew Hitler didn't like Jews, but they might not realize how much. When it came to the men from the boxcar, I knew a lot about what type of food they fantasized about and almost nothing about their religion. But at least one of them had thrown his dog tags with an *H* for Hebrew in the religion slot out the train vent. I willed him to stay still. I'd grown up with stories about dying for one's beliefs, mostly from the scriptures, but this wasn't the time or the place.

The commandant paced in front of us, his lips turned down and his hands clasped behind his back. "Should you be found lying on this matter, the consequences will be most severe—for the entire group."

My stomach had to be nearly empty, but something inside churned around uncomfortably as we waited for the commandant to give up his search. I kept my eyes straight ahead, looking at neither the commandant nor my fellow prisoners. I didn't want to call attention to myself or make the commandant think I was looking at a Jew.

Time stretched out. The shadow from the nearest barracks crept over me, and the temperature plummeted. The commandant repeated his threats and waited a little longer.

Finally, he turned on his heels and strode away.

I relaxed. One of the guards addressed us next. It was time to be processed.

The Germans wouldn't go through the trouble of feeding us regular meals, but they kept record of name, rank, and serial number and assigned us all a prisoner number. I glanced at the new ID tag when they gave it to me, wondering if they wanted us to memorize our number. They didn't put our name on the tags, just our number. I stood in front of the camera with three other prisoners so the Germans could document it. Then I was interrogated again, but the questions were simple, and the interview was short.

When we were official residents of Stalag IVB, they led us through one of the wired-off sections. The sun was gone, and as darkness engulfed the camp, searchlights on the towers began probing the ground. A guard assigned me to the third barracks we came to, along with Winterton, Samson, and seventeen others.

I blinked in the electric light, taking in the men lounging on three-tier bunks or gathered around an odd assortment of tables. One of them put his cards down and approached us. He was average height, but he seemed taller because his back was ramrod straight. Not a strand of his receding hair was out of place, and his chin had only a five o'clock shadow. I felt my own cheek, rough and scratchy with two-weeks' growth.

"Welcome, Yanks. I am Sergeant Kingston, the senior NCO in this barrack. No doubt things have been rather rough for you lately, but I am certain the rest of us could match you when it comes to tales of hardship. I think we can all take comfort in the fact that 1945 will begin in a few hours. Perhaps the coming year will see the end of the war."

"You didn't see all the Tiger tanks the krauts were throwing at us," one of the guys from the train said.

Kingston clucked his tongue. "Shoulders back and chins up, lads. The German offensive has been halted. Victory has been delayed, but it will come."

"How do you know what's going on with the German offensive?" Samson asked.

A slight smile pulled at Kingston's lips. "Why, we listen to the BBC, of course. The Battle of the Bulge is hardly over, but the tide has turned against our Nazi foes. Soon enough, Monty and your Patton will be crossing the Rhine and running their tanks through the wire. Unless the Red Army gets here first. In either case, Hitler's days are numbered."

Samson felt in his pockets for a cigarette, just like he had on the train every morning, afternoon, and evening, and most hours in between. He didn't find one. "They let you listen to the BBC?"

"Do you think we let them know we're listening? You lot have a great deal to learn about being a kriegie."

"Kriegie?" Samson asked.

I knew the answer to that. "Comes from *Kriegsgefangene.* 'Prisoner of war.'"

Kingston nodded. "You've arrived just in time for the New Year's festivities. We've cleared out those four bunks for you." He pointed to a total of twelve mattresses for the twenty of us. "We're a bit crowded, I'm afraid."

I poked one of the mattresses to figure out what was inside. Wood chips.

"You guys got anything to eat around here?" Samson asked. "It's been a couple days since they handed us our last scraps of food."

Kingston smiled. "We've been stockpiling for the occasion."

As Kingston motioned to the tables, my mouth watered. Compared to diluted cabbage soup, the crackers, jam, tinned cheese, herrings, and choice of tea or hot chocolate represented a feast.

"Looks like the Germans feed you guys pretty decently," Samson said as he eyed the food.

Kingston huffed. "The Germans give us black bread and soup. Occasionally potatoes. This is from our Red Cross parcels. Frankly, the Red Cross is the only thing standing between us and starvation."

"How often do the parcels arrive?" Winterton accepted a cup of tea. I grabbed some hot chocolate and took a sip. It could have used more sugar, but it was still the best thing I'd had to drink in months.

One of the British soldiers piped up. "We used to get one a week, sometimes all to ourselves. But since the landings in Normandy, they haven't been getting through like they used to. Now we have to share them three or four ways."

"Are there any cigarettes in those parcels?" Samson asked.

"Yes, but these came nearly a week ago, old boy. The cigarettes were divvied up quite some time ago."

"Old boy?" Samson's lips formed the words, but no sound came out. His brow wrinkled in confusion until Winterton handed him some tea. Samson accepted the mug. "Tea?" He sniffed it and frowned.

"The American parcels have coffee, but it's been a few months since we had those." The British soldier turned his attention to a pair of men bringing out a bucket that unleashed a slightly fruity smell.

"I'm guessing that didn't come from the Germans either." Samson stood on his toes to get a better look.

"No."

"British moonshine." Samson chuckled. "I'll take some. And I'll have Ley's share too." He gave me a wink.

"Fine with me. As long as I get one of your crackers."

After the feast, I wasn't full, but my stomach didn't ache with hunger anymore. It was good to know the Germans hadn't broken through all the way to Paris. They'd surprised us, and they'd overwhelmed my company, but they hadn't routed the entire army.

I ended up sharing a mattress with Winterton. The British had given us one blanket per man, so the benefit of sharing a bunk—other than not having to sleep on the floor—was that we had two blankets on top of us. Since there were two of us, we got the bottom bunk because bed boards were one of the few sources of wood in the camp, and most of them had been whittled down to half their original thickness. The lighter prisoners slept up top.

A few minutes after lying down, the contentment in my stomach turned to a mutiny.

Winterton groaned beside me. "I think I'm going to die."

"Me too." I gasped. "Where're the buckets?"

We ran to make use of the facilities, but there were only two holes, and all the other Americans needed to use them at the same time we did. Someone opened the barrack door a crack, trying to escape outside. One of the British men slammed it shut. "They shoot anyone seen outside after dark."

My guts cramped in pain as I glanced at the line. It was too long. Disaster was inevitable.

* * *

Early the next morning, I was by Winterton again, this time sharing a wash bin, scrubbing out our underwear.

I put my wet pants back on because I didn't have anything else to wear and wrapped my overcoat around me to keep from freezing. A few of the British troops from our barracks passed us, disgusted. "Why did Jerry drag us all the way to Mühlberg? They could have shot us in Luxembourg. It would have been a lot easier than dying of dysentery."

"Our systems had a shock," Winterton said. "Almost nothing to eat for days, then all that rich food. But I don't think we're going to die from it."

"Why does the Red Cross send stuff that's so hard to digest?"

Winterton scratched at his arm. "Well, they have to send something that doesn't spoil easily. I think the parcels were designed to make up for deficiencies in nutrients and calories. Whoever made the menu assumed the Germans would give us potatoes and bread. They didn't know we'd be starved for a few weeks before we ate it."

"Maybe now that we're in camp, we'll at least get more than we got on the train." My stomach itched, and I pulled my fingers away. But after borrowing a razor and shaving so that Kingston would stop calling us "a rather scruffy lot of Yanks," I found myself scratching my stomach again. I tugged my shirt up and discovered red welts from my belly button to my chest.

Winterton glanced at me, then rolled his sleeves up. He had welts all along his arms, even bigger than the ones on my torso.

"What is it?" I asked.

"I don't know."

"Bedbugs," someone said in passing.

Winterton frowned. "Guess we get to spend the day looking for bedbugs. After roll call and breakfast."

Roll call, or *appell*, consisted of standing at attention while the German guards counted all the prisoners from our section. The senior British

NCO stood at the front, facing us. A few of the British prisoners moved lines, I suppose to make it harder for the Germans to get an accurate count, but my pants were damp, so I wished they would have stayed still. Instead, it took over an hour.

"Dismissed!" When the count finally finished, the British man saluted the guard, but something about the set of his head and the line of his lips showed no real respect. The German guard disgusted him.

I was eager to eat, but when we got back to the barracks, the only thing we had for breakfast was a drink that looked a lot like coffee. I skipped it.

"Ley, you can't skip breakfast. You need all the calories you can get." Winterton took a sip and nearly choked. "On second thought, I might join you. This isn't real coffee. For all I know, it's made from ink."

"Is it warm?"

He made a face. "Mostly."

"Maybe tomorrow I'll use it for shaving."

Later that morning, I was given three postcards with little red crosses on them.

I knew what I wanted to write:

Dear Mom, I'm miserable. I'm starving to death, but everything I eat goes right through me. We had a long march here, and some of the guards used me as a punching bag. If that wasn't degrading enough, I've got dysentery. I haven't stopped shivering in days. The bites from all the bedbugs itch, and the cut in my arm from a piece of German shrapnel is festering. My clothes are filthy, and they're getting too big. The British prisoners look down their noses at us because our buttons aren't polished and our morale isn't so great after being stuck in a boxcar for a week with less food than we'd usually get at one meal. I think we're safe from mass execution for the moment, but what will happen when a friendly army gets closer? Will they release us, or will they shoot us?

I didn't write any of that. It wouldn't have fit on the postcard, and I didn't want my mom to worry. Most of the other men were saying things like "am unwounded and in good health." That wasn't entirely true for me, but my arm would probably be better by the time the postcard reached Virginia. Maybe the dysentery too. I finally settled on:

Dear Mom. Got captured awhile back. Currently in a camp near Mühlberg but expect to be moved soon. I'm doing all right. No need to worry about me. Please tell Bastien, Hannah, Stefanie, and Belle. I'll write as often as allowed. Love, Lukas.

I wrote about the same thing to Bastien and Belle, but with Belle's new job, I wasn't sure she still got the mail, and I doubted her dad would pass it on.

Our meal that day was cabbage soup and a slice of bread. The cabbage was starting to spoil, and I was half convinced the bread had sawdust in it. I ate it anyway. Then I ran for the latrine, along with most of the other new kriegies.

I passed one of the British NCOs on the way back to the barracks. "That a wound, there, Yank?"

I nodded. The bandage on my arm was red, and the wound underneath ached.

"Well, off to hospital with you. Have it stitched up."

I followed his directions to the tiny hospital building. I stepped inside and looked around. I hadn't been in many hospitals, but this one had to be the worst-stocked one I'd ever seen. The nurse at Fairfax High School had more to work with.

The British doctor gave my arm a painful scrubbing. I gritted my teeth because the cleaning hurt almost as much as the initial injury had. He used a knife to trim part of the flesh away, and finished with seven stitches, all using no anesthetic.

"There you are," he said. "Come back if you develop a fever, feel light-headed, or notice angry red streaks coming from the wound."

"I've been mostly dizzy most days the last week."

He pressed his hand to my forehead. "Hmm. No fever. Or not much of one."

"It's not because I'm sick. It's because they haven't given us enough to eat."

He nodded. "That seems to be typical as of late. Everyone is hungry when they arrive."

"How long have you been here?"

"Since Dunkirk."

"I thought everyone got evacuated after Dunkirk. All the British troops anyway." It had been four and a half years ago, but I'd read all the newspaper accounts.

"Most. Not all."

Four and a half years. It seemed an eternity, but I'm sure he knew that a lot better than I did. "Do you have anything for dysentery?"

"Just charcoal."

"Charcoal?"

"Dysentery is usually caused by contaminated food or water. Charcoal absorbs poisons." He handed me a chunk. "It's easiest to digest if you grind it into powder first."

I was desperate enough to try it. "Thanks, Doc."

He chuckled. "I'm not a doctor. I'm just a medic." He moved on to the next patient.

I checked my new stitches a little more closely. The lines were even and tight. Not bad for a non-doctor. I rolled my sleeve back down and put my greatcoat on. The medic looked slim, but he didn't look like he was starving. If troops from Dunkirk were still alive, sane, and relatively healthy, then life in the stalag couldn't be all that bad.

On the way back to my assigned barrack, I saw something that killed my budding hope. A long line of men plodded along on the other side of an internal camp fence with shovels and picks slung over their shoulders. Only they didn't look like men. They looked like skeletons with skin. They wore mismatched clothing. Scraps of newspaper peeked from their collars, and rags with bits of hay sticking out bound their feet. Several of them limped, and the ones I saw speaking to each other had mouths full of rotten teeth.

They were under guard, so I didn't dare call to them, but I followed their progress, walking parallel to them.

I stopped a British NCO on my side of the fence. "Excuse me, Corporal?"

"Yes?"

"Who are they? Did they break the camp rules or something?"

He glanced at the walking skeletons, then back at me. "Let me guess, you just arrived?"

I nodded. "You've been here awhile?"

"Since '42." He tilted his head toward the other prisoners. "They're Russians. The Soviet Union didn't sign the Geneva Conventions, so they don't get Red Cross parcels. And Hitler considers Slavs subhumans, so they get substandard rations."

The Russians turned at the end of the compound and walked out of sight. The last man in the column lagged behind, and one of the German guards swatted at him with a rifle.

The NCO cursed the Germans under his breath. "Mark my words. The Germans will lose this war. And the Red Army will show them no mercy when that happens."

* * *

I saw my first Red Cross parcel five days later. Inside was soap, cigarettes, chocolate bars, raisins, crackers, jam, coffee, sugar, and cans of Spam, tuna, cheese, condensed milk, and powdered milk. None of the items by themselves would have caused much excitement a month ago, but now my mouth watered, and my stomach rumbled.

"We have to share it four ways," Winterton said. He picked up the can of cheese and pointed to a small hole. "The guards punctured all the cans so we can't hoard them for escape attempts. As if we'd have energy for that."

I took the tinned cheese, holding it reverently. "That sure looks better than barley and maggot soup."

"They aren't maggots; they're little worms." Samson looked up from the cigarettes he was dividing.

"Whatever they are, they're gross." But that didn't stop me from eating them. And with a little help from powdered charcoal, I was actually keeping the food inside long enough to digest it. But there was never enough of it.

The fourth man to share our parcel was another American, from the 99th Infantry Division. He had black hair, but everyone called him Red. I'd wondered why for a day and a half before I figured out he was part Iroquois, and Red was short for Private Redhawk.

I shoved my cigarette rations in my pocket. Cigarettes were almost as good as money around camp. I'd seen lots of men—like Samson—value a smoke over a meal. The question was how long to wait. Trade now while everyone had food? Or trade later, when the cigarette supply dwindled?

I spent an hour looking for bedbugs and lice. Winterton and I made daily searches, but I still woke each morning with new welts and new itches. Maybe they were falling from the bunks above us. I started working on those mattresses too.

Winterton knocked a bedbug to the floor and smashed it. "Wouldn't it be nice if we could dump some in the guards' barracks?"

I cracked a smile as I scratched behind my left ear. Some of the guards were mean. A lot of them were stupid. Others were old. None of them were

front-line troops for one reason or another. They may have only been following orders, but giving them a taste of the misery they'd inflicted on us
sounded appealing.

After the next *appell*, I saw the Russians again. I fingered the cigarettes
in my pocket. German guards liked cigarettes, especially the kind that came
in Red Cross parcels. The Russians might get something useful with a fistful
of cigarettes—potatoes, bread, even watery soup had to be an improvement
over the scraps they normally ate.

I strung the cigarettes together with a piece of twine I'd picked up the
day before. When the Russian column was as close at it would come to the
British section of camp, I threw the bundle into the center of the group. It
hit within a foot of where I'd aimed, not a bad throw for a guy down on
his muscle weight and missing his glasses.

The Russians dove for the cigarettes, and a second later, the guards
began yelling. They didn't stop with shouts. Rifles swung into the prisoners,
and even from twenty yards away, I heard the sickening sound of bone
being snapped in two.

More guards came running at the Russians. I stood there, horrified.
Then something grabbed the back of my neck and half pulled, half pushed
me into the shadow of the nearest barrack.

"What were you thinking?" Samson demanded.

I glanced around, grateful none of guards had noticed us. "I was about
to ask myself the same question."

"Huh?"

"I thought they could trade for food or something." From where Samson had dragged me, I could no longer see the melee I'd caused, but the
shouts of the guards and cries of the prisoners still sounded. "I figured they
needed the extra food more than I did. I didn't know it would make the
guards attack them."

Samson relaxed his grip on my neck. "Ley, you may not have noticed,
but that ain't how things work around here. The British run a tight ship.
The food's divided up equally, and if anyone steals, they're punished. But
that's discipline, not compassion. You can't look out for the whole camp.
Ain't you noticed that most everybody's broken off into groups of two or
three?"

I nodded.

"Look out for your buddies. Look out for your squad mates. Anything
more than that is gonna leave you without enough to eat. And throwing
things at the Communists ain't gonna help 'em survive the war."

"What do you mean?"

"They're starving to death. You could give 'em all your food all the time, and you know what would happen? They'd still be hungry. You'd starve to death, and then they'd starve to death. You wanna sacrifice your life so they can have one more week of misery?"

"I gave them cigarettes, not food."

"Cigarettes you could've traded for more food or for medicine if that arm gets infected." Samson looked round the end of the barrack and motioned me in the opposite direction. Part of me wanted to see what had happened to the Russians. Part of me was scared to look. Either way, Samson was pushing me away from them. He sighed. "Maybe it doesn't matter. I've got a rotten feeling the Germans are gonna gun us all down before they hand us back to our own side anyway."

I looked up at the nearest guard tower. "Why would they keep us alive now if they're planning to kill us later?"

"Reciprocity. We've got a lot of kraut prisoners. I have a cousin who lives near a POW camp in North Carolina. Told me all about it. The krauts take English lessons, go to movies in their spare time, get plenty of rations, work union hours." Samson clenched his jaw in frustration. "If they treated us half as well as we treated them, this might not be so bad."

"They said they're sending us to work camps in a few days."

Samson shook his head. "I doubt a new camp will be much different. Rotten food, fleas, a bunch of limey soldiers acting all superior. I've gotta get outta here."

I glanced around. We'd turned onto the main dirt path between the rows of barracks, but no one was close enough to overhear us. "Are you thinking of escape?"

He nodded. "As soon as I have a plan."

"Have you run that past the escape committee?" Kingston had told us in clear terms that all escape attempts had to be run past the British. The SS had a nasty habit of shooting escaped prisoners, so current orders from London and Washington were to stay put.

Samson huffed. "We fought a couple of wars to get out from underneath British rule. I'm not gonna submit to it here."

"But how?"

"I don't know yet. I doubt it will happen in Mühlberg. But when we get to a new place—maybe there."

CHAPTER 21

ONE WEEK AFTER ARRIVING AT camp, a German guard took out a paper at the end of *appell* and started reading. "The following prisoners will prepare for transfer: Ley, Lukas."

I gulped and stepped forward. Were they calling out German-born POWs? And if so, where would they send me?

He read off a few more names, and I started to relax. I recognized some of the men from the train, and eventually, he called Winterton, Samson, and Red.

They gave us a few minutes to gather our things. I said a prayer of thanks that I'd gotten my stitches out the day before, because they hadn't told us where we were going, and I had no idea what type of medical help they'd have there.

We marched back to the train station. I dreaded another trip inside a boxcar. Winterton stopped completely and looked like he was about to bolt. A quick glance at the guards told me how that would end. "Come on," I told him. "We can survive this. Maybe we won't be crammed in so tightly this time."

His feet began moving just as one of the guards started toward us. To my relief, the guard backed off.

The boxcar stank of sick POWs and horse droppings. I did not want to get inside, but I did because the alternative was getting shot, and if I didn't climb in, I didn't think Winterton would get in either, and then he'd get shot too.

The guards used chalk to write the number of prisoners on the outside of the boxcar before they locked us in. There were fifty of us. That was a lot better than sixty-five. Once we shoved the filthy straw to the side we could all sit down at the same time; we just had to sit between each other's legs. Or we could take turns with half of us standing and half of us lying down to sleep.

I had mixed expectations as the train rolled through the nearby town of Mühlberg. I wouldn't miss Stalag IVB and its bedbugs, lice, and cesspool of a latrine pit available only during daylight hours. But no one had told us where we were going or how long the trip would last. Would we get any food? Most days, they served only two meals at the stalag, and the first one was just a cup of ersatz coffee, so it didn't really count. But at least in the stalag we'd been able to walk around, and we'd had space from the guards. Twice during my week-long stay, the Germans had thrown in a few potatoes for an extra meal. Now that we were registered with the Red Cross, it was less likely that the Germans would take us into the woods and shoot us, but that didn't mean they wouldn't work us to death.

It was hard to tell how far we went, but it didn't seem long before the train pulled to a stop. We waited, but no one unlocked the door. Red and Samson lifted me to the vent to take a look.

"We're on some siding again. No signs."

Everyone groaned. We all remembered sitting locked in boxcars for hours at a time, waiting for other trains to pass.

"I can't see any civilians, just the guard."

"Ask him where we're going," Samson said.

I didn't want to stir up trouble, but I was curious, and the vent gave me the safety of anonymity. "Where are we headed?" I yelled in German.

The guard took a pull on his cigarette and glanced around. Maybe he wanted to make sure no one could see him answer. "Work kommandos. Somewhere between Chemnitz, Leipzig, Dresden. Where they need workers, we'll take you off."

"What type of work?"

"Everything. Lumber, mining, sorting through rubble, unloading trains."

"How long are we going to be at this train station?"

The guard shrugged.

"Can we get out and stretch our legs?" I didn't mention it aloud, but it would be nice to take care of a few other things too without having to make use of the bucket in the corner of the boxcar. I'd used up all my charcoal powder, and my guts were acting up again.

The guard finished his cigarette and tossed it to the ground.

"Please?"

"I'll ask." But he didn't leave his position. Maybe he wasn't allowed to.

"You done yet, Ley?" Samson asked.

"Yeah."

Red and Samson lowered me back down.

"The guard said they're taking us south, toward where the border with Czechoslovakia used to be. They'll pull us off wherever they need workers in the triangle between Chemnitz, Leipzig, and Dresden. Manual labor."

"If they expect us to work, I sure hope they're gonna give us more to eat than they did back at Mühlberg."

"Yeah." I found a spot on the floor and sat.

"What, kid? You look kind of gloomy." Samson felt in his pocket for a cigarette, but maybe by now he knew he needed to ration them, so he didn't light it.

I scratched an itch—probably a louse—on the back of my neck. "I think a lot's going to depend on where we end up."

"And what we can scrounge." Red's words were spoken in a matter-of-fact tone. I almost asked if he had experience with scrounging, but I thought better of it and kept my mouth shut.

"According to the Geneva Conventions," Winterton broke in, "we're supposed to get more food if we work."

Samson gave a huff. That was as close as he ever came to laughing. "Well, we know how well they follow the Geneva Conventions."

"Maybe we can work on a farm. Might get more food there." I pictured rows of potatoes, a cow to milk, chickens to gather eggs from, pigs to slaughter and turn into sausage. "What I wouldn't give for bacon and eggs right now."

"Yeah, with white bread instead of that sour black stuff they give us." Samson frowned. "But I'd take that black stuff over nothing if they'd just give us enough to fill up on."

The air raid siren halted our conversation. Red and Samson pushed me back up to the vent. "I can't see anything yet . . . but the guards are taking off."

Some of the other prisoners beat on the door, demanding to be let out. The same thing happened in the cars in front of and behind us.

"How many cars are in this train?" Winterton asked.

"Enough to make it a target." We weren't even moving. We were like sitting ducks, but the truth was, ducks could move, and they were small enough that it would be hard to hit them from a few hundred feet above ground. A line of boxcars parked on a railroad siding was a whole lot more vulnerable.

"Do you see anything yet?" Samson asked.

"No."

"You're half blind anyway; get down."

I wasn't half blind, but I wasn't about to argue with him. A scrawny guy from Ohio got boosted up next. I heard the whine of the engine at about the time he called out, "Enemy fighter! Me-109!"

The engine noise grew from a hum to a torrent, and the crack of large-caliber bullets ripping through railcars grew closer and louder. It was like being in an artillery barrage again, only it was worse because there was nowhere to hide. We huddled on the floor of the car, trying to make our-selves as small as possible. The first pass left holes in the sides and roof of the train, but miraculously, no one in our boxcar was hit.

"Why are they shooting up their own trains?" I asked.

"They aren't." Winterton peered through the ripped side of the boxcar. "That's not an Me-109. It's a P-51 Mustang. Probably on its way back from escorting bombers."

The guy from Ohio stood and found a hole to peek through. "No. No way is our own air force trying to kill us."

"They can't see what's inside. For all they know, they're shooting up artillery shells." Winterton shielded his eyes from the sun. "Look—two of them now, circling back for another pass. You can see the white stars on their wings."

The first pass had been bad. The second pass was going to be worse because there were two planes, and I knew how big of a hole they could put through the side of a boxcar—or a body.

"Don't the Germans have any antiaircraft guns?" Ohio asked.

No one answered. I'd been thinking the same thing, but I didn't really want American pilots shot down. Yet as the bang-bang-bang of the guns cracked and tore up everything in the rail yard, I knew I'd be relieved if a German 88 took out the Mustangs.

The bullets crashed through our boxcar again, and splinters of wood exploded all around me. Half of us screamed in terror, but the planes and the bullets drowned out the noise. Only when the planes left and the cries continued did I realize there were severely wounded men right next to me.

Blood streamed from the Ohio man's arm. I grabbed at his shirt, try-ing to figure out how bad it was.

"Put pressure on the wound," Winterton said. "I'll get something for a tourniquet."

I pressed a wad of shirt into the bleeding wound. The poor guy whimpered. A few other wounded men were nearby. At least I hoped they were wounded and not dead. "Hang in there," I said.

Winterton wrapped a shoelace just above my hands and snugged it in. He went to help the next wounded man. I wrapped Ohio's arm with his shirt and wiped my hands off on my greatcoat.

"Ley?"

Samson's voice was tense, but he didn't sound wounded. I turned around, and he motioned me to a hole in the side of the boxcar.

"The guards are coming back. Will you tell them we've got some wounded and some dead?"

My stomach lurched. Dead? I glanced around and counted four men bleeding and breathing. Four others who had bled and breathed their last. All this way to get killed by their own side. I almost threw up, but the men who were wounded needed aid. I couldn't waste time being sick, no matter how helpless and vulnerable I felt.

I didn't need anyone to lift me to the vent because the boxcar was now speckled with holes. "Hey!" I shouted in German when a guard came into view. "We've got wounded men!"

* * *

The next day, we pulled into a village train station near Chemnitz. The guards counted out twenty prisoners and handed us off to a pair of local guards. Winterton, Samson, and Red were with me. The other sixteen I knew only from the train.

It didn't take long to figure out why the new guards weren't on the front line. Unless he'd dyed his hair gray, the older one was past military age. The younger one was probably about thirty. He towered over us and looked capable of snapping a rifle in half with his bare hands, but he limped when he walked.

"Do any of you speak German?" the older one asked.

I didn't answer immediately because I didn't want to pass orders to my fellow prisoners, but when no one else responded, I cleared my throat. "I do."

The wrinkles on the guard's forehead relaxed. I guessed that meant he needed me to translate.

The younger guard had walked out of view, but his hand whacked the back of my head with enough force to send me stumbling forward. He came around to stand in front of me, his lips curled into a smile under his narrow mustache as if he'd told a joke worthy of Bob Hope or Red Skelton. "You will address Feldwebel Neubau as *sir*."

I took a few moments to bite back my temper. The sight of the younger guard's carbine helped. "I speak German, *sir*."

"Better." The younger one put his hand on my chest and pushed. "Get back in line."

The senior guard looked over the twenty of us. "You have no luggage?"

"No." The younger soldier moved, and I added, "Sir."

"Follow me, then."

I turned to my friends. "We're supposed to follow."

Winterton pulled beside me as we walked. "What was that all about?"

"They asked if anyone spoke German."

"Yeah, but why'd the big guard with a mustache push you around?"

I glanced behind me to where the younger guard limped at the end of our column. He was far enough away that he didn't notice our conversation. "I forgot to say *sir* when I answered the other guard."

"What rank is he?"

"Feldwebel. It's like a sergeant or a staff sergeant."

"Huh. Did they say what we're doing?"

"No."

Samson was just ahead of us. "Ask, will ya?"

I nodded.

The feldwebel pulled to a stop, still in the train yards, and we gathered around.

"Excuse me, sir," I said.

For a guy who limped, the younger guard managed to get beside me with lightning speed and drive the butt of his carbine into the back of my knees. I crashed to the ground.

"You do not have permission to address the feldwebel." He raised his carbine again, aiming for my head, but the feldwebel called out and stopped him.

"Enough." Neubau turned to me as Samson gave me a hand up. "You will load the items from this lorry"—he patted a nearby truck—"and that one"—he pointed to another—"into this boxcar. Do you understand?"

I nodded.

"Tell them." He waved a hand at the others.

I explained our task, and once we were organized, the guards backed off a bit. We formed a chain to move the boxes from the truck to the boxcar. I kept an eye on the mustached guard, hoping he'd stay on the other end of the rail yard.

"What's in the crates?" Samson asked.

I'd read the words stenciled in black paint. "Bullets."

"What?" Winterton took a box from me and paused before handing it to Samson. "That's against the Geneva Conventions."

"I don't think they care."

"Great. Now we're helping the Nazi war effort." Samson glared at the mustached guard.

"Careful," I said. "I got a feeling if he sees you doing that, he'll beat you over the head with something."

We worked until dusk. Our hands were raw, our limbs were sore, and our stomachs were empty. The feldwebel counted us and told us to follow him. The mustached guard took the back of the line, and I stayed in the middle, away from him. At the edge of the yard, we saw another group of men who looked almost as run down as we did, escorted by two more guards. The feldwebel told us to follow them, so we did, through streets that grew darker and darker as we passed. The civilians inside closed their blackout shades and disappeared from view. The civilians on the street ignored us. I preferred that to the spitting and the rock throwing, but a little compassion would have been even better.

The other workers marched to a warehouse surrounded by a chain-link and barbed-wire fence. We followed them in, and the guards locked the gate and chained the warehouse door shut. None of them came inside, and the mustached guard was nowhere to be seen. For the first time in hours, I relaxed a little.

"You Yanks?" one of the men from the other column asked.

Samson answered for us. "Yeah. You?"

"I'm from Australia. Private Daniels." He pointed to the other men. "One from South Africa, two from Canada, and the rest from Britain proper."

I counted the men from the other column. There were ten of them.

"You fellas got any food?" Samson asked. "Or cigarettes?"

Daniels seemed to be in charge, and he filled us in. "A *frau* brings in breakfast and supper. She'll be here soon. Nothing else, so save a bite tomorrow if you want anything for dinner or tea. Guess I better show you the place." He pointed to a wall with shelves full of mugs, plates, and razors. "Two sinks over there. The water and electricity work more often than they don't, but it's going downhill lately. The loo's through that door."

We followed him to a back room. Straw pallets lay in neat rows beside a stove. "All right, cobbers, make room for the yanks." One of the Canadians and two of the Brits shifted the pallets around. It looked like they had been doubling up on the bedding, but they spread the mattresses out and divided up the blankets so everyone had a place to sleep.

Red opened the stove. Nothing burned inside, but the men had been gone all day. Maybe they hadn't had a chance to light it yet.

Daniels gestured at the empty coal bin. "Jerry gives us enough coal for a fire once a week, but sometimes we can scrounge a bit more."

"What's the work like?" Samson asked.

"We hike out an hour after sunrise. Come back at dusk. We have a break at the yards midday. Sometimes fifteen minutes. Sometimes an hour. Depends on what's come in and how the guards feel. We have Sunday afternoon off."

Samson felt his pocket like he was searching for a smoke. "Any Red Cross parcels?"

"Not lately."

The guards unlocked the door and escorted a middle-aged woman inside. She pushed a cart holding a steaming pot and a pile of black bread. The Commonwealth prisoners lined up, and we followed their lead. It was pea soup, and it was a lot better than the cabbage soup or the barley soup I'd survived on the past few weeks, and the portions were slightly bigger than what we'd had at camp. I glanced at the men from the other column. They were lean. They didn't look as bad as the Russians had back at Stalag IVB, but they were on the sickly side. Hard labor balanced out the slightly larger rations.

"How long you guys been here?" I asked.

"Six months for me," Daniels said. "Longer for some of the others. Last week our old barracks was smashed in an air raid. Killed a dozen men. One of the guards too. When they moved us here, they let Monson scramble onto the roof and paint POW in big white letters. But the RAF can't see that at night, can they?"

If I hadn't been so hungry, I might have lost my appetite. A dozen men killed by their own air force. Add in the men we'd lost the day before—

five, because one of the wounded had died before the Germans could evacuate him. We could get strafed by our own air corps, bombed by our allies, beaten by the guards, and executed by the SS. We weren't even halfway through January yet. Last I'd heard, the Americans were counterattacking through Belgium and Luxembourg, but they still hadn't taken back all the ground we'd lost in December. Peace was a long way off.

"Is it always the same guards?" Samson asked.

"They change from time to time, but mostly we see the same five. Feldwebel Neubau's in charge, but he's hard of hearing, and his eyesight is none too sharp. He's not cruel, but he's not in full control of his men either. Most of them aren't too bad, but you'll want to watch out for the bloke who was limping along at the end of your column today. Little Adolf, we call him."

I could see how his narrow, dark mustache had earned him the last part of his nickname, but the first part was a mystery. "Little?"

Daniels shrugged. "Just watch out. He likes to beat people and doesn't need much of a reason to do it. So don't get in his way or let him catch you looking at him, 'cause the other guards might pull him off you but not until you've got a few broken bones, see?"

That night, the British prisoners posted two lookouts, and then they removed a small radio from its hiding place behind a loose wooden board under a sink. They tuned it to the BBC. It was comforting to listen to our own side again. The men at Mühlberg had a secret radio, but only the camp leaders listened to it, I suppose to make sure the guards didn't catch them. Here, everyone except the lookouts gathered around the radio's slight volume. According to the announcer, there was heavy fighting in the Vosges, where the Germans had launched another attack into the American lines.

The next morning started off with bread and ersatz coffee. Then we spent all morning loading and unloading boxcars, or wagons, as the British called them. We got a short break at noon. The guards pulled out sandwiches for themselves. The rest of us pulled out leftovers from breakfast. Thanks to Daniels's warning, I'd saved half a slice of bread. The afternoon was more of the same.

As we shuffled home, I put my blistered hands in my greatcoat pockets. The thirty of us had been split into two groups, and I'd been lucky enough to work under guards who were content to sit on crates and watch. As long as we kept working, even at a snail's pace, they didn't do anything other than observe. I was sore and tired, but it could have been worse.

We joined the other column, and Little Adolf came into view. I looked away, but before long, he was walking right next to me.

"One of the prisoners said you speak German because you were born here. Is it true?" he asked.

"No."

He cuffed the back of my head. "He heard you on the train. You're a traitor."

Anger surged through me, at Little Adolf and at whoever had told the enemy I wasn't a native-born American.

"Where were you born?" he asked.

Lying wasn't going to work, so I told the truth. "Frankfurt."

Little Adolf whacked me again. "You will respond with a *Frankfurt, Gefreiter Metzger.*"

"Frankfurt, Gefreiter Metzger."

Next the end of his carbine jabbed into my side. "Stand up straight. You may be a filthy traitor, but you have German blood, and Germans don't slouch."

I did my best to comply, praying the warehouse would come into sight soon.

His next hit was the small of my back. "Straighter."

"Yes, Gefreiter Metzger." I was tempted to turn around, break his nose, and steal his weapon. But then my mom would get one of the dreaded telegrams from the War Department telling her I was dead. I bit my lip together to keep from saying anything more.

I almost lost it when he purposely tripped me and I landed in the gutter in a pile of slime.

Little Adolf looked even taller than normal as he glared down at me, his carbine pointed at my face. "If you left the Fatherland for America, then you are nothing but garbage, and you belong in the gutter."

"I'd rather be garbage than a Nazi," I mumbled. At least I'd had the sense to mutter in English instead of German.

"What's that?"

"Nothing, Gefreiter Metzger."

"Get up." He emphasized what he wanted with a kick in the pants.

One of the other guards offered Little Adolf a cigarette, distracting him. As we trudged along to the warehouse, my anger boiled. What idiot told Little Adolf I was born in Germany?

Winterton slipped in behind me, making one more body between me and the guards. "What's he got against you?"

"Somebody told him I was born in Germany."

"What?" Winterton looked at the other prisoners with narrowed eyes. "We'll find out who."

"It won't do any good. He knows now, and if he keeps it up, either he's going to kill me, or I'm going to kill him."

"Ley, don't say that. He'll get bored soon, and then he'll leave you alone."

"What if he doesn't?" I didn't know how long it would take for the war to end, but it was more days than I wanted to spend under Little Adolf's thumb.

"We'll figure something out. We're going to make it through this, remember?"

Winterton was right—I couldn't kill Little Adolf, not if I wanted to live through the war, but I was still ready to lash out at someone, preferably whoever had spilled the fact that I was born German. I took a deep breath. I wanted to get back home. I wanted to see my family again. And I wanted to see Belle again. So I had to stay alive. And for now, that meant letting Little Adolf bully me.

We made it back to the warehouse without further attention from Little Adolf. The water was working, so I scrubbed the gunk off my greatcoat. If I'd had any money, I would have paid a lot for a bar of soap. I would have paid even more for a change of clothes. I looked at the tiny pile of kindling next to the stove and decided against washing my pants or shirts. I didn't want to sleep in wet clothes.

While I waited for supper, I warmed myself by the stove. Red had somehow gathered enough sticks to double the pile of firewood. It still wouldn't last past the time we went to sleep, but I was impressed. "Where'd you find all this?" He'd worked the same group of boxcars I had that day.

"You gotta learn to look for opportunities. Practice. You'll get better. Or keep distracting Little Adolf. I got most of these while he was giving you grief."

I grunted. I suppose I should have been glad my misery had led to something good, but I ached to strike back at the guard, to return some of the hurt and humiliation he'd given me.

Down the line of mattresses, one of the British prisoners knelt next to a blanket. I had to look twice before I realized there was a man under the blanket.

"Come on, lad, you've got to get up and eat."

I couldn't hear the reply.

"Remember what you told me about Wales and how beautiful it is? You want to make it home, don't you? Come on, you've made it this far. We're winning now."

Eventually the friend was able to get the sick prisoner out of bed. His face had a distinct yellow tint, and he looked almost as skinny as the Russian POWs back in Stalag IVB. As soon as supper was over, the man from Wales went back to his mattress, rolled over, and faced the wall.

"Bad sign when they start pit-bashing like that," Daniels said.

"I didn't see him on the work crew today." Winterton kept an eye on the sleeping Welshman.

Daniels nodded. "We can claim we're too sick to work. Feldwebel Neubau has to approve it. If it goes on too long, he says he'll send the man back to Mühlberg."

"How long is too long?" I asked.

"Don't know. It hasn't happened yet."

Winterton turned to Daniels. "Do they let us see a doctor if we need one?"

"No."

I hoped someone in the warehouse knew more about first aid than I did. "But everyone so far has gotten better?"

Daniels's face told me I'd said something absurd. "Lately we've had a funeral every other week."

"What happened to him?" Winterton motioned to the Welshman.

"He said hello to one of the local girls, and Little Adolf broke his ribs. And I'd guess he has a bad case of hepatitis."

It was easy to imagine Little Adolf smashing someone's ribs. I was sore, but nothing was broken. Maybe I'd gotten off easy.

CHAPTER 22

THE NEXT MORNING AT THE rail yards the guards divided us into three groups. I was surprised when Winterton purposely went to work on another team, Samson and Red too. Winterton and I had stuck together since the Siegfried Line. I stood in my row, stock still, biting my lip to hide my disappointment. I understood. Little Adolf was dangerous, and I drew him to me the same way a muzzle flash drew sniper fire. But it hurt. Almost as much as my nearly empty stomach did. So much for Winterton's promise that we were going to make it together, no matter what.

I was still swallowing back the bitterness of abandonment when Little Adolf took his place at the head of my group. I closed my eyes for a few seconds, trying to summon up a little extra courage. I imagined Bastien giving me a pep talk. *Keep your head down, stay as far away from him as you can, avoid eye contact.* I thought back to our lessons in the backyard. We'd gone over all the wrong things. But as smart as Bastien was, I doubted he knew how to survive something like this any better than I did.

I was five men back. Little Adolf saw me, and his lips curled up like he was some type of animal. A mean, predatory animal. It was hard not to feel like a cornered rabbit. I couldn't let him get to me so much, not if I wanted to stay sane.

Feldwebel Neubau had one of the other guards count us, then gave the order to move forward. Little Adolf turned his back to us and led the way.

Winterton grabbed my elbow and yanked me out of line. "Trade spots with me." He shoved me toward the line he'd been in, the line led by one of the more laid-back guards. And he took my place, volunteering to work an entire day under Little Adolf.

I was speechless as I realized that was why he'd gotten in a different line. He hadn't ditched me to avoid Little Adolf. He'd planned ahead to give me an out.

His group was gone before I could tell him thanks.

Every time I hauled a crate that day, I thought of how wonderful it was not to be on Little Adolf's crew. The day was long, the weather was cold, and my stomach was mostly empty, but my apprehension stayed at worried instead of terrified.

The terror returned during our march home. Little Adolf zeroed in on me almost at once. By the time we'd reached the warehouse, I had a new bruise on my hip and my left eye was well on its way to being swollen shut, both from the end of his carbine because I wasn't quick enough to grovel.

"Let me look at it." Winterton stood on his toes to see the swelling on my face. He cursed.

"Now Samson will be right when he says I'm half blind."

I'd thought my joke was pretty funny, but Winterton didn't even smile.

"Thanks for trading with me," I said. "Although you're kind of making me wonder. You're supposed to be a smart college kid. Don't know what volunteering to work under Little Adolf says about your intelligence."

Winterton shrugged. "He ignores me. Ignores all the others too as long as we look like we're working. He just has it in for you."

I rubbed my eye and winced. "Yeah, I've noticed."

"This week's been rough so far. But hang in there. Maybe he'll find someone new to pick on."

* * *

The next day, Winterton figured out which prisoner had told Little Adolf about my birthplace. He and Samson had a long talk with him, but there wasn't any way to take back the truth.

When we divided into work parties, Winterton switched lines with me again. When we finished for the day, Little Adolf walked beside me on the way back to the warehouse and shoved his carbine into my back because I wasn't standing up straight enough. Then he elbowed me in the chin because I wouldn't say I was sorry I'd left Germany.

I had sore muscles, a bruised back, and a bloody nose. But when we got back to the warehouse and were free of the guards, I realized that in comparison, I'd had a good day. The Welshman with hepatitis was dead.

* * *

The days soon settled into a mind-numbing, body-crushing routine. We put in long hours at the rail yards, hours that grew longer as the sun rose earlier and set later. The middle-aged lady brought bread and ersatz coffee every morning and something warm every night, usually soup but sometimes potatoes or sausage. She was a skilled cook, but the meals weren't enough to live on. After two weeks, I could see each of my ribs, and skin from my upper arms was starting to hang around my elbows. Lice crawled through our straw mattresses, and rats scurried through the warehouse shadows.

We got five Red Cross parcels the last Saturday of January to share among the twenty-nine of us, and another six the second week of February. It helped, but my stomach never felt satisfied. Five prisoners had sick days. Three of them got better. One died of hepatitis. He was from Nova Scotia. One died of pleurisy. He was from Michigan, and he happened to be the one who'd snitched on me. He'd caused me a lot of grief, but his death was still an unpleasant shock. He hadn't been a prisoner that long.

We scrounged what we could at the rail yard. One day, seven of us unloaded bags of potatoes and all of us shoved a few dozen down our pant legs while the guard flirted with a local girl.

For the most part, I didn't have to work under Little Adolf. Winterton and Samson were quick to trade places with me when he stood at the head of whatever group I was in. But most days he amused himself by pestering, pummeling, and punching me on the march back to the warehouse.

"Wonder when they're gonna give us a break," Samson mumbled as we settled another crate in the boxcar we were loading.

I leaned out of the boxcar and found the sun behind the hazy clouds. The air corps and the Royal Air Force had been busy lately, and smoke from the nearby cities they'd bombed still trailed into the sky. "It's past time." I'd saved half a piece of bread from breakfast. I was itching to eat it, but I'd probably be hungry again as soon as I swallowed the last bite.

"You know what I wish?" Samson asked.

"What?"

"I wish we woulda stripped down the corpses of some of those officers we buried or nabbed their dog tags. Then we wouldn't have to work."

"Yeah." They gave us more food than they gave the officers, but they worked us pretty hard too. "Would it get boring though, sitting in camp all day?"

Samson huffed. "You ain't bored loading and unloading boxcars all day?"

We bent to take the next crate from another pair of Americans and hauled it to the top of the stack. "Yeah, good point."

"And at the stalag, they had lectures, classes, an acting group, and cricket equipment."

"That's the last one," the prisoner who'd been bringing us crates said.

We crawled down and looked for the guard. He wasn't paying much attention, so we could relax.

"Well, that's a small break, at least." Samson leaned against the train, waiting for Red to drive the unloaded truck away and bring a new one in next to the boxcar. "Wonder what they hit over there."

I followed his eyes to the smoke in the distance. I tried to picture a map in my head. We were in a little village not far from Chemnitz, and we often watched huge groups of B-17s and B-24s fly past on their bombing runs. The smoke today was to the northeast. "Might be Dresden."

"They got any big factories there?"

I shrugged. "Don't know. Probably."

Samson turned from the smoke and looked past me, his eyes widening. "Look out, kid!"

I glanced behind me and instantly wanted to scurry under the train and sprint for the other side of the train station, but the warning had come too late. Little Adolf was heading right for me.

In the two seconds it took him to reach me, I straightened my torso and pulled back my shoulders. That had never stopped him from complaining about my posture before, but maybe it would stall him.

"Why are you not working?"

"Gefreiter Metzger, we're waiting for the next truck to pull up so we can unload it."

He slammed the end of his carbine into my stomach, and when I bent forward, he smashed it into my nose. It didn't matter that he'd been giving me a couple bruises every day for weeks—each new one still hurt. His strikes were a little more vicious than average, and it was earlier in the day than normal, but it wasn't surprising.

His next move usually involved finding something else to complain about. Today he skipped that step and went right into the next blow. He whacked my legs, and between the pain of his first hits and the fact that I was halfway starved, it wasn't long before I was on the ground with my arms pulled up to protect my head and my knees curled up to protect my stomach.

Over and over again, Little Adolf shouted German obscenities about the Americans. He was usually bitter and sadistic, but today he was out of control. If I fought back, he'd shoot me, but as he hurled his foot into my spine and pain shot up and down my back, I thought he might kill me anyway. And if I didn't do something soon, I'd be too injured to defend myself. I had to act.

Then Little Adolf kicked the back of my head, and I knew I'd waited too long. My vision blurred, and pain howled at me from a hundred different places. It was all I could do to keep my arms near my face. I heard shouts and boots running along the ground, saw Little Adolf lifting his weapon up again and again, but mostly everything turned gray, and I heard only his insults and felt only the unending agony of blow after blow after blow.

He stopped for a few moments. I'd been careful to protect my eyes, but it took some time to focus.

Little Adolf wasn't hacking away at me anymore because he was wrestling with Winterton, and Winterton was losing.

For two seconds I debated whether I should crawl away and hide, or help my friend. Little Adolf's weapon lay on the ground only a few feet from me. I reached for it, but pain shot through my arm the instant I moved. Who was I kidding? I wasn't fast enough to crawl away and hide, and I wasn't strong enough or skilled enough to help Winterton. But I had to do something. I took a deep breath, set my teeth, and inched toward the carbine.

Little Adolf kneed Winterton in the gut, making him groan and collapse into the dirt. Then Little Adolf stood and kicked his defeated opponent. He turned around and saw my arm extended toward his weapon. He yanked it from the ground and swung it into my head.

* * *

"Ley? Ley? Wake up, kid."

I forced my eyes open and squinted in the dim light. I looked past Samson to see where I was, but moving set off a bitter chorus of agony from every part of my body. "Where . . . ?" I could barely talk.

"You're back in the warehouse."

"What . . . ?" I licked my lips, still working on getting my voice going.

"When Little Adolf went nuts, I went for Neubau. Winterton heard me trying to tell him what was happening and ran ahead so he could end up with a cracked rib. I got Neubau there about the time Little Adolf gave you the knock-out. He ended it, for today, said they need you to translate so they can't beat you to death."

"You hungry? Thirsty?" It was Red's voice, but I couldn't see him.

"No, don't give him that," Samson said. "Get him some water."

I tried pushing myself into a sitting position. If my bruises had been a bitter choir before, now they were a pack of banshees. Samson helped me lean against the wall.

"Here." He handed me a cup of water and stayed long enough to make sure I could drink it by myself, then he walked back to the front of the warehouse. It sounded like the food cart had arrived.

Winterton lay on the next pallet over. His face has been spared, but I'd seen a few of the hits Little Adolf had given him. He was damaged elsewhere.

"Cracked rib, huh?" I said.

"Yeah." His voice sounded strained, like he wasn't inhaling enough air.

I wasn't sure whether to thank him for helping me or apologize for drawing him in.

When I hesitated, he spoke. "Rumor is we flattened Dresden. Maybe that's why he was worse than normal today."

"Huh?"

"The RAF's been going in at night, our air force during the day. Couple days in a row. Most of Dresden's on fire or smashed. Maybe he knew someone there."

"I wish he'd been there."

Winterton cracked a smile. "Yeah, me too."

"I'm sorry."

He glanced at me. "It was my choice."

With a few extra minutes, Little Adolf could have done a lot more damage. Winterton's distraction might have saved my life, but it had cost him. "Thanks."

He nodded.

Samson came back with soup and bread. "Ley, you probably didn't hear, but Neubau gave you two days off. Winterton got one day."

I sighed with relief, but sighing hurt my torso, so it turned into a wince.

"Take it easy, huh?"

When the food lady left and the guards locked us inside, Daniels got the radio out. The BBC reported wide success on the targeted rail yards in Dresden. When the channel grew fuzzy, Daniels switched it to a German station and asked me what they were saying.

"The normal stuff about terror-fliers."

No one wanted to listen to German propaganda. Monson, one of the British prisoners, switched the station. From the look of concentration on his face, he was hoping for something specific.

"It's been off the air for months, old boy," one of the other prisoners said.

"What's he looking for?" Samson asked.

Monson sighed. "Lili Marlene. Radio Belgrade used to play it right before ten every night. But the Russians don't play anything, not on that station." He switched the radio to classical music, and I fell asleep to that.

I didn't sleep long. When I woke, I could hear Samson's deep breathing on one side of me and Winterton's shallow breathing on the other. Across the room, one of the British prisoners was having a nightmare again and muttering in his sleep.

The warehouse was drafty, my blanket was thin, and I couldn't stop shivering. Hunger gnawed at my stomach. Red had a talent for picking things up without anyone noticing, and he shared the food he scrounged. But I was losing weight faster than Red could steal. Winterton kept saying things might get better, but they never did. Even my smart college friend doing his best couldn't keep Little Adolf from almost killing me.

Part of me wished Little Adolf had just stuck a bullet through my head, because the daily beatings were worse than a quick death. I had two days off, and then I'd have to face him again. I couldn't keep doing this. I wasn't sure how long the war would last, but I'd been a prisoner for two months, and there wasn't any way I could survive the same things again.

I was cold. I was hungry. I was lonely. Every inch of me hurt, and the more I thought about it, the more certain I was that I was going to die a prisoner. Either Little Adolf would kill me, or I'd waste away like the Russian POWs, or the SS would machine gun us all down as the front line drew closer. I thought about each option. I didn't look forward to any of them, and I didn't see any reason to keep trying. If I was going to die anyway, why keep struggling? Life as a POW was misery. The most I could look forward to was a better-than-normal dish of soup or a good joke from Samson.

I wouldn't commit suicide. I'd been taught that was wrong. But what would it take to get Little Adolf to kill me? Not much. I had two days off, and then I was certain he'd be in my face again. I'd slouch, forget to use his title, maybe talk out of turn. It wouldn't be hard to make him mad enough to pull the trigger. And then I'd be done.

And then what?

Death was so final. I believed in heaven, but death held a sting, a horror. Was I ready to give up, to never see my mom or my brother or my sisters again? And what if I worked Little Adolf into a frenzy but he didn't kill me? What if he crippled me instead?

My favorite person in the whole world was a cripple. It was odd to think of Bastien that way because he was still so capable, so confident, so in control. What would he do? I tried to imagine it for a while, but I gave up. I had a feeling if my brother the spy had been in Luxembourg, he would have stolen the German plans, gotten himself an appointment with General Eisenhower, and somehow stopped the German offensive all by himself. I couldn't do what Bastien would have done. But I knew what he'd tell me to do now. He'd tell me to pray.

I didn't at first. Before I prayed, I had to convince myself that I wanted to survive, that I wanted to make it home, that somehow the future would be worth it if I could just make it through my current hell.

Eventually I found it, the combination of memories and hopes and images of the people I loved. The look on my mom's face when I planted a patch of pansies for Mother's Day. The way Belle could play footsies and solve geometry problems at the same time. Bastien and Gracie smooching on the front porch.

I turned over and pushed myself to my knees, and a rush of pain swept through my stomach so strong I could barely breathe. I huddled over on my knees, with my forehead on the pallet. Had Little Adolf made something inside me burst apart? "Please, God," I whispered through the sharp ache. "Please help me." My pleas turned into sobs, and I covered my mouth to stifle them so I wouldn't wake anyone. But in my mind, I didn't stop begging for help until I drifted off to sleep.

* * *

I rolled over the next morning and groaned in pain.

"You okay, kid?" Samson asked.

"I think I got ran over by a panzer."

Red rubbed a hand over his face, yawned, and gave me a quick look over. "After we surrendered, I saw someone who got ran over by a panzer. Tried to move the body off the road 'cause it was one of ours, but the guards told us to keep marching. You look bad, but trust me, not that bad."

That was a sight I was glad I hadn't seen. Maybe that was the trick—being grateful. I tried it for a few seconds. I was grateful I hadn't seen an American body squashed by a tank. I was glad that only nine of my fingers hurt instead of all ten. I was thankful I had a blanket and a pallet to sleep on, even if both were infested with lice and bedbugs. Most of all, I was overjoyed that my mom and my brother and my sisters and my girlfriend weren't here because I'd hate for them to be as miserable as I was.

I managed to hobble to the food cart when the woman came with our breakfast. While most of the group marched off, Winterton and I went back to our mattresses.

"How's the rib?" I asked.

He grunted. "Could be worse. It's not a jagged break. Daniels said he thinks if I wrap it, I'll still be able to work. Red said he'd keep an eye out for something to use."

We spent the morning listening to our illegal radio and picking lice from the seams of our clothes.

"I wonder if this is what my dad did when he was in prison. Sat around and picked nits."

"Your dad was in prison?" Winterton asked.

"Yeah. In Germany, before I left. He didn't like the Nazis. Wrote some stuff and printed it in a Swiss newspaper. He used a pen name, but I guess they found out who he was, and they weren't too happy."

"So they arrested him?"

I nodded. "I didn't even get to say good-bye. They took him at night, and I slept through it." I flicked a few cooties from the sleeve of my coat. "We kept thinking he'd come home. My dad was a good man. I thought only bad people went to jail, so they'd realize they made a mistake and let him out. But a year later, we found out he was dead."

"Executed?"

"No. He got sick. Typhus or something. But they immunized us against that, right?"

"Yeah."

"I always wondered if it was worth it, him dying, leaving Mom and four kids. He might have changed a few people's minds, but he would have changed a few more people's minds if he'd been alive longer." I didn't ask it out loud, but I wondered if he'd ever cried like I had. Surely he'd wanted to get home again. Had he clung to the hope that one day he'd be free? Or had he known he'd said his last good-byes?

"Ley . . ." Winterton's voice trailed off.

"Huh?"

"I um . . . I heard you praying last night."

I concentrated on the seam in my greatcoat because finding lice on my clothes was less humiliating than knowing my friend had heard how desperate I'd been.

"Ley? Are you all right?"

I finally met his eyes. I had something else to be grateful for because he wasn't mocking me or looking at me like I was crazy. He showed the same concern I would have expected from my mom or my brother. "I don't know. Last night I had a hard time believing I'll ever make it home. Even if Little Adolf doesn't kill me, the SS might, or I'll get sick . . ."

"We'll figure out a way to keep him off you."

"How?"

"I'm not sure yet. Maybe we'll ask Red to scrounge some poison or something. But we will figure it out. And we'll make it through this together."

In the daylight, it was easier to believe I might survive, but it still seemed like the odds were stacked against us. "My dad didn't. And he was strong, and he was good, and he had a lot of reasons to live."

Winterton put his lice-free shirt on and started working on his pants. "Daniel made it out of the lion's den. And Joseph made it out of Pharaoh's prison."

"You quoting scripture to me?"

Winterton's lips pulled into a smile. "I figure you'll believe it if it's in the Bible."

"They're plenty of people who went to prison in the Bible and didn't make it out."

"Like who?"

I rolled my eyes. "Didn't you ever go to Sunday School? Jesus. Paul. Most of the Apostles."

"That was different."

"How?"

Winterton picked at his pant seam. "That was a time for martyrs."

"And this isn't?"
"No. This is a time for survivors."

CHAPTER 23

THAT EVENING, ONLY EIGHT MEN marched into the warehouse. The British prisoners were back, but none of the Americans.

"Where is everyone?" I asked as I scratched at an itch on my arm.

Daniels sat on the pallet next to mine. "They needed more workers in Dresden. They sent them there."

"Are they coming back?"

"Don't know, mate." He pulled a dirty potato sack from under his shirt and handed it to Winterton. "Red sent this for your rib." He turned to me, and a genuine smile spread across his lips. "Little Adolf went with them."

I closed my eyes. *Thank you, God.* I wasn't glad Samson and Red were gone, but nothing could beat the relief of finding out Little Adolf had left with them. Not even a hot bath and a full meal could have made me feel better.

The next morning I tied strips of the sack around Winterton's cracked rib. He'd washed the fabric the night before, but he'd had only a sliver of soap, so it wasn't clean, and the fire hadn't lasted long enough to dry it completely, so it was damp. But maybe it would keep the pain down.

The rest of the day was strange for me. It wasn't completely quiet—the wind blew through the warehouse joints, and from time to time, I heard noise from the street. But I was alone, which hadn't happened much since I'd joined the army and hadn't happened at all since I'd been captured. I had nothing but the bedbugs and lice to interact with, leaving me lots of time to think.

Winterton had mentioned a few righteous people who'd been in prison and lived, but I could think of just as many who'd been in prison and died.

For every Shadrach, there was a Stephen; for every Meshach, there was a Matthias; and for every Abednego, there was an Abinadi. And there was my dad. But if Little Adolf stayed in Dresden, I might have a chance. I thought of home and longed for my family, but most of the day, I day-dreamed about having a full belly.

I was sore when I went back to work the next day, but it was a Sunday, so we only had to work until noon. Sunday had always been a special day back home. Here it was different. Mom would have never done wash on Sunday, but we shook out our blankets, beat a few of the bed-bugs from our mattresses, and stocked the stove with plenty of wood so we could wash our clothes and not freeze while they dried.

By the middle of the next week, my muscles still pulled with pain every morning when we loaded or unloaded our first boxcar, but things were mostly back to normal—if slaving away from sunup to sundown and doing it all on barely enough food to keep a cat alive could be called normal. They stayed that way for another week.

Samson and Red and all the others came back ten days after they left. They arrived late at night, tired, dirty, and trailing the scent of death. They carried Red Cross parcels tucked under their arms, but even their food didn't seem to cheer them.

We'd listened to the radio while they were gone and heard what the Germans had said about Dresden. The Nazis claimed there weren't any war industries there. I didn't believe them. They also said the city was full of refugees. That I did believe because we saw constant trickles of civilians moving from one place to another, hauling their belongings in suitcases, potato sacks, even baby carriages.

Samson sat on his pallet. I'd seen him during the Battle of the Bulge, during a week of being locked in a boxcar, and during an attack by our own fighters when we couldn't move, but he'd never look as troubled as he did then. His cheeks were drawn in; his eyelids were tight as if in pain; his mouth was clamped shut.

"We heard all sorts of stuff about the raid. Was it as bad as they're saying it was?" I asked.

Samson looked up. He didn't speak at first, and when he did, his voice was hoarse. "It was worse, kid. Worse than anything they could describe on a radio. Imagine hell. That'll get you in the same neighborhood."

Samson was quiet the rest of the night, but bits of what they'd seen came out from the other prisoners. So many bombs had been dropped so closely together that a huge swath of Dresden was flattened. Fire had raged, and those who hadn't died in the flames had died when the firestorm had sucked away all the oxygen. My friends had been collecting corpses from the rubble.

Red gave me a handful of cigarettes and a four-ounce tin of coffee. I stared at the gift. I didn't smoke, and I didn't drink coffee, but he'd handed me Lucky Strikes and real Nescafé. I looked up in amazement.

"The lady that brings food in will give you two potatoes for each cigarette. Samson and I figured you were gonna need a miracle when Little Adolf came back. We're out of miracles, but we aren't out of Red Cross parcels. Almost as good, right? Maybe you can strike a deal with him. He was pretty upset about Dresden. Wouldn't trade with us, but maybe . . . Well, maybe you can at least have a full stomach next time he beats the snot outta you."

Fear gripped me so tightly that I could barely choke out a whispered thanks. Six cigarettes and four ounces of coffee. For a POW, that was practically a fortune. But it wouldn't do me any good against Little Adolf.

I didn't sleep well that night, and it wasn't because the stench of decomposing bodies had followed the other prisoners back from Dresden. It wasn't even because of the descriptions they'd given about the corpses they'd found: shrunk, melted, or turned to charcoal in the firestorm. The deaths were horrible, but it wasn't horror for a bunch of German civilians dying in their bomb shelters that kept me awake. It was terror at Little Adolf's return.

The next morning, Winterton switched work groups with me so I wouldn't have to work under Little Adolf, but all day, I dreaded the march back to the warehouse. When the last crate was unloaded from the last boxcar, fear filled me so completely that Red had to nudge me forward. I forced myself to breathe, tried to think of something happy. Belle's laugh. Mom's pies. The way Bastien looked at Gracie. The images helped but only for a second or two apiece.

I'd avoided looking at Little Adolf when we'd lined up for *appell* and received our assignments. But I couldn't avoid looking at him now. If anything, he seemed wider and taller. His mustache needed a trim, giving him a wild, animallike air. I looked away as he got closer, praying for deliverance, even though I knew it wouldn't happen. Little Adolf put the stock of his carbine under my chin and forced my head up.

"Your posture has not improved since I last saw you, traitor." He pushed with his carbine, ramming it into my neck.

He caught my ear with his elbow next. "Must I remind you that you are to address me as Gefreiter Metzger?"

"Yes, Gefreiter Metzger. I'm sorry, Gefreiter Metzger."

He huffed and smiled his sadistic smile.

I turned away. I couldn't duck, even if I saw him swinging, couldn't block his blows or fight back. If I wasn't looking, at least I wouldn't have to feel the anticipation that came before each strike, that instant when I knew what he was going to do and couldn't do anything about it.

My eyes caught sight of a German teenager with braided hair wrapped around the top of her head and tied with a yellow ribbon. She was beautiful as she waved and called out to our group. At first I thought she might know one of the British prisoners, but she walked straight for Little Adolf.

Funny, I'd thought she was pretty, but when she went to Little Adolf, I dismissed her. I wasn't going to think any Nazi girl was pretty. If she'd looked good from across the street, it was probably because she was clean and healthy. Yet as she strolled beside our guard, taking up his attention so he didn't pick on me, a plan began forming in my head.

That yellow ribbon just might be my salvation.

* * *

When I told Winterton my plan, he frowned. "That's crazy. If Little Adolf sees you anywhere near a girl he likes, he's going to break bones. And I'm not talking about a cracked rib; I'm talking about a flattened skull. Remember that Welshman?"

"Yeah, I remember. I'll make sure he doesn't see me. But I can't keep doing this. Unless the BBC is dead wrong, we've got at least a month, probably more like two or three before the war's over, maybe another year. I can't survive that long with him taking a swipe at me every time we walk home."

Winterton shook his head and coughed. "I still say it's crazy. But it's worth a try, and I'll help."

I saw her twice more that week but never where I could talk to her privately. Little Adolf continued to shove the end of his carbine at me on the way back to the warehouse each night, but I had hope that it would end soon, and that kept me going.

It was eight days before I finally had the chance to talk with Fräulein Yellow Ribbon without Little Adolf or anyone else seeing. I spotted her on the other side of the rail yard. She waved to someone in a passenger train as it pulled from the station, then watched it fade from sight.

"Cover for me, Red." Most of us prisoners still had dysentery more often than not, so the guards were used to us running off to take care of urgent business. I blessed my luck that I was working on a crew headed by one of the more laid-back guards and hoped he'd think it was desperation of the gut driving me away.

I watched the direction she walked and went ahead of her, anticipating where she'd go. I climbed between two boxcars, in the shadows, where no one to either side could see me.

"Fräulein, a moment, please." I waved her closer, hoping my German sounded polite, hoping she wouldn't get frightened and bolt.

She turned my direction, startled, then she folded her arms across her chest and glared.

"Please? Just a minute."

She took a step toward me, close enough that I could lower my voice but still distant enough that she could run away. She lifted her chin slightly. "You're filthy. Why would I want to talk to you?"

"Because I've got real coffee from a Red Cross parcel and American cigarettes. And I've got an easy way for you to earn them."

She stepped back. "I'm not that type of girl."

"I'm not asking you to do anything wrong."

She raised an eyebrow, and one side of her lips pulled up. "Maybe I don't smoke."

"Then you can trade. They're worth a lot."

She stuck her nose a bit higher and straightened her shoulders, making it clear that she thought I was a lower form of life. But she didn't walk away, so something I'd said must have caught her interest.

"Your boyfriend likes to beat up on prisoners on the way back from the rail yards. He really hates us, especially me."

"Of course he hates you," she said as if it was the most obvious thing in the world. "You've killed his entire family."

"What?"

"His parents are from Leipzig. They died in an air raid the first week of January. So did his sister and her two children. His brother died in France last summer. And his only surviving grandparents, plus an aunt and her entire family, died when you fire-bombed Dresden."

It had never crossed my mind that Little Adolf might hate Americans because of what we'd done rather than because of propaganda.

"Look, are you going to give me that coffee or aren't you?" she asked.

"You have to earn it."

She frowned. "How?"

"I want your help with your boyfriend."

"If you think I'm going to convince him to give you time off or a bath or real butter, then you're going to be sorely disappointed. Even if I suggested it, I doubt he'd help you. He'd like nothing better than to execute the lot of you."

"He might listen if the suggestion came from you, but you don't have to talk about us at all." I glanced around. We were still alone.

"Oh? Then what?"

"Come meet him at the end of our shift, before we leave the rail yards, and walk with him until we're safe in the warehouse."

"What's that supposed to help with?"

"When you're around, he's so busy trying to impress you that he ignores us."

She smiled, then tried to hide it. I'd seen the same look in high school when one of my friends had asked a girl to a dance—a girl who was crazy about him, according to Belle, but pretending it was no big deal. My new Nazi acquaintance with a yellow ribbon was pleased by the power she had over Little Adolf. I thought she could probably do better than a limping, unintelligent brute like him, but I doubted she wanted my advice.

"Coffee and cigarettes first," she said.

I didn't trust her, and I could get a fair trade from the woman who cooked for us. I needed more food almost as much as I needed Little Adolf distracted. It was a Monday. "You start distracting him today. Payday on Wednesday. A cigarette a day or half an ounce of coffee. I need you every evening about sunset, midday on Sunday. If you're late, we'll trade our cigarettes ourselves. Or smoke them."

She nodded.

I almost stuck my hand out so we could shake on it, but I glanced at my fingers. They were gray with black streaks under the fingernails and dark lines crossing my palms, staining the skin where it had cracked. No girl would want to touch me. "On Wednesday, meet me at the fence behind the warehouse about an hour after sunset. I'll give you the stuff then."

"Won't the guards see?"

I shook my head. "After we're fed, they go eat real food and play cards."

She stuck her chin up again and walked away.

I made sure no one was looking and ran back to the boxcar.

* * *

The next thirteen days still involved long hours of hard work with insufficient food and filthy living conditions, but Fräulein Yellow Ribbon turned out to be a good employee. She was on time every day, she distracted Little Adolf so completely that my only bruises were from banging my shins on crates, and she was discreet when collecting payment.

For her first payday, I gave her an ounce and a half of coffee. The next one was the rest of the coffee and two cigarettes. On the morning of her third payday, I owed her seven cigarettes. I had only four.

Prisoners were supposed to get one Red Cross parcel each week. That hadn't happened regularly since early 1944, according to Daniels. A full American parcel had five cigarette packages, so I should have had eighty cigarettes a week—more than enough to pay Little Adolf's girlfriend and trade for food. With that many cigarettes, even sharing the parcel would have left me with enough to pay my debt. But as February turned to March and my supply of coffee and cigarettes disappeared, no new parcels arrived.

I shifted uncomfortably on my mattress and jerked my hand up to scratch at a flea. What would Fräulein Yellow Ribbon do when I could pay her only half? Would she tell Little Adolf? If she did, he'd probably pound me.

"Ley, you awake?" Winterton's voice was groggy, and I wondered if I'd woken him.

"Yeah."

He grunted and coughed. I thought he'd go back to sleep. The crack between the roof and the wall was gray instead of black. Dawn was coming, but we had a few more minutes of rest.

"You okay?" he whispered.

"For now, I guess."

"Then what's with the fidgeting?"

I sighed. "I owe Little Adolf's girlfriend seven cigarettes. I'm three short."

"She seems to like him. Maybe she'll walk with him anyway."

"Maybe." But I thought it more likely that she'd purposely see him another time—after work, for example—just to spite me. Or tell him about our deal and how I'd cheated her. He'd probably beat me once because I'd talked to his girl and then again because I hadn't delivered what I'd promised. She wouldn't know I couldn't pay until that night, so I had one more day without the end of Little Adolf's carbine ramming repeatedly into my torso. But Thursday was a different story. Thursday was going to be brutal.

Eventually the sun rose on my last day with a bruise-free body. While we washed and shaved, I overheard Winterton asking Samson if he had any cigarettes.

"Ha," Samson said. "I stretched them out a week. Wasn't that long enough?"

Once we got to the rail yards, Feldwebel Neubau told us to line up in three different groups. Little Adolf, as usual, went to the head of the column I'd lined up in. He turned around to lead us to our assignment, and Winterton and I switched groups. And as we switched, he handed me three cigarettes.

"Where did you get these?" I asked.

Winterton just smiled and marched off.

Thursday no longer seemed like the end of the world.

* * *

That night, we had mail call. I sent the regulation four postcards and two letters we were allowed every month, but I hadn't heard from anyone since Luxembourg, and the most recent mail call was no exception. They were probably writing; the letters just weren't getting through.

After supper, I sneaked through one of the warehouse's partially boarded up back windows and waited by the fence. We were supposed to be locked in, other than when we were using the privies, but before the rest of us arrived, the British prisoners had found a way to get to the loading grounds in the back of the warehouse. It didn't do anyone much good. The chain-link fence was topped with barbed wire and its cement foundation would take days to tunnel under. Even if we got past the fence, where would we go? We were too skinny to blend in with the local population, and we wore enemy uniforms. Sneaking outside was good when we wanted to trade with civilians. That was about it.

When Fräulein Yellow Ribbon arrived, she held her hand out. I put seven cigarettes there and prayed a Red Cross parcel would come soon because, otherwise, what I'd feared would happen tomorrow would happen next week instead.

She glanced at them and held one up to show me. "This is a different brand."

"It's the best I could do."

She frowned and stuck them in her pocket. "I'm not sure I can keep doing this."

"Doing what? Walking home with your boyfriend?"

"He's not my boyfriend." She crossed her arms and sulked. "And I don't want him to be my boyfriend, not anymore. He's not very smart once you get to know him. And he's not very thoughtful either. So if you want me to put up with him, you're going to have to do better. Ten cigarettes a week."

I let out a low whistle. "I don't know where I'm going to get ten cigarettes a week."

"Figure it out. Or you can distract your guard yourself." She marched off.

Later, I asked Winterton where he'd gotten the extra cigarettes.

"I had one left. Bummed one off Red and one off the Canadian."

I thought about how many times Little Adolf could jab his carbine into my ribs on an average walk from the rail yards to the warehouse and about how hard he'd hit if his girlfriend put him in the brush-off club. Winterton had saved me again.

* * *

By the next Tuesday, I was starting to get nervous. I owed Fräulein Yellow Ribbon ten cigarettes. I didn't have any, and no one else did either. But that night, the twenty-seven of us got three American Red Cross parcels. My share included nine cigarettes and an ounce of coffee. As I feasted on biscuits slathered in margarine, I said a prayer of gratitude. I was safe for another week.

Winterton handed me his share of smokes too, minus the cigarettes he'd repaid the Canadian and Red. That was almost enough for another week, but Winterton was starting to look a little like the Russian POWs, and his coughing fits were getting worse.

"Are you sure you shouldn't keep these?"

Winterton shook his head. "Inhaling deep enough to smoke hurts. It's not worth it."

"Yeah, but seven cigarettes could get you a lot of potatoes."

He held up a can of Spam. "I've got this for now." He nodded toward an empty powdered-milk can. "And I can fry it in that."

Later that night, I saw Winterton talking to Samson and Red. Not long after, Samson gave me his coffee, and Red gave me four of his cigarettes. I was safe for another two weeks, with a start on payment for a third.

The next few days were better than average. We had extra food from our parcels and no beatings from Little Adolf. Sunday afternoon, we boiled water and had warm baths with Red Cross soap. For the first time in months, I smelled like a human instead of an animal.

Fräulein Yellow Ribbon kept doing her job, but she looked at the ground more than she looked at Little Adolf, and her part in their conversations went from exuberant to merely polite. Little Adolf didn't seem to notice, but everyone else did.

"She doesn't look very happy," Winterton whispered on the way back to the warehouse. She had taken Little Adolf's arm when he'd offered it, but her face was expressionless.

"Maybe she figured out he's mean and stupid."

Winterton coughed, then winced. "I hope she can last until the army gets here."

The BBC had good news almost every night. The Soviets were pushing in from the east, and the British and Americans were pushing in from the west. Germany was losing. It just wasn't losing fast enough.

CHAPTER 24

WHEN FRÄULEIN YELLOW RIBBON'S NEXT payday rolled around, I was afraid she'd ask for a raise, since she obviously wasn't excited about Little Adolf anymore. When we met by the fence, she took the combination of coffee and cigarettes and shoved them in her pocket. "I'm finished. I can't do this anymore."

"I'm paying you the best I can," I said. "I can't get you any more because the Red Cross parcels aren't coming like they should. I'm already begging and borrowing from the other prisoners. So, please, take what I can pay, put up with Gefreiter Metzger a little longer, and enjoy your coffee and whatever you can trade the cigarettes for."

She sighed and put her fingers through the links in the fence. "How did I get myself into this mess?"

I had two older sisters, so I knew better than to answer her question, but I also knew she wanted to talk. "What mess?"

"Metzger. I met him the day before I came by the rail yards that first time. I was on my way home, and he offered to carry my bundle of wood for me. You can't know what it's like, growing up this way. Half the boys I went to school with are dead, and the others are missing or wounded so horribly they'll never have a normal life. Do you know how scary that is— to realize the war is going to end, and Germany is going to lose, and everyone my age is going to be dead? They're calling up fifteen-year-olds now!"

"How old are you?"

"Seventeen."

"How old is Gefreiter Metzger?"

"Thirty."

If some thirty-year-old had tried to date one of my sisters when either of them was seventeen, Bastien would have broken both the man's legs. The best advice I could give Fräulein Yellow Ribbon was *run*, but that wasn't what I said. "Can you put up with him just a little longer? The war might be over in a week or two." I'd given her a ridiculously optimistic time frame, but I was desperate.

She shook her head. "I don't know where you're getting your information, but the war isn't going to be over that soon. Not here. And Metzger's getting pushy. I've been so afraid that all the men will die and I'll live my whole life and never even be kissed, but his kisses are rough. I'd rather kiss a lice-ridden kriegie."

At the mention of lice, I was tempted to scratch an itch behind my left ear, but I stopped myself. My legs were tired though, so I turned my back on Fräulein Yellow Ribbon and sat, leaning against the fence. "I've never seen him try to kiss you while he's guarding us. You don't have to see him other than on your walks, do you?"

She sat on the other side of the fence, only inches away from me. I hadn't been that close to a girl since I left for the induction station. An ache grew in my chest. I missed my mom, and I missed Belle. I wanted to be home in Virginia, not stuck behind wire in some dinky town in Germany.

"My name's Ilsa."

I glanced over my shoulder at her. My first impression of her had been right. She was pretty. If women were flowers, Belle would be a daffodil. Gracie was a lily. Ilsa was a rose. And she probably had thorns to match the ones on Mrs. Thompson's big pink rose bush. I frowned. I had to stop thinking about home. The memories hurt too much.

"What's your name?" Ilsa asked.

"Private Ley."

"No, your first name."

"Lukas."

"How old are you, Lukas?"

I almost said eighteen, but I realized I wasn't sure. "What day is it?"

"March 14."

"Nineteen." I'd had a birthday, and I hadn't even noticed. "Thanks for distracting Metzger. He didn't give me a black eye or a bloody lip for a birthday present last week."

Ilsa sighed. "It's not that I want Metzger to beat you up—I don't. But I don't want him to hurt me either."

"Will he hurt you if you keep walking him from the rail yard to the warehouse and stay away from him the rest of the time?"

"Maybe. Maybe not. But he might hurt me anyway if I tell him to get lost. Mostly I'm worried about what he'll do if he gets me alone somewhere."

I had firsthand knowledge of how mean Little Adolf could be. I couldn't picture him being gentle with anything, not even a girl. I wanted him distracted but not at Ilsa's expense. Nazi or not, no girl deserved that.

"Where did you learn German?" she asked.

"I was born in Frankfurt."

Her eyes widened. "And you left?"

"Yeah."

She tilted her head toward me. "Maybe you were the lucky one."

The air-raid siren sounded. I thought about the destruction I'd seen throughout Germany, about Ilsa's desperation, about the coming defeat. Yep, I'd been the lucky one.

Ilsa rushed to her feet. "I better go. I'll try it another week because I like you better without scrapes on your face and because I've almost saved enough cigarettes to trade for a new dress. But if he gets too pushy, I'm done."

* * *

When I crawled back into the warehouse, Samson was waiting.

"You out there talking to that kraut girl this whole time?"

I nodded, preparing myself for a lecture on fraternizing with the enemy.

He grunted. "Well, if you ever want to do more than talk, let me know. I think I can get you through the fence and back."

"What?"

"Red snagged a pair of wire cutters."

"When?"

"In Dresden."

"What are you still doing in here, then?" I asked. Samson had wanted to escape since Stalag IVB. Now it was possible, so why was he waiting?

"Where're we gonna go in dirty American uniforms? I soaked up what I could in Mühlberg. If we want to get out and stay out for more than five minutes, we need civilian clothes or German uniforms. A compass or a weapon would come in handy too. So would food, but it's not like we get much in here anyway."

"What about papers?"

He pursed his lips. "We're hoping we can make it without papers long enough to get to the front lines. They're getting closer."

"Not close enough."

"Not yet, maybe. But do ya think you could ask that girl to get us some civilian clothes? We'll find something to trade, even if we have to rob those boxcars we're unloading. Red and I are taking off for sure. You and Winterton can come too."

"And the others?"

He shook his head. "Big groups always get caught. They can take off if they want, but they have to come up with their own plan."

Escape. Simply thinking the word made me stand a little taller. I might run out of cigarettes and coffee to pay off Ilsa, but when that happened, there was suddenly an option other than being Little Adolf's punching bag.

The next day, I caught Ilsa looking at me more than once while she walked beside Little Adolf. She must have been pretty desperate. I hadn't glanced in the mirror much lately, but I assumed I looked like everyone else: dirty, skinny, with sunken cheeks and dirt-encrusted hands. Maybe it didn't take much to seem more appealing than Metzger.

Samson cornered me in the warehouse that night right before supper. "I think she likes you."

I shrugged. "And?"

"Stay on her good side. It might be useful."

I nodded, but if Ilsa was interested, it was only because Germany had a dwindling population of young men and I was in the right age group and spoke the right language.

I sat next to Winterton for cabbage soup. His skin was pale and his breathing shallow. "Are you all right?" I asked.

He shook his head. "Must have a cold or something. Nothing liberation can't fix."

Liberation. According to the BBC, the British and American troops were well into Germany now. The western part of Germany. We were to the southeast.

"What was Samson bugging you about?"

"Little Adolf's girl. She wanted to chat last night when I paid her. She's seventeen and desperate for romance, but she doesn't like Little Adolf."

"But she likes you." He stated it as a fact rather than a question.

"Even if I wasn't locked up in a warehouse, I wouldn't want some Nazi girl."

Winterton had a bad coughing fit. I refilled his tin of water, and eventually, his lungs calmed down. "Is she a Nazi?"

"Ilsa? I don't know. Maybe not. But I've got a girl back home."

Winterton took another sip of water. "What's she like?"

"Belle? She's smart. Probably as smart as you." Talking about her made me miss her, but I didn't stop. "She's got a laugh that makes me feel like everything in the whole world is going to turn out all right. She's pretty, and she always smells good. Quiet but passionate about what she feels is right. And her fingers are magic when she's giving neck rubs."

"She sounds perfect."

I inspected the night's soup, then glanced away when I noticed the weevils. It was better to swallow them without looking. "She's not perfect. When she's reading a good book, it's like she goes into a trance or something and doesn't remember anything you say to her. And she burns stuff all the time when she cooks." I finished my soup. "But I'd take her burned pancakes over this stuff anytime."

Winterton smiled. "I wonder if charred pancakes would help with dysentery the way charcoal does?"

I snickered. If the portion was enough to fill my stomach and if Belle was involved, I'd eat burned food every day for the rest of my life without complaining.

Four days later, Winterton's cough took a sharp turn for the worse.

"I think it's pleurisy," Daniels said.

Winterton frowned but was otherwise calm. More calm than I was.

"What can we do?" I asked.

Daniels shook his head. "We can't do anything here. He should be in hospital."

When it was time to report for work, Feldwebel Neubau excused Winterton for the day.

"Can you get him into a hospital?" I asked as I followed Neubau out to the yard in front of the warehouse.

He shook his head. "I'm not allowed to move anyone without orders."

"Can you talk to your superior and ask?"

Neubau glanced back at the warehouse. "I can ask. But the answer will be no."

As he walked away, I understood. He didn't *want* Winterton to die. But he didn't care enough to fight. Just like he didn't *want* any of us to be abused, but he wasn't going stop Little Adolf from having a little fun.

I heard a step and a rush and felt a whack on the back of my head that knocked me to the ground.

Metzger stood over me, his carbine gripped in his hands. "You are not to address Feldwebel Neubau without permission."

I forced my clenched fists to relax. "Yes, Gefreiter Metzger," I said through gritted teeth.

One of the other guards called to him, distracting him. I took a few deep breaths, trying to calm down. I couldn't help Winterton if I provoked Metzger into crippling or killing me.

When we divided into teams at the rail yard, Metzger went to the head of my group. Samson switched with me. All day long, I pestered the other prisoners for anything they knew about pleurisy. It was an inflammation of the tissue around the lungs involving lots of pain and sometimes fluid retention.

"My granddad had it," one of the British prisoners said. "They drew out some of the fluid with a needle, but it got infected, and he died anyway."

If I had pleurisy, Winterton would do everything he could to help me. I intended to do the same. When the lady brought us supper that night, I ignored the food and went to talk to her.

"One of my friends needs a doctor. Can you help?"

"I am sorry for your friend, but there is nothing I can do."

I held up a cigarette. "Please?"

She glanced at the Lucky Strike and hesitated. "I will ask."

The next day when we returned from work, I rushed to Winterton's straw pallet. His breathing was shallow, his face pale, and his muscles set in a grimace of pain.

"How bad is it?"

He turned his face toward me, the movement slow and labored. "Nothing liberation can't cure."

"Yeah." I felt his forehead. He had a fever. "Not much longer now. The war's almost over, and you're going to make it through, remember?"

"That's right." His voice was soft and raspy.

I sat beside him until the German woman brought our food. A gray-haired man in civilian clothing followed her into the warehouse. The cook motioned for me, and I practically ran.

"This is Herr Meyer. I told him you would pay with cigarettes."

"*Herr* Meyer?"

"He works with sick horses."

I wanted a doctor, not a veterinarian, but the pleading look in the woman's eyes told me she'd done the best she could do. "My friend's this way." I led him to Winterton's pallet.

Herr Meyer, the horse doctor, listened to Winterton's breathing, checked his temperature and pulse, and did a few other tests. I translated his questions about when various symptoms had begun and how severe they were.

After a thorough exam, Herr Meyer stood and turned to me. "I believe it is pleurisy, advanced to a dangerous level. He needs to be in a hospital. The fluid around his lungs has built up, and that puts pressure on his chest, making it difficult to breathe."

"Can you get him to a hospital?"

Herr Meyer shook his head.

"Can you remove the fluid here?"

"No. I've never removed fluid from a human before. I might kill him." Meyer looked around. "And the conditions here would likely lead to infection, even if I succeeded. I'm sorry. Unless you get penicillin in those Red Cross parcels, the best you can do is make him comfortable."

He took all my remaining cigarettes as payment.

* * *

"Ilsa?"

She approached the fence the moment I called her name. "Hello, Lukas." Her lips curved into a smile and the scent of perfume wafted toward me.

I waited for her to lean into the fence. "I need your help."

"With what?"

"I need penicillin for a friend."

She gave a short laugh. "Do you have any idea how impossible it is to get penicillin around here?"

"Someone in town has to have some. If not penicillin, then something else that would help him fight his infection. For the right price, they'll sell."

She tilted her head as she thought. "Maybe . . . No, they'd never trade with a POW."

"Who?"

"Obersturmbannführer Wagner. His son was injured on the eastern front. He's home recovering, and I heard his wounds are infected. If anyone in town has medicine like that, he does. There's his father's rank, and his mother's family all have party connections."

"Where does he live?"

"You walk past it every day. The big house near the library with all the pine trees. Not that it matters. Even if you got permission to trade, they'd never give up their son's medicine for an American prisoner. Not unless you have gold bars to trade with."

I knew the house. "Would he trade with you if I sent you?"

Ilsa shook her head. "They'd want to know why, and I'm obviously healthy."

"You can make something up. You don't have to tell them it's for a POW."

"What's in it for me?"

I had nothing to bargain with. No coffee, no cigarettes. I couldn't even offer letting her off the hook when Little Adolf marched us back to the warehouse because I already owed her a week of back pay. "My undying gratitude?"

She huffed. "Gratitude won't buy me a new dress or get me extra bread."

"Please! My friend is dying!"

She stepped back from the fence. "People are dying all over. I can't save everyone, not if I want to survive. I'm sorry about your friend. But you better give me those cigarettes before one of the guards catches us."

"Um, Ilsa . . . I don't have anything for you today. I'll pay you as soon as the next Red Cross parcel comes."

"When will that be?"

"I have no idea."

"So maybe never?" The skin around her eyes tightened in anger. "I should have known better than to trust a filthy POW!"

Ilsa's temper flared, and so did mine. "You're worried about a few cigarettes? My friend is dying!"

"I walked Gefreiter Metzger from the rail yards to the warehouse seven times last week, and I hated every second of it, but I put up with him for you because I thought you were different." She shook her head. "But you're just like him! Using me, and never once thinking about what I want, what I need." She stormed off.

I let my head fall into the chain-link fence. Winterton's fever was spiking, and every breath he took looked like it caused him pain. He needed help, and I'd just lost my most promising contact. I had a feeling Ilsa wasn't going to distract Little Adolf the next day. If she told him she wasn't interested, he might have more frustration than usual to work out on me, which meant I couldn't count on being able to walk tomorrow evening.

If I wanted to save my friend, I had to act tonight.

CHAPTER 25

SAMSON SAT NEXT TO WINTERTON while everyone listened to the radio.

"Samson?" I said.

He caught my urgent whisper and joined me in a back corner of the warehouse. "What is it, kid?"

"Can I borrow your wire cutters?"

He raised an eyebrow. "That pretty little kraut girl wants your extended company, huh?"

I blew out a frustrated breath. "You think I'd be chasing a skirt at a time like this?" I glanced back toward the row of mattresses. "How is he?"

Samson looked at the floor. "Bad."

"Ilsa told me where I might find some medicine. I'm going to go get it."

"Where?"

"That big house with the pine trees we pass every day. A guy named Obersturmbannführer Wagner owns it, and his son is ill. Ilsa thought he might have penicillin."

"Obersturmbannführer . . . What rank is that?"

"It's like a lieutenant colonel in the SS."

Samson looked around to make sure no one was close enough to hear us. "You want me to risk our escape plans so you can go ask some SS lieutenant colonel if he'll give you penicillin for a sick POW?"

"No. I want you to lend me those wire cutters so I can go steal it."

"Little goody-two-shoes Ley is going to burglarize an SS lieutenant colonel's house? Kid, you aren't thinking straight. Have you ever stolen a thing in your life?"

"I filched my share of potatoes when we unloaded that shipment awhile back. And I've grabbed plenty of firewood without the guards noticing."

Samson folded his arms across his chest. "That's a lot different than breaking into an occupied home."

"I know. But I can't sit here and watch Winterton die and not do anything to help. We can't get him to a hospital. So he needs medicine. And Ilsa's not too happy that I gave her stash of cigarettes to the vet. That means Little Adolf is going to wallop me tomorrow, so it has to be tonight."

Samson sighed and looked away. "Wait here."

He came back a few minutes later with Red.

"I'll come with you," Red said. "I've, uh . . . Well, I grew up in a rough neighborhood. We didn't have much of anything, not even food. I've done this type of thing before."

I never thought I'd be grateful to have an experienced thief for a friend, but I was more nervous than I wanted to admit. Having Red along made the excursion a lot more likely to succeed.

He looked back to make sure no one had followed. "We should wait till the others are asleep. If they don't know what we're up to, they can't try to talk us out of it or decide on a mass escape that would get the whole town out looking for us."

I nodded. "All right. It's just a normal evening till everyone settles down."

We listened to the BBC's report on the Red Army taking Hungary and the Marine Corps securing Iwo Jima. What I really wanted to hear was that the Americans had crossed the Rhine and were advancing at breakneck speed toward the Elbe, but they weren't that far east yet.

"How was Ilsa?" Winterton asked. There was a pause between each word, and even then I could barely hear him.

"I think I've probably seen the last of her. But I think Little Adolf has probably seen the last of her too, and he's going to miss her a lot more than I will."

"That's not good."

I shrugged. I knew the consequences of angering Ilsa, but I was trying not to think about them. "How do you feel?"

He sounded awful, and he looked awful, but he closed his eyes and said, "Not too bad."

I didn't believe him. I was relieved when his breathing relaxed and he drifted off. Sleep had to help, didn't it?

I was even more relieved when most everyone else fell asleep and Red slipped away from his mattress. I waited about a minute, then I followed.

Samson joined us a few moments later. He pried a loose board from the wall and took out a bundle. The wire cutters were wrapped inside a pair of civilian pants. He'd said they'd picked them up in Dresden. They must have come from the bottom of a rubble pile. The stripped handles and spots of rust didn't give me much confidence, but I was desperate, and sometimes desperation was more powerful than confidence.

Samson came with us to the back fence. He handed me his cigarette lighter. "Since I can't give you a flashlight." I slipped it into my pocket while he grabbed the bottom of the chain-link fence and grunted as he tried to compress the handles.

"Are they dull?" Panic sank in. Without working wire cutters, Winterton was dead.

Samson strained as he worked the beat-up tool. "I don't know, kid. They ain't so sharp, and I'm not as strong as I used to be."

It ended up taking two of us, each pushing one side of the handles in from the opposite direction. Red kept watch to make sure the guards hadn't suddenly incorporated patrols into their night-time routine. We clipped a two-foot-high line. Samson pulled on one side while I pulled on the other. Red slithered out and held the hole open for me to escape through.

"Good luck," Samson whispered.

I fingered the clipped fence, wondering if the guards would notice. Samson would hide his wire cutters as soon as Red and I took off, but if the guards searched, would they find them?

I shrugged off my worry. I had enough to be nervous about without thinking of something that might not even happen. I followed Red along the alley at the back of the warehouse. He crouched in a shadow as we reached the main road.

"We've got all night," he whispered. "Better to wait and take it slow than to rush and make a mistake."

"All right."

"I'm gonna be surprised if the krauts have their own penicillin. They don't make it, so they'd only have it if they stole it from us. But they might have something useful, even if it's just aspirin for the pain. Medicine's on the top of our list, but I'm also hoping to get civilian clothes. And food."

Stealing an SS officer's supper sounded appealing, so appealing that I should have been worried by how weak my conscience was. "Should we go?"

"Let's watch the road awhile first."

I dampened down my impatience and put my trust in Red. The moon was a half circle, sinking toward the horizon. It would disappear before we finished. Blackout curtains blocked any light from nearby buildings, but it wasn't completely dark. In the distance, rumbles sounded, and the glow of bombs and antiaircraft searchlights lit the horizon. The Royal Air Force was busy tonight.

Eventually, we moved off. I stepped quietly, like Bastien had taught me, and kept my eyes moving, searching for anyone who might thwart us. Remembering Bastien's advice to always have a weapon, I picked up a sturdy stick.

Obersturmbannführer Wagner's house was quiet when we arrived. Red led us around the edge of the property to the back of the building. It was a two-story structure, large enough that I guessed it had at least eight rooms, maybe more if they were small. A sliver of light shone in one of the upper story windows through a wrinkle in the blackout curtains. Someone was still awake.

"Do you think that's where the sick son is?"

Red pursed his lips. "Maybe. If I remember right, most antibiotics have to be given every few hours. Maybe he's getting a dose now."

We waited. Eventually the light dimmed. Then we waited again. The moon had slipped beneath the horizon, so it was darker. I guessed it was past midnight.

Red put his hand on my shoulder to get my attention. "No talking while we're in there unless you absolutely have to," he whispered. "Move slowly; move quietly; don't take unnecessary risks."

I nodded.

He led me to the back door and tested the knob. It was locked. We went to a nearby window and got it open an inch. Red took the stick I'd picked up and forced it into the crack to unfasten the latch. On the third attempt, he pushed the hook from its socket. He opened the window, and I cringed as it let out a squeak. Red stopped. My heart pounded, and I strained to hear a reaction from someone in the house. But the noise hadn't been that loud, and whoever was inside probably slept on the upper floor.

After a few minutes of silence, Red motioned me in. I gripped the window ledge and pulled myself inside. The window was about hip height, but clambering up without making any noise was a challenge. I'd had more muscle when I was twelve. My right knee came to rest on a countertop, and my left knee sank into a sink. Cold water soaked through the thread-bare fabric of my pants. At least I hadn't landed on a butcher knife. Even though Red had asked for silence, I turned around to whisper a warning. "The sink is right under the window, and it's full of water."

I helped Red through, and when the blackout curtains were smoothed to block our light, I lit Samson's cigarette lighter. In the dim glow, the kitchen seemed tidy. Red opened a door and discovered a pantry with bread, potatoes, and jars of preserved fruit. My mouth watered. Why hadn't we broken out of the warehouse before to raid local pantries?

The next door led to a corridor with a dining room, a study, and a spacious parlor all branching off of it. The downstairs was deserted. A staircase wound up from the side of the parlor. I took the carved railing in one hand and stepped onto the first stair, staying on the side, where it was less likely to creak. Red followed behind me as we slowly made our way upstairs to a long hallway.

Red motioned for me to put the lighter out, and I complied. The hallway was black, except for a dim crack of light shining underneath a door. Red tugged on my shoulder. "That's the room. Follow me."

I couldn't see or hear him, so when the door with the glow under it silently opened, I was several feet away. Red's shadow crossed in front of the light, and I waited for someone to demand who had broken into their house. But silence greeted us. I slipped into the room behind him. On the bed lay a man of about twenty with a bandage wrapped around his fore-head. His pale skin held a grayish hue despite the warm light of a candle burning on a nearby dressing table. The man's eyes were closed, his breathing labored but steady.

I went to the table, hoping to see syringes and vials of penicillin. There were no needles. But a metal tin of sulfa tablets that looked like it came from an American medic caught my eye, and I slipped it into my pocket. I grabbed one of the clean washcloths too but left the shallow bowl of water.

Red opened the wardrobe. It let out a squeak, and the patient mumbled and turned in bed. Red and I stood completely still, waiting to see if he'd wake. After a minute, his breathing returned to normal. Red grabbed a fistful of clothes from the cracked wardrobe and motioned toward the door. My muscles were so tense I had to force them to relax before I could move. We'd gotten medicine, but I'd about had a heart attack.

I lit Samson's cigarette lighter, and we both tiptoed to the stairs. A door across from the patient's room opened, and I smothered the light.

"Erwin, are you awake?" the German voice asked. It was a woman, but we couldn't see her in the pitch black. I hoped that meant she couldn't see us either, and I prayed she hadn't noticed the glow of the lighter in the instant after she'd cracked her door and before I'd doused it.

She went into her son's room, so I continued down the stairs slowly. Red bumped into the back of me, and I stepped a little quicker.

"Rudolph!" the woman shouted.

If I had to guess, I'd say Rudolph was Obersturmbannführer Wagner, and his wife had noticed something was missing.

We reached the bottom of the stairs before I heard another door opening and shutting upstairs. We felt along the hallway of the dark, unfamiliar house, wanting to run but afraid of making too much noise.

"Light," Red whispered.

I cupped my hand over the lighter to hide as much of the glow as I could. When it flashed to life, Red unlocked the back door and the two of us sprinted for the edge of the property. When we'd first arrived, we'd approached from the front, but I wanted to put distance between me and the SS Obersturmbannführer as quickly as I could, and I think Red felt the same way.

That meant scaling the back fence. It was made of iron rods five feet high. I'd barely been able to climb into the kitchen window, but Red gave me a leg up, and I was over in a matter of seconds. I grabbed his arms and helped him over next, and then we ran along the next yard until we reached a residential street.

"That was close," I whispered.

There was hardly any light outside, but I thought I heard a smile in Red's voice. "I've had closer."

* * *

"You know what I wish?" I said when we got back to the fence surrounding the warehouse.

"What?"

"That we'd put a few bags of food by the back door so we could grab them on the way out." My stomach was cramped into a knot. Part of it was tension from the near discovery by an SS officer, but I was also hungry. I couldn't remember the last time I hadn't been hungry.

We sneaked back to our mattresses, and for the first time, I really looked at the tin of sulfa pills. They were definitely American. I thought it fitting that they'd be used to save an American POW.

Samson sat up when we arrived and lit a misshapen candle—I wasn't sure where it had come from. "Well?"

"Got a few things. Not as much as we wanted," Red whispered. "Someone heard us, but they didn't see us."

"So is a search party out looking for you?"

"Not that we saw."

Samson nodded. "I'm going to tie up that fence so it doesn't look cut."

Red held up the handful of clothes. "We need to hide these."

The two of them headed off. "Wait, Samson, you were in a hospital," I said. "How often should I give Winterton a sulfa pill?"

Samson was a few mattresses down, but he turned back. "How many are in there?"

"Nine."

"Give him two now, with lots of water. Two more in the morning."

One of the other prisoners grunted, no doubt unhappy to have his sleep interrupted. I went to the sink. The plumbing hadn't worked the day before, but now water poured from the tap, filling a mug that I took back to Winterton. His forehead was hot, and his breathing was shallow and strained.

"Winterton?"

He groaned.

"Winterton, wake up." I grabbed his shoulder. "Wake up, buddy."

He opened his eyes and squinted at the candle light. "What?"

"I've got some medicine for you." He grimaced as I helped him sit. "Swallow these." I handed him two pills.

He winced as he moved his hand to his mouth, but he followed my directions, washing them down with water. "What is it?" Each word was an effort.

"Sulfa pills."

"Where did you get sulfa pills?"

"Never mind. Just get some sleep and start getting better."

He nodded off again. I listened for a while, waiting for his breathing to sound less pained, but maybe sulfa pills didn't work that fast. By the time Red and Samson returned, I was exhausted. I had a feeling the next day would have its challenges, including an empty stomach and some unwanted attention from Little Adolf, but for now, I could sleep with ease. Winterton was going to get better. He had to.

CHAPTER 26

WHEN DAWN CAME, I WANTED to roll over and go back to sleep. But there was more commotion than usual, and when Samson shook my shoulder, I couldn't ignore it.

"Up, kid. The guards are searching everything."

"Do they think . . . ? Do they know about last night?"

Samson looked around. His voice was quiet when he spoke. "I don't think they know about the burglary. But they saw the cut fence."

I hid the tin of sulfa tablets in the ankle of my sock. Then we stood to attention at the edge of our mattresses while Feldwebel Neubau and one of the other guards counted to make sure none of us had disappeared overnight. Everyone stood except Winterton. Samson hadn't been able to wake him, and he wouldn't have been able to stand anyway. I watched with concern. How was I supposed to get his next dose of sulfa in him if he wasn't awake to swallow?

"Out," Feldwebel Neubau commanded when he finished his count.

We went to the courtyard in front of the warehouse and waited.

"What's going on?" I asked Daniels.

"They're looking for anything we shouldn't have."

"Do you think they'll find the radio?"

"I hope not, mate. Probably a capital offense."

We shivered in the early morning cold for what I guessed was an hour. Finally, Neubau and the other guard came out. They had neither radio nor wire cutters with them, so our secrets were safe, for now.

"You have an hour to eat and tidy your quarters," Neubau said.

I translated, impressed with his generosity—our single slice of bread would take a minute to eat, not an hour. Then we walked back inside. He wasn't being generous; he was being practical. They'd torn the place apart. A few of the men cursed. Monson, one of the British prisoners, walked to one of the upturned boxes we'd been using as a table and set it upright. The rest of us followed his lead and got to work. I straightened a few things, but as soon as I found a mug, I went to fill it with water so I could give Winterton his medicine.

Something was going on back by the mattresses, but I ignored it. The guards had probably ruined a few pallets when they'd searched the place. Being short on bedding was a problem, but for now, I needed to focus on getting Winterton his pills before we were marched off to the rail yards. I let myself hope that Little Adolf was sick and that was why Neubau hadn't brought him, but I didn't really believe it, and fear of an undistracted Little Adolf gnawed at my stomach.

"Ley!" Samson called.

"Yeah?"

"You better get over here."

Something in his tone sent icicles down my spine, chilling me as thoroughly as the Ardennes Forest. I took the partially full mug back to our sleeping area. A group of POWs had gathered around Winterton's mattress. They parted as I arrived. Winterton lay completely still, his eyes staring unblinking at the ceiling. Samson crouched over him with his fingers pressed into Winterton's neck. He held his position for a long time, then shook his head and reached up to close Winterton's eyes.

I knew what that meant, but I couldn't believe it. "What's wrong?"

No one answered.

"But we got him sulfa pills! He's supposed to be getting better!" I knelt by his mattress and shook his shoulder. "Come on, wake up."

He didn't move.

I shook his shoulder again.

He still didn't move.

I grabbed the tin of pills from my sock, wondering if we'd stolen the wrong thing. "These are really sulfa, aren't they?"

Daniels took them and licked one. "They're sulfa. But sulfa pills can't do anything about the fluid buildup. I'm sorry, mate." Daniels and most of the others left to finish tidying up.

Samson had already checked for a pulse, but I checked again. "No. No. No!" I grabbed both shoulders and shook him hard. "You said we were going to make it through this together! You can't die!"

"Ley." Samson's hand rested on my arm, but I jerked away from his grasp.

"You lied!" I shouted at Winterton's body and beat my fist into his chest. "We were going to hold out no matter what they did to us, and you lied!" I choked on the emotion building in my throat and pounded his chest again.

Samson grabbed my arm again, harder than before. This time I couldn't shake his grip. "Ley, it's too late. You did the best you could, but he's gone."

I threw him off and stomped away. I wanted to run. I wanted to punch someone. I wanted to yell. And I wanted to sob. But what I ended up doing was nothing at all.

* * *

The rest of the day was a blur. I unloaded box after box, carton after carton. The splintered wood cut at my hands the way the pain cut at my heart. In some ways, it was good to work. I could focus on the cargo we were shifting from one spot to another, on the ache in my stomach, on the cold wind that bit into our skin. Our midday break was worse because I kept seeing Winterton's lifeless body lying on a cheap mattress in a run-down German warehouse.

We finished as the sun sank below the horizon. Ilsa was absent as the guards rounded us up for the march back. With no girlfriend to distract him, Little Adolf walked beside me instead. Two blocks from the rail yard, he stuck his foot out, and I tripped into the gutter. He smirked as he walked off. I was tempted to run after him and smash his face into the brick wall of a nearby shop, but I kept my anger in check as I got back to my feet and shook off the clumps of mud.

A few minutes later, Little Adolf was back. The end of his carbine smashed into my ribs and almost knocked me to the ground.

"Stop being so clumsy," he said.

I gritted my teeth. He brought his carbine up again and swung it in a wide arc. The idiot didn't know the first thing about surprising his opponent, and I was done meekly waiting for him to strike. I blocked his swing with my left arm and thrust the heel of my right hand into his nose. The moves I'd practiced over and over again with Bastien came as easily now as they had last summer. Little Adolf's nose cracked, and he stumbled into the wall of the nearest building and slumped to the ground.

As shouts sounded all around, I dashed after him, frustration snapping my better judgment. I kneed him in the face and was about to pound his head into the wall when the other guards poked the business ends of their carbines into my back.

Striking a guard was suicide. The only reason they hadn't already shot me had to be because I was too close to their comrade. They yanked me off Little Adolf and pinned me against the wall. I knew I was going to die, and part of me was too mad to care.

Neubau strode over.

"Should we shoot him?" one of the guards asked. I was surprised he needed permission.

Neubau hesitated. The other prisoners stood around in various states of dismay. One of the British prisoners had a hand on Samson's shoulder, like he was holding him back. Red stared at me, jaw slack. He was missing a perfect scrounging opportunity.

Little Adolf pushed himself to his feet. Blood streamed from his nose, and his left eye was starting to swell. "I have a better idea." He picked up a broken brick from the gutter. "Hold him," he told the other guards.

He stood in front of me, weighing the rock in his hand. If he wanted to scare me, he was succeeding. He took his broken brick and smashed it into the side of my head. I reeled in pain. That strike alone would have been enough to send me to the ground, but the other guards held me up. He hit me in the jaw next, and something cracked. Pieces of at least two teeth cut into my tongue before I managed to spit them out. His revenge didn't end there. He spent the next couple of minutes using the brick, his fists, and the end of his carbine to show me how stupid I'd been to strike him. By the time he was done, I wished he would have just shot me.

Samson dragged me back to the warehouse because I couldn't walk. Red spooned watery barley soup into my mouth because my arms trembled too much to hold the bowl. Daniels found an extra blanket for me because I couldn't stop shaking.

Samson and Daniels looked at the cuts and bruises and wiped as much blood from my skin as they could. We didn't have an X-ray machine, but based on the pain and the swelling, Daniels thought I had two cracked ribs, a broken collarbone, and a fractured left jawbone.

"Anybody know how to give stitches?" Samson asked as he examined a gash across my forehead.

"What would we stitch it with?" Daniels sat back on his heels. "You're lucky they didn't shoot you. Or shoot all of us in retaliation."

I didn't feel lucky. Death sounded a lot better than the pain shooting through my limbs and the aches screaming from my ribs. I glanced at the empty mattress next to mine. They'd already taken Winterton's body out and buried him next to all the other dead POWs. Were any of us going to get out of the war alive? I'd thought I wanted to live, that each additional day was one step closer to liberation, one step closer to being home, but nothing was worth living through the last twenty-four hours.

* * *

The next day, Feldwebel Neubau took one look at me and excused me from work for the day. Same thing the day after and the day after that until a week had passed. I moved only when I had to, spoke only when I was spoken to, and used only one syllable unless two were needed.

Little Adolf had beaten me before, but his brick had been worse. Now I barely had enough energy to walk to the soup line. Everything seemed pointless. The army might be coming, but I doubted I'd be alive when they reached Chemnitz. Either I'd starve to death, or Little Adolf would get his wish and execute us before freedom arrived.

Home was so far away that I could barely even remember the sound of my mom's voice or the smell of Belle's perfume.

After ten days off, I went back to work. Little Adolf jabbed the end of his carbine at me on the way back to the warehouse, and most days he threw in a few kicks too. I spent the evenings after we'd eaten lying on my mattress, staring at the rafters, trying not to breathe in too deeply so my cracked ribs wouldn't hurt so much. Red scrounged rags to use as bandages, and he passed me some extra food, but it hurt to chew. Even when I just used the right side of my mouth, staying away from the broken teeth, the jawbone itself fluctuated between misery and agony.

March turned to April, but the weather didn't improve much; it was still cold all the time. To make it worse, our rations were cut. They were hardly worth climbing out of bed for. We were going to die anyway, so maybe it was better to accept the fact and stop fighting the inevitable.

"Ley?" Samson called out early one morning.

I didn't answer.

"Ley!"

I turned over to face him. I hadn't really studied him for a while. His cheeks were leaner, and his eyes had sunk even further into his face.

"Get out of that bed." He didn't say it loud, but he said it firmly.

I huffed. "What's the point?"

"The point is you're acting like you've given up. And that's not acceptable. Get out. Now."

I turned away. "Leave me alone."

"Look, four-eyes, you get off that mattress right now and go get your measly breakfast, or I'm gonna drag you out."

"I'm not hungry. I haven't had glasses since December. And this lousy sack of wood chips is hardly a mattress."

I thought maybe he'd go away, but instead he knelt behind me, grabbed my shoulder, and pulled me over so I was facing him again. "Get up, Ley."

I shoved his hands away and just about cursed when the pain in my collarbone hit. He let his hands fall to his side. Good thing, or I might have taken a swing at him, despite my cracked bones. I didn't like being manhandled. It was hard enough to take it from Little Adolf every day. I wasn't going to take it from Samson too. "Go away."

"Nope. I'm staying right here until you get your sorry self outta bed." He stood beyond my fists' range and folded his arms. "I'm waiting."

"What do you care?"

"I care because you're turning into a sorry excuse of a soldier. You're a discredit to the entire US Army."

I glared at him.

"And you're a disgrace to the state of Virginia."

Seething, I folded my arms across my chest. I was pretty sure I'd be dead in a week or two anyway. I didn't care what Samson said.

"Or maybe you ain't really a Virginian. Not even an American. Maybe you still got more in common with those kraut pigs who're starving us to death."

"I'm not a Nazi." I enunciated each word clearly.

"Oh yeah?"

"Yeah."

"Then prove it."

I got up and ate my measly breakfast. Most of it, anyway. I always skipped the coffee, but I wasn't sure why. It wasn't really coffee, and I didn't think the Word of Wisdom applied if a guy was starving to death. We marched to the rail yards and stood around, waiting for orders.

"Ley!" Samson waved me over to stand with him and Red.

"What?" I was beginning to understand why he'd dragged me out of bed and ended my pit-bashing session. I was even a little grateful, but I still hadn't forgiven him.

"This morning the guards are gonna ask for volunteers to work in Chemnitz. I'm gonna volunteer. And you're gonna volunteer with me."

I looked around to see who else was nearby. No one was close enough to hear. "How do you know?"

Samson patted his pocket. "I traded a cigarette for news. Little Adolf and one of the other guards are taking a crew to sort rubble today."

I remembered the stories they'd told of digging through rubble in Dresden. "Why would I want to go to Chemnitz to dig through bombed-up houses for rotten corpses when I could stay here and unload railcars while Little Adolf's in a different city?"

"Because Chemnitz is a few miles closer to the Rhine."

"So?"

"You may not have noticed, but ever since you and Red went out for those sulfa pills, the guards have been patrolling at night. Escape from the warehouse got a lot harder."

Some of the British prisoners walked toward us, and Red headed them off, making some remark about the weather.

I waited until they were out of earshot. "Look, even if we get away in Chemnitz, where are you planning to go?"

"Patton and Monty both crossed the Rhine around the time . . ." He trailed off, and I guessed he'd been about to say *around the time Winterton died.* "About two weeks ago."

"The Rhine is two hundred miles away."

"Yeah, but we've got enough civilian clothes for three of us, and you speak German, so I'm betting you can talk us out of a few jams."

I held back a huff. So that was why Samson dragged me out of bed. He wanted a translator.

The guards ended their discussion, and Feldwebel Neubau waved one of them forward.

He spoke in broken English. "I need ten men. We go to Chemnitz for special work duty. Step forward, or we will assign."

Samson and Red stepped forward. So did a prisoner from New Zealand. Samson looked back and eyed me. Did I want to be free? Of course I did. Did I think we could travel two hundred miles across Nazi territory without getting caught? Wasn't much of a chance. But it was a chance. And risking it sounded better than starving to death in the warehouse.

I stepped forward.

CHAPTER 27

THE SOUND OF THE LOCK clicking closed on the boxcar brought back bad memories, but there were only ten of us inside. We had almost as much room as we'd had at the warehouse.

I sat next to Samson. "All right. I'm coming. What's your plan?"

Samson took off his greatcoat and his Eisenhower jacket. Underneath he had a blue button-down shirt. It wasn't part of a uniform. He stripped it off and gave it to me. He had a gray pin-striped one underneath it. "Put this on under your coat. We might have to leave a few layers behind, but this way we won't be in olive drab. It should get warmer soon, right?"

"I don't know. This winter's worse than any I remember from growing up. But I wasn't starving and sleeping in an unheated warehouse back then." I put the shirt on slowly, trying not to irritate my ribs and collarbone. They were improving, but they were still tender. "I don't know how well this is going to work. Most men have ties and suit coats."

"Yeah, I know. And they're cleaner and fatter than us, and if they're our age, they're fighting. But this is the best we could do."

As I replaced my layers, one of the other prisoners, Monson, scooted to our side of the boxcar. "What are you planning?"

Samson and Red looked at each other, then at the British prisoner.

Monson leaned forward, his eyes sparkling with anticipation. "Escaping?"

Samson nodded.

"May I come with you, please?" He gripped and relaxed his hands rhythmically. "I can't last much longer."

Another of the British prisoners overheard and shook his head at us. "Don't be daft. The war's almost over. Sit tight a few more weeks, and wait it out. You've survived this long. If you're caught, they'll shoot you."

"We might be shot if we stay," Monson said. "You think they'll hand us over peacefully when the time comes?"

"They haven't killed us yet." He looked us over. "I won't impede you. But you're making a mistake." He stood and staggered to the opposite side of the boxcar.

The pleading tone of Monson's voice deepened. "May I come? I've picked up a little German. And I've been a prisoner for almost four years. I'm ready to get out, no matter what the risk, and this might be the best chance we'll have."

Samson looked at Red, who nodded slightly. "All right. You can come. I don't know how we're gonna scrounge food for four people, but you can come."

Monson's thin face lit up in a grin. "Thank you. You won't regret it. I promise. What is your plan?"

Samson sighed. I'd asked the same question. "We're going to be flexible. Look for an opportunity. If none comes, we'll make one. Then we'll try to stay outta sight as much as we can and head west."

Monson frowned. "That's more of a strategy than an actual plan."

"Do you want to come, or don't ya?"

Monson nodded. "Yes, I want to come."

* * *

Little Adolf and the other guard assigned us to a flattened block of apartments once we arrived in Chemnitz. "Find the dead. Pile them here." The kinder guard pointed to an area already lined with several corpses and partial corpses. One of them belonged to a child, and I turned away as soon as I finished translating.

We pulled at the nearest pile of rubble, trying to unearth a collapsed bomb shelter. I felt sick to my stomach every time we came across a body. The remains weren't fresh, and some of them were falling apart. Even in the cold air, the stench was almost unbearable. As we shifted bricks and stacked bodies, I stayed close to Samson and kept my eye on Red and Monson. By noon, it was warm enough to take off our greatcoats. Unfortunately, the warmth made the stink even stronger.

A few hours and a few basements later, I began doubting we'd ever escape. There were two guards and ten prisoners. If four of us took off, they'd notice.

"I think we might have to make an opportunity," Samson said as we moved to another flattened building. He, Red, Monson, and I went to the far side of the pile. Little Adolf followed. We were out of sight from the rest of the crew and the other guard, but Little Adolf was armed.

I picked up a brick to move it away from a sunken staircase. Bastien's rules floated through my head. *Get a weapon.* I was surrounded by weapons. Each piece of brick, each broken length of pipe was something I could fight with.

Little Adolf stood ten yards away. The other half of the crew walked farther down the street and disappeared behind another rubbish heap. The five of us were alone, but could I take Little Adolf? I ripped away a piece of pipe and kept it nearby.

"Samson," I whispered.

"What?"

"I need someone to get his attention. Get him closer."

Samson nodded.

Two minutes later, Red bumped into Samson, and Samson pushed and shouted back. They yelled nonsense, but Little Adolf didn't speak English, so that didn't matter. Monson tried to break up the fight, and Red shoved him away. I hoped Monson's collapse was planned, because it looked like it hurt.

"Stop!" Little Adolf shouted.

Samson and Red kept it up.

I watched our guard from the corner of my eye. Would he come closer, or would he shoot?

Little Adolf yelled again and took his first step. I had hoped he would walk within range of my pipe, but he stayed out of reach. He brandished his carbine and looked like he was about to fire a warning shot.

I took a deep breath and remembered my first sparring session with Bastien. I picked up a brick and backed out of Little Adolf's periphery. Then I moved up on him from behind. Samson and Red made enough noise to block the sound of my footsteps.

"Stop, or I'll shoot!" he yelled at Samson, stepping closer.

When I was a foot behind him, I swung the pipe around into the front of his neck. At the same time, I rammed a brick into the small of his back. A strangled sound escaped his throat and he fell backward. I dropped the pipe and the brick and yanked his gun away, then pummeled his temple with the stock. Two strikes, and he lay still.

It was just like when Bastien had taught me how to sneak up on a sentry, except with a pipe and a brick. And Little Adolf had been too uncoordinated to throw me to the ground like Bastien had.

I took a deep breath and tried to control the tremor in my hands. Underneath the bandages my ribs screamed in pain, and my collarbone didn't feel so great either, but Little Adolf was down. Red and Samson stopped arguing, and we looked around nervously in the sudden silence. No one had seen us. I exhaled slowly. "You know, I've been wanting to do that for a long time."

Samson slapped me on the shoulder. "Well done, kid. Red, take his uniform off. Monson, keep a look out. Ley, help me find a place for his body."

We shifted bricks to make a body-sized ditch and by the time we were done Red and Monson had Little Adolf ready. He wasn't dead, but I had a feeling he was going to be out for a long time. I had no regrets.

"He had some cash." Red held up a few bills.

I looked at the Reichsmark. "It won't buy much. But it feels pretty good to take it from him."

"Put these on." Samson handed me Little Adolf's clothes. "If we run into trouble you can claim you're our guard."

I slipped his pants on over mine, then looked down at the cuffs dragging on the ground. When I tucked the shirt in, it went almost to my knees. I thought about looking for a rope to use as a belt, but our situation was hitting me with full force. We might be free, but we were in enemy territory. We needed to put as much distance between us and the rest of the crew as possible. "Let's get out of here." I handed Monson my greatcoat. I slung Little Adolf's pack over one shoulder and put his helmet on my head.

Samson nodded. "Stay by the rubble as long as we can, and when it gets dark, we'll find a place to sleep."

For the first time in months, there were no guards to threaten us with guns, no barbed wire, no roll call. We had taken one giant step toward freedom.

We headed west, away from our worksite, stopping a few times when we approached busier areas to give the impression that we were a guard and a few workers rather than a pack of escaped prisoners. The moon set at around ten that night, and with the blackout curtains, it was too dark to continue, so we hid in the partially flooded basement of a destroyed home near Chemnitz's outskirts. I checked Little Adolf's weapon. The Mauser carbine had a five-bullet magazine, but there were only two rounds inside. Maybe we could use them for hunting.

We raided Little Adolf's pack and found half a loaf of bread, a piece of sausage, and a piece of cheese. When divided four ways, it was slightly less than we would have had at the warehouse, but the quality was better, and we took satisfaction knowing it was his.

I had the third shift of guard duty that night. Nothing moved, except the lice in my hair, and not even an air-raid siren broke the silence. I was used to being locked up all night. I'd missed the stars, missed seeing them unimpeded by barbed wire or the cracked roof of a boxcar or a warehouse. With little other light, they seemed brighter than normal.

A calm night should have put me at ease. But peace was more elusive than freedom. If the SS caught us, would they shoot us? Would normal soldiers do the same? Would civilians? We were still a long way from safety.

I woke Red a few hours before dawn. "Red?"

He blinked away his fatigue and stretched. "We leaving again as soon as it's light?" he asked.

"Yeah. Wake us then." I handed him the carbine. "Do you suppose Little Adolf's woken up yet?"

"Unless that other guard found him and got him to a doctor, he might never wake up."

I shivered as I settled onto the cold, bumpy floor. It wasn't much colder than the warehouse, and it was more comfortable than the boxcars the Germans had shoved us in after we'd been captured, but I still had a hard time falling asleep. Would Little Adolf really die? I'd killed before, but it seemed different if it wasn't in the middle of a battle.

Something else bothered me even more than the slight strain on my conscience. It was the unknown. I didn't like being trapped behind barbed wire, but there was a pattern to our lives as POWs, a bit of security, and that pattern and security were both gone.

A few hours later, we left Chemnitz with its bombed-out buildings and streaming refugees and moved into the countryside. We were starving, but I was too skinny to pass as a guard at a bakery, and we didn't have ration cards, so we waited until we were in a less dense area before we sought out food.

"That house is off by itself." Samson pointed to a tidy building with smoke rising from the chimney.

"Good." Red turned toward it. "Let's have Ley act like a guard and demand some food."

We pounded on the back door. A frail-looking woman and a boy of about three answered it.

"We would like food," I said in German.

She shook her head. "No, we have so little."

I bit my lip to keep from laughing in her face. *So little* was a relative term, and the boy showed no signs of malnourishment. "We are not asking. We are demanding."

She stepped back, keeping her son close, and the four of us pushed past her.

"Come to the kitchen with us," I ordered. I didn't want her running off to a neighbor or finding a group of soldiers while our backs were turned.

She hesitated.

"We don't want to hurt you. We just want food."

She took her son's hand and led us to the kitchen.

"Monson, take the front window and watch the road," Samson said. "Red, go check the barn."

There were at least twenty pounds of potatoes in a box in the kitchen. I grabbed a small one and ate it like an apple. It was the first hard thing I'd tried to eat with my injured jaw, and it hurt, but I was hungry enough to chew through the pain. Samson found a frying pan and some lard. Then he started washing and slicing potatoes.

"Cut them thinner and they'll fry faster." I finished my raw potato and helped.

Red came back with three eggs. "They've got a pig and four chickens."

If we hadn't been in a hurry, I would have suggested we fry one of the chickens or slaughter the pig, but I wanted to put as much distance between us and Chemnitz as we could. Eggs and potatoes would do for now.

Red went through the cupboards and discovered jars of preserved pears and a loaf of bread. It wasn't white bread, but it was lighter and softer than the stuff they normally gave us. He found three more eggs in the icebox.

"Find a bag and get some stuff for later, will ya?" Samson asked Red.

I found another pan and fried all six eggs. When the food was done, I divided it onto four plates and took some to Monson.

The boy and his mother had watched us in silence while we ransacked their kitchen, but when I came back, the little boy began to cry.

"Is he scared of us?" I asked.

"No. He is not scared. But you are eating all our food. He is hungry."

I looked at the box of potatoes and glanced at the still-opened cupboard full of canned and bottled food. We were eating our fill now, and Red had packed potatoes, bread, and several cans in a bag, but we were leaving far more than we took. They had a pig they could slaughter and a bunch of chickens that would give them eggs in the morning. "Ma'am, you don't know anything about being hungry."

* * *

The switch from prisoner to fugitive was exhausting, with its constant hiding from passing troops and endless maneuvering to avoid refugees. By the next evening, we'd eaten through all the food we'd taken from the woman. We'd been free for two days. We needed another meal, and we needed a place to hide.

"That looks promising." Red pointed to a small home in the distance.

No one answered the door when we knocked. Monson stood watch while the rest of us went inside. Stale air greeted us. Murky light shone through dirty windowpanes, revealing a thick layer of dust coating the sofa and end tables in the front room. A spider's web clung to the corner of a framed portrait of Adolf Hitler. The kitchen, two bedrooms, and water closet showed the same signs of abandonment.

"We could sleep in real beds tonight." I felt the bed in the larger of the two bedrooms. A puff of dust came up as I patted the pillows. One end of the curtain rod had broken off the wall and showed a sinking sun. I went into the bathroom and turned on the faucet. No water came out. But I'd noticed a well out back, and there was an old cake of soap dried on the ledge of the sink. The kitchen stove was a coal-burning type, but there was no coal. No food in any of the cupboards either, but Samson found a handful of wrinkled potatoes in the cellar.

If we waited until dark, we could light the stove without anyone wondering why a previously abandoned house had smoke coming from the chimney. We could have a hot meal, a hot bath, and a soft bed.

Samson assigned us tasks. "Red, you and Monson see if you can find something to burn. Ley, start on food. I'll get water, and then I'll fix those blackout curtains."

I searched the kitchen. It wasn't fully stocked—the people who'd left had probably taken all the stuff they used the most, but I found a dull paring knife, a cracked cutting board, and a handleless pot. Ash packed the stove, and it took some digging to find a brush and dustpan, but I had the stove cleared out by the time Samson came back with a pail of water.

"Potato soup?" I asked. "With potatoes . . . and potatoes?"

"Better than that barley and weevil stuff they gave us at the stalag."

"I could probably throw in a little sawdust or ash if we want a reminder." Samson chuckled as he went off to fix the broken blackout curtain.

I cut out the bad spots on the potatoes and removed the eyes. I kept the skins on because I didn't want to waste anything edible. I could hardly believe I was in a real home, working in a real kitchen. It felt so different from the warehouse or the stalag. We'd made good progress so far. In another week, we might be free.

"Kid!" Panic sounded in Samson's voice. "Take off that kraut uniform now!"

"What?"

"German soldiers have us surrounded."

I ripped Little Adolf's shirt off, sending buttons flying every direction. "How many?"

"Five."

Five soldiers. Two bullets. We couldn't beat them. I shoved the shirt, helmet, and carbine in the broom closet and slammed the door. I stripped off the German pants, using the paring knife on the ankles, and stashed them under the stove as the soldiers broke through the front door.

"Out! Now!" Two soldiers appeared from around the corner with rifles aimed at me.

I was a prisoner. Again.

CHAPTER 28

IF THE GERMANS WHO CAPTURED us had been decent people, they would have let us eat our food before marching us out. They weren't decent people.

"Stupid Americans," the feldwebel said in English as he pushed me out the front door to stand beside Samson. "Where are the others?"

"What others?" I asked.

"The woman you robbed yesterday said there were four of you. One wore a German uniform, but he deferred to one of the prisoners and served them first, so he couldn't have been a real guard. Where are the other two? And where is the one impersonating a German soldier?"

"You must be mistaking us for a different group," I said.

A mirthful grunt escaped his lips. "No, we tracked you directly from there. Where are the others?"

"We split up yesterday. It was too hard to find food for four of us." I glanced at Samson. He'd had a smile on his face when he'd brought in the water. The smile was gone, replaced by deep lines of worry and disappointment.

The feldwebel stared at me for several long seconds. I had the feeling he didn't believe me. He turned to two of his men. "Sommer, Ziegler, see if you can find them." I resisted the urge to look behind the house, where Red and Monson had gone to gather wood.

The feldwebel prodded me with the stock of his rifle. It hurt my ribs. "March."

We walked in silence. I had only the two thin shirts I'd been doubling up with since November to warm my torso. The sun disappeared, and I missed my greatcoat. Even Little Adolf's thick tunic would have been welcome. Thinking of Little Adolf created a new fear. If we went back to the warehouse, and if Little Adolf was still alive, then I was dead. It was a miracle he hadn't killed me when I'd bashed his nose in. There was no way I'd survive if he got a hold of me after I'd knocked him unconscious.

"Where are you taking us?" I asked the guard.

"Shh." He glared at me and didn't answer.

It grew dark, and the feldwebel herded us into a barn. He didn't give us any food. Then he and one of his men left, leaving a single guard to watch us. But that single guard was alert as he held his rifle in his lap and smoked a German cigarette.

"Do you think Red and Monson escaped?" I whispered to Samson.

"No talking!" the guard shouted.

Eventually, I fell into a light sleep. I woke when the feldwebel returned with the other members of his squad. They hadn't caught Red or Monson. I was glad for that but frustrated to be in Nazi custody again.

The next morning they marched us to a well and let us drink as much as we wanted. No food. We'd stayed off the main road as much as possible while fugitives, but the guards had us on parade in front of the civilians rushing to church, the soldiers moving toward the front lines, and the refugees clogging the roads in their search for safety. A few people sneered at us in passing, but most of them were occupied with their own problems.

The guards stopped at noon. The feldwebel left and returned with bread and sausage. The guards divided it among themselves. Samson and I watched. I thought we'd be on the road again soon, but two of the guards chatted while the rest napped. The sun shone brightly, and even though I was ravenous, I stretched out and closed my eyes.

When one of the guards kicked me awake, it was midafternoon. My ribs had been feeling better, but his boot reawakened an intense agony, and I had to hold my side when I stood and take a few shallow breaths to get the pain under control. At least none of the bones in my legs were broken, so I could walk. I said a silent prayer for help and managed to put one foot in front of the other for the next few hours.

While we marched, I maneuvered next to the shortest of the bunch, the guard with a chipped tooth and a cocky swagger. "Where are we going?"

He looked at me in surprise. "You speak German?"

"Yes."

"Hmm."

"Can you tell me where you're taking us?"

He waved his hand eastward. "A camp."

"Which camp?"

He shrugged.

"A big camp or a work kommando?"

"A big camp."

I tried not to show my relief. If we were away from Little Adolf, maybe I could hold out until the end of the war. "Are we walking the whole way or taking a train?"

He looked around to make sure none of the other guards were watching our conversation. "If we're guarding you, we won't be sent to fight the Russians, so we're walking. Taking a nice, easy pace. Are you in a hurry?"

"No. But some food would be nice."

"Weak prisoners have a harder time escaping."

That might have been true, but it didn't make my stomach feel any better.

They marched us for almost a week. The pace was reasonable, ten to fifteen miles a day. The food situation was awful. They gave us one meal a day, usually a quarter loaf of black bread, sometimes cabbage soup. Once, a group of French laborers shook our hands and left us each an extra slice of bread. But for most of the trip, thirst and dizziness threatened to overwhelm me.

Whenever Samson and I tried to speak, the guards yelled at us, so we didn't communicate much through words. I could tell he was as exhausted, hungry, and discouraged as I was. It would have been better to stay in the little town and unload boxcars. The work was long, but at least we could count on two meals a day. They might be pitiful, but they were consistent.

Six days after our capture, the attitude of the guards shifted. They'd been desperate men trying to stay busy so they wouldn't be sent to the Eastern Front; now they were jubilant. One of them filled me in. "President Roosevelt died yesterday. He committed suicide because America will never beat Germany."

I didn't believe him.

"What's going on?" Samson asked.

I shook my head. "It's just propaganda."

"What did they say?"

"They said President Roosevelt's dead."

I saw my own emotions reflected in Samson's face. I'd never known another president. If he was really dead, would the Nazis win?

When we finally arrived at the camp, I looked up at the familiar gate. The sign above the entrance read M. Stammlager IVB. We were back in Mühlberg.

* * *

When the Germans captured escaped prisoners, they punished them.

Starving us on the march wasn't official discipline, so they put Samson and me in solitary confinement. For five days, I was given one pint of water and one thin slice of bread. That was it. I couldn't talk to anyone, not even the guards, but by the second day, I didn't have energy to talk anyway. I spent the first half of solitary wondering how long it would take to starve to death. I spent the second half in a slow, fuzzy stupor, too lifeless to think about anything more complicated than whether it was night or day.

When they released us, Samson and I were assigned different huts. Maybe they thought if we spent too much time together, we'd try to leave again. Escape was a long way from my mind. Every time I stood, I was dizzy, and my stomach hurt even worse than usual. Lesions marred my skin and refused to heal. My muscles were withered, and it took effort to keep upright.

From my capture in Luxembourg to my capture at the abandoned house, I'd lost about fifty pounds. During the march back to Mühlberg and my time in the cooler, I'd probably lost another ten. I had to hold my pants up when I walked because I was afraid they'd fall off. I was never warm. Striding across the barracks was exhausting.

"Is Roosevelt really dead?" I asked another prisoner when we lined up for *appell* my first day out of the cooler.

"Yeah."

"Did he commit suicide?"

The other man, an American, gave me a funny look. "Of course not. Why would you think that?"

"That's what some of the guards said."

"Don't believe 'em. They're losing. The Russians will be here soon."

"How soon?" I was going to starve to death if it was more than a week or two.

He shrugged. "Soon. You've seen all the planes strafing the krauts, haven't you?"

I shook my head. "I've been in solitary."

"Well, you can still see the results." He pointed out smoke in the distance. "Not long now."

That night, there weren't enough beds in my assigned barrack, so I had to sleep on the floor. The barracks were a few feet off the ground, and the guards let their dogs loose at night. One of the mongrels woke me twice, sniffing and grunting at me through the cracks in the boards.

The next morning, as I stood for roll call, I felt like a sapling in a windstorm, so weak that anything stronger than a mild gust would tip me over. I wasn't sure what to believe anymore. The Germans were losing, but they hadn't lost yet. And conditions in camp were worse than I remembered.

Most of the guards still acted like we were animals. How could real men with real lives and real families treat people the way they treated us? I spent most of the morning on that question as I sat outside the barracks in the sunlight, picking at lice. Maybe to them, we weren't human. We ate food scarcely fit for animals, and sometimes we fought over it. The latrines constantly overflowed, and the food caused havoc to our guts, so most of us soiled ourselves. And we never stopped smelling like animals because they didn't provide enough places to wash.

It was a horrible, undignified cycle. The more they treated us like animals, the more we behaved, looked, and smelled like animals. Except I didn't think animals could recognize how pathetic they were. That was among the more depressing aspects, seeing how far we'd fallen. The army had trained us to follow officers, but the Germans sent officers to different camps, so there was no one with rank to impose order. As a group, we were desperate and undisciplined.

Some of the men had more to deal with: physical wounds that hadn't healed, nightmares and memories of combat that wouldn't go away, regret that they'd surrendered too soon, regret that they'd surrendered at all, guilt that they were alive when so many of their friends were dead. I tried not to think of Winterton, but it was hard to keep my mind occupied when all I did was sit around all day. I didn't have the energy to do anything else.

Ever since being captured, I'd been mostly certain about two things: the Allies would win the war eventually. And at any time, the Germans might slaughter us. Which would happen first? Liberation? Or execution?

"Ley? That you?"

I looked up from my spot in the sun to see Samson. "Yeah."

He sat next to me. "You don't look so good."

"I don't feel so good."

"Solitary confinement wiped me out. Some fellows in my hut found an extra potato. Today's a little better."

I closed my eyes, wishing the sun would soak me up and take me back to Virginia. "The fellows in my hut found me a blanket. No bed. No extra food."

"Hang in there."

"For how much longer?" My stomach hurt, and my energy had reached a new low.

"Just listen, kid."

I listened, and I was surprised I hadn't heard it earlier. Mortars. Rifle fire. Explosions. I stood and stumbled closer to the warning wire. I couldn't see anything other than a long haze of smoke, but a battle was taking place within earshot. I was so relieved that I wanted to cry.

I turned to Samson, who'd followed me over.

"You've been through a lot, kid. Don't let the krauts beat you now that it's almost over."

Samson left, but I stood there awhile longer, looking into the distance, thinking about his advice. The Nazis had been taking things from me for a long time. I had first noticed it ten years ago, when Bastien and my parents would have tense conversations about politics that would end abruptly if my sisters or I walked into the room. First, the Nazis had taken our freedom to talk, our freedom to disagree. Then they'd taken my father. They'd taken my brother's leg, and they'd put me through hell as a POW. But now the end was in sight.

My father had fought them with words. My brother had fought them with espionage. I'd fought them with bullets, but my time in Luxembourg hadn't been the only battle I'd waged against them. As the rumblings in the distance grew louder, I knew my time as a prisoner hadn't contributed much to a military victory. But living through everything the Nazis had thrown at me had contributed to something else: a crack in their iron grip on Europe, a chink in their belief that they alone were right, some small sign that despite their power and their anger and their ruthlessness, they were not invincible. Freedom and humanity were stronger, and they always would be.

Sometimes survival was the ultimate act of defiance.

CHAPTER 29

THE FOOD RATION WAS LATE that day. It didn't show up until dark. My stomach hurt, but I refused to get depressed over it. I was going to survive. No matter what.

But the next morning, the pain in my stomach was worse, and I had trouble finding the strength to walk to *appell*. There were different guards, members of the Hungarian SS. They reminded me of Little Adolf, so I spent most of the day sleeping inside Samson's barracks because Samson let me borrow his bed. When I finally got some food, I threw it up.

The morning after, *appell* was even harder to get to. I was well-acquainted with hunger pains, but this new ache in my stomach was different. I wasn't sure I could stand long enough for the guards to count us.

It turned out I didn't have to. The guards were gone, and commotion surged through the camp faster than a P-51 Mustang.

"Where did they go?" I asked one of the other prisoners.

The man's face broke into a grin. "I think they were running away from them."

I looked where he pointed. Sturdy men with fur caps and submachine guns rode to the camp astride healthy horses. The Soviet Cossack Cavalry had arrived. We were free.

My face broke into a grin that didn't relax until I found Samson. "We're going home!" I yelled.

All over camp, men were dancing, laughing, crying, and shouting. The Soviet flag went up a flag pole, followed by a Dutch flag, a French flag, a British flag, and then the Stars and Stripes. I had a feeling that if I looked closely, I'd see a few irregularities in the homemade flags, but from where I stood, they looked absolutely perfect. I closed my eyes for a moment to keep tears from forming and to say a quick prayer of gratitude.

The Russian POWs raided the camp's potato stores. The Germans had starved them even more than they'd starved the rest of us, so I didn't begrudge them, but the pain in my stomach made me wonder when our next meal would come. The Red Army was here, but the Cossacks were a fighting unit, and I doubted they could feed thirty thousand ravenous ex-prisoners.

The camp's population dropped quickly. All the Soviet POWs healthy enough to march left that morning. One of their officers told the rest of us to stay put because there were still SS units nearby.

I had every intention of obeying the Soviet officer until midafternoon when my hunger got the best of me.

"Ley," Samson whispered. Another American was right behind him. "Some of the other guys tore holes in the wire so they can scrounge at local farms. Let's go."

I nodded. The camp was big, and there were only a few Soviet troops around, and they weren't really guarding us. Getting out sounded easy. But actually leaving was a little trickier. I paused at the warning wire, and my eyes automatically went to the guard tower. It was empty. I looked at the other guard towers too, making sure they weren't manned. They weren't. I stepped across the wire, and then I followed Samson through the cut double-fences. I'd known I was free when the kraut guards had disappeared and the Cossacks had ridden in, but now I *felt* free.

The elation didn't last long. After half a mile, I hunched over in pain. "What is it, kid?"

I took a deep breath and slowly straightened. "Just my stomach."

"It'll get better when we get some food."

I nodded and let Samson help me stand upright.

We came to a farm a few minutes later. The owners had fled, probably to stay ahead of the Red Army. Inside the barn were four milk cows mooing in pain. I found a stool and a bucket and got to work. The poor cows practically milked themselves. Samson found potatoes, and the other ex-prisoner found cans of green beans and sardines. We skimmed the cream from the milk and drank it warm. We ate the beans and fish cold because we didn't want to wait to heat them up, and then we started on the potatoes.

After two bites of potato, I vomited it all up. I sat on the ground, weak and miserable. Had I eaten too much too fast? Samson and the other guy had eaten just as much as I had, and they weren't barfing. I tried another swallow of cream and was soon nauseated again, but at least I didn't puke.

"Let's rest before we go back." Samson made himself comfortable on a pile of hay outside the barn, and soon the three of us dozed off.

Soviet soldiers prodded us awake with the end of their rifles. I didn't understand the words they used, but I followed Samson's example when he lifted his hands in surrender. We showed them our POW tags, and they patted us on the back and motioned for us to go back to camp.

"I think I'd rather sleep here than the stalag," the other prisoner said.

Samson looked back at the barn. "Yeah, until the SS shows up."

We passed a few other farmhouses on our way back, not all of them abandoned. A handful of Red Army troops were looting one. And they weren't just taking jewelry and silver. Two of them dragged a woman toward a barn. She shrieked in horror as they laughed.

We paused, but we had no weapons, and we couldn't exactly turn against our ally to protect our enemy. Samson cursed and shook his head. One of the Soviet soldiers waved us on, and we left, but we could hear the woman's cries for a long time after that, and even when they stopped sounding in my ears, they kept sounding in my mind.

I'd been wary of the Communists before. Now a mix of fear and foreboding cemented itself inside me. They weren't as bad as the Nazis, but that was only because they were on our side.

* * *

Back at camp, the scent of roasting pigs and cattle filled the air. We weren't the only ones who'd gone out to find food. Later that night, someone gave me a piece of beef. It was the most delicious thing I'd ever eaten, but it didn't taste so great when it came back up five minutes later. Maybe my stomach wasn't up to meat just yet.

As the week progressed, the Soviets grew more organized. They brought in a grain-heavy diet, and I was able to keep it down about half the time, but the hunger never left. Samson suggested another trip to a nearby farm, but the longer the Red Army stayed, the harder it was to sneak out.

"I'm starting to feel like we exchanged one set of guards for another," Samson said.

"Is our army coming?" I sat in the sun between one of the barracks and the outer fence, too tired to even scratch at the lice.

Samson shook his head. "Word is they stopped at the Elbe. The Soviets are supposed to take us there, but some of the others said they ain't gonna do that until our side hands over all the Soviet POWs they've been liberating."

"How far away is the Elbe?" An idea floated into my head. I doubted it was unique, but it was strong.

"Six, seven miles at most. If we left tonight, I bet we could make it tomorrow."

The war was nearly over. It seemed silly to risk trouble during the final days, but my stomach felt like it was holding an unexploded mortar shell. "What do you suppose the Russians would do if they caught us?"

"Yell at us and bring us back."

"Do you think there are still kraut soldiers out there?"

"Probably." Samson looked around. "Look, kid, I'm sick of this place. And you're starting to look a little yellow."

I huffed. Just because I was thinking through his plan before agreeing to it didn't mean I was too scared to try it. "Oh? And what exactly does a coward look like?"

Samson shook his head. "Not yellow-bellied." He grabbed my hand and held it in front of my face. "Look at your fingers, kid. It's hard to tell under all that grime, but your fingernails are yellow. So are the whites of your eyes."

I could guess what that meant. "Jaundice?"

"Yeah. Or hepatitis."

I thought back to the first prisoner who'd died in the warehouse, the man from Wales. He'd had hepatitis. I couldn't remember if he'd had symptoms like nausea and stomach pain, but he'd been listless. Was hepatitis the reason I was so weak?

"The way I see it," Samson said, "we can make a dash for our lines tonight, and you can be in a nice American field hospital by this time tomorrow, or we can wait here and see how well the Red Army takes care of you and the thousands of other men that need a hospital."

I closed my eyes and thought about home. "I'll be ready as soon as it's dark."

"Good. 'Cause I ain't staying, and I don't wanna leave you behind."

I didn't want to be left behind, not now, not when I didn't know anyone else in the entire camp. Samson and I might have gotten off to a rough start, but five months later, there wasn't much I wouldn't do for him. "The crazy thing is, I was pretty sure you hated me back in November."

Samson chewed on his lip for a bit before answering. "It wasn't hatred."

"Irritation?"

"No. You reminded me of my cousin. Especially when you had a helmet on and I couldn't see your hair."

"A cousin you didn't get along with?"

Samson shook his head. "No, Randy was my best friend. We joined the National Guard together—he wanted to impress a girl with his uniform, and I thought two weeks in Virginia Beach or New York every year sounded good, even if it did involve training." He glanced at the wire, then at his hands. "We were still in the same company on D-Day. He was first off our landing craft. Got hit in the shoulder, so I dragged him to shore, patched him up. Then he got hit again, and he didn't make it." He blew out a breath. "Looking at you reminded me that I couldn't save him or any of the other boys I grew up with. They all ended up dead in the sand that day or dead in the hedgerows a few weeks later. I couldn't do nothing for no one."

"You saved me."

Samson raised an eyebrow.

"After Winterton died, I was ready to give up, and you knocked some sense into me. And you helped me after we got out of solitary. And you're helping me tonight."

Samson looked away. "I don't know how much I did, but we're survivors now, and I think we better stay that way."

* * *

"Ready?" Samson shook me awake.

I blinked and looked through the barracks window. The sun had set, and its light had faded, but we had a full moon to guide us.

This escape was different from our last one. Our adversary was technically our ally. But that didn't mean I trusted the Soviets. If I trusted them, I wouldn't be trying to escape. I didn't think they'd give me the Little Adolf treatment or slam me in the cooler for a week with nothing but bread and water, but I'd heard about the Communist-run camps in Siberia, and I doubted the food was much better there.

"They took a bunch of bodies out today," Samson said.

"Sick or executed?"

"Typhus, I think."

"That's another reason to leave now." There were too many ill men, too few doctors, not enough food or medicine. I was nervous, but I felt compelled to leave. Part of it was my desire to get home, part of it was the pain in my stomach, but it went deeper than that. I needed to leave the way I needed to breathe.

We crouched under the barracks on the side by the wire, watching for our chance. There was a hole in the fence a few yards ahead of us. We waited about ten minutes, long enough for a Soviet soldier to walk around the perimeter, then we waited some more. He came around again twenty minutes later. When he was out of sight, we walked to the fence and stepped through.

"If anyone asks, we're coming back," Samson whispered. "We're just off to a farm to scrounge food."

I nodded and jogged along with him to put some distance between us and the camp. When we were far enough from the stalag that we didn't think anyone could see us, we slowed and turned west. West to freedom.

CHAPTER 30

WE WALKED THE REST OF the night, taking breaks when we needed them. The ball of lead in my stomach seemed to grow as the hours passed, but I did my best to ignore it. Nothing was going to keep me from the American lines, especially not a little case of jaundice. Yet as the moon set and the eastern horizon grew light, I knew I couldn't keep going indefinitely. "I need some sleep."

Samson glanced at me. "All right. Do you want to play it safe and sleep in the woods, or do you think you can talk some German farmer into letting us borrow his bed?"

"You'd trust a German farmer while we sleep?" We didn't have money or cigarettes or weapons, so bribery and intimidation were out. A bed in a house or a pile of hay in a barn sounded a lot better than sleeping on ground lumpy with roots, but I didn't want to risk a civilian turning on us. "Let's lay low for now. We'll save talking to the German farmers for when we're hungry."

"You ain't hungry now?"

I shook my head. I should have been hungry, but my stomach hurt too much to eat.

We found a mostly flat stretch of ground and curled up under some trees. Before I drifted off, I thought we probably should have stopped earlier. Now we were too exhausted to keep watch. We'd have to trust nature to hide us.

The sun was high overhead when Samson shook me awake. He pressed a finger to his lips and pointed. A group of seven German soldiers marched along a road roughly twenty yards away. They were young. If I'd had my BAR, I would have hollered at them to surrender, but since I was unarmed,

I followed Samson's lead and stayed hidden. Just because they were young didn't mean they weren't fanatical.

I gave them time to get out of sight before I spoke. "I thought the Red Army would have rounded them up by now."

"If we're not careful, we'll end up in the middle of it when the Russkies catch up to them."

The group had been going due west. "Maybe we should angle south."

Samson nodded. "How's your stomach feel?"

"About like yesterday. Let's go."

* * *

I knocked on a German farmhouse door and waited. A wizened old man opened the door.

"We'd like some food, please," I said in German.

"We have almost nothing." He started shutting the door, but I put my foot out to stop him.

"We just want enough for one meal." I forced the door open and pushed past him. I stopped when I saw the front room. It was like it had seen battle, only it didn't smell of explosives, and there were no bullet holes. But the furniture was overturned, the pictures torn from the walls, and the lamps smashed into the floor. "What happened?"

"The Communists came."

That would explain why he'd said he had almost nothing, but Samson and I didn't want much, and I could smell fresh bread. I went through the room into the kitchen. It showed the same amount of upheaval. The man's wife watched as I poked through cupboards. Her gray hair was neat, and her clothes clean. She stayed on the opposite end of the room from me, doing her best to straighten her kitchen.

The bread I'd smelled was in the oven. I peeked inside, and the loaf was a golden brown. "Is this almost done?"

The woman nodded.

Samson came into the kitchen. I doubted he cared if the center of the bread was still doughy. I sure didn't. I found a dish towel and took the pan from the oven, then dumped out the loaf and wrapped it inside.

"But that's our last food!" the woman protested.

I didn't believe her. "Then go see your neighbors."

We left out the back door. I tore into the bread while it was still hot enough to hurt my hands, then handed the bundle to Samson.

"They didn't seem too happy about that."

I blew on a piece of bread until it was cool enough not to burn my tongue. "Yeah, they said the Red Army ripped their place apart and this was their last food."

Samson looked at me, then looked away.

"What?"

He took his time answering. "I don't know. Yesterday you said I helped turn you into a survivor, and I'm glad for that. But I'm sorry I had to change part of you to do it."

"Change part of me?"

He gestured to the bread in my hand. "You wouldn't have stolen that back in December."

I huffed. "We weren't starving back in December. Besides, we stole it from Nazis. One of the pictures on the floor was of Hitler." They might have had the picture more to keep up appearances than because they liked him, but regardless of the reason, they had it.

"I'm not saying you were wrong. You've just changed."

I tried not to roll my eyes as I chewed another bite of bread. I didn't know what Samson was talking about.

* * *

"Is that the Elbe?" Samson pointed to a bit of sunlight reflecting off water in the distance.

"I think so." The Elbe. Freedom. I focused on the shimmer for the next ten minutes as we walked toward it, chanting *Almost home* in my head whenever my stomach hurt or my feet ached.

When the shouting started, I didn't understand the words, but the anger and authority were clear as a Soviet officer and squad of men ran from a group of trees and surrounded us. I looked at their rifles pointed at Samson and me. We raised our hands and stood there until the officer strode closer.

"You are Americans?" He spoke English, but his accent was so thick I could barely understand him.

"Yes."

"Why are you on this side of river?" He came closer and fingered our torn and faded uniforms. Then he raised his chin. "You are prisoners?"

"That's right. We're working our way to the American side of the river."

He smiled. "Oh, no. It is not safe for you to be away from camp. Diplomats will agree on release. Until then, you must stay at camp."

I wasn't about to let him send us back to Stalag IVB when we were within sight of our goal. "But I'm sick, and the camp doesn't have enough doctors."

He raised an eyebrow. "You look healthier than many Soviet prisoners we liberate. You wait until official release. Orders are orders." He switched to Russian and called out two of his men and gave them instructions. Then he turned back to me. "These will escort you back."

I didn't want to go back to the stalag, but they weren't asking my opinion. One of the Russians pushed me forward, and I started moving. With each step, anger boiled inside me. We were walking the wrong way. After being treated like a slave, after starvation and sickness, after putting up with Little Adolf and bedbugs and permanent dysentery—I wasn't going to let some Soviet ally hold me prisoner. I didn't care how far they'd come or how hard they'd fought or how many Germans they'd killed. Nobody was going to stop me from going home.

We quickly settled into our march, Samson and I in front and the two Russians behind. They held their rifles in front of them but didn't aim them. The few times I looked back, they seemed relaxed but alert as they chatted with each other.

"Samson?" I whispered.

"Yeah?"

"We can't go back."

He glanced at the guards. "Hey, do you think we could stop for a rest?"

The blank stares told me neither of them understood.

Samson motioned to his legs and then turned off the road to sit in a patch of grass. I followed him. The guards followed me.

I mulled over our choices. If the guards had spoken English, I might have been able to reason with them, but that wasn't an option.

The safest bet was going back to camp and waiting for liberation. But it wasn't as safe as it sounded. There were only two Soviet soldiers. If we got attacked by a group of fanatic Hitler Youth, we might all die. Or we might make it back and I'd starve in Stalag IVB. That, or die of hepatitis.

The last choice was taking the guards out so we could cross the Elbe. I didn't like the thought of hurting supposed allies, but I liked the thought of going back behind wire even less.

I needed to be standing, and the guards needed to be sitting. "Samson?" I whispered.

"Yeah?"

"Stay here for a second, but follow my lead when I get back." I stood and walked off a few yards. The guards watched me but stopped paying attention when I unzipped my fly and answered the call of nature.

After I finished, I meandered back, doing my best to look relaxed and harmless. The thought crossed my mind that maybe I should pray, but there wasn't time for that. Both guards had rifles across their laps. The taller one sat with his legs stretched in front of him and his hands to the side for balance. The shorter one crossed his legs. His hands were closer to his rifle. I gazed around, making sure none of their friends were nearby.

As I reached the shorter guard, I pretended to stumble, snatched the rifle from his lap, and drove its stock into his buddy's head. Samson dove for the shorter guard and kept him on the ground long enough for me to knock him in the head too.

I checked their vital signs. They were unconscious but alive. "We better tie them up and get across the Elbe as quick as we can."

We used their shirts as ropes and left them in a ditch a few yards from the road. They'd have to make noise if they wanted anyone to find them. I stripped off their boots and shoved their socks in their mouths so making noise would be more of a challenge.

I debated putting on a Red Army uniform but decided against it. I didn't speak Russian or Ukrainian or Tajik. And while the Germans *might* shoot us in our American uniforms, they'd *definitely* shoot us in Soviet uniforms. We left the Mosin-Nagant rifles behind too. It would be hard to explain how we'd come by them honestly if anyone stopped us.

If my stomach hadn't been so sore, I would have run. I had to be content with walking. We kept to the woods, even though the terrain was more difficult there. Eventually my walking turned into stumbling, but the shimmer of water in the distance gradually turned into a thick line glowing orange in the light of the sinking sun.

Freedom was just across the river.

"Can you swim?" I asked Samson.

He hesitated. "Not very well."

I wasn't sure I could make it either. The river looked calmer than the Potomac, but not by much. "Let's go south, see if we find a bridge or a ferry."

We followed the river around two bends. We kept our distance from the open fields along the banks, preferring the shadowed, forested bands farther back.

The sun had disappeared, and its light was growing dim when we sighted a bridge. As we drew near, we picked out a Soviet soldier on our side of the river and an American sentry on the opposite bank.

I looked at Samson. "Should we risk it?"

He nodded.

When we walked up to the Soviet soldier, he blocked our path.

"Do you speak English?" I asked.

"*Nyet.*"

He obviously understood enough to answer no, but I tried a different approach. "Do you speak German?" I asked in German.

"*Nyet.*"

"Can we go across?" I said in English, using motions to show him what we wanted.

"*Nyet.*"

Samson started across the bridge, and the soldier stuck his rifle in Samson's stomach. Samson backed down. "Should we try a different bridge?" he asked.

That sounded better than waiting for the man's officer and getting sent back to the stalag, but the American sentry on the other end of the bridge had crossed over to our side. "Is there a problem?" he asked.

"Yeah. We've been prisoners for four months, and we want on that side of the river." Samson pointed.

The American soldier spoke a few Russian phrases. Then he handed over a Hershey bar and a pack of Pall Malls. The Soviet soldier slipped the gifts into his pocket and stepped to the side.

A minute later, we were on the west bank of the Elbe.

PART FOUR: A FREE MAN

SPRING 1945

CHAPTER 31

It took awhile for it to sink in, but when it finally did, relief that I was back with my own army was so strong that I had to blink hard to keep from tearing up.

The American sentry sent us to another American soldier with a jeep and a radio. Before long, another jeep came to pick us up and take us to a company command post, where we were showered with cigarettes and C rations. Samson lit up and told a youngish captain our story while I dug into a package of SOS. Had I really thought chipped beef on toast was bland? It was incredible.

"Hey, buddy, take it easy," a passing medic said. "You aren't the first POWs we've seen. In your condition, eating too much too fast can make you sick."

I glanced at the food. I wanted to shove it all in, eat so much it hurt. But I believed him, so I slowed down. There were plenty of C rations for later. Besides, my stomach already churned in protest. I lurched out the door and found a bush to catch my vomit.

One of the other soldiers eyed me when I came back. "How long you been wearing that uniform?"

"Since I hopped off the Red Ball Express in Luxembourg. End of November." I glanced at the other men. Combat troops weren't exactly known for being clean, but this was a headquarters group, and according to the comments I'd heard, all the hard fighting had ended a few days before. I was suddenly aware of the rips in my collar, the holes in my knees, and the splattered vomit on the side of my boots. The back of my neck started itching, and I remembered I had lice and fleas. I was a mess.

The captain called a corporal over. "See if you can get these men cleaned up."

"Yes, sir."

The corporal was a miracle worker. Samson and I were deloused in a cloud of DDT powder, and soon after that, I was soaking in a bathtub in a commandeered German cottage. I used an entire bar of army-issue soap and changed the water three times because the house had running water.

When I got out of the bath, I put on a clean uniform. It was too big around the waist. I held my pants up with one hand and went to find the squad staying in the house, planning to ask them for something to use as a belt. But in the hallway, my stomach cramped again, even worse than usual. I sank to the floor and groaned.

One of the soldiers found me. A few minutes after that, I was in a jeep on my way to the nearest aid station.

* * *

"Hepatitis," the doctor said. He pinched my fingernails and nodded to himself.

"Are you sure it's not just jaundice and a case of eating too much too soon?" I asked.

The doctor bent over a clipboard and wrote something on it. "No. Frankly, I'm surprised you were able to walk all the way from that stalag given the advanced state of your case."

"So do you give me medicine or something?"

"No. In most cases, it's something your body has to fight on its own. Rest and proper nutrition will help, and I think we've caught it in time to prevent permanent liver damage." He turned to an orderly and handed him a clipboard. "Start an IV."

When the doctor left and the patients beside me drifted off to sleep, I stared at the ceiling of the big hospital tent. I wore clean clothes, and I was tucked between clean sheets. But I had trouble sleeping, and it wasn't because an uncomfortable IV was stuck through the inside of my elbow. The phrase *permanent liver damage* kept running through my head. The memory of the POW who'd died of hepatitis didn't help. I was finally free, but that didn't mean I was going home.

Eventually, I did sleep, but I woke up feeling worse than ever. A pair of orderlies had to shift me onto a stretcher and carry me to a jeep because I couldn't walk. They took me to an airfield and loaded me onto a C-47.

I finally got to fly in an airplane, but I was too sick to enjoy it.

I fell asleep again and woke up in a real building with a long row of hospital beds stretching in either direction. I stared at my fingernails. Yellow. An

IV bag was connected to a pole on the headboard and was hooked to my left wrist.

A few beds away, a nurse checked another patient. She had a gap between her front teeth when she smiled. As she moved from one bed to the next, she wiped a few wisps of hair off her forehead.

"Private Ley, are you feeling well enough to stand on a scale?" she asked when she reached my bed.

I fumbled with the sheets. "Maybe." My stomach hurt, and even the thought of getting out of bed was exhausting.

She brought a scale to me so I only had to take two steps.

"What's your normal weight?" she asked as she helped me back in bed.

"At the end of training, I was about 180."

Her mouth opened into a perfect *O*. She shut it with effort and cleared her throat. "Well, we've got our work cut out for us then, haven't we?"

"How much do I weigh now?"

"105. And you're a hepatitis case, so you're on a no-fat diet. But don't worry, we'll get you better."

She made a few notes on my chart and glanced at the next bed over.

"Ma'am?" I said.

"Yes?"

"I had a few broken bones. I think they're mostly better now, but do you think someone could look at them?"

She wrote something down. "We'll take a few X-rays."

"Can I get glasses again?"

"Of course. I'll have the optometrist come see you sometime in the next few days."

"Can I write to my family?"

"Didn't they let you send a telegram when they liberated you?"

I shook my head. "We weren't really liberated. And then I got sick."

"I'll send someone to help you with it. Anything else?"

"Yeah, where are we?"

"Paris."

Paris. I'd always thought leave in Paris would be nice, but I'd pictured myself staying in a hotel, not a hospital.

They let me send a telegram to my mom, and then I slept.

Ten days later, my stomach still cramped, my body still ached, and I still threw up about half of what I ate. The ward was full of other hepatitis cases with similar symptoms. But at least I was free, and the doctors didn't think I was going to die. The X-rays had shown complete healing in my ribs and jaw. My collarbone was slightly crooked, but it wasn't bad enough that I wanted them to break it again so they could reset it. I was scheduled to see a dentist in a couple days about my missing teeth.

That afternoon, I got a new pair of glasses and a pile of letters. As I flipped through the stack, I recognized the different handwriting without even looking at the return addresses. Belle. Bastien. Mom. Belle. Hannah. Stefanie. Belle. Bastien. Belle. Belle. Mom.

I was overjoyed to open the first three, but the more I read, the more I realized the letters had been written for someone who no longer existed. The Lukas they'd written to was eager to fight the Nazis; he wasn't afraid of anything, not even death, because he knew for certain that there was a God and that no matter what happened to him physically, everything would work out in the end. He knew what was right, and he knew what was wrong, and he always tried to do what was right. But sometime between getting pushed back through Luxembourg and walking across the bridge over the Elbe, that Lukas had disappeared.

I was still alive, but the Nazis had won. Not the war. That had ended a few days ago, in Europe anyway. On the battlefield, the Nazis were vanquished. But they'd treated me like an animal, done everything they could to destroy my inner discipline and my dignity. What was once black and white seemed gray, and though my faith wasn't gone, it didn't seem to matter anymore.

I'd killed men in battle. I'd walked by people who were hurt or starving or about to be assaulted and hadn't lifted a finger to help them. I'd clobbered Little Adolf, maybe killed him, and it hadn't been in battle, so that made it murder. I hadn't done a thing to help the woman the Soviet troops had raped. I probably couldn't have stopped them, but I hadn't even tried, hadn't even reported it to one of their officers. I'd stolen medicine from a sick soldier, food from an old man and an old lady, more food from a mother and her son. She could have been my mother in the last war—young, with my dad off to war and Bastien and Hans to take care of. German, but good. And desperate to keep her son from starving.

Over time, my actions had aligned with my treatment. The Nazis hadn't killed me, but they'd changed me. I was a thief, maybe a murderer. I'd seen evil, and I hadn't stood for the right. The postwar Lukas was different, and I didn't like him much.

* * *

Letters continued to trickle in over the next week, with everyone saying how worried they'd been and how relieved they were to finally hear from me. I didn't write back. I'd have to reply eventually, but I wasn't ready to introduce my family to the new Lukas.

The stomach cramps kept me in bed, so I had a lot of time to think. I was terrified of what my mother would say when she realized how I'd changed. I worked up the courage to send a letter, but I wasn't brave enough to confess.

Dear Mom,

Sorry to scare you by giving a hospital as my address. I've been ill, but I'll get better. They didn't give us much food while I was a prisoner, so I lost a lot of weight. I've got some vitamin deficiencies and a little case of hepatitis. They're taking real good care of me, so you don't need to worry. I get clean sheets and lots of baths and lots of fruit and vegetables. No, you don't need to send any food. I'm on a restricted diet until the hepatitis is under control. Remember Hannah's husband saying how servicemen in the South Pacific get yellow skin from the antimalaria tablets? I look like I've been on a double-dose of Atabrine, but they say it will go away after awhile. I miss you, and I love you, and I'm looking forward to seeing you again real soon.

Love, Lukas

I lied to my mother. I wasn't looking forward to going home. Home was for good people, for brave people. I didn't feel very brave, and I wasn't good, not anymore.

I wrote roughly the same things to my sisters, telling them I'd be fine in a while and that they shouldn't worry. If they ended up in Kansas and Colorado, where their husbands had grown up, maybe they'd never find out where I'd gone wrong.

The next day, I reread all of Belle's letters. It would have been easier to write her if she'd fallen in love with someone else. Then I could have wished her well and kept it short. But her letters were heartfelt, as if we were still sneaking into her barn every morning to talk about school and our families and the war that we had thought we'd known so much about. We hadn't known anything, not really.

I reread the part where she explained how little they'd heard about me.

It was horrible when you disappeared. The Germans pushed so far west back in December, and I knew you'd been on the line. Your letters had come so consistently, and then they stopped. In January, three of my letters for you were returned. Someone had written MIA across the front of two of them, and KIA across the front of one. I think that was the worst day of my life. No one knew for sure what had happened to you until the end of March. Your mom got a postcard from the Red Cross, and she came over to tell me that night. But by then, the newspapers were full of information about the type of camps the Nazis ran, so I was still terrified for you.

I'm enclosing one of the letters that came back to me. It had part of the story we were working on. Do you remember that? You don't have to finish it now. I somehow thought if we had an unfinished story you'd have to come home again, and now I know you're coming home, so the story doesn't matter.

The other letter had been written in December, mostly about Christmas, with a few lines of the story about the knight. It seemed like so long ago that it might as well have been written during medieval times. I smiled as I remembered. I'd said she cried every night because she missed me, and I'd told her about finally getting along with the other men in my squad. My smile faded. The only other member of my squad who was still alive was Samson, and maybe Martinez, if the Germans had taken care of his wounds.

Belle's part of the story picked up right where I'd left off.

After a few tearful nights, the lady drew upon a reserve of inner strength and ceased her weeping. She knew her knight wouldn't want his maiden to turn into a sniveling weakling. She devoted herself to her work and faithfully said her prayers morning and night, trusting that the Lord would keep her knight safe.

I didn't feel like a knight. The knights in Belle's stories were supposed to be strong. I was so weak I could barely walk to the other end of the hepatitis ward. Her knights did good deeds and fought evil and protected women from rampaging soldiers. I'd just survived. That was all. And I'd done a lot of things that weren't so good in order to do it. I wasn't sure what to tell Belle at first, but eventually I figured it out.

The dragon let the knights think he was wounded. He stayed in his position and breathed fire at them from time to time, but the fire was always the same. It was dangerous for the knights closest to the dragon, but most of them learned how to hide behind their shields when the dragon started smoking.

Then one day the dragon blew more fire than any of the knights had ever seen before. It killed a lot of them and hurt a lot of them. And some of the knights got captured. The dragon put them in his prison, and then even more of the knights died.

The lady's knight tried very hard to be brave. And he tried very hard to be good. And he tried very hard to survive. But it turned out that the only way he could survive was by turning into a goblin. Goblins aren't nice, and they aren't good, and they don't win the approval of fair ladies. They just survive, and sometimes they make ugly choices because they don't want to die.

And then some other knights finally slayed the dragon, and the knight was free. Except he was a goblin now, and he didn't know how to turn back into a knight. At one time, the knight had known that death wasn't the end and that it was better to be good than to be alive. But somehow, in the prison, he forgot. And now he was stuck as a goblin.

With Bastien, I was more direct.

You were right. War is hell. I'm not sure which was worse—the battle or the prison camps. Either way, I'm afraid I've turned into a devil.

* * *

After four weeks in the hospital, I'd regained ten pounds. I still had a lot of stomach cramps, but I didn't barf after every meal, and I felt strong enough to walk around the whole hospital instead of just the hepatitis ward.

A couple other patients were starting a card game. "Want to join us?" one of them asked.

I nodded, but before I sat down, I heard a familiar voice. "Hey, four-eyes!"

Samson rushed down the hall and grabbed me in a bear hug. "You up and disappeared when we crossed the Elbe. I thought maybe after you scrubbed all the dirt off, there wasn't nothing left."

I grinned. "Not much left." Samson looked healthier, his skin filled out instead of sagging and a contented look on his face instead of the worry I'd so often seen there. "You look like a human again instead of a skeleton."

"Yeah, been up at a camp near Le Havre. All the food I can eat all the time." He lowered a bag from his shoulder and rested it on the ground. "But I wanted to see Paris before I sailed home, so I snuck out and thought I'd come check on you. How ya feeling?"

"Not as bad as I felt that last week in Mühlberg."

Samson studied me as if he wanted to make his own diagnosis.

"I'm still kinda yellow."

He smirked. "It's a good look for you. Glasses and yellow skin. The French women are gonna fall all over you."

I laughed.

"I ran into Red."

"Yeah? Did he and Monson make it?"

"They got captured about two hours after we did but by a different group. Ended up in Stalag VIIA outside of Moosburg. Liberated by General Patton at the end of April."

"How bad was Moosburg?"

Samson shrugged. "Like Mühlberg. Maybe a little worse 'cause it was more crowded."

"Are they all right?"

"Skinny, but yeah, they're all right. Monson didn't want to get stuck waiting for the bureaucrats to process him, so he stayed away from the British and planned to hop a ride across the Channel with the Americans and make his way home himself, surprise his parents. I hope he made it. Red shipped home last week. Have they said how long you're staying?"

"No." I wasn't ready to face my family yet anyway. I wanted to be with them again, but I didn't want to see disappointment in their eyes when they found out how I'd changed.

"Well, I figure if you can escape a work kommando and a stalag, you should be able to get out of a hospital for a night. Wanna get supper?"

"I don't have any money."

"Yeah, me neither. They sent all our records back to the States after we were captured, so they can't pay us. But I got these." Samson pulled a carton of cigarettes from his bag. "They work on French civilians almost as well as they work on German guards."

It turned out that I didn't have to escape. The nurse gave her permission, along with a stern warning. "No meat, no alcohol. And you come back right away if you start to feel nauseated. Got it?"

I nodded. "Yes, ma'am."

She turned to Samson. "You make sure he makes it back. Tonight. In one piece."

"Yes, ma'am."

Walking onto the streets of Paris was like walking into a party. The war was over, and surviving it was something to rejoice over. People laughed a little too loudly, skipped instead of strolled, flirted instead of talked. It was as if they had to live more fully now to make up for all the war years.

Samson had a place in mind. It was close, which was good, because I couldn't have walked more than a few blocks. He paid for our bread and cheese with cigarettes. But the cheese was too rich, and my stomach cramped up again.

"Should I take you back?" Samson asked, his eyebrows scrunched up with worry.

"No, I'll just stop eating." I watched the people go past on the street outside. Everyone seemed to be celebrating, but when I looked closer, their eyes told a different story. The war was over, and everyone was happy for that, but a cease-fire couldn't erase the war's damage.

"Did you hear anything about the rest of our company?" I asked.

Samson nodded but didn't answer.

"Well?"

"Martinez was listed as killed."

I thought about him for a while. "He should have got a medal."

"Yeah, but the thing about medals is it don't matter how brave you are if all the officers die before they can send in a report."

I watched a few more people walk by.

"Kid, how you really doing?" Samson leaned forward, his eyes intense as he studied my face.

I took my time answering. "I don't know. I wanted to go home so bad, but now . . . You were right. I've changed. And not for the better."

Samson fingered the edge of the table. "Kid, the important thing is you survived. You can go home and start over, and you never have to tell anyone about what happened. Do your best to move on. If you did things you regret, just do better from here on out. That's the best any of us can do."

We said good-bye that night with plans to meet again when we were both back in Virginia. I thought a lot about what he'd said. I was lucky to be alive. I couldn't change the past, but I didn't have to dwell on it. No one needed to know. But in the back of my head, Samson's reasoning fell apart. Even if I fooled everybody else, I couldn't fool God.

CHAPTER 32

I stayed in the Paris hospital for two more weeks. Then I transferred to Camp Lucky Strike near the French port of Le Havre and spent a few weeks there. It was almost July. I was up to 130 pounds and I could eat anything I wanted. I still had stomach cramps from time to time, but they weren't as common. I'd stopped vomiting, and I could walk around for twenty minutes straight without feeling worn out.

I continued to get letters from home, but I didn't get replies to the ones I'd sent until two days before I sailed back to the States. Bastien and Belle both said pretty much the same thing. But they said it in different ways.

Belle used the story. She was smart like that.

After a time, the knight-turned-goblin remembered the legends he had heard about the king. The knight had known the stories so well that he'd told them to his lady, and the lady knew they were true because the king had helped her. The king was wise, kind, and powerful. He had the ability to turn goblins into knights, trolls into dukes, and brokenhearted girls into courageous women. He could even turn evil dragons into placid princes. Perhaps the most wonderful thing about the king was that he was always willing to help. When called for, he sought out the supplicant and agreed to meet them midway. But the king always went more than midway. And whenever someone wanted to change, he was able to change them.

The knight-turned-goblin went to the king and pleaded for help. The king transformed him back into a knight. The knight went home, past the burned-up villages and across the gray sea to his own land that was still picturesque because the knight and his allies had kept the dragon from ruining it. His lady waited, eager to see him again because she knew a secret. The knight wouldn't be the same, not exactly, for when the king transforms you, he doesn't put you back as you were before. He always leaves you better than when he found you.

Luke, I don't know what you've been through or what you've done. You can tell me as much or as little about it as you want. I know things will be different when you get home. You've changed, and I've changed, and the whole world's changed. But everything you taught me about the Savior and the Atonement and the Resurrection is still just as true now as it was back when my mom died. Please get better, body and spirit, and come home soon.

It was strange how I could know something so completely and then forget it. I'd believed in repentance and forgiveness my entire life. But sometime in the past few months, I'd let in a nagging doubt. The Savior was perfect and all-powerful. He *could* do anything. But why would someone perfect and all-powerful care about someone like me? The Nazis had held me for four and a half months, and they'd thought I was worthless. Maybe I'd started believing them.

Bastien's letter came with a package. I opened the letter first.

Dear Lukas,

I wish I could come see you in person. Every man fights a different war, and every man has his own set of wounds. I don't know what your circumstances are, but I hope you'll think of your struggles as wounds. They're painful, and they're scary, but they will heal.

I did a lot of ugly things while I was away at war. They were necessary, but it's hard to move past them. I don't like to talk about them, nor am I allowed to, but I imagine we've experienced similar things and had similar reactions. Whatever you're going through is hard, but you are strong enough to come out of it.

A year ago, I was in a dark place. I can't fully describe what it's like to wake up and realize your leg is gone. And then to go through the same process day after day. It took weeks before it stopped being a shock each time I remembered. I wasn't sure I wanted to live, especially that first week when the pain and the surprise were still so raw, so new. For me, it was Gracie who pulled me out of it, but I was almost too stupid to let her. Even now I sometimes worry that I'm not good enough for her, that I was selfish to marry her when I wasn't whole, but she convinced me that we were better together, that she needed me as much as I needed her. And I did need her, every time I woke in the middle of the night and remembered anew the loss of my leg. It would have been so easy to give up, but with her there, I had a reason to go on.

I don't know what it will be for you. But I have faith that the Lord will send you what you need to heal the wounds to your soul. And, Lukas, believe me, there are no wounds He can't heal.

I love you, Lukas. I've loved you since Mom placed all seven pounds of you in my arms the day after you were born. I kept loving you when you were a baby who woke me in the middle of the night, a toddler who chewed on my homework, a five-year-old who bent my puzzle pieces, and a seven-year-old who snitched on me for staying out too late with a girl. None of those feelings went away as we grew older, and they never will because you're my brother.

No matter what you've done, I'll still love you. And something tells me that whatever you've done won't seem quite as bad with a little distance and a little understanding. You've been good before, and you've been strong before. I know you can be both again, especially if you turn to the Savior.

Yes, war is hell. But your participation in war doesn't define who you are. You may have made some mistakes. We all have, especially in war. Leave it to the Lord, and move forward with the faith that He can fix it because He loves you just as much as I do.

I did a lot of thinking after I read the letters. Eventually, I opened the package and found a copy of the Book of Mormon. It was a lot like the one I'd lost in Luxembourg but without the scratches and bent corners.

The trip across the Atlantic took eight days. I spent most of my time on deck, walking around without worrying about stepping over the warning wire, looking at the sky without any barbed-wire fences or guard towers blocking my view. When I wasn't walking or eating, I was reading. Before leaving France, I'd asked a chaplain for a New Testament, so I had two books. I read a lot of stories about people who had messed up. And a lot of them had messed up even worse than I had. But they'd gotten another chance. And the closer to the US we sailed, the more I knew I could have another chance too.

Belle had convinced me the Savior could help, and Bastien had convinced me that He would help. Gradually, I felt a sliver of peace again. It wasn't the type of peace that had come with the German surrender; it was an internal peace, a knowledge that God was in charge and that somehow everything would be all right in the end. I'd grown up with that feeling, but I'd lost it somewhere in Luxembourg. I'd missed it. By the time I saw the US again, I had confidence that the fragile bit of peace I clung to could someday be strong again.

* * *

I arrived in Boston Harbor and was assigned to Camp Myles Standish for a few days of medical checkups and debriefings. A few army men asked questions about my time overseas, and a WAC clerk typed out what I said. When I told them about Winterton's death and the scuffle I got into with Little Adolf, the stenographer started crying. They got a different WAC clerk to replace her.

Reliving everything at the debriefing was like ripping the scab off a partially healed wound. Everything started bleeding again. I took a deep breath as I left the room, searching for calm and remembering lines from my letters until I found it again. The pain was raw, but it wouldn't last.

The WAC clerk from the debriefing dabbed at her eyes as I passed her in the hall.

"Are you all right?" I asked.

She nodded. "I'm the one who should be asking you that." She put her handkerchief away. "I ought to be used to it by now. I've been listening to RAMP debriefings all week."

"RAMP?"

"Recovered Allied Military Personnel. You're all so skinny. And you've all been through so much. One of the men was Jewish, and they sent him to a different camp, and it was even worse than the stalags. He said they gassed people and burned their bodies in ovens. They had a system down as efficient as a factory. Men, women, and children murdered because they didn't have a place in the Nazi empire. I hate them."

"Don't hate them."

"What?"

"Don't hate them. If you start hating them, you become a little bit like them, and they've changed you for the worse."

She stared at me for a few seconds before answering. "And I suppose you've forgiven them all, even the guard who hit you day after day?"

I pictured the tall, limping soldier with a mustache and a snarl. "If I get angry every time I think about him for the rest of my life, I'm going to be angry a lot. I don't want him to have that kind of pull on my future."

Her forehead wrinkled in concentration, and then she nodded. "Maybe you're right. You're doing better than a lot of the other RAMPs."

I thought about Little Adolf as I walked around the camp. Had I killed him? If I had to guess, I'd say no. Other than his limp, he'd been healthy.

The other guard wouldn't have left Chemnitz without him, so he would have made it to a hospital within an hour or two. I doubted I'd hit him hard enough to maim him. I'd probably given him a concussion and a few welts, and he'd probably needed stitches. I pondered the WAC's question again. Had I forgiven Little Adolf? No, but the hatred was fading, and that was a start.

Across a fence, I saw a line of men walking from one building to another, laughing and joking with each other in German. The backs of their dark jackets were marked with large white letters: PW, and they were escorted by armed guards. German prisoners of war were being held at Camp Myles Standish.

I wasn't sure how I felt. They seemed healthy; they looked happy. Their clothes were clean, and their faces lacked the pinched look I'd seen so often in Europe. Life as a prisoner at Camp Myles Standish was a stark contrast to life in Stalag IVB and the warehouse guarded by Little Adolf. It seemed unfair that we were treating German prisoners so well when they'd treated American prisoners so horribly, but my resentment soon passed.

My time as a prisoner had been hard, but I was home. And my house hadn't been bombed into rubble, and my family wasn't worried about starving to death, and my girlfriend wasn't threatened by a rampaging army of occupation.

All of Germany, in contrast, was reaping the bitter harvest Hitler had sowed. The country was in ruin, food was scarce, and the Red Army was in charge of a big chunk of it. I wouldn't trade Mühlberg for Myles Standish, not if it meant returning home to a country destroyed by war.

That night, I wrote a letter to Bastien. I'd see him in a few days, but the letter would make it home before I would.

The truth is, Bastien, I did some ugly things too. And I got to the point that I didn't like myself much. Belle reminded me that the Savior could help. But I didn't know why He'd bother. I'd had the light. I'd lost it. Why help someone like me, even if He could? But I get it now. He wants to help because He loves me. He doesn't love me because of what I've done or because of what I haven't done. He loves me because He's my brother, and that's the only reason He needs. I don't know if I would understand that if it wasn't for you, but I've always known you'd do just about anything for me. Having a brother like you makes it easy to believe Christ when He promises He'll fix all my mistakes and save me, no matter what I've done.

I'm taking your advice and treating it like a wound. I feel like my soul has been stitched up again, but it will take time to fully heal. So far, I don't see any signs of gangrene, so eventually, the sutures will come out, and eventually, the scars will fade.

It's strange. I went to war and found out I was a lot weaker than I thought I was. But I was also a lot stronger than I thought I was. I'm not sure how both can be true, yet somehow they are. I had a lot of friends die. I often wonder why I lived and they didn't. One of them had a son that he never got to meet. Another was brave enough to run in front of Nazi tanks and hardly think twice about it. And one of them could show compassion in the middle of combat and kindness in the face of cruelty. They would have made good lives had they survived. Sometimes I don't feel ready to put the war behind me and move on. But I'll take it one day at a time, one prayer at a time. And somehow, I'm going to make it.

* * *

Before I left Massachusetts, they gave me my back pay. It included a dollar for each of my days as a prisoner.

"I thought I was a prisoner for a hundred and twenty-five days?"

The corporal shrugged. "You escaped twice. Those days don't count."

"And I guess those days when the Red Army was in charge of the stalag don't count either?"

"No."

I didn't argue with him, even though that policy had to be among the army's most ridiculous, and the army had ridiculous regulations by the truckload. Being a fugitive had been just as bad as being a prisoner. But I was ready to put it in the past, and even if I wasn't, I doubted a corporal could change anything.

The army got at least one thing right: a bus ticket back to Fairfax and sixty days' leave.

When I got off the bus, my mom was waiting.

"Lukas, Lukas, Lukas!" She hugged me hard enough that I wondered if I'd have bruises the next day. But I didn't mind. She brushed a few tears from her eyes and stood back to look at me. She had more gray hairs now, but her face, despite the tears, displayed pure joy.

She patted my shoulder. "I'm going to have to fatten you up."

I grinned and gave her another hug. "I missed you, Mom."

* * *

My mom drove to the three-bedroom brick rambler with a big porch out front and a service banner with two blue stars hanging in a front window. It was the address I'd mailed letters to, but I hadn't expected Mom to park there. "Weren't you going to move to the bakery?"

"Bastien and Gracie couldn't find an apartment until April. And then I thought it would be nice for you to come home to someplace familiar."

When I went inside, everything was just as I remembered it. My room still had the same blanket on the bed, the same baseball bat in the corner, but Mom must have been in there, or the dust would have piled up. I sat on the bed and smiled because I had a mattress of my own again, one without bedbugs or fleas.

I walked through the rest of the house, trying to convince myself I was really home. Things I'd always taken for granted before stood out: soap in the bathroom, clean clothes in the closet, screens on the windows, running water, lightbulbs, toothpaste.

Mom met me in the front room. "In one of your letters, you asked about your father."

I thought back, barely remembering.

She handed me a pile of folded papers. "We couldn't bring much when we left Germany, but I brought these. Some are letters, some are things he wrote to himself, if you want to see them."

I took the papers, cradling them reverently in my hands. I spend the next few hours reading them. One part, not addressed to anyone, hit me hard.

The last four years have been a form of hell. The war is over now, and soon we'll go home, but I worry. How can I return to an angel wife and innocent children and pick up my life again as if the past four years haven't transformed me? Will the horror that clings to me somehow tarnish my family? I've prayed, and I hold to a small shred of hope that God can help me, but it may take every last drop of blood that was shed on Cavalry to make me clean again.

My dad's words cut right to my heart. I had never seen him waver in his faith, never seen him doubt what was right and what was wrong, never thought he was anything but perfect as a father. But he'd felt the same way I had at the end of the war. Yet despite that, he'd made it—he'd somehow put the war behind him and been a good man in the years that followed. And that was one final sign that I could make it too.

CHAPTER 33

I JOINED MY MOM IN the kitchen and inhaled the smell of chicken roasting in the oven. She looked up from the gravy she was stirring. "It's good to have you back."

"It's good to be back." I leaned against the back door.

"You've grown taller, I think."

"Yeah?" I stood up straight. There had been a knot in the door frame at eye level when I left. Sure enough, it was a little lower now. "Must have happened during training." I was certain it couldn't have happened in the stalag or on the work kommando. I glanced out the window. "How are you taking care of the yard?" The grass was mowed and the bushes neatly trimmed, but Mom wasn't up to that type of work, and I couldn't imagine Bastien pushing the lawn mower and holding his crutches at the same time.

"One of the boys from church comes. I pay him in pies. Bread if I don't have enough sugar for pies."

"So if I start mowing the lawn, will you make me some pies?"

"*Ja.*"

I grinned as I spotted an apple pie sitting on the countertop. "You know, I think I dreamed about your pies at least once a week while I was over in Europe."

The doorbell rang.

"That's Bastien and Gracie. Will you let them in while I finish the sauce?"

I nodded.

My mom's guess was right. It was my brother and his wife, and they immediately smothered me in hugs.

After the initial greetings, Gracie excused herself to go help my mom. As she walked away, I did a double take. Gracie had a nice shape. And it had changed. There was a distinct bump on her abdomen.

I turned to my brother. "Do you two have some news you haven't told me yet?"

Bastien stuck his hands in his pockets. "The baby's due in about three months."

"Why didn't you tell me?" We must have exchanged a dozen letters since I'd been liberated.

"It seemed like something to tell you in person. And it's a big change."

My brother was usually too serious for his own good, but this was the type of thing I'd have thought even he would grin about. "Aren't you happy about it?"

"Of course I'm happy about it." His answer was immediate, but his face was still serious.

"But?"

He frowned. "On the drive over, I saw a man giving a little girl a ride on his shoulders. I might never be able to do that. Another man was running along after his son's bicycle. I won't be able to do that either. Or play baseball or teach my child how to ski."

"You'll still be a good dad, even if you can't do those things." Bastien was quiet, so I kept talking. "I mean, you did a good job with me. You got the letter I sent from Camp Standish, right?"

He nodded.

"If you can dig me out of the hole I was in with just one letter, imagine what you can do with someone living in the same house as you."

He cleared his throat and blinked a few times, probably to keep tears from forming, and I finally got it. My brother, who was never scared of anything, was nervous about being a dad. He was vulnerable, but that only made my regard for him grow.

"Thanks, Lukas," he whispered, and I knew I'd said the right thing.

A cane leaned on the wall off to the side of the front door frame. "Where're your crutches?"

Bastien grabbed the cane. "I graduated to this." He motioned toward the kitchen, and we both went back.

My mom's cooking was like a bit of heaven. It was so much more filling than the prison rations, and so much better tasting than army chow. "I don't remember the last time I had a meal this good." I ate until I was full. So full that it was almost painful, but it wasn't the pain I'd gotten from hepatitis, and that made it wonderful.

Gracie cut a huge piece of pie and handed it to me.

"I don't think I can eat that now."

Gracie eyed me. "It looks to me like you could use a piece twice this big, served hourly for about a month."

"Yeah, I know. Give me a half hour."

"Have you given any thought to what you'll do when you're discharged?" Bastien asked.

"Haven't decided yet." I wasn't strong enough for full-time farm work, not yet, and I didn't want to go back to a paper route, at least not permanently. But I wasn't sure what I wanted to do instead.

"Have you heard about the G.I. Bill?"

I shook my head. "Someone mentioned it, but they didn't say what it was."

"The government will pay for college or occupational training for veterans. I'm using it when I go back to school in a few weeks. I'll finally have a chance to finish that architecture degree I started in 1940." Bastien looked at his wife and took her hand. "But first we're taking a trip to Utah. I'll meet Gracie's family, and Gracie and I will go to the Salt Lake Temple together."

"That's right." Gracie grinned as Bastien moved their hands over the baby. "Make this marriage permanent before Bastien changes his mind."

I laughed. "I've seen the way he looks at you, Gracie. I don't think he's ever going to change his mind."

"Good." Gracie leaned over and kissed my brother's cheek.

When Bastien finished the cuddles, he retrieved his cane and stood. "Lukas, while you're waiting for your pie, will you come outside with me?"

"More sparring lessons?"

"No, something else."

I followed him out the front door. "You know, some of those things you taught me did come in handy." I almost told him about it, but I didn't want to talk about war right then. There would be other times for that.

He seemed to understand. He nodded and led me to the garage, limping slightly as he used his cane for balance. When he pulled the door open, I noticed a 1937 BSA M-20 motorcycle propped up on its kickstand. Bastien pulled a key from his pocket and held it out to me.

"What's this?"

"It's your new motorcycle. Newly restored, anyway."

"You rebuilt it?"

Bastien nodded. "Half the parts are new, but yes."

"For me? After I took it without asking and crashed it?"

"Try not to crash it again." He winked.

A smile tugged at my lips. I had no idea what to say, so I ended up just saying, "Thank you."

"You're welcome. I'm afraid no one's tested it yet. I'm not that skilled with my prosthesis, and Gracie hates motorcycles. But it has a full tank of gas. And there are two helmets on that shelf over there." Bastien pointed across the garage.

I went over to get them. "Why two?"

Bastien shrugged. "If I remember right, Annabelle Montgomery usually gets back from work about now."

I glanced at the Montgomery property. "I wonder what her daddy would say if I knocked on the front door."

"I have my pistol in the car, if you'd like to borrow it."

I ran my fingers over the BSA's handlebars as I considered Bastien's offer. "I think I'll leave it in your car. But maybe you should leave the windows open and listen out for shotgun blasts."

Bastien nodded, then motioned to the motorcycle. "Take it easy the first few times, eh? Especially if you pick up a passenger."

* * *

Five minutes later, I straightened my army tie and knocked on the Montgomerys' front door for the first time in nineteen months. I glanced at the barn. I would have felt more comfortable there. Mr. Montgomery answered the door. It took him a few seconds to recognize me, and then his lips tensed and pulled into a frown.

I hadn't expected him to roll out a welcome mat, but I'd been hoping for something better than the grim scowl currently lining his face. I wasn't going to apologize for being there though. I wasn't a kid anymore, and I'd proven my loyalty to America. "Good afternoon, sir. Is Belle home?"

He folded his arms across his chest. "She went out."

"Oh." I tried to hide my disappointment. In my last letter to her, I'd said I was in Massachusetts, but I hadn't known my release date, so for all she knew, I was still there.

Mr. Montgomery rolled his eyes at me and started to shut the door in my face.

I held it open with my foot. "Sir, I know you don't like me. I can live with that. But Belle and I wrote while I was gone, and we're planning to see a lot of each other now that I'm back. I'm willing to turn over a new page, for Belle's sake, because I think it would be easier on her if we could at least be polite to each other. But no matter what you do, you won't chase me away."

"You say you won't be chased away? Isn't that how you ended up a prisoner? Turning tail and running the second the Germans attacked?"

My fists balled up, and I forced them to relax. I thought through my words carefully so I wouldn't say something I'd regret. "No, sir. My company and I held off a force ten times bigger than us for two days. We only surrendered when we ran out of ammunition, and by then, we had ruined the German timetable and given the 101st Airborne time to fortify Bastogne. I know the papers didn't report much about us, but that's because we were mostly dead or captured, not because we didn't put up a good fight. And let me tell you, sir, after being on the receiving end of a German offensive and enduring a POW camp, I'm not going to let anyone intimidate me with a shotgun full of rock salt."

Mr. Montgomery opened his mouth and then closed it again.

"Good evening, sir." I turned to go.

"Ley?"

"Yeah?" I turned back.

"She went to the post office."

He was telling me where to find her? I wasn't sure I believed him, but his sneer had disappeared. Maybe he was willing to turn over a new page too. "Thank you, sir."

I grabbed my motorcycle and headed into town. The last time I'd ridden a motorcycle, I'd been frustrated and gone too fast. This time I was more content and kept it at a reasonable speed. The wind blew past me, cutting the sticky summer air and cooling my skin. I didn't mind the muggy weather. I preferred it over a German winter.

Fairfax had changed a little, but it was still familiar. I parked my motorcycle near the post office and slipped inside. Belle wasn't there, so I searched along the shops, wondering if she'd had another errand or if she'd gone home.

It took a few minutes to find her. She wore a dress with little white polka dots on a baby-blue background and a navy-blue hat. I'd seen the dress before; the hat was new. She read a newspaper as she walked. I crossed the street to meet her and waited for her to get closer. With every step she took, my smile grew larger.

She glanced up from the paper, scanned the sidewalk and the people ahead of her, and strolled right past me.

My smile fell. Her eyes had been on me for at least half a second. I'd never worn glasses in front of her, and my skin still had a yellow tint, but to have her not even recognize me was like taking a piece of shrapnel in the heart.

Belle paused, waiting for the traffic to clear before she crossed the street. I swallowed back my disappointment. I almost called her name, but instead I started whistling "She Wore a Yellow Ribbon."

I picked out the exact moment she recognized the tune. Her foot stopped midstride, and a look of concentration crossed her face as she turned around. It melted into a grin when she finally recognized me. "Luke?"

I nodded. In three strides, she was in my arms, laughing and throwing her hands around my neck. That type of momentum would have knocked me off my feet a month ago, but I managed to keep my balance, and all disappointment that she hadn't recognized me disappeared. She buried her face in my neck, and I felt something warm and wet.

"Are you crying?"

She pulled me closer. "Yes."

"Why on earth are you crying?"

"Because you're here, and there were so many times when I thought I'd never see you again." We held each other for a long moment, then she pulled away to get a better look at me. "When did you get back?"

"This afternoon."

She folded her paper and stuck it under her arm. Then she pinched my waist. "You look awfully skinny."

"Ow." I brushed her hand way. "I've put on about forty pounds since liberation, thank you very much."

Belle's eyes widened. "How much weight did you lose?"

I shrugged. "Seventy-five. Something like that."

Belle looked me over from head to foot and blinked away a few more tears.

"Hey, don't get all sad on me. I'm getting better. With my mom's cooking, I'll probably be back to normal by harvest time."

Belle reached up and put her hand on my jaw. "Your face is a little different. Either because you're older or because you lost so much weight. But it's still the face of my best friend, and that makes it my favorite face in the whole world." Her lips turned up; her smile was exactly as I remembered it:

sunshine and freckles. We were blocking the sidewalk, so she threaded her arm through mine, and we strolled past a few stores. "Are you feeling better?"

"Mostly."

"Can I buy you some food or something?"

I chuckled. "Everybody else is trying to fatten me up too. I ate something about a half hour ago, but if you're hungry, I'll buy you something."

"Maybe later." Belle pulled me to a shady bench. She turned to face me, one finger on her cheek and the rest on her chin.

"You look like you're brainstorming topics for an English paper."

She laughed. The sound still made me feel like everything in the whole world was going to turn out all right. "No, not that."

"Then what are you thinking about?"

She shrugged. "Just that you don't look much like a goblin. I'd say you look almost like a knight. A skinny one."

I glanced down at my uniform. "Knights don't wear olive-drab uniforms. Or glasses. And they don't have jaundice."

"Well, if you aren't a goblin and you aren't a knight, what does that make you?"

I shrugged. "Just a normal man, I guess."

"You'll never be *just normal* to me. You'll always be a little better than that."

"Yeah?"

"Yeah." She put a hand on my knee and slid her feet next to mine.

I put my arm across the back of the bench and leaned into her. She was close enough to kiss. I touched one of her curls and ran a finger along her neck. Her hair and her skin were so clean, so perfect. And her mouth looked every bit as pristine.

"What are you waiting for?" Belle whispered.

"I'm just trying to remember what a sunshine-and-freckle smile tastes like."

Belle's cheeks grew pink. She ran a finger along my shirt until she found the part of my collarbone that wasn't quite perfect. "It's going to taste like freedom, Luke."

I hesitated a moment, and then she sat forward and pressed her lips into mine. I kissed her back, and all that seemed to matter were Belle's soft lips and Belle's sweet perfume and Belle's trembling fingers holding my shoulders.

Freedom tasted great.

NOTES & ACKNOWLEDGMENTS

I WOULD LIKE TO BEGIN my notes with a disclaimer. Many of the character names came from suggestions on my Facebook author page. I would like to assure readers that I received permission to kill off characters named after high school buddies and other friends, and I would like to clarify that characters named after real people in no way resemble them. A friend with the maiden name of Wood has a very pleasant voice, I am sure the real Higham has beautiful toenails, and I've never slept in the same room with either of the Broyles, but if they snore, I doubt it resembles a tank.

Readers may find it strange that President Roosevelt ended voluntary enlistment partway through WWII, but executive order 9279 was issued in December 1942, and the paragraph ending voluntary enlistment for men between ages eighteen and thirty-seven was not revoked until the end of the war. The reasoning behind the change was a desire to decrease competition between service branches for the most desirable recruits and ensure the right balance of manpower for military, industrial, and agricultural needs.

I've read numerous incidents of Americans stationed in England driving on the right rather than on the left side of the road, so for Lukas's crash, I simply reversed the pattern. I didn't want to besmirch the driving reputation of anyone real, so Captain Cunningham is a fictional stand-in for W. E. Fairbairn and E. A. Sykes, two former members of the Shanghai Municipal Police Reserve Unit who spent part of WWII instructing American OSS agents.

Belle and Luke's relationship is partially inspired by my family history. My great-great-grandparents didn't approve of the poor neighbor boy's interest in their daughter. She offered to milk the cows morning and night to get out of the house. If she was alone, she sang "She Wore a Yellow Ribbon," and my great-grandfather came and milked the cows for her. They were married in the Salt Lake Temple in 1922, so their story predates the time period of this novel, but only by a little. For the book, I chose a version of the song used as a military cadence, though the lyrics have varied throughout the years and between branches.

I patterned Luke's training and transport to Europe and into Luxembourg after what was common at the time for replacement soldiers. His unit's norm of manning foxholes during the day and pulling back to a stronghold at night with frequent patrols was common for the 28th Division. Though the German attack in the Ardennes is normally reported as a surprise, that wasn't the case for the men on the front lines. In my research, I found examples of front-line squads hearing engine noises, observing bridge construction, and being warned by civilians.

I kept Luke's unit vague for two reasons. First, it gave me more wiggle room when it came to the plot. And second, I didn't want to give Luke's fictional squad or fictional company credit for something real men did. Almost everything Lukas experienced during the Battle of the Bulge was experienced by a real American soldier, but I took literary license to combine events from several different units to create his story. Overall, my goal was to make his experience true enough to what someone in the 110th Infantry Regiment of the 28th Division would have experienced that if the story were told at a reunion of men who fought there, they would find Luke's experiences believable for someone in the next company over.

There were times when various sources were in conflict about the details of the battle. One source, for example, said the 110th had fifteen miles of front. Another said it was ten. For the novel, I went with the regiment's official history and said fifteen.

SS troops were responsible for multiple massacres during the Battle of the Bulge. The most famous instance involving African-American POWs took place in Wereth, Belgium. The Wereth Eleven were members of 333rd Field Artillery Regiment, supporting the 106th Division rather than the 28th Division. The POWs Winterton saw should be considered fictional but patterned after real events.

Readers familiar with German POW camps through films such as *The Great Escape* may wonder why I depicted Stalag IVB as such a dire place. Prisoners of the German Air Force were generally treated better than prisoners of the German Army. Also, officers received better treatment and better living conditions than enlisted men. But the biggest difference between Lukas Ley and Steve McQueen is the years depicted. As Germany struggled against defeat on several fronts and as more POWs came under its control, camps became more crowded, transportation and communication broke down, and conditions for those held in captivity plummeted.

Sadly, the scene when Luke's boxcar is strafed by friendly planes is based on multiple real incidents. Conditions on trains varied, but the overcrowding and hunger depicted in this story were typical for prisoners captured during the Battle of the Bulge.

Charcoal was often used to treat dysentery and diarrhea during WWII, but I discourage any readers from trying the same thing without the advice of a doctor.

Prisoners sent on work kommandos lived through diverse experiences. Most guards were fair, but there were many who abused their prisoners. Little Adolf is fictional but inspired by historic figures, particularly a guard nicknamed Big Sloop.

I tried to depict the liberation of Stalag IVB as accurately as possible. Unfortunately, each POW remembered things slightly differently. Details mentioned in the story come from at least one POW account. Many prisoners left camp without permission after the Red Army arrived, and aspects of Samson and Luke's final escape is patterned after their experiences. The Soviets eventually released the remaining prisoners to the Western Allies, but not until a month after its initial liberation.

Most details, like the deduction of escape days from a POW's back pay, come from history books, likewise, information about uniforms, food, medicine, and weapons. Throughout the book, I've chosen to base Lukas's impressions about other nationalities on the prevailing opinions among US soldiers in similar circumstances during that time period. Slang such as "kraut" and "Jap" is based on common 1940s usage. No disrespect is intended toward any nationality or group of people.

And now for some thank-yous.

Thank you to my editor, Sam, for making my books better. Thank you to Robby, Kathy, and Stephanie and to other members of the staff at Covenant who faithfully do their part to ensure my manuscript reaches readers.

Thank you to Briana Shawcroft for creating beautiful maps and for being such a pleasure to work with.

Thank you to Paul Sowards for explaining the differences between bird shot and buck shot and for bringing up the possibility of shells loaded with rock salt instead.

Thank you to my test readers: Linda White, Terri Ferran, Melanie Grant, Shanda Cottam, Bradley Grant, Teresa Bills, and Ron Machado. I also wish to express thanks to Kathi Oram Peterson and Jeanette Miller for their help with portions of the manuscript.

Thank you to my family and to my Heavenly Father.

I love writing, but while working on this book, I was extremely aware of all the things I was giving up in order to find the time to complete it. Normally, I'm content with writing books that mostly just entertain, but with this novel, I felt it needed to be something more. I hope I've achieved that, at least for a few readers.

ABOUT THE AUTHOR

A. L. SOWARDS HAS ALWAYS BEEN fascinated by the 1940s, but she's grateful she didn't live back then. She doesn't think she could have written a novel on a typewriter, and no one would be able to read her handwriting if she wrote her books out longhand. She does, however, think they had the right idea when they rationed nylon and women went barelegged.

Sowards grew up in Moses Lake, Washington. She graduated from BYU and ended up staying in Utah, where she enjoys spending time with her husband and children or with her laptop. She does not own a typewriter. She does own several pairs of nylons.

Defiance is Sowards' sixth novel. Her previous books include several Whitney Award finalists and a Whitney Award winner. For more information, please visit ALSowards.com or connect on Facebook, Goodreads, or Twitter.